THE LUCKY WIDOW

SAMANTHA VÉRANT

To request permissions, contact the publisher at rights@stormpublishing.co

Ebook ISBN: 978-1-80508-642-0
Paperback ISBN: 978-1-80508-643-7

Cover design: Blacksheep
Cover images: Depositphotos, Shutterstock

Published by Storm Publishing.
For further information, visit:
www.stormpublishing.co

This book is dedicated to those of you who dream of flying free.
(Just don't take the law into your own hands.)

The flapping of the wings of a butterfly can be felt on the other side of the world.

—Chinese Proverb

ACT ONE: NOW AND THEN
THE BUTTERFLY EFFECT

*We delight in the beauty of the butterfly,
but rarely admit the changes it has gone
through to achieve that beauty.*

—Maya Angelou

FACT: When looking at the concept of chaos theory with a closer lens, the butterfly effect suggests that when a butterfly flaps its wings on one side of the world the result may stimulate tiny atmospheric changes that could influence the weather on the other side of the world. Essentially, small actions have the possibility of creating much larger and unexpected influences.

ONE

EMMA

Sunday, May 26th, 2024: 8:32 a.m.

I'm a woman on the verge of reclaiming her life.

And I can't stop fantasizing about my husband's death.

Struck down by lightning on the golf course. Careening over Bear Mountain Bridge in his bronze Bugatti. Slipping off a subway platform as an oncoming train approaches. Or a personal favorite—rotting in prison for the rest of his twisted life with no chance of parole.

So many ways Nate could meet his demise.

To be clear, I'm not a heartless sociopath. What I *am* is terrified of all the nasty measures he'll take once he finds out I'm about to slap him with divorce papers. And I know I need to strike first. Because if Nate even suspects what I was up to when I was in Paris he'll hit back and—with his money and connections—a hell of a lot harder.

Better for Nate to go down in flames, not me.

Envisioning Nate's death is like cognitive therapy for my mental health, it takes the edge off. I know I'm not the only woman on the planet who has these kinds of fantasies: escape without repercussions.

On the ride home from JFK, I'd like to nod off for a couple of minutes, to get my head together for the fight of my life, but the way Abby drives is wreaking havoc on my already whacked-out nervous system. She swerves into another lane, honking her horn, and I stomp my right foot down on the floor mat. "For crying out loud, slow down!"

Abby flips a lock of red hair over her shoulder and shoots me an amused smirk, pressing her foot down on the accelerator. "Emma, you do realize that there are no brakes on your side of the car."

A truck rumbles by and the huge iPad-sized screen lighting up the dashboard of her Tesla beeps out warnings. I shriek and brace my hands on my knees. "I really don't know why you insisted on driving us to and from the airport when I could have hired—"

"I like driving," she says with a wicked grin and then her voice goes deadpan. "I'm an excellent driver."

"Oh no, Rain Man, you're a speed demon," I hiss, after catching my breath. "A redheaded speed demon with a lead foot."

"Rain Man? No, I'm Thelma. And you're my Louise," she cackles.

I groan. "Do I have to remind you that they die at the end of the movie?"

Abby sways her body, humming along to "Love is a Battle-field." I know she put this song on purposefully for a little musical motivation, both of us die-hard fans of music from the eighties and early nineties. But, as much as I'd like to become inspired by Pat Benatar's female-positive anthem and pump my fist to the chorus, today I'm not feeling so strong. Love isn't a battlefield. Divorcing a monster is. Bring on the reinforcements because I need all the ammunition I can get. I exhale a deep breath and lower my sunglasses to the bridge of my nose to re-read the text the private investigator sent me:

STELLA:

> Got the bastard. (And his sick and twisted friends if you ever need dirt on them.) You'll have everything you need to negate the prenup you signed and more. Video is not for the faint of heart. Cleaning it up—although I'd rather not re-watch it.

I'm pinning all of my hope on whatever is on this video; for now, it's the only bomb I have to drop. Leaning my head against the side of the car, I stare out the window, willing the chill of the AC blasting from the vent to cool down my boiled nerves.

We pass a sign indicating the exit for Katonah is ten miles up ahead. Two exits before mine, this is also the route one would take to get to the Bedford Hills Correctional Facility—an all-women maximum-security prison in Westchester County. Abby—like she always does at this mile marker—starts spouting off the names of its most infamous inmates. "'Fatal Attraction' teacher Carolyn Warmus, 'Salt Mom' Lacey Spears, 'Long Island Lolita' Amy Fisher, 'To Die for Teacher' Pamela Smart—"

I swallow and cut her off. "Keep driving and drop me off there. Hey, I might even make some new friends—"

Abby blurts out a donkey-like laugh. "At least you designed *your* prison and know every nook and cranny of it—no hacksaws or grind disks needed for your escape."

"An eighteen-thousand-square-foot glass and cement prison—"

"That you love."

"When he's not there," I say.

"And you're getting rid of him. Your PI caught him in the act on video, right?" She shoots me a concerned side-glance when I respond with a guttural groan.

I pick at my cuticles. "I hope it's enough."

"It will be." Abby sighs and slaps my hand. "Don't do that. Look, I know you're about to face a real shitstorm, but just promise me one thing—"

My eyelids flutter with fatigue. "What's that?"

"You'll see the divorce through to the end," she says, gripping my hand tightly. "You're doing the right thing, Emma. Finally. You just need to keep calm and carry on with your plan."

Easier said than done.

I'd been so self-assured when we were in Paris, knew exactly what I needed to do, but the closer we get to my home the harder I'm finding it to breathe. Every nerve, every bone, and every muscle in my body pulses and throbs. Even the Xanax I'd swallowed back with a glass of bubbly on the seven-plus-hour flight back to New York didn't stop my mind from racing with all of the what-ifs. What if he finds out what I've been up to? What if my plan doesn't work? What if? What if?

I'm mentally and physically exhausted. Paris wasn't the only long-haul trip I'd recently taken. The last one was a lot longer. Just two weeks ago, I'd bounded from New York to Bangkok to Chiang Mai to Phuket searching out Thai Rattanakosin pieces for one of my celebrity clients as well as ideas to construct her Hamptons' summer home—ideas she adored—and I'd run myself ragged.

It's hard to think straight.

A minute later, we careen onto the off-ramp, and the car winds down the bucolic roads of Bedford with its horse trails and huge estates, the leaves of the trees blurring into a haze of green, Abby now singing along to Alanis Morissette's "Ironic." And, yes, as I listen to the lyrics, I'm thinking life is full of twisted, mind-bending, soul-sucking irony. Isn't it ironic, don't you think? Nate is a heart surgeon and instead of healing or fixing mine he's broken it so many times I'm surprised it's still beating.

"Tell me what you told me on the plane," Abby demands.

"You slept like a baby on the flight," I point out. "A giant snoring baby."

She lightly nudges my shoulder. "What you told me before I fell asleep."

Abby Hoffman: fashion designer for Zala, happy divorcée, best friend, and future motivational speaker. I squeeze my eyes shut, trying to find an ounce of the wavering bravado I'd had before we left Paris, repeating my mantra. "I'm going to float like a butterfly. And then sting like a hundred killer bees."

"That's my girl." She pats my hand. "And you're keeping the house you put every ounce of your creative energy and soul into designing and you're—"

Abby taps her magenta-painted fingernails on the steering wheel, waiting for me to complete the sentence.

"Going to kick out the evil warden and he won't know what hit him."

"I think we said evil bastard. But I really love the prison reference. See, you've got this." She nods perfunctorily. "Say it."

"I've got this," I mumble.

We pull up to my estate and when Abby screeches the Tesla to a stop my breath rattles in my throat. I punch in the code to open the gates on my phone and as we jostle down the gravel driveway my stomach lurches with every crunch. The phone I'm clutching in my hand like a lifeline vibrates and my heart rate speeds up. I glance at the screen. It's just an alert from my personal shopper about a sale. Nothing from Nate—thank God.

He knows I'm coming home today and, although he did stay at the house while I was away, he'll either be at the hospital or our loft in the city. Wherever he is—and, truth be told, I'm currently envisioning him six feet under—we've been avoiding one another—no texts, no calls. I'd told him I was going to Paris to get my head together, that I needed space. Which is a half-truth. I'd needed to give *him* space so he could hang his own noose. The tighter the better.

Abby pulls up to the front of the garage and we're about to get out of the car when the giant screen on her dashboard lights up. "Damn, Emma, I have to take this. It's my manufacturer in Hong Kong. I'll meet you up at the house. Leave your bags in the trunk. We'll grab 'em in a minute." She holds up two fingers, mouths "coffee," and answers the call. "Abby Hoffman—"

I throw my phone into my purse, exit the car, and slowly push my legs forward to the front entry, each step like I'm trudging through quicksand. Steadying my breath, I punch in the alarm code and the steel door opens with a groan. A heavy moan works its way out of me too. I walk into the bright, modern foyer, where every detail, from the mirrored side console to the polished travertine floor, to the flow leading off to the grander rooms, is sheer perfection. I blink rapidly, trying to clear the little spots dancing in front of my eyes, and focus on the Picasso Nate had purchased on one of his whims during a private auction at Sotheby's for the bargain price of 16.6 mill: *Nature morte au panier de fruits et aux fleurs*—a basket of fruit and a pitcher of flowers painted in shades of blue, red, gold, brown, gray, green and black.

My relationship with Nate is more like this cubist work of art—beautiful to look at, beyond expensive, the subject completely broken up and reassembled into an abstract reality, the brush strokes purposeful and out of kilter. A still life in need of analysis, fractured.

I can't believe I'm about to shatter this life, just like the painting.

Hello, hello, hello. Anybody here? I'm back. I'm ba-ack.

Can you hear me? Nope. Because the house is empty and

only my voice echoes off the slick, cement walls. No answer—not even a "Mom you're home," my twin girls, Ava and Grace, turning down the music they like to blare—Rihanna or Taylor Swift—from every speaker in the house when I'm not around. But I'd let the girls stay in France, where they'll have the time of their lives while I untangle mine one sticky thread at a time, starting with Nate.

I take in a steadying breath.

Next to a massive basket of cymbidium orchids, a stack of *Hamptons Life* sits on the side console—me on the cover, styled like the elegant woman people always compare me to: Jackie O. Even my shoulder-length hair is curled into her iconic bouffant, the ends flipped up. Not one wrinkle. No smile or frown lines or crow's feet. Glowing skin.

Somebody clearly airbrushed the hell out of my face.

As I reach for the magazine, my gaze lands on my ring finger and the giant—could save a small country with its worth—six-point-five carat diamond resting on it. My God, I hate the ring because it's a constant reminder of the life I chose when I was young, dumb, and full of hope. I stare blankly at the glossy image on the cover. I can't believe I'm turning thirty-nine in a couple of months. I feel older, even my hands are showing my age, and I wonder how time flew by so quickly. You blink. Then —poof—it's gone.

A ripple of laughter bubbles in my throat when I read the headline: "Everybody Wants Socialite Interior Architect Emma Landon."

Sure. Everybody but my husband.

I suppose the joke is on me because I don't want him either.

I gnash my teeth together and flip through the pages of the article, complete with photos of my *perfect* life—my *perfect* husband, Nate, our beautiful twin girls, Ava and Grace, and our bear-sized Tibetan mastiffs, Harry and Potter. Isn't our home and our extravagant existence the absolute model of perfection? Instagrammable? Of course, it is. Don't we all lead perfectly styled lives? Of course, we do.

Oh yes, poor little rich girl, you're living the dream.

Aside from my girls, the house I designed, and my business, the rest of the world I live in is one twisted lie. I lick my finger and turn a page, my eyes latching onto a photo of Nate.

Still as charismatic as he was then, now his salt-and-peppered hair gives him a distinguished vibe. His boyish, dimpled smile and crystal-blue eyes gleam with mischief. The poster man of perfection, with his buff body—the six-pack abs, the sculpted arms, he doesn't look his age of forty-nine, almost fifty, and the photos of him jumping into our award-winning pool with a come-hither grin don't let me forget it.

I scoff at his image. Nifty-fifty, Nate? Not really. You can put lipstick on a pig to try to make them more attractive, but, in the end, a pig is still a pig. And Nate's a master of deception. I'm not the naive girl he'd married fifteen years ago and then brainwashed into thinking I wouldn't have a life worth living without him.

He'd had five days without me to do whatever he'd wanted —five days where I couldn't accuse him of the cheap perfume saturating the collars of his crisp, white Prada shirts, five days where I couldn't harp on him for coming home late or not at all, choosing to stay at our loft in the city. And I'd had five days to get more dirt on him, thanks to the PI.

I never thought it was humanly possible to hate somebody you were once hopelessly in love with with so much intensity, yet I do. Because he's not just a cheater, he destroys lives.

Heaving out a disgusted grunt, I slam the publication down and a breeze blowing in from the entry causes the pages to flutter open to his image, as if to taunt me. I slap the magazine shut. Abby saunters up behind me and peers over my shoulder.

"You look fantastic, as usual, but what the hell died in here? It stinks to high heaven."

I've been holding my breath since I walked through the front door, thinking over what's about to happen, and for the first time, I inhale deeply through my nose. The scent of expensive cigars and whiskey lingers in the air with something else rancid.

"Nate must have had people over," I say.

"When the cat's away—"

"I'm not a damn cat. And I'm going to kill Nate." It's not the first time I've said something like this in front of Abby. Not even close.

"Before or after you serve him divorce papers?" asks Abby with a snort.

A small smile tugs at my lips. "Not funny."

"But it is."

She hooks her arm into mine and we stride through the corridor, the eerie silence punctuated by our heels clicking on the slick, travertine floor. As we turn the corner to head into the kitchen for Abby's much-needed caffeine fix, my left shoe slides into what appears to be a trail of vomit.

I stomp into the kitchen, Abby following. More vomit. It's everywhere, coating the counters and the floor in thick chunks of putrid disgust. A fly the size of a dime, one of many swarming like angry dive-bombers, almost smacks me in the eye. The sink is overflowing with dirty whiskey glasses, one with blood-red lipstick smudges on the rim, and ashtrays filled with cigar butts. I throw my purse on the counter next to a bottle of George V limited edition vodka, nearly toppling it over. Even though it's priced at $24,500 a bottle because it's filtered through champagne limestone, infused with 24-karat gold flakes, and it's encased in gold-plate with a leather label, I don't care if shatters on the ground.

The stench of Nate's extravagances is a mix of rot and decay.

"Christ," Abby mutters, pinching her nose.

It's like Nate left this mess for me to discover on purpose. *Welcome home, honey, I hate you as much as you hate me.* Beyond livid, I don't want to talk to the bastard, can't face hearing his arrogant drawl right now, so I send him a text.

> I'm going to kill you.

I stare at the screen, waiting for a response. Nothing. And I'm not expecting one.

The doors to the terrace are ajar and I open them wider, desperate for fresh air, trying to shoo the army of flies away. Our Tibetan mastiffs, Harry and Potter, run around the yard in circles, playfully nipping at each other's ears, and ruining recently planted flowers in my butterfly garden.

Nate knows how hard I work on my little slice of happiness, digging into the earth with my bare hands planting flowers to attract my obsession, and the dogs should never be left on the grounds unsupervised. In fact, they should be in their run, not desecrating my thirty-by-ten-foot oasis of a personal escape.

"I'm taking pictures of this disaster zone," says Abby, swallowing hard. "Might help your divorce. And I'm passing on the coffee, no matter how much I need it—"

I choke back a heavy wheeze. "I need something stronger. How about a mimosa?"

"You're a bad influence." She grins and then grimaces, batting a fly away with her hand. "But only if we drink them poolside. I can't stand one more second in your house."

Mumbling out an agreement, I step onto the terrace to call out to the dogs before they destroy my blazing star plants, and I freeze mid-step. Shards of a smashed whiskey glass sparkle on the ground and glint in the sun like a kaleidoscope of broken dreams. My gaze locks onto a human-like form floating face down in the water among the reeds and lily pads, silver-speckled chestnut hair glimmering pearlescent in the sun. The heat of the previous anger rushing through my veins turns ice cold and my stomach churns, bile rising up in my throat. I choke out a whimper and scramble backward, my hands clasped over my mouth.

"What's going on?" asks Abby, rushing over to steady me before I fall to my knees.

I lift a shaky finger and point to the water. "It's Nate. I think he's—"

Abby's eyes go wide with shock. "Oh my God."

I repeat her phrase, the words coming out in a breathless whoosh. "Oh my God."

We stare at his form, floating, not moving. In stunned disbelief, neither of us can move a muscle either, the pond's glassy surface mirroring our glazed expressions. More vomit trails on the terrace and one of the glass panels is shattered. He'd obviously fallen over the side. A gentle breeze rustles the reeds and one of his arms twitches ever so slightly.

"You should call 911 immediately," says Abby, and then she blinks rapidly, her voice unsteady. "But..."

My heart feels like it's going to jump out of my ribcage. "But what?"

"His freaking arm just moved! Did you see it?" She pants. "What if he's alive?"

We exchange a panicked look and then bound onto the terrace, racing down the stone steps. It's like we're both moving on autopilot, not really thinking, just reacting. After kicking off our heels, we trudge knee-deep into the pond, grimacing while making our way over to Nate, the sludge at the bottom thick and slimy with God only knows what.

A couple of leopard spotted and fiery orange koi nip at his arms and legs, jumping and splashing. There's a gash on the back of his head, curdled with brown blood. My fingers fly to my temples and my voice comes out as a wheeze. "We have to move him. Koi fish are omnivores."

Abby gags, closes her eyes, and tilts her head back. She lets out a blood-curdling scream. "I can't believe we're doing this! I'm a really good friend!"

Took the words right out of my trembling mouth. Our gazes lock. We blink. On one, two, three.

Panting, we grasp him by his slippery armpits and drag his stiff, heavy form onto the grass, flipping him over. His lips are blue and swollen. His eyes are open, but glassy and unblinking. His skin is a whiter shade of pale, prune-like and speckled with a rash, his body bloated. This person, this ghost of a corpse, doesn't resemble Nate at all. But I know it's him, thanks to the dog-shaped birthmark on his left thigh. And I know he's dead. There is no rise and fall of his chest.

Not like ours. We're both on the verge of hyperventilating.

The hot sun beats down on my back as Harry and Potter plod over and sniff my hair, and then Nate's lifeless form. The furry beasts shake their bodies, pond water and drool flying into the air, droplets of muck landing on my lips. Nate's red-tinged eyes stare me down. The air smells of rotten eggs, sulfuric like overcooked cabbage. My stomach churns and I hunch over, retching my guts out. The dogs growl, low and deep.

Before they edge in to lick up my vomit or attack Nate, I wipe off the corners of my mouth. "Abby, you know how the dogs are around strangers. Get them in the run. Now!" I screech as I finally manage to scramble up from the ground, tripping over my feet, and race to the house.

With my breath coming hard and fast, I cautiously make my way back to the kitchen, doing my best to avoid the broken glass and the vomit. I grab my purse off the counter; my first instinct to get outside because the smell of decay is about to make me lose it again. I also snatch the bottle of vodka because I could really use some liquid courage right now. Soaked to my waist, pond scum dripping onto my pristine floor, I stumble through the foyer and out the front door, my mind spinning.

Funny, I'd envisioned so many scenarios in which Nate could die. But this wasn't one of them. And, honestly, I'm happy he's gone.

TWO

EMMA

Sunday, May 26th, 2024: 9:25 a.m.

I pace under the shade of a large willow tree, trying to keep my wits about me. My toes wiggle in fresh-cut grass, grounding me in this messed-up reality for a moment. After downing a shot of vodka, I wipe the sweat from my forehead and once I regain control of my trembling hands, I dial.

"Nine-one-one. Please state the nature of your emergency."

"I-I just got back home from a trip—Paris—and found my husband—Nate, Nathaniel Booth Landon, floating face down in the pond. He's all bloated and puffy and, and—"

"Take a deep breath. I'm here for you. Who am I speaking to?"

"Emma. Emma Landon. His wife."

"Your address?"

"Twin Ponds Lane, Bedford; 1850, second home in. There are only four homes on the road—"

"And where are you now, ma'am?"

"I just told you where I was, for crying out loud!"

"Please, try to stay calm, Mrs. Landon."

"I'm being as calm as possible, given the situation!"

"Situation? Do you think there's anybody in your home? A break-in?"

"No. Definitely not. We have a pretty extensive security system. Plus, our dogs are aggressive around strangers—"

"OK, Mrs. Landon, don't touch anything and please stay on the line until the paramedics and responding officers arrive—"

"Excuse me? What? This is my house! And I'm not supposed to touch anything?"

"Ma'am, that's correct. You came home to your husband, now dead, that's right?"

"Yes—and I pulled the lying cheating bastard son of a bitch out of the goddamn water—"

I clamp my free hand over my mouth. *Shit. Shit. Shit.* I didn't mean to say that. I slam the line to a close and slump onto the ground, leaning against the trunk of the willow tree, the bottle of vodka I'd commandeered from the kitchen by my side.

THREE

EMMA

Sunday, May 26th, 2024: 9:35 a.m.

Every last detail of this day is going to be burned into my memory forever. I can't shake off the vision of Nate's unblinking eyes. I can't believe I touched a dead body. My husband's dead body. I can't believe he's gone. I can't believe my kitchen is a vomit-covered war zone. But, aside from these stomach-turning thoughts and my heavy wheezes, I'm wondering why I'm not in a complete state of panic—screaming and crying. Perhaps my brain is blocking out this trauma like a self-defense mechanism.

Everything around me is in sharp focus—each perfect blade of grass, the ants crawling up the bark of the tree, the spiderweb glistening with drops of condensation. I'm here, I'm present, but I'm not. This doesn't seem real.

"Emma!" Abby bellows from somewhere inside the house. "Where the hell are you?"

"I'm in the front yard... by the willow tree," I yell back and end up coughing so hard my eyes water.

Once the fit subsides, I look up to find Abby leaning against the frame of the front door. She visibly blows out a sigh of relief, her curly red hair glimmering in the sunlight like coils on a lit burner. She staggers over to me. "Why are you sitting outside?"

"I'm waiting for them to arrive," I mumble, sweat pooling at the nape of my neck, dripping down my back to the base of my spine.

It's only the end of May. Maybe all those rumors about global warming and climate change are true. My clothes are almost dry from the pond water but will be dampened soon from perspiration.

"Where the hell are they?" Abby asks, scooting down next to me, her voice quivering.

I swallow and clear my throat. "I don't know."

Her eyes shoot to my side, to the bottle nestled in the grass. "Vodka?"

I nod. "After what we just did, I needed it." I hand her the bottle. "Want some?"

She grips the neck and chugs straight from the bottle like I did. Then she swallows and coughs. "Oh my God, I hate the stuff, but that did the trick." She pats my knee. "But you, my dear, are alcohol intolerant—especially with the hard stuff. Do I have to remind you about—"

"You don't."

That time we attended a glamorous party with friends where vodka cocktails flowed freely, and I may have or may not have hooked up with a guy whose name I can't remember for the life of me, or the time we went to Sing Sing, a karaoke bar in the East Village and, apparently, I was convinced I could belt out tunes like the rest of them. (I couldn't). At least I was saved from the aftermath of embarrassment by not remembering a thing.

"And I only get out of control when I have more than one." I take the bottle from Abby, chug a rather large sip, and Abby's eyes go wide. "Right about now, I'd like to black out and pretend this never happened."

If only I could do the same for the rest of my life, namely my marriage to Nate.

"Me too," she says, after swigging back another gulp. "But maybe this was a bad idea."

"Why do you say that?" I ask.

"The police will be here any minute."

I roll my eyes. "I think they'll understand."

My gaze drifts to the kaleidoscope of butterflies flitting around in the distance at the side of the house. As they flit gingerly from flower to flower in my butterfly garden, their beauty contrasts with the horror of the day. I used to wish I could fly away from Nate. Freedom.

Be careful what you wish for, lest it come true.

"You're zoning out," says Abby, nudging me with her shoulder.

"Sorry. Just thinking," I manage to croak out, lacing my fingers within hers, both of our hands damp and sweaty. "Are you OK?"

Her response is hesitant, measured. "I'm not," she says. "We just—"

"I know what we did." The words are like a weight on my chest. I clear my throat, the taste of bile still fresh in my mouth. "And don't say it."

Of course she isn't OK, neither of us are. I don't know why I asked her that. In a sick and twisted replay, the actions of what we have done this morning sting my mind like bullet ants. I remember the emergency bottle of Xanax I packed in my suitcase. I could really use one right about now, but I can't move. It's as if I'm glued to the ground.

"I don't want to say it, let alone think about it," she responds, her voice just barely above a whisper. "I'm trying to breathe, to do anything to find my Zen. But, besides the obvious, what's going on inside that head of yours?"

My tongue thickens in my mouth as I struggle to find the right words to say. If anything, Abby deserves the truth.

"Honestly, I think my heart is made of stone," I confess through gritted teeth while clenching my hands so tightly my fingers cramp up. "I'm a terrible person—a cold, heartless bitch—"

"No, you're not—" Abby interjects.

"But I am, Abs." I cut her off with a pathetic sob. "I wished, even prayed, Nate would die and now he's—"

"Both of us joked about your black widow fantasies. I think I even came up with a few scenarios." Abby lets out a derisive snort. "And you're not a terrible person, Em-Dash. I wouldn't be your best friend if you were."

Silence settles between us for a moment as we sit under the blue sky grappling with this morning's cataclysmic event. Our clothes are moist with pond scum. Our feet are covered in dirt and sludge. We'd dragged a dead body—Nate's body—out of my pond.

"Do you think he got drunk and slipped over the balcony?" asks Abby, her voice just above a whisper.

"I don't know what happened," I mumble, shaking my head. "All I know is that you've gone above and beyond the call of friendship duties." My lips pinch into a trembling frown. "And I'm so sorry you've had to deal with all this—"

"That's the understatement of the year," she says with a sigh, leaning her head on my shoulder. "This is a supremely messed-up situation. You're a victim of circumstance. We both are. Besides that, I really have no words. None whatsoever." She clasps my hand, stopping me from picking my cuticles raw. "Did you get in contact with the girls yet?"

My eyes go wide and I snatch my phone off the ground and try calling the twins. No answer. I send a text and then another one. And then I call both of them again. "Call me back. Immediately. It's important." I sit up straight, twisting my body so I can face Abby. "I'm not telling them that their dad died in the pond over a text or a voice message."

"Right. Good idea," Abby says and then looks at her watch. "Jesus. They're taking their sweet time getting here."

An onslaught of anxiety sucker-punches my stomach. I really messed up. My words come out in a whoosh. "Abby, when I called 911, I may have said something I shouldn't have. About Nate."

Abby places her hand on my back. "What?"

"I pulled the lying cheating bastard son of a bitch out of the goddamn water?" I swallow so hard my throat burns. "And then I hung up the phone—"

"At least you were honest." She blurts out a surprised laugh and wraps her arm around me, pulling me in for a tight hug. "You're in shock. Nobody, not one person on this planet, will take that seriously."

Funny, because I'd meant every word.

"I love you, Sugar Pie," I say with a sniffle.

"Love you more, Honey Bunch—"

A siren wails in the distance. They're almost here. Minutes. Maybe seconds. Along with the nerves sparking every pore in my body, I feel like I'm baking from the inside out, the heat flaring from the top of my head down to my toes. Nate's body is splayed out on the grass. Baking. I shouldn't have touched him, moved him. I shouldn't have married him. I glare at my house. I may have designed a beautiful home, but I should have designed a better life.

FOUR

EMMA

Sunday, May 26th, 2024: 9:43 a.m.

Three vehicles screech into the driveway. Emergency lights flash, pulsing strobes of red and blue, making me lightheaded. Dazed and dizzy, there's no mistaking the police cars, but the third one is a coroner's van—obvious because the word CORONER is painted on the side of the vehicle in big, bold letters. They turn off the sirens, but the ringing in my ears still buzzes and hisses.

A blond man barrels up to us like a Mack truck and Abby and I go as rigid as the statues we'd seen at the Louvre the previous day. Tall at over six feet, a closely shaved goatee brings attention to his square jaw line and in his blue uniform with all the badges and bulging muscles he exudes an intimidating air of authority. His body looms over us, dimming out the light of the sun, and the branches of the willow tree form vein-like shadows on his face. "Emma Landon?"

It's like I'm paralyzed from the neck up. I can't speak, utter out anything but tiny grunts.

"Her," says Abby, waving a tentative finger in my direction.

"And you are?"

"Abigail Hoffman. Best friend."

Both of us scramble up from the ground, shifting our weight from side to side. My knees feel like they're made of jelly and I'm certain my legs will give out. Abby squeezes my hand and then shoots her arm out to him in greeting. He ignores the gesture with a frown, his eyes locking onto the vodka bottle by my feet.

"Have you been drinking?" he asks, and Abby nods.

"Kind of freaking out. Finding a dead body. Not something we expected. And it must be five o'clock somewhere—"

His lips pinch together into a tight line and I lower my head.

"I see," he says with his eyebrows raised, muttering "straight vodka from a bottle" under his breath and my throat catches. "And were you with Mrs. Landon when she discovered her husband's body?"

She tenses beneath his stare while nodding her head yes very quickly several times in succession. The movement causes the triple gold hoop earrings she wears to bobble and clank together like little bells.

"Um, we both kicked off our shoes and waded into the pond." Abby gestures outward with her hands and brings them back toward herself. "We dragged Nate out of the water before the fish ate him." She clears her throat and cocks her head to the side. "Koi fish are omnivores—did you know that?"

"I didn't," he replies, looking at Abby like she's nuts.

Although she's in nervous babble mode, spouting out one breathless sentence at a time, I'm just happy she's explaining everything, no matter how nonsensical she sounds, because all I can do is let out little grunts.

"Emma threw up." Her shoulders rise into a shrug. "That's what happened."

He just blinks slowly. "And where do you live, Ms. Hoffman?"

"Katonah."

"That's over fifteen minutes away—"

"Not if you speed like a bat out of hell," says Abby, and then quickly corrects herself. "We were together. We just got back from Paris this morning. I drove. I mean not from Paris—"

"What airline?"

"Air France to JFK."

"You parked there?" he asks, pulling out a pad of paper and a pen as she nods. "For how many days?"

He's fact-checking, glancing at me every few seconds, and this makes me nervous. By his stoic demeanor, the way he's eyeing my every reaction, he thinks I had something to do with Nate's death. Maybe I've read too many thrillers my mother bought over the years, but they always focus in on the wife and what I said on the call cast me into the murkiest of waters. While Abby rambles out a reply, I try to focus on my breathing. In through the nose, out through the mouth, my back pressing into the rough bark of the willow tree, the trunk anchoring my weight so I don't tumble to the ground.

"We left last Tuesday night, the red-eye, and arrived back in New York this morning—another red-eye." Abby emits a high-pitched squeak. "Oh yeah, Emma's girls, Ava and Grace, went to Paris with us too."

He raises a brow and locks me in his gaze. "What time did you say you arrived here?"

I lick my lips and swallow.

"A little before nine," I say, the words sticking in my throat. My posture straightens when his brows lift and he motions for me to carry on. "Our flight got in at ten past six. We went through security. We got our bags. Went to the lot—"

"OK, I don't need to know all that," he says with an exasperated sigh. "What I do need to know is why you waited over twenty minutes to call 911?"

"We didn't notice him at first," I stammer and shift my weight. "I wasn't exactly expecting to find him floating in the pond when I got home. And then we had to get the dogs in the run."

"They're aggressive around strangers," explains Abby. "Really aggressive. Harry and Potter are Tibetan mastiffs and they are enormous. Protective of their masters—"

His eyes float to the right, then the left. "I don't see any dogs."

I point to the run at the side of the property. "It's hot out. They're probably in their house. It has air conditioning—"

His lips twitch. I shut up. The dogs live better than most people, in a five-hundred-square-foot "home" with custom-made iron beds with memory foam mattresses covered in a chocolate-colored brocade. Nate's brilliant idea, which I acquiesced to in order to avoid the thick clumps of tumbleweed hair rolling around in every corner of the house.

"Uh-huh," the officer finally says, jotting something down on his notepad. His blue eyes meet mine, his gaze intense. "And where are your girls—it's Ava and Grace, right?—now?"

"They're still in France with Taryn. In Cannes," I say and continue explaining. "Taryn Flynn was with us in Paris too—"

"Taryn Flynn, the model, daughter of Gordon Flynn?" he asks, a spark of recognition flashing in his eyes.

No surprise there. Everybody knew Gordon Flynn's name and, more importantly, how the "sex king of New York" made his fortune. Worth around thirty billion, Gordon is a purveyor of porn, websites, and sex toys, among other savvy and unsavory deals, run by his company creepily named G-Spot Enterprises. Revolting. I couldn't stand the man, but, the best friend of my girls, I adored Taryn.

"Yes, she's like a third daughter to me." I wave a hand

toward the distance. "Gordon is our neighbor. We—Nate—bought this land from him over two decades ago—"

"How old are your girls?"

"Fourteen."

His eyes bug out. "And they're with Taryn Flynn?"

"She's like their big sister. They worship her. And I trust her like one of my own."

"I see." The officer nods and scribbles something down and then looks up. "Do your girls know about Mr. Landon?"

"I-I can't get in touch with them."

Abby coughs and repeats my earlier words. "It's not exactly the type of news one delivers over a text or voicemail, is it?"

I shoot her an appreciative side-glance.

"No, I suppose not."

"And, officer, your name is?" I ask, my nerves in a tangle.

"It's Sergeant," he states gruffly. "Sergeant Kowalski."

Numb, I can only nod because two men wearing lab coats are pulling a gurney out of the van and it slams down onto the driveway. A third, and then a fourth man, exit the cop cars. Sergeant Kowalski's gaze follows mine. My shoulders shake and I choke back a low moan. Abby places a tender hand on my shoulder. Although I haven't shed a tear, I know my heart is definitely not made of stone because it's beating furiously.

"I'm sorry for your loss. I understand a shock like this could be a jolt for the system." He scratches his chin. "But, I do need to know, where is Mr. Landon's body?"

Keep calm, I tell myself. *You didn't do anything wrong except wish him dead.*

But the officer definitely doesn't need to know that.

"In the backyard at the side of the pond." I point to a flagstone path, my entire arm trembling. It takes effort to lower it. "You're welcome to go through the house, but that might be an easier route for the—the—"

"Gurney." He turns and gestures to the men. "Around

back," he instructs and then meets my petrified gaze. "Are you coming?"

"Do I have to?" A bitter taste fills my mouth and I try to swallow it down. "This is all so devastating. I don't think I could take seeing him again. N-n-not like that. I... it... I..."

"I understand. Finding the body of a loved one is a traumatic experience, but you'll still have to identify his body before we take him to the morgue," he says, and I flinch. "Just wait in the house for now. It's boiling hot outside, like soup. I'll come find you when we need you."

The heat of the blistering sun has nothing on the wave of nausea roiling in my stomach. I stifle the urge to gag. Now I'm thinking about how Abby and I discovered Nate's body. Maybe boiling in the pond like soup. No. Why on earth did he have to say that?

"She doesn't want to go into the house," says Abby, latching onto my obvious discomfort.

"Why? Did something happen? Do you think there was a break-in?"

I shake my head no slowly. "I think Nate had people over when I was out of town. Uh... the kitchen is swarming with flies—"

"And there's vomit everywhere," interjects Abby. "Plus, if there was a break-in, the Picasso is still hanging on the wall—"

"And he's wearing a two-million-dollar watch."

"Uh-huh." He scribbles rapidly on his pad and then his gaze sweeps the property. "I'm going to have to take a look around. For now, just stay in the shade." His eyes narrow with suspicion as my spine stiffens and I straighten my back to full attention. "Standard protocol," he says with a lift of his massive shoulders. "We need to rule out foul play."

My heart thuds in my chest as Sergeant Kowalski's gaze rakes over me, his eyes steady and cold. "Oh?" I mutter.

He tilts his head to the side and places his enormous hands on his hips. "Do you have a problem with that?"

The skepticism in his tone is unmistakable.

My throat goes dry as I stammer out a response. "N-No. Not at all."

Sergeant Kowalski turns on his heel and meanders down the path, the other members of his crew following, leaving me trembling with fear. I shudder, the words foul play chilling me to the bone. Any loose threads I've been hanging onto are about to snap.

FIVE

DETECTIVE ROSSI

Sunday, May 26th, 2024: 10:17 a.m.

The news of Nathaniel Landon's death buzzes through the station in excited murmurs.

Although there are many wealthy families in Bedford—the jurisdiction also comprised of Bedford Hills and Katonah—there are only a couple of billionaires and Nathaniel Landon is one of them. Everyone knows his name—including me.

I was fourteen years old when I'd found out who he was—the new prince of New York, his picture plastered on the cover of every tabloid magazine—the kind my ma bought—and I'd developed one of those adolescent crushes. I didn't hang his pictures on my walls or anything like that, but I did develop a little obsession. Dream big or go home, right?

My friends would click a Chinese fortune-teller open after I'd picked a number (click, click, click): a mansion and a yacht, driving a Mercedes convertible, and you're marrying Nathaniel. Granted, I cheated and made sure I got what I wanted.

But Ma always brought my little-girl fantasies crashing down to reality.

"A man like him from high society," she'd say, waving a dismissive hand, "would never go for the likes of you. Men like him are way out of your league. Stick to your own kind."

I cried (way to crush a prepubescent girl's dreams, Ma), but I knew she was right. Nathaniel Landon was definitely in a league of his own and I stuck with people from the same social circles as I was. Like my pa, I became a cop. Unlike him, thanks to a full scholarship, I'd studied criminal justice at NYU and I'd moved on quickly from patrol to detective.

I'm a critical thinker. And I'm thinking right now.

Pure and simple facts roll around in my head. Nathaniel Booth Landon. Age forty-nine. A highly respected cardiothoracic surgeon, and beyond rich—old money rich. His family wealth came from a steel and aluminum fortune in Pittsburgh. Body found by his wife, Emma Landon, floating face down in a pond. As I grab my fourth cup of joe from the kitchen, an undercurrent of electricity pulses in the air and the house is already placing bets, the pungent scent of sweat and testosterone wafting up to my nostrils.

"I met Emma Landon at a Boys and Girls Club charity event. She was a standoffish bitch. I'm betting she offed him or hired somebody to do it."

"How much?"

"Twenty bucks."

"Let's make it forty."

"Motive? Love, lust, loathing or loot?"

"She may have a *billion* reasons to have wanted him dead, but I'm going with loathing."

Officer Diaz adjusts his balls (I swear he has to check them every five minutes to make sure they're still there). He catches my eye as I pour milk into my mug. "Rossi, what do you think?"

"We all know that a death investigation is comprised of three stages: examination, correlation, and interpretation. So, I think, in this case, Emma's words are open to interpretation. Beyond suspicious."

"So if she did it, what was her motive?" asks Sergeant Smith.

"I think you're all jumping the gun," I say, which makes everybody chuckle. "It's not a homicide." My lips curl into a grin. "Yet."

Diaz guffaws. "You're placing a wager, I take it?"

"I'm not."

"Buzzkill," says Diaz with a laugh.

"Not exactly. I'm saving my cash for a pitcher or two of margaritas."

Shaking my head, I meander to my desk. I'm back to listening to Emma Landon's words on repeat, primarily her last statement before she hung up on her call to Dispatch.

"Yes—and I pulled the lying cheating bastard son of a bitch out of the goddamn water—"

Her voice, her tone, is filled with anger, her words spitting venom. Trouble in paradise? Didn't they have the perfect marriage, the perfect life? Was he cheating on her? I want to know more about Emma Landon so I pull up Google.

Thirty-eight years old, Maiden name Novak. Grew up in Bushwick, Brooklyn. Member of the drama club in high school. Dad, Mark, is a veterinarian, retired. Mom, Olivia, runs a cleaning service, Dust Busters. I cackle at the name—and the tagline: "Who you gonna call? Dust Busters!"

Her parents currently live in Pound Ridge—kind of a pricey area and above their means. I open up Zillow in a new window, to find the house was purchased by Nathaniel Landon in 2003 for 295k and currently valued at 1.5 mill. Interesting. I close the window and continue investigating Emma. Graduated high school at seventeen. Went to Parsons for undergrad, Columbia for her masters' degree in interior architecture. Married Nathaniel in 2008 when she was twenty-three. Gave birth to twin girls, Ava and Grace, when she was twenty-four. Esteemed interior architect.

I blink back my astonishment as I click through photos of their magnificent estate. Set on twenty-three acres, the eighteen-thousand-square-foot glass and cement 'architectural triumph' is partially built over a pond, each and every room decorated impeccably. Add in the pool, pool house, guesthouse, ten-car garage, tennis court, driving range, and, damn, this woman is living the good life.

I'm chewing the cap on my pen. Emma Novak. Why does her maiden name ring a bell? She went to Parsons for undergrad. I pick up my phone, dialing my best friend, Francesca. She picks up on the first ring. "Gabriella! I was wondering if you'd forgotten about me—"

"Frannie, we'll catch up on everything later—life, all that. Sorry, I've been busy." My brain tingles with my hunch. "What was the name of the girl that received the financial aid from Parsons? The one that you needed? The one that you thought might have been screwing the counselor in charge of it?"

The sound of something crashing on the floor. Barking. Frannie screams, "Kids, take Balboa outside! Now!"

I laugh. "You named your dog after Rocky?"

"Better than Sly," she says. "What'd you ask me?"

"The name of the girl?"

She takes in a deep breath. "Emily something or another. I dunno. I kind of blocked her out of my memory ever since she stole my life away from me. She got what I needed. And now look at me. I mean, I would have slept with that counselor too." She pauses. "Kidding, of course. You know me—raised in the strictest of Catholic families."

I let her words sink in. I was raised the same way. Ma saw to that, chasing boys away from the front drive of our home with a baseball bat if they seemed sketchy—and most of them were.

No wonder I didn't date much in high school. I shake the thought off.

"Was her name Emma Novak?"

A silence settles between us for a moment. I hear a sharp intake of her breath.

"Yeah, that's it. Why?"

My eyes go wide. "Frannie, I'm going to have to call you back—"

"Meet up for margaritas later this week?"

"You bet."

I hang up the phone. My hunch was right. Emma Landon does whatever she wants to get what she wants—tipping the scales so they lean in her favor. Sleeping with a counselor? Killing her husband? I'm going to prove that Emma Landon is a fake, a fraud, and an opportunist. She'd screwed over Frannie, who was wronged and denied opportunities that were rightfully hers. Who knew what else she was capable of?

The more I dig online, the more pictures of the perfect couple show up in the highfalutin society pages—dressed up at galas at charity events or posh gatherings, him wearing a tuxedo, her in outrageous designer dresses. In the beginning, she's all smiles in wedding photos, looking up at Nathaniel with adoration, but I notice about two or three years later, things change. Emma's body language, the way her torso twists away from him, conveys repulsion. Her eyes are distant and cold, like she's not really there. Nathaniel smiles at her, but it doesn't reach his eyes and feels fake as shit. It's like they can't stand one another and are simply acting out roles of the perfect couple.

I open a new window and google the twins, Ava and Grace. Not much comes up, save for a couple of photos of them in matching dresses—tiaras included—at charity events, or competing at horse shows. Well, la-dee-da. Aren't they just the perfect little princesses in their emerald green Ivy Crest school uniforms, which they've been attending since they were twelve years old? What kind of mother sends their kids away so young? Not a good one.

Groaning with utter disgust, I close out of the window and play Emma's call again while clicking through photos of the deliriously rich and happy couple. The cars. The house. The clothes. The trips. An illusion of luck and fortune, nothing about the way they live seems real.

Questions prick at my brain. Would a woman in her position kill when she has everything? Wouldn't it be easier to divorce him if he was cheating? Why did he marry her? How did they meet? I want answers and I'm champing at the bit.

Chief Davis meanders out of his office. Fifty years old, he's tall at over six feet, on the thinner side (choosing exercise instead of eating doughnuts) and has salt-and-pepper hair, graying at the temples. Distinguished. I cross my fingers as he swaggers up to me, looking up expectantly. "I see you're already doing research on the Landon death."

"Yeah, well that call was suspicious as hell, CD," I say, using his nickname like we all do. "Particularly her last statement." My eyes go wide with anticipation. "And? Anything?"

"Kowalski found a bunch of weird shit in the kitchen and the pool house," he says, and I cackle softly, rubbing my hands together. "You're on the wheel. A couple of investigators will join you."

I squint. "And is Emma Landon a person of interest?"

"Won't know until we get the coroner's report back." He knocks my desk twice with a sturdy fist and then shakes a finger. "Rossi, be careful with this one. We need to tread lightly."

I blink with confusion. "What do you mean by that?"

"This is a high-profile case and once the news outlets get their grubby hands on the story, and they will, we can't take any chances. Don't jump to any unwarranted conclusions until the evidence is processed."

"Got it," I say. "I'll gather my gear and be on my way."

"Radio in if you need anything."

I salute him. "Will do, CD."

As he saunters back to his office, I tap my fingernails on my desk, my eyes locking onto pictures from the past, specifically the one where Emma is twisted away from Nathaniel with revulsion. Based on the call and what I know about Nathaniel's vast fortune, if I'd placed a bet on her motive, mine would be on both loot *and* loathing.

SIX

EMMA

Sunday, May 26th, 2024: 10:35 a.m.

Abby and I have been staying out of the way, finding relief from the heat in her car with the AC blasting. Thankfully, I have a charging station for her Tesla, so we're all plugged in, no worries about her car dying. Parched beyond belief, while I was in the garage hooking the car into the outlet, I also managed to snag us bottles of Voss water from the refrigerator along with two pairs of gardening Crocs. Both of us are physically and emotionally drained. We are not talking about Nate or his death, just listening to the music we bonded over when we were in our glory days.

With her eyes closed, Abby hums along to Romeo Void's "A Girl in Trouble (Is a Temporary Thing)" and I'm hoping my troubles are temporary, although every fiber in my being tells me they're only beginning. I look over at her—fierce, strong Abby, thankful some of her strength, her inner confidence, rubbed off on me.

We may have been cut from different molds, but it only solidified our initial opposites-attract friendship. She's a hard-nosed, doesn't take crap from anyone, tells-it-like-is Jewish girl from Brooklyn and damn proud of it. L'chaim. I'm, well, me—a girl who let people walk all over her—that is, until I met Abby.

"Abs," I say with a sigh.

"Mmm-hmm," she responds.

"Do you remember the day we met?"

She nods her head, a small smile curving on her lips. "How could I forget? What did I call you?"

"A pushover."

"Ha. That's right. And right about now, I'd kill for a pitcher of those margaritas." She licks her lips. "Guac and chips? Those were the good ol' days, huh?"

"They were."

Prior to obtaining my masters' degree for interior architecture at Columbia, I'd attended Parsons for undergrad and in my third year of studies I slammed into Abby in the stairwell. A student of fashion design, she was carrying a bolt of silk fabric, which she dropped, and it unrolled down the stairs like a red carpet.

"For crying out loud," she'd screamed as I scrambled to help her roll it back up. "This cost me twenty bucks a yard! If there's one speck of dirt on it, one blemish, you're buying me more. Ten yards. That's two hundred bucks if you don't know how to do math."

Her eyes shot daggers at me and if proverbial looks really could kill I'd definitely have been dead, all bloody and twisted on the floor. I'd thought she was so cool and fierce. Dressed in an eggplant flower-patterned Bohemian-chic dress with brown boots that laced up at the ankle, she really had her own sense of style. Her long red hair, also streaked with eggplant, was tied in a side braid that reached the middle of her stomach. A mash-up of Stevie Nicks and Cyndi Lauper, she pulled off her look and, the kind of woman who commanded attention, she had mine. I stood on the steps with my mouth open.

"Do you speak?" she'd asked. "Or are you a mute?"

"I speak," I'd said, hands raised. "I'm so sorry. I wasn't looking where I was going." I pulled out a twenty from my pocket, saying a silent goodbye to the hard-earned funds from working for my mother's cleaning service, scrubbing down toilets with bleach until my hands were raw and red. But at least I lived at home and qualified for financial aid. "Here's enough for one yard."

She looked at me like I was nuts and grabbed the bill.

"It's all I have on me. I'll give you more when I can."

"Are you always so agreeable?" she'd asked with a sneer, turning to inspect the silk. "I haven't even checked the fabric out yet. It might be fine."

"But it might not be. You said one speck of dirt—"

"I can be a little overly dramatic." She laughed. "You should meet my mother. And my sister." She brushed off the now rolled-up silk. "The five-second rule, right? I can steam off any imperfections," she'd said, and then placed her free hand on her hip. "Anyway, I'm Abby. A piece of advice, watch where you're going next time. And, while I'm at it, don't be such a pushover."

I gave her a blank look.

"Aren't you going to ask for your twenty back?"

"Can I have it back?"

Abby grinned, highlighting the little gap in between her two front teeth. "No, we're going to put it to good use. I'll store the fabric and then let's go grab a drink somewhere. My treat." She waved the twenty. "I don't know about you, but I need a break from all the stress."

Stunned, I nodded my head in agreement. "I'm only nineteen."

"Good thing they don't card. And that I have my sister's fake ID. We kind of look alike. I know of a place around the corner. Best margaritas in the area. Killer guac and chips too."

She pursed her lips, squinting at me. "OK, you pushover, what's your name?"

"Emma."

And that's how Abby and I became friends. Over a pitcher of margaritas, we laughed and talked, her teaching me the finer points of sticking up for myself, me telling her not to curse so much. She also encouraged me to come up with a style more of my own. She'd eyed me up and down. "You know who you remind me of?"

"Who?" I asked.

"A sassier Jackie O. You've got a really classic look, sophisticated. Get some inspiration from her, play up her look and make it your own. I know of a great fabric shop on the Upper East side," she'd said.

"Fabric shop?" I'd parroted.

"Yeah, you kind of need an overhaul," she'd said, circling her finger in front of my blue-and-white checked dress with a white bow that tied at the neck. I'd purchased it at a thrift store. "You're way too young to dress like a little old lady. And I need somebody to make clothes for. A real-life mannequin. You'd be doing me a favor—and I'd definitely be doing you one."

I should have been insulted, but for some odd reason we really clicked, and from that day onward we'd become inseparable, which was a blessing because I didn't have many friends. Most people thought I was aloof or snobby or simply an overly competitive, uptight bitch. I knew this because I'd overheard them talking about the professor's pet: me. Same thing happened in high school, but without the rumor of me sleeping with a financial counselor whispered behind my back. But Abby got me—my drive and my ambition.

Although we're both older now, and our styles have changed, her curly hair now styled so it brushes over her shoulders, we're also wiser. I should have taken her advice to heart years ago when she'd warned me about Nate.

I wish I could press the rewind button on time and do everything all over again. But I'm reminded of the fact that I can't when more cruisers tear into the driveway, sirens blaring. Abby turns the music off. Frozen, we watch the scene play out in her rearview mirror. A half-dozen men and women jump out of the vehicles like a SWAT team, carrying equipment and boxes and who knows what. Kowalski ushers them into the backyard. I lock onto a woman wearing a navy blue suit and a white shirt as she steps out of a black Chevy Impala.

Panic blooms in my chest. Thanks to Nate's obsession, I know more about cars than I'd care to. The veins in my neck pulse with fear. "I think they've called a detective in."

Abby rubs the sleep out of her eyes and mutters, "Damn, Emma. That can't be good."

"I know," I say, and then frantically instruct her. "If they question you, you can't tell them about my plans to divorce Nate. It's why I was skittish to call 911 in the first place." I take in gulps of air—like a fish fighting for its life, flapping around on the ground when they need to get back into the water. "Wife planning on divorcing billionaire husband and comes home to find him dead. What I said on the call. Think about it."

Abby studies my face intently. Her hazel eyes narrow, darkening to more of a brown than green. "Am I your alibi? Did you hire someone to—"

"Oh my God, Abby! I can't believe you'd even suggest that." I slam my hand on the dashboard. "No! I wanted to divorce him. I wanted to hit him where it hurts—financially. I wanted to humiliate him by striking first. Kill his ego!" I rub my eyes with the tips of my fingers. "What kind of person do you think I am?"

Her expression softens. She clucks her tongue. "Jesus, Em, you better find out what's going on."

We jump out of the car and I march to the backyard, Abby trailing behind me. Nate's lifeless corpse—the centerpiece of the scene—is all zipped up in a black body bag, lying on a gurney. A crew of people in white lab coats are taking measurements, or photographs, or placing objects in containers. Sergeant Kowalski turns when he hears our approach, his eyes blazing with curiosity. "Did you need something, Mrs. Landon?"

"Can you please tell me what's happening?" I gasp, hunching over and placing my hands on my knees.

"We're securing the scene and collecting evidence," he says.

Abby's mouth drops open. "Y-y-you think Nate was murdered?"

"I didn't say that." He fixes his gaze on Abby. "But that's what we're going to find out."

My heart rate revs up to a new dangerous level. My lungs feel like they're going to burst. "Should we leave?"

I want to.

Somebody in the distance waves and taps their wrist.

"No, not yet," he says, squinting toward the sun. "They're about to take Mr. Landon to the morgue." He meets my eyes. "It's time to identify his body."

SEVEN

DETECTIVE ROSSI

Sunday, May 26th, 2024: 10:42 a.m.

Sweat beads on my forehead. It's only the end of May and it's already hot as hell, not a cloud in the sky, just the sun beating down on the ground like it wants to destroy the grass and burn me right along with it. I've been watching her, observing. Emma Landon barely flinches when they unzip the body bag. She just nods, lips pinched, and turns around when the coroner wheels her husband's body into the van.

She's of average height, maybe five-foot-six at best, a whisper of a woman, thin to the point of being seemingly anorexic. Her designer dress is black, contrasting her pallid complexion. Her shoes? She's wearing Crocs now, but her Chanel kitten heels were found in the yard—and have been marked as evidence. At least she's somewhat appropriately dressed for a funeral.

Her friend, Abigail Hoffman, is wearing a black, flared-leg jumpsuit with a wide, studded black belt. Every time she moves her head, her giant gold earrings clang like little chimes. Large black sunglasses cover her face.

Sergeant Kowalski walks up beside me and, like a laser, his eyes follow mine.

Momentarily stunned, I straighten my shoulders and shake my head with disdain. "Do you see her? The way she's acting? It's just not right."

Kowalski nudges my rib with his elbow. "People grieve in different ways. I tried ruffling her feathers by acting all tough. It didn't work. I think she may be in shock."

"Whatever she is, she's not acting like a grieving widow."

He holds back a laugh. "She'll be a happy widow with that money."

I tap his chest with a pointed finger. "Motive. And I believe she was already celebrating his death with that bottle of vodka."

Along with inheriting all of Nathaniel's assets—the stock in his family's steel company worth a couple billion, Emma will definitely benefit from his twenty-million-dollar life insurance policy and their monstrosity of a house, worth thirty mill, maybe more. Give or take, she and her spoiled brats get it all.

Abigail leans toward Emma, whispers something. I swear a tight smile passes across Emma's lips. They're probably planning a vacation to the islands to celebrate Emma's great fortune. On a yacht. With champagne. And a crew of tanned studs catering to their every need.

"People are innocent until proven guilty," whispers Kowalski.

"And I'm going to prove she's guilty."

"Gabby, you'd think you had a vendetta against this woman." He rolls his eyes. "The facts are the facts. She was out of town. In Paris."

Before I'd left the station, I'd read an article that Nathaniel had been quoted in: *Emma can do anything she wants with her 50k monthly allowance.* I tilt my head, watching her closely. The paramedic slams the back of the van closed and her mouth forms a tiny *o* followed by what looks like a sigh of relief. "Maybe she hired someone to bump him off."

"You're grasping at straws," he responds with a scoff.

"Alex, I'm not." I wave my hand toward the perimeter of the estate, specifically to the bushes with smooth dark green leathery leaves and red flowers. "Look at all the oleander surrounding the property. They are highly toxic. Can kill a person—"

Kowalski lifts an eyebrow. "And she was force-feeding him leaves? Brewing it in a tea? Or had somebody do it?"

I know he thinks I have an overactive imagination, that I watch too many cop movies, read too many detective novels and thrillers, but I'm trusting my instincts.

"Didn't CD warn you?" Kowalski continues. "Let forensics do their job before you jump to conclusions."

"Exactly." I arch a defiant eyebrow. "And that's why I'm calling in for tox."

"Fine. But you'll be waiting at least two to six weeks to get it." His face goes serious for a moment and then he grins, laughing softly. "In addition to oleander, you might as well put Polonium-210 on your list. And cyanide."

"Not a bad idea," I respond, knowing he's trying to egg me on. "And aren't you the one who told CD to tell me to get my ass over here?"

"Maybe I missed you. And your sexy ass."

I glare at him and then send one in Emma Landon's direction. She has something to do with his death. I know it.

"Look, something definitely isn't adding up. But I'd cross her off your list." He raises a brow. "Are you searching for justice? Or are you jealous?"

"Jealous? Why? Because I live in a two-bedroom apartment in Mount Kisco and she lives in this monstrosity? She has maids and cleaners and doesn't lift a finger? Probably has somebody wipe her ass after she shits?"

"I'd do that for you."

"Stai zitto, cazzo, you nutjob." I exhale a sharp breath. "Remind me why I like you—"

"Because we work well together, Gabby." He wiggles his brows and winks. "You dating anybody?"

I snort into my hand. We've been dating on the sly for about six months. Me, a sassy Italian girl from the Bronx. Him, a Polish dude from Brooklyn. We'd fallen into like at a department picnic, me drooling over his homemade pierogis, him with my stuffed manicotti. I'd say opposites attract, but the more I got to know him I'd realized we had more in common than I'd initially thought—namely we were both true and tried New Yorkers born into a second generation of families of hard-working immigrants. Pomylony! Pazzo! Crazy! Plus, we're both cops and believe in justice.

I tap his chest with my index finger. Shoot him a mock glare. "Sergeant Kowalski, sometimes I want to strangle you."

"There are witnesses," he says, waving his hand toward Emma and her friend. "And there's no such thing as the perfect murder."

"Tell that to Emma Landon."

He's about to respond when I shush him. The woman in question sashays by us with her friend, Abigail. Emma stops when she notices us. Her spicy and decadent perfume infiltrates my nostrils—almonds and leather and something floral. She lowers her sunglasses to the bridge of her nose and I can finally see her eyes and they're not red from tears; they are cold, devoid of emotion like a sociopath. Dead.

"Mrs. Landon, can I have a word with you?" I ask.

"I already told him everything," she says, nodding toward Kowalski. "We came home this morning from a trip to Paris and found him floating in the pond. We pulled him out. I called 911. What more do you need to know?"

"Just covering all my bases. The conditions surrounding

your husband's death are very suspicious," I say, and then lower my voice. "And so was your call to Dispatch."

Her jaw unhinges ever so slightly and her friend lets out a gasp. "I understand. But, as you can imagine, it was quite the shock. Finding him like that."

"I'm sure it was. But I do have to ask you and your friend some questions. Is there somewhere inside we can speak? Out of the heat and away from the investigation? They're collecting evidence on the terrace, the pool house and in the kitchen. They've already swept the living room—"

"Can't it wait?" she asks with fatigued annoyance.

"I'm afraid it can't."

"And your name?" she asks, lips pinched.

"Detective Rossi." I offer a sympathetic smile, wanting her to think I'm on her side. The woman-to-woman vibe. "I'm sorry to be a nuisance. I just need to be clear in my report."

EIGHT

EMMA

Sunday, May 26th, 2024: 10:56 a.m.

I let out a puff of irritation I can't contain and then nod, leading the detective to the flagstone path, taking us to the front door. As she gives me the once-over, I also survey her. Pretty in a rough and tumble way, her chestnut hair is unkempt, her eyes dark brown and intense. She's probably in her mid-thirties. She's around five foot three, but makes up for her tiny stature with her gruff demeanor—the way she walks, stomping behind me like she's one of the boys.

We bat away flies, heading into the living room. After I slide the iron and glass pocket doors to a close and open a window, Rossi settles into one of my favorite chairs, white linen with carved platinum-painted armrests, Abby and I on the couch. She scans the room, a bushy eyebrow raised, her dark eyes locking onto the coffee table displaying magazines I'd been featured in like *Vanity Fair* and *Elle Décor*, overly stylized and airbrushed representations of my actual life. "You have a beautiful home. I understand you're an architect and you designed this place."

"I am. I did. And thank you." Something about her gaze is unsettling and I'm not lulled by the fake kindness in her voice or the thinly veiled compliment. I'm on edge. "I'd offer you a coffee or something to drink, but—"

"I'm fine." She raises her chin and pulls out a digital tape recorder, placing it on the coffee table. "Mrs. Landon, before we start, are you OK if I record our conversation?"

My throat tightens with dread and I clasp my hands on my lap, my legs crossed at the ankles. "Do what you need to do."

"Would you like an attorney to be present?"

The hair on the back of my neck bristles. My left eye twitches. I know what she's getting at. With an edge of defiance, I reply, "Do I need one?"

"If you think you do—"

My mouth goes dry.

"I don't," I say with exasperation. "How many times do I have to explain this to you people? The girls and I went to Paris. We left on Tuesday night and arrived back home this morning— when we found him, my husband, floating in the pond face down, dead."

Before Rossi speaks again, she leans forward, balancing her elbows on her knees. Her chair scrapes the floor and my eyes drift to her dirt-covered shoes and then to the strands of fur and lint on her jacket. My lips pinch into a tight sneer, which she picks up on. Her eyebrows raise and her lips slightly part with offense. She blinks and I continue, "What more do you need to know?"

Her posture straightens. "Forgive me for being frank, but you really don't seem too upset about your husband's passing."

Her voice is tinged with malice, a threat. A shimmer of fear scurries its way up my spine. I can feel the blood rushing out of my face and my breathing becomes shallow. If she knew the truth about Nate, what he was really like, she'd want the twisted bastard locked up in prison and she'd swallow the key.

"Forgive *me*, but, honestly, I'm in shock. I mean, how would you feel? How am I supposed to act? You're not even giving me a moment, a second, to breathe. I'm doing my best to retain my composure," I say with a shaky voice. I hastily lift my sunglasses to the top of my head and choke back an angry sob. "I'm sorry. This wasn't the homecoming I expected."

Abby clasps my hand and eyes the detective. "Is all this really necessary? We're pretty shaken up."

"I'm just doing my job," says Rossi with false sympathy. "And, for the record, I know this is uncomfortable and I'm truly sorry for your loss. But I really do need some answers before I can leave. We think something happened to your husband and we hope you can shed some light on the situation."

Light. I'd left Paris, the City of Light, only to come back to a world of darkness. I'd wanted to reboot my life, but this new one came with glitches and I don't know how to press the restart button. I just want her to leave. I look up and wipe the tears off my cheeks, and then swallow. "Maybe he drank too much with his friends and fell over the terrace. He had a gash on his head."

"The wound was superficial—not the cause of death."

I blink. "Then, I don't know what happened."

"That's what I'm trying to find out."

I huff out a sigh. "Can we please just get this over with?"

"Nathaniel had a strange rash covering his body. Was he allergic to anything?"

I nod and lift my shoulders into a slight shrug. "Anything with a stinger. Bees, wasps, and hornets."

"Mrs. Landon, I'd like to speak with you alone," she says. "Is there somewhere Ms. Hoffman can wait until I'm ready to speak with her?" She tilts her head toward Abby. "And I do need to speak with you."

Abby shoots me a concerned frown and stands up. "I'll be in my car."

I watch her leave the room, rubbing the base of my throat with my fingertips, trying to quell my nerves.

Detective Rossi coughs and I sit up straight, locking my hands together. "So, Paris. You said you were also with your twin girls, Ava and Grace, and Taryn Flynn. Where are they now?"

"They're still in France. With Taryn. They went to Cannes," I say. "For the film festival."

Her chin tucks into her collarbone. "You allowed two young girls to gallivant around the south of France?" she scoffs. "With a model?"

I know this doesn't look good. But I'm happy they're not here to deal with this.

"Look, I trust Taryn, OK? She's like the girls' big sister. And Taylor Swift was performing. Plus—"

"I see," she says, cutting me off and jotting something down in her notebook. "Since your girls are minors, I'll need Taryn's contact information to corroborate your story."

"For Pete's sake, Abby was with me." I throw my arms up in the air in exasperation. "We just got back this morning. There's your story."

"Noted. I'm just making sure that all angles are covered," says Rossi. She leans forward, eyeing a photo of the twins on the side table. She shoots me the fakest of smiles, highlighting her sharp canine teeth. "How do you tell your girls apart?"

What a stupid question. How is that going to help her find out what happened to Nate? She's wasting my time.

"I'm their mother. It's not that hard, and they're not exactly identical," I say, and Rossi lifts a brow in question. "Ava has freckles, Grace doesn't."

"Good to know." She scribbles something in her booklet again, pressing her pen hard into the page, and the sound is like nails on a chalkboard to me. So is her saccharine tone. "I still need Taryn's contact information."

After I blurt out her telephone number, I sit back into the couch, growing more irritated by the second. "Good grief. I feel like I'm being interrogated. And I haven't done anything wrong."

Except marry the bastard. He's probably laughing at me from his spot in hell.

Got you, Emma.

"You don't have to speak with me right now if you don't want to," she says, her New York drawl grating on my every nerve. "But you will have to eventually—either right here, right now or down at the station. As I've mentioned, we think Mr. Landon's untimely passing could be the result of foul play."

Just like the big Kowalski cop, I can tell by the suspicion lighting her eyes, the way she's scanning me, the room, everything, she definitely thinks I had something to do with Nate's death. Foul play? His past—all his lies, all his shady side businesses—caught up with him. I adjust my weight, straightening my posture, and inhale sharply. "Right now is fine."

"I know this is hard." She cocks her head to the side. "You and Mr. Landon had quite the romance," she begins and pauses when I shoot her a confused look. "I've done a little bit of research. Lots of articles and photos of the happy couple with the perfect life online."

Happy couple? Perfect? She's baiting me. And I won't lie; our lives were fantastic in the beginning. "Yes," I say. "We had a wonderful life. This is all so—"

"Why didn't Mr. Landon go to Paris with you?"

"It was a girls' trip and he was busy at the hospital." Instead of meeting her intense gaze, I look toward the fireplace, focusing on a picture framed in platinum. In it, I'm wearing a sleek Vera Wang dress and Nate is whispering in my ear: *I can't wait to rip this dress right off you. I own you now.* That should have been the sign to run, but I thought he was joking around, the reason my head is thrown back in laughter. I shake the thought off and get back on track because Rossi is staring me down. "He's a cardiothoracic surgeon."

"Yes, I'm well aware of that." She pauses, eyeing the wedding photo on the mantel. "And you were married for how long?"

"Fifteen years."

Fifteen years. Two of them amazing. Six of them decent. The rest hell. I'd only stayed with him for the girls. My eyes lock onto the butterflies, mounted in deep-boxed acrylic frames, on the walls. Like them, I feel trapped with no escape.

Rossi snaps her fingers in front of my face. "Mrs. Landon, I lost you there for a moment."

"Sorry," I say and her gaze follows mine.

"I noticed the tattoo on the back of your neck and the art on your walls. So, you have a love for butterflies, yes?"

"I do," I say, shifting uncomfortably. A drop of perspiration trickles down my back. "And I really don't understand this line of questioning."

Rossi nods and writes something down again. She steps up and walks over to the custom-built bookcase, running a finger over the leather-bound spines, organized by color. "Mr. Landon was a reader?"

"He was, but that collection is mine—mostly design, architecture, antique gardening and butterfly books."

She pulls out one of the volumes: a first edition of *Favourite Flowers of Garden and Greenhouse*, circa 1896. Olive green art-nouveau cloth bindings with top edge gilt, the book is in mint condition, complete with tissue-covered lithographs, and I'd like to keep it that way.

"You certainly have a lot of oleander surrounding the property." I exhale a sigh of relief as she places the book back on the shelf in its proper place and turns. "And, by this collection, unless they're just for show, you should know that oleander isn't favorable for the species—"

"Which is the reason I have a butterfly garden." I want to say the one the officers are probably trampling all over, but hold my tongue. "This year I've planted coneflowers, asters, zinnias, English lavender, and goldenrods, the plants attracting species like swallowtails, viceroys, and, one of my personal favorites, the *limenitis arthemis*—an electric-blue winged beauty, which I think I just saw outside of the window."

"Yes, your garden." She can't hide the glimmer sparking up in her eyes; it's unnerving. "Don't the plants also attract bees and wasps, which"—she looks over her notes—"Mr. Landon was allergic to?"

"He doesn't go to that part of the yard," I say. "That's the one area that's truly mine."

She lets out a caustic snort. "But bees, wasps, and hornets do fly, don't they?"

"He wasn't afraid of being stung," I say, thinking about his God complex. No bee, no hornet, no wasp would dare! "But if he was, we keep EpiPens in a drawer in the kitchen and he knows where they are. Besides, like you said, creatures fly, regardless of my plants." I take in a breath. "Do you think a wasp killed him?"

Ha! Killed by one of his own kind. I blink to clear my thought before I burst out laughing and meet her eyes. The glare she sends in my direction, the slight smile twisting her lips, tells me that she thinks I killed him. She scribbles fast and furiously in her notepad and then looks up.

"Back to the oleander. You do realize the shrub is toxic to both pets and humans?"

What the hell is she getting at? She thinks I poisoned Nate with oleander? Or sent a hive of wasps or hornets to attack him? Come on, I may have had my share of black widow dreams, but I'm smarter than that. Rossi clicks the top of her pen like she's gearing up to unlock the clip of her gun so she can shoot a perp.

"Mrs. Landon, I asked you a question."

"I know all about oleander and plants. The dogs have been trained not to go near it. We have an electric fence. And the oleander was on the property when we—" I correct myself. "When Nate bought the land. It was a wedding gift." I hesitate, wondering how much I should share with her, deciding on a half-truth. "He gave it to me so I could design our home and launch my business—Atelier Em."

The whole truth: my name is not on the deed; his is.

"Wow," she says, letting out a gulp of surprise. "That's quite the gift. I read that they called Mr. Landon the catch of the century. And"—she eyes me up and down—"you caught him, just like a bee to honey."

I see the look of judgment flickering in her eyes, hear her lame idiom. She made up her mind about me the moment she set foot on my property. I've been picking up on it ever since she first opened her mouth, questioning me with her harsh New York drawl. One thing is certain; she despises me.

"He was quite the catch," I respond, leaving out the rest of my thought: *Until he wasn't.*

"I'm curious. How did you meet?"

She thinks Nate is—was—perfect. I'm the problem. I'll bring her into my so-called ideal life bit by bit. She can come to her own conclusions. "You really want to know?"

"I do," she says.

NINE

EMMA

Then: September, 2007

My future husband smiled at me from the newsstand on the corner.

New York City was in the midst of a heat wave, with hazy wisps of gray smoke billowing out of the subway grates. Although a thin sheet of sticky perspiration already coated my body, I raced toward him and grinned right back—ignoring the lanky brunette and imagining myself, not her, wrapped in his arms. Good news for me: the tabloids rarely photographed him with the same woman twice.

Well, that was definitely going to change once I actually met him.

Labor Day had come and gone and all the high rollers were back in town from their summer vacations—the Hamptons, the islands, or yachting somewhere dream-worthy in Europe, and I think the city was just as excited as I was. I stood amidst the thick of it all—the people rushing by, the honking taxis, the life.

All of the outlets called him the new prince of New York,

comparing him to JFK, Jr. I'd cried buckets the day John-John had died—July 16, 1999, to be exact—with his wife, Carolyn in a catastrophic plane crash. Considering I was only thirteen years old, I'd never have stood a chance with him. Well, there was that, and two very big complications: he'd married another woman and, more important, he was now six feet under.

No matter. There were other big fish in the sea. There was a new prince of New York. A way more age-appropriate one. I had my eyes on him.

Nathaniel Booth Landon, thirty-two years old, handsome, with a jaw line that could cut you, thick brown hair, and piercing blue eyes. A heart surgeon. Thanks to his trust fund from his family's steel fortune, he turned from millionaire to billionaire when his father passed over to the other side from a heart attack. One of the reasons he'd become a heart surgeon. (Such a dream!) His mother, Brigitte "Gigi" Landon, a French showgirl back in the day, presumably suffered from severe depression after his brother, Andrew, died in a car wreck—but, no wonder, she'd lost one of her sons. My research in the libraries' archives pulled up her obituary—cause of death unknown.

Armed with information from the press, I knew he golfed and played tennis. I knew he collected watches (the best of the best for him), and I even knew what his favorite movies were (*American Beauty*, *Eyes Wide Shut*).

"Lady, you gonna buy that, or what?" bellowed the vendor.

"I already have this one," I said with a saccharine smile and he sneered. "I'll take a pack of Tic Tacs. Mint."

I paid, popped a mint in my mouth, and dashed around the corner, from Thompson to Spring, heading over to Sullivan, looking at my watch. I was running a couple of minutes late for work and I picked up my pace. Not because I worried about being late. Tonight could be the night I finally met him.

I knew Nathaniel frequented Pearl & Prime in Soho, the buzzy restaurant where all the chefs in the city went after hours because it was open until four in the morning, and all the trendsetters went for its succulent oyster bar or savory steaks during regular hours or clubbing too late.

And I got a job there.

Sure, I was a bit obsessed, but I wasn't stalking him, hiding in the alleys behind garbage cans with cat-sized rats. No, I wasn't doing anything all that bizarre or neurotic.

Now attending Columbia to follow my dream of becoming an interior architect, I also needed to pay off my tuition. Three extra bonuses: the tips at Pearl & Prime were killer, especially when the Wall Street crew came in, the hours were perfect, and I didn't have to clean toilets with my mom or her staff.

Dressed in my uniform, a short black skirt and a crisp, white button-down top, my hair bobby-pinned in a French twist, I straightened out the back seams of my thigh-highs (a little sex appeal never hurt anybody, especially when it comes to tips). Before entering the restaurant, I touched up my lipstick—L'Oréal's Deep Black Red—and smacked my lips.

"You're five minutes late," said my boss, Aaron. He whipped a kitchen towel over his shoulder. "But you look cute."

I winked. "Thanks, Aaron. I believe that's why you hired me."

"And you can shuck oysters. We've got some nice ones in. Want to try 'em? Your meal before the dinner rush?"

Oh, boy, did I nick my fingers, learning how to shuck before my interview. But, with the potential of meeting my dream man, another bonus of working here—free food. "That's exactly what the doctor ordered."

And, according to the tabloids, he *always* did.

Aaron set a chilled glass of wine—only half full—and an iced plate of succulent Kumamotos before me. I swallowed back an oyster—sweet, slightly salty and, oh so delicious, the honeydew finish.

"Amazing," I said.

"And when you're finished with your meal, get to shucking."

I grinned, pulling out one of the jokes that never got stale in this restaurant. "Shuck off."

Aaron sauntered back into the kitchen. Over his shoulder, he said, "If I shuck off, who is going to bring pearls to the party? Or, for that matter, write your checks."

I was behind the bar, chain mail glove on hand, knife slipping gingerly into a shell, when the restaurant filled with whispers of his name.

My spine stiffened and my heart skipped a few beats. My research had finally paid off. Before he noticed me gawking at him over my shoulder, I went back to my oysters, willing the ice I was placing them on to cool me down.

"Excuse me, what does a guy have to do to get a dozen around here?" he said, and when I turned he grinned. "I haven't seen you before. Are you new here?"

"No, I'm old," I said, and he lifted a brow.

"Not that old."

"I mean, I've been here for a couple of months."

"I've definitely been missing out."

Even better in person than in pictures, his smile devastated me. His crystal-blue eyes gleamed, penetrating. I breathed him in—a light clean, musky scent. Citrus. The sleeves of his navy button-down shirt were rolled up to his elbows, highlighting tan skin and glorious forearms. *Play it cool*, I reminded myself. *Don't look desperate*. I struggled to keep my facial expression neutral, probably landing somewhere in between resting bitch face and constipation.

"What can I get you?" I asked.

"Those are my absolute favorite," he said, pointing to the display of iced oysters. "They're an aphrodisiac."

"A myth," I said, picking up an oyster and letting it slide down my throat. I met his gaze. "See? Nothing. I didn't shimmy out of my clothes and roll around on the floor like a cat in heat."

He belted out a laugh and leaned against the bar, angling his body toward me. "I really hope you know CPR because you just took my breath away."

I raised a brow.

"If you're having trouble breathing, you really should get your lungs checked out." A bit snarky, yes, but it was the wittiest response I could come up with on the fly. "Sorry, too rough of a comeback to your lame pickup line?"

He blinked and sat silent for a moment—probably surprised I showed no signs of recognition. I mean, how dare I? How could I not know who he was? Why wasn't I fawning all over him, the new prince of New York?

He cleared his throat, taking a step back, and placed a hand on his chest. "And now you just sliced my heart in half," he said. "Which is pretty ironic—"

"Oh, why's that?"

"I'm a heart surgeon," he said with a low chuckle.

"Good for you. My dad's a doctor too," I said, but didn't divulge that my dad's an animal doctor.

"I bet we'd get along," he replied.

"A bit premature for introductions to the parents, don't you think?" I lifted my eyebrows, tilted my head to the side, and pointed. "Did you want to order something? Or step outside? Might give you some breathing room. You know, for your lung problems."

His gaze shot to the oysters, then back to me. "I like it here."

He smiled at me again and the fantasy of him—our marriage, our kids, our life—took my mind hostage. It was as if I was the only person in the place. I didn't know if rejecting him would reel him in, make him want me more, like an article I'd read in *Cosmopolitan* had suggested, but apparently it did. This was going way better than I expected and the playing hard-to-get approach seemed to be working in my favor. I decided to take it one step further. I slipped a knife into the side of the oyster and headed over to the end of the bar to take care of a few other customers—businessmen dressed in well-tailored suits. When I returned a few minutes later, his eyes went wide with amusement.

He laughed and I loved the honey tone of it. "So, what do you do when you're not shucking?"

It took a second or two to gather my thoughts. "Not that it's any business of yours, but I'm attending Columbia for my masters."

"Columbia. I went there too," he said, his eyes lighting up—such a deep, clear blue and hypnotizing like an ocean I wanted to dive right into. "Let me guess? Fashion? Publishing?"

"Wrong and wrong. I want to be an interior architect," I said, thinking with his looks he must give his female patients heart attacks, or at least palpitations, because mine was racing.

"Oh, a designer—"

"No, I don't want to be a designer. Like I said, I want to be an architect." I narrowed my eyes into a glare and lifted up my chin. "I want to design every detail of the interior of a home, from where the closets, light switches, and staircases are placed to every plug and, of course, the flow from room to room. Yes, this also includes interior design—paint colors, throw pillows and the like—but I do much more than that and I'm damn proud of it."

"Hmmm," he said, tapping the sexy cleft in his chin. "It's fate that we ran into one another. I'm thinking about remodeling my place. It's just around the corner. A loft. Maybe you could stop by and give me your thoughts? We can talk about my renovation plans—"

I forced my lips into a closed mouth smile, needing to think quickly. "Oh, you're one of those nouveau riche types looking to gentrify a neighborhood?"

Maybe I was pushing too far?

"Wow, you're tough." He chuckled. "No, I'm a fan of a supremely good deals and of culture."

"Culture? Know of Maya Angelou?"

I knew he did. He'd been quoted in a magazine and I'd studied up on her.

"Of course," he says.

I raised a finger and spouted off the first stanza from "And Still I Rise", which I related to on so many levels. Then I paused and batted my eyelashes, ending with the perfect verse that would keep him on his toes. "Does my sassiness upset you?"

He gazed into my eyes, not breaking contact. "No, your sassiness doesn't upset me, it amazes me." He shook his head with disbelief and smiled, revealing perfect white teeth. "I can't believe you know that poem."

"I do. And I really need to take your order. The restaurant is filling up."

"I'll take a Scotch on the rocks, a dozen of any of the oysters you recommend with a mignonette sauce." He met my eyes. "And your phone number."

With my stomach feeling like it was on a roller-coaster ride, I held back my inner squeal. "You don't give up, do you?"

"Nope, never." He shrugged. "Not in my nature, especially when I'm intrigued."

"I'm not on the menu," I said, turning my back on him. I poured his Scotch. "And, if you think I am, maybe you should skedaddle—"

"Don't worry, I'll get out of the way when it gets busy," he said and then snorted. "Skedaddle?"

"Don't make fun of me," I said, placing his drink order on the bar. "I like old movies—the classics."

"So do I. What's your favorite?"

I tapped my chin with a pensive finger, pulled my finger down just a little bit on my bottom lip. "Hmmm. Let's see. I adore *Casablanca*."

And I knew he did too. He smiled, lowered his lashes. "To think, of all the gin joints in all the towns in all the world, you've walked into mine."

"I don't believe this is your restaurant—"

"It isn't, but I do come here a lot so it should be."

"Hmmpf," I said. "Everybody wants to rule the world, or maybe a restaurant."

"Are you quoting Tears for Fears?" He paused when I shrugged and eyed me up and down. "One of my favorite bands, but a little before your time."

"Maybe I like the classics and not living la vida loca." I leaned forward and met his eyes. "And I don't want no scrubs."

He cut me off with a laugh. "I may be a doctor, and I may wear scrubs, but I'm definitely not a busta."

I thought I'd thrown him for a loop. "Wait. You know TLC?"

"Doesn't everybody?" He took a deep breath. "I prefer Chris Isaak's 'Wicked Game,' though, if we're on the subject of music. And, I think, you're playing the wickedest of games with me," he began and then his tongue ran over his lips, "aren't you? You still haven't given me your number."

I scratched the back of my neck, nonchalantly, trying to think. *Don't lose your chance. Reel him in.*

"I don't even know your name," I asked with a slight squint, which hopefully came off as cute and sexy. "I mean, I may have to run a background check on you before I agree to a stranger-danger encounter. Plus, you might be married."

"Nathaniel Landon—Nate. Single and not at all dangerous." He grinned, holding up his left hand and wagging his ring finger. "No tan lines. No need for a background check. I'll tell you anything you'd like to know about me over dinner. But I don't know the name of the captivating—and sassy-pants—woman standing before me."

"Pants? I'm wearing a skirt."

His gaze shot to my legs. "I noticed."

I went dead silent, my heart stuttering.

"And your name?" he persisted.

"Novak. Emma Novak. Like James Bond, but female. Also single, but slightly dangerous."

"Emma Novak," he repeated my name in a whisper, leaning toward me. "Do you have a fear of heights?"

I stared at him, my expression blank.

"*Vertigo*. The Hitchcock film? With your namesake Kim Novak?"

I twiddled my fingers behind my back. "Right, her, we're not related. Such an amazing movie, a little twisted though."

"It's one of his best," he said, and I nodded. "What are you doing after work?"

My mouth twisted to the side. "Going out with some friends to a hot new club, but that's not until later..." I lied.

I'd probably go home after this encounter to my tiny apartment—a one-bedroom converted to two with a rental wall—on the Upper West Side, drink a bottle of cheap wine with my roommate, Abby, and turn a movie on—maybe *Vertigo*. I'd never seen it.

His eyes made an unabashed loop over my body. "Don't take this the wrong way, but you don't seem like the clubbing type."

"What can I say? Sometimes I like to have fun, let my hair down." I grinned and leaned forward, setting his plate of oysters in front of him, and then I licked my lips. "We just met. There's a lot you don't know about me."

"Which is why I'd like to take you to dinner, Ms. Novak."
He smiled again and a feeling of triumph rushed through me.
"If you're not interested, that's fine. But, if you are, I'd really like
your phone number."

Smooth. Real smooth. But I was smoother. He'd taken the
bait: me.

TEN

DETECTIVE ROSSI

Sunday, May 26th, 2024: 11:36 a.m.

As Emma rambles on, I settle back and listen to her supremely deranged story, taking in all of the details of the living room while jotting down the important nuggets laced within her words. Save for the art on the walls and the throw pillows in varying shades of blue, the colorful butterflies in the acrylic frames, and silver accessories like the lamps and decorative bowls, everything is white. Pristine. Modern and elegant. To her, I'm a speck of dirt.

She smiles in melancholy remembrance, flashing her pearly whites—probably has 50k worth of veneers. Aside from her teeth, I don't think she's had any other work done. Finally, I have to stop her nervous babbling. "So, that's how you and Mr. Landon met," I say with force.

She goes quiet, picking up on my not-so-subtle hint. My ears are thankful.

She fidgets with one of the diamond studs on her left ear, bringing attention to the massive rock on her ring finger. A dispersion of rainbow-colored flashes reflects on the white walls.

She clasps her hands in her lap. "Yes, that's how we met. Do you have what you need?"

Oh no, Emma, I'm only getting started. I thumb through my pages of my notes. "Let me get this straight. You stalked Mr. Landon?"

She chokes and spittle flies out of her mouth. "No! What? No, I researched him. Big difference! I wanted to meet him and I did."

I jot the word *obsessive* down on my pad, underlining it three times, followed by *mentally unbalanced.* If she thinks her little tale has painted her in a positive light, she's highly mistaken.

"Fine. You researched him and then seduced him." I scoff, trying to get another rise out of her. "Were you after his money?"

She haphazardly twirls a lock of hair that has fallen down from her updo. "No, like I said, I was dreaming of the perfect life."

"With him?"

"Of course with him! I was head over in heels in love." She leans back. "Oh my God, you sound just like Abby."

I pause because hurt feelings can be an opening into a perp's mind; sometimes something they toss out is exactly what we are looking for. So when she grows quiet and still as if scared by her outburst, my eyes dart around the room looking for some sign of who Emma truly is beneath the surface: someone obsessed with perfection, or someone truly delusional who will do whatever it takes to achieve that goal no matter how many people it might hurt along the way? Ah, who am I kidding? She's a nutjob.

"OK, you were mildly obsessed with him and that obsession turned to love," I say, and her eyes bug out in shock. "What did Ms. Hoffman think of Mr. Landon?"

"She wasn't his biggest fan."

"Why?'

"You'll have to ask her." As she says this, I can't help but note the tension in her voice. She speaks slowly and deliberately, like she wants to say more. Then she lifts up her pointy chin defiantly and I know not to push the subject any further.

"I will."

Nathaniel could have had his pick of practically any woman in the world. Why Emma? I mean, she's attractive enough if you like that type, but I'm starting to think she's also borderline psychotic. I glance down at her hands. She's been pulling at her cuticles until they're raw and red. Her nail polish is chipped. She's trying to present herself as a well put-together woman, but underneath the surface her veneer is cracked. I note: *Don't forget: talk to Abby.*

I am so tempted to ask her how she got the financial grant for Parsons, but stop myself. She can't know that I know what an opportunist she is, not to mention the guilty verdict that should be stamped on her crazy forehead, which she keeps rubbing nervously. I tap my pen on my pad. "I'll need a list of Nathaniel's known associates—his friends, his co-workers, anybody you can think of."

"For the most part, he was at the hospital or with his club."

"Club?"

"His friends. Ben and Becks Stark, Gordon Flynn, Harold Katz, Jeff Cox, Claire Woodbridge—"

"The congresswoman running for governor?"

"Yes, her." Emma grimaces. "I don't know her all that well. Honestly, I really didn't care much for any of his friends and I tried to avoid them. If something happened to Nate, I'd look at them."

"Anybody in particular?"

"Becks and Ben Stark or Gordon Flynn."

She doesn't even pause, take a moment to think. Just blurts their names right out. "Why them?"

Emma's eyes narrow into slits. "There's something really off about Becks and Ben—like their moral compasses are broken." Her jaw clenches and her gaze shoots toward the window. "And Gordon? He's repulsive. He doesn't have one moral bone in his body."

"Uh-huh," I say. "I'm well aware of Mr. Flynn's reputation. But why would you think any of them had a problem with Mr. Landon?"

"Because dirty people do dirty things," she mumbles.

I lean forward, placing my elbows on my knees. "Care to expand on that thought?"

"Based on first impressions, I came to that conclusion. And you would too."

Her mouth twists to the side and her eyes lock onto mine. I know exactly what she's implying. She's accusing me of judging her. Excuse me for coming at her with predetermined opinions but, thanks to her phone call, her snotty demeanor, and *doesn't give a rat's ass* attitude toward her husband's death, it's no wonder I'm not her biggest fan.

"And your first impression was that Mr. Landon's friends were seedy? Up to no good?"

She nods so slowly it's almost as if she's a frozen character on a video game when you hit pause. I know she wants to tell me all about how horrible his circle is when a spark lights up her eyes. "I have to tell you about the first night I met Ben and Becks Stark." She pauses. "And Gordon Flynn."

Here we go again. I sit back in my chair and wave her on with an impatient hand.

ELEVEN

EMMA

Then: November, 2007

Nate and I had been dating for a couple of months and he was finally introducing me to his friends, which meant our relationship was going places. I was so nervous getting ready because I'd wanted to dress to impress, to fit in. I wore one of the Chanel knockoffs Abby had made—a cute skirt suit, white with a black border—and, to be more modern, white over-the-knee boots. I'd put my hair up in a French twist, smacked on my L'Oréal lipstick, and blew myself a kiss before the car Nate was sending for me arrived.

Abby, as usual, was working in the living room—sewing outfits left and right with the hope of leaving her current job working at a mass market chain for Zala, an up-and-coming designer who was supposed to give Stella McCartney a run for her money. Sequins littered the floor. Fabrics in every color covered our couch. I twirled and then curtsied. "How do I look?"

"Like Barbie vomited Chanel," she said, grimacing.

"You made this for me," I'd replied.

"And you insisted on the sparkly tweed." She sighed. "You look nice. Have fun tonight. You know what I'll be doing."

I kissed her on the cheek and left our apartment with the rumble of Abby's sewing machine and her screaming, "Fuck!"

When I arrived at La Dolce Vita, Nate was waiting for me at the bar. He waved me over and I raced toward him. He stood up and kissed my cheek and whispered, "You look beautiful."

"Chanel," I said with a curtsy, leaving out the fact it was a knockoff made by Abby.

"What would you like to drink? The usual?" he asked, and I nodded.

He called the bartender over and ordered me a Sauvignon Blanc. While his back was turned, a man dressed in a Brioni suit, complete with suspenders, and an unlit cigar hanging out of his mouth, approached us. His eyes scanned my body like a laser and he cackled. "Har-har-har. So this is the new girl. Now I understand why you keep blowing me off for this piece of—"

I cringed and my upper lip involuntarily lifted into a sneer. I mouthed *shit* to myself, shaking my head. Nate handed me my wine and the veins in my neck pulsed as he made the introductions.

"Ben, this is Emma Novak. Emma this is Ben Stark, a great guy. And I use that term loosely." He slugged Ben on the shoulder.

I sat numbly as Ben focused his attention on me. "My wife owns a gallery. I really hope you know about art. None of the women Nate carries on with can put a sentence—"

"Ben, play it cool," said Nate.

"Bah! I'm the king of cool."

"In your dreams."

I swallowed a sip of wine, straightening my posture. "Ben, I'm studying to be an interior architect. I know all about art. Which gallery does your wife—Becks, right?—run?"

"The 44." Ben smiled, his gaze shooting from me to Nate. "I

like her already. A smart cookie. Where on earth did you find her?"

"I'm right in front of you," I said with a wave. "See, I'm right here."

"That you are," said Ben, running his tongue over his lips. "And what a spitfire."

"She definitely is," said Nate with a chuckle.

"Somebody, that's me, doesn't like being talked about in the third person," I said with my teeth clenched.

"What are you drinking, princess?" asked Ben, shooting Nate a grin.

Misogynistic pig. I absolutely despised men like him—their weak chins, the way their bellies hung over their belts. The way he called me princess—as if I needed a man to save me from a tower. "Oh, Ben, believe me I'm not a Disney character."

"What's your poison, Snow White?"

"Sauvignon Blanc," I said, trying to hide my sneer.

"Such a girly drink. Bah." He bellied (literally) up to the bar, waved the bartender over with an impatient hand, and ordered a Scotch and a vodka gimlet. "Becks's gallery is a couple of blocks away. Should be here any minute. A little piece of advice: don't let her talk your ear off." He took a swig from his drink, set it down, and ran his hand down my back, making me shudder. "You look so sweet and innocent. I like that."

"Being touched by strangers could be my trigger. Can you please take your hand off my back?" I demanded and he did.

"Har-har-har. Good one. Sweet and salty. You've got bite. Like my wife."

"What kind of woman would marry this jackass?" I muttered under my breath.

I didn't have to wonder for too long. The answer to my question came when an intimidating brunette with cropped short hair wearing a red dress –so tight I could see the lace pattern of her bra underneath it—pushed through the crowd. Ben handed her the waiting gimlet.

She gave me the once-over, her gaze lingering on every detail, before taking a large sip of her drink. "Ah, I needed that," she said and then waved a manicured finger at me, circling it. "Is this charming girl Nate's date?" she asked and I raised my shoulders into a slight shrug. "I'm Rebecca, this not-so-charming man's wife," she continued with an eye roll aimed at Ben, "but most people call me Becks."

"Emma," I said, pasting on a smile. I tucked a loose strand of hair behind my ear. "Lovely to meet you."

"I like the tattoo on the back of your neck. The butterfly. It's pretty."

"Thank you." Although I loved it, I honestly regretted getting the tattoo, but Abby had convinced me to head down to the parlor below our apartment one night after we'd shared a jug of Gallo, Abby choosing a dragonfly on her ankle. Unfortunately, we should have gone the temporary route, a trial period, but, buzzed beyond belief, we didn't think of that and now we're marked for life.

"A good girl with a hint of crossing over to the dark side— just Nate's type," said Ben. "He's a WASP—white Anglo Saxon Protestant. A wasp *always* dominates over a butterfly. Survival of the fittest at its best."

My head snapped in his direction as I'd tried to come up with the perfect comeback line like "you'd never survive in the wild" or "evolution clearly skipped you," but Becks continued before I could.

"Ignore my dolt of a husband," she said. "I understand you're studying to become an interior designer?"

"Architect," I replied. "Interior architect."

"Same thing," she said with a shrug.

I blinked with annoyance and cleared my throat. Instead of biting her head off like I'd done with Nate, I switched gears into kiss-ass mode. "I'd love to stop by your gallery, see what you have."

This was a lie. I'd passed by it many times. The paintings in the window and on the walls were reminiscent of slasher films, complete with blood spatters, or over-the-top erotica. Like, I got what that painting of a sliced peach dripping with wetness was supposed to represent.

"The art in my gallery is for people with the most discerning of tastes."

"I didn't know you had any," said Ben.

"True," she'd replied with a snort. "I married you."

I coughed and placed my purse in my lap, which Becks focused right in on. "I love your bag. I have the same one, but mine's a little different—"

"Different how?"

"Mine's real," she said with a snigger. "Don't get me wrong. You bought a fairly decent knockoff—"

My face flushed with embarrassment. "How did you know?"

"We wealthy can always spot a fake," she said, eyeing my outfit with a raised eyebrow.

I couldn't stand either of them and wanted to feign an illness to get out of having dinner with them. But my eyes met Nate's. He smiled and I swooned. The hostess sauntered up to Nate, and said, "You're ready to be seated."

"I have to pay for my wine," I began, pulling my wallet out of my purse, and Becks lightly slapped my hand.

"It's already taken care of," said Nate. He ran his hand down my back and winked. "They're putting it on my tab."

"Thank you," I said, thinking, *Thank God.* Between paying off my student loans and my rent, money was tighter than tight.

"Just being chivalrous."

"Or trying to get into your pants," said Ben with a bois-terous har-har-har.

Diners stared at the loudmouth and us, some glaring, some whispering Nate's name. On the way to the table, Becks nudged Nate in the ribs and whispered, "Don't let this one get away. She's exactly what you need—the perfect catch for a doctor's wife."

Why, thank you, Becks.

A waiter came over and we ordered another round of drinks. Ben waved a limp hand toward me. "She'll have a Sauvignon Blanc."

Becks leaned forward and whispered, "If you stick around with Nate and Ben's billionaire boys' club, your tastes might become stronger." She turned toward the waiter. "Vodka gimlet. A double. Extra lime."

"Wait, what?" I asked, all wide-eyed when she not so casually dropped Nate's net worth into the conversation.

"Come on, unless you've been hiding under a rock, you know *exactly* who Nathaniel Booth Landon is. Everybody in New York does."

"Don't tell me you're after his money," said Ben.

Becks scoffed, nodding to Ben. "I sold my soul to you, the devil. Good thing we're filthy rich."

Thrown for a loop, I didn't know how to wiggle out of this one without looking like a gold digger. "I think Nate is handsome and charming. I, uh—"

"Charm and looks only last for so long. Diamonds are a girl's best friend, yada, yada, yada," she said, holding up her hand, flashing a diamond so enormous it could have been a weapon. She wiggled her fingers. "Anything under five carats is a plaything—a toy."

"I just met Nate." I took a sip of my wine. "I barely know him. I'm not thinking about marriage—"

Such a lie. And she knew it.

"If I wasn't married to Ben, I'd be all over Nate." She licked her lips. "He's quite the catch."

"Only if she's adventurous," said Ben, and Becks nudged his rib with her elbow, glaring at the loudmouth. "We could take her to one of Gordon's parties? There's one on Friday night."

Nate cleared his throat. "I really don't think it's Emma's scene."

"Who is Gordon?" I'd asked, although I knew exactly who Gordon Flynn was. All over the news, he was recently under investigation by the FBI for hosting a revenge porn site, which allowed users to post sexually explicit photos of people online without their consent, and Gordon wasn't charged with anything. Which was appalling and sickening. And Nate was right—not my scene.

"If it weren't for him, none of us would ever have met," said Becks.

"What a man," said Ben, his gaze shooting to the door. "And he's here now."

Gordon and his paunch hobbled into the restaurant, tapping a carved wooden cane with an ornate silver handle. The man behind the myth smiled, revealing cigar-stained teeth. He wore a burgundy velvet smoking jacket that tied at the waist with a black silk sash—which matched his pants and ascot. The overall vibe: Hugh Hefner from the Crypt.

He came over to the table, taking his seat. "Sorry, Irina couldn't make it. Has the flu or something." His eyes raked over my body and I shifted uncomfortably in my chair. "I take it this is the famous Emma. Nice to finally meet you."

His voice, his manner of speech, sounded like he had a ball of phlegm stuck in his throat.

"Nice to meet you too," I said with a fake smile. I took a dainty sip of my wine and set the glass down. "I understand Irina is from Russia. How did the two of you meet?" I asked, searching for anything to say. The man was staring me down and gave me the creeps.

"I bought my beautiful doll from a catalog," said Gordon

with an obnoxious laugh that turned into a hack. He leaned forward and winked. "Best investment I ever made."

My eyes went wide and volleyed to Nate. He shrugged nonchalantly like it was no big deal.

After a torturous three-hour dinner with Becks downing vodka gimlets like water, and the conversation leaning toward investments (Ben) and the latest blowup dolls and dildos (Gordon), the server came over for our dessert order. I was hoping everybody would say no, but Nate ordered a round of sambuca for the table—with three coffee beans in the glass for good luck.

Nate grabbed my hand. "Do you want dessert?"

"The salted caramel one."

"See? Sweet and salty, just like I said," Ben guffawed with an obnoxious har.

I didn't know why Nate associated himself with these people. But, at the time, I didn't really care because I had my *in* and I was focusing on the big picture—a life with him.

TWELVE

DETECTIVE ROSSI

Sunday, May 26th, 2024: 11:47 a.m.

When Emma finishes telling me about her impressions of Ben, Becks, and Gordon, I can't help but cringe. Through her twisted tale, she's basically admitted she's a liar and a phony, not to mention a stalker.

"Let's move on," I say. "Did Nathaniel have any enemies? Anybody who would want to harm him?"

"I don't think somebody as wealthy as Nate is—was—wouldn't." She cracks her neck, rolls her shoulders. "I did receive somewhat of a threatening text about a week ago. It came from a blocked number. And then it vanished."

She meets my eyes and we sit in silence for a moment. I'm waiting for her to continue. But she doesn't.

"And it said...?"

"You don't know who your husband is and what he's done." She sniffs and then reaches over for a tissue from a silver holder on the side table. "It didn't concern me at the time because we, both of us, have received weird messages and threats over the years."

I love how she's shifting the attention off herself. I'm getting somewhere. "From who?"

"I don't know! Psychos? People trying to get under our skin and rile us up."

"Give me your cell. I'll see if somebody on our team can trace the message."

She jolts upright and snatches her phone off the couch, holding it close to her chest. "No, no, and no. I need my phone to get in touch with my daughters."

Hiding something she doesn't want me to see?

"It should only take an hour or two," I insist.

"Sorry, if Ava or Grace call I need to speak with them—don't you think?" She clutches the phone tighter and her knuckles turn white. "Like I said, the text vanished and I'm not all that concerned about it."

"Then why did you mention it?"

"I thought you should know." She leans back on the couch, eyes closed. "Maybe David Clark sent the text."

"David Clark?"

She's instantly alert, nodding vigorously. "Yes, he and his wife, Audrey, just moved back to town. Years ago—I forget how many—he and Nate had a huge falling-out."

"Over?"

She lifts her tiny shoulders into a shrug and lowers her head, shaking it from side to side. "I don't know. Nate wouldn't talk to me about it."

By her rigid posture and extremely guarded answers, she definitely knows something, but she's not going to tell me. I circle David Clark's name, even though she's probably looking for a diversion.

"I'll check him out." I tap my pen on the table and Emma looks like she wants to rip it out of my hand.

She yawns, not bothering to cover her mouth, and slumps

deeper into the cushions of the couch. "Are we just about finished here?"

Is she kidding? I get that she's tired. Her eyes are glassy with fatigue. I get that she just flew back from Paris (poor thing) this morning. I get that she wants me to leave. Heck, I want to leave too. What I don't get is why she isn't taking her husband's death more seriously.

"No," I snap. "We're not finished. I think figuring out what happened to Mr. Landon is more important than sleep, don't you?"

She hunches over and starts to babble in between sobs, bringing on the waterworks. "Yes, I'm sorry. You're right." She swallows. "You have to understand, I haven't slept in weeks. I came home to this mess. Nate's dead. I don't know what's going on. I... I..."

... *am a neurotic sociopath.* I underline this four times.

She may be showing signs of human emotion instead of a Bedford robot now, but this act of hers is giving one of those soap opera stars my ma watches a run for their money. It wouldn't surprise me if she were to flop onto the couch, pretending to faint, one hand on her forehead.

"I'll give you a minute to pull yourself together, Mrs. Landon."

She whimpers out a dramatic sob and whispers, "Thank you."

Emma Landon thinks she's fooling me with this performance, but she's now given me four names, clearly trying to shift the focus off of her and onto people she doesn't like. And then I remember. She was part of the drama club in high school; this could all be an act for me. Which makes me even more suspicious of her. I study people for a living, their body movements, their reactions. Her facial expressions, the way she stumbles over her words, tell me everything. I'll play along with her little game, see where the dice lands.

Finally, Emma settles down. She grabs another tissue and daintily blows her nose. "I'm sorry," she whispers.

Blinking back my disbelief, I reach into my pocket, handing over my card. She scans the details before she sets it down on the coffee table, her hand shaking. "If you think of anybody else I should look into, please email me a list when you can," I say, and she snuffles out her agreement. "Who has access to the house and the property?"

"Me, the girls, Abby, Taryn, my parents, the dog walker, Ryan, the pool guy, Eddie, the landscapers, Diego and Company, and the house staff."

"House staff?"

"Our house manager and my personal assistant, Luisa, our two cleaning ladies, Homa and Kom, and our cook, Alba—"

The woman has a cook? A cook? Why design a kitchen like that if you're not going to use it? The appliances are high-end. The white stove with copper knobs is one of those fancy French ones—Lacanche. The pots and pans are polished copper and the cast iron pieces are from another French brand, Le Creuset, white in color, and in pristine condition like they've never been used. I'd taken a quick peek inside the cabinets and everything is organized—the spices in glass jars with chic labels. It's a dream. And her kitchen is bigger than my apartment.

I shake the twinges of jealousy off and get back on track. "Where are your staff now?"

"They live in the guesthouse at the far end of the property."

"I'll speak with them after I'm finished with you and Ms. Hoffman." She nods. "I noticed that you have a pretty extensive surveillance system."

"We do, and I'd be happy to show you any footage."

"Yes, please."

"But Nate turned it off when I was away."

"How do you know that?"

"I logged in when I was in Paris." She rolls her eyes. "Nate doesn't like to be monitored; he feels like he's being spied on."

So she was trying to spy on him? This is getting more suspicious by the second and I haven't even gotten to the hard stuff yet.

"Pretty convenient," I say. "I'd like access to the footage anyway."

"I'll give you the codes and log-in information," she says, and I wave an impatient hand, raising up both my eyebrows and a pen. She's being too agreeable. She must not realize she doesn't have to tell me anything right now. And I'm taking advantage of the situation.

She reels off a bunch of numbers and letters, and after scribbling down the information, I hold up a finger and unclip my radio from my belt: "Officer Roberts, bring it in now."

Emma's face blanches.

I'm about to get to the good stuff and want honest answers.

"Can you explain the scratches on Mr. Landon's back?"

"I'm pretty sure the dogs had something to do with that. They were running around the pond when I arrived home and soaking wet—I, uh, I—"

Her chest rises and falls and she's fighting for breath. Or she's making it look like she is. Her eyes tear up again. She's like a roller coaster of emotions—up, down, and crazy all over the place. She should get an Academy Award.

"I understand. People grieve in different ways. And, for the record, I know this is uncomfortable and I'm truly sorry for your loss, but on the 911 call, you said, and I quote, 'I pulled the lying cheating bastard son of a bitch out of the goddamn water.'"

She covers her face with her hands. "I didn't mean to say that. I don't know why I said that. I-I—"

"But you did say that." I lean forward and tap my pen on the coffee table. "Was he cheating on you?"

Her head snaps up. She wipes her tears away and shoots me a death glare. "Look, I really don't think that's any of your business and I refuse to talk about it."

"So he was."

She stands up swiftly, stomps her foot, and points to the door. "I'm just about finished here."

"I'm not finished with my questioning. Please sit down, Mrs. Landon, unless you want to continue our chat down at the station."

She slumps onto the couch, clenching her hands, her gaze focused on the window.

Officer Roberts strides into the living room, placing a plastic container by my side. Emma's eyes lock onto him and then the box. I know she sees her shoes and all of the prescription bottles we'd commandeered from her medicine cabinet. I reach into the container, rifling through it. Then, I hold up a plastic envelope marked EVIDENCE. "This was found in the pool house."

"What is it?" she asks, squinting.

"A red thong with a sequined butterfly on the crotch. Is it yours?"

"No," she says. "I don't wear thongs. Never have."

"One of the twins'?"

"Are you kidding? They're only fourteen," she says, appalled. "But what do I know? I'm not the underwear police."

Oh, you sarcastic little bitch. Ignoring the obvious dig—I'm not backing off—I grab three more envelopes, holding them up one by one. "What about the peacock feathers and plumes? The masks? Did you have a costume party? Or did you and Mr. Landon like to dress up? Maybe role-play?"

Her entire body freezes and her face flushes red.

"Oh my God, no!" she finally spits out. Her voice bloats from a low wheeze into a wail. "This line of questioning is absolutely absurd. I'd really like for you to leave."

"Moving on," I say, registering that I've hit a nerve. "Can you tell me what Mr. Landon's daily routine was like?"

She huffs and leans back into the couch. "He's a creature of habit. He usually wakes up at around four thirty in the morning, sometimes six on the weekends, depending on his schedule. He'll make his daily juice blend, drink it, and then clean it up. He's fastidious like that—he even pre-measures all his ingredients. Then, he'll go for a run with the dogs, work out in the gym, and swim laps in the pool."

"Fastidious? The kitchen is in quite a mess."

"That's not like him. He's a neat freak like me. Everything has its place," she says and then cuts herself off, straightening her posture. "It's very out of character for him."

"I'll have our team look around. Did he work this weekend?"

"Not that I'm aware of."

"Did you speak with him or text while you were in Paris?"

"No."

"Why?"

"Because of the time change," she says defensively. "It was a moot point."

It doesn't take a rocket scientist to figure this one out. They probably had a fight before she left for Paris. I don't bother asking; she won't tell me. I scribble: *Not on speaking terms*.

"So, you mentioned he worked out a lot. He was in prime form?"

"What do you mean by that?" she bleats.

"Did he have any health issues? Any addictions?"

"No. I mean, he smoked the occasional cigar and drank an occasional Scotch, whiskey or bourbon. Nothing out of the ordinary. For the most part, he was a bona fide health nut."

Earlier, she'd suggested Nathaniel had had too much to drink and had fallen over the balcony. She's just implicated herself again.

"To your knowledge, did he ever do cocaine for a diversion?"

"No. Never. He's a doctor. A cardiothoracic surgeon, as you know."

"Then can you explain the cocaine residue we found on the coffee table by the pool?"

She recoils and presses her knuckles against her lips. "No, I can't."

"Do your girls do drugs? Party? Maybe get involved with a bad crowd?"

"No. No. And, for crying out loud, no. For Pete's sake, can you please stop with these outlandish insinuations."

And I've hit another nerve—and this one is more raw than the others. Clearly, she's a protective mother.

The doorbell rings twice and Emma's body jolts forward.

"Are you expecting somebody?" I ask.

Emma scratches the back of her neck and then her hand shoots to her armpits, drawing attention to the sweat seeping through her dress. "It's Ryan, our dog walker. He always rings twice before letting himself in so we know he's here."

"I'd like to speak with him. Alone." I stand up, brushing invisible dust off my thighs to watch her cringe, which she does. "I'll meet him out front." As I leave the room, I look over my shoulder. "Wait here."

"Do I have a choice?" she mutters.

I'm standing on the front steps by stone planters. Beside me, black and green-striped plants, reminding me of bamboo, wave in the breeze. I'll give Emma props: she really does have excellent taste in all the details, including dog walkers. I laugh and shake my head as Ryan makes his approach. He's a young, buff, handsome stud, wearing a tight T-shirt and running shorts, his sandy hair tucked underneath a baseball cap. I've heard of bored housewives having affairs with their pool guys or tennis pros, so I'm not ruling out a dog walker. Perhaps Emma is the cheater. Maybe that's why she and Nate weren't speaking. I wave him over.

"What's going on?" he asks, racing up to me. "Why are there so many cop cars here? Did something happen?"

"Nathaniel Landon was found dead this morning," I respond, waiting for his reaction. "I'm Detective Rossi."

"Holy shit," he says, clasping a hand over his mouth. "Am I walking onto a crime scene?"

"Maybe," I say and he startles. "How well did you know Mr. Landon?"

"N-n-not that well. He was never really around. I-I take care of the boys, Harry and Potter. He had me drop them off here on Thursday morning and then he sent me a text on Friday to come by midday today to walk them..." He pauses. "He said he was heading back into the city and Emma can't walk the dogs because they're a bit unruly..." He swallows and rubs the stubble of his chinstrap beard, which accentuates his square jaw. "Man, this is a lot to digest—"

"Understandable. It's quite the shock." I meet his eyes—a strange color, sea foam green. "What's your relationship with Mrs. Landon like?"

"Emma? She's awesome," he says, worry creasing his brow. "Is she OK?"

"She's fine."

From the side of the house, the dogs must hear his voice and start barking up a storm.

"And Harry and Potter?" he asks, shaking his head from side to side. "They really don't like strangers and there's so much activity going on. I can hear them panicking." He swallows with worry. "Can I speak with Emma? I'm thinking I should get the boys out of here, back to my farm." He paces in front of me, lightly banging his sides with his fists. "Oh, man, I can't believe this is happening. The poor hairy dudes. Have they eaten? Oh God, they're probably starving."

And there goes my hunch. He's more worried about the dogs than the woman. "Wait here," I say, holding up a finger and heading back into the house. "I'll ask her."

Emma sits on the couch, wringing her hands in her lap. She looks up expectantly. "Mrs. Landon? Ryan wants to know if he can take the dogs to his farm. He thinks they're stressed."

She nods and sniffles. "Good idea. Tell him I said thanks. I'll send him a text, letting him know when he can bring them home."

"I'll be right back," I say, heading outside to give Ryan the go-ahead to take the dogs.

A couple of minutes later, Ryan leads the gigantic beasts to a black pickup truck. They stop and growl at me, hackles raised. If somebody harmed Nate, they definitely knew him because these dogs would have attacked a stranger for sure. Momentarily stunned by their size, their manes of lion-like black fur streaked with tan highlights, and enormous paws, I watch the dogs jump right in the back and off they go. After Ryan leaves, I notice Ms. Hoffman sprawled out in a white Tesla. She rolls down the window and waves me over.

"Is this going to take much longer?" she yells as I make my approach. "I'm a redhead and the sun is killing me."

I do feel kind of bad for her. Her face is red and blotchy with some kind of heat rash. But I also need information. "I just have a few questions for you."

"Shoot," she says and then covers her mouth. "I mean, don't shoot *me*. Ask me anything."

"I knew what you meant." With a perfunctory nod, I hold up my notepad and a pen, cutting straight to the chase. "What was your relationship like with Mr. Landon?"

"My relationship with Nate? Ha. I didn't have one. I hated him on sight." She shakes her head with dismay, lips pinched. "I tried convincing Emma not to marry him, warned her, but she did anyway."

"Hate is a pretty strong word. But I get it. You sound like you're a protective friend."

"Not protective enough," she scoffs. "When she married Nate, he almost ruined my friendship with Emma."

"How?"

"He tried paying me off to stay away from her."

"And you took the money?"

"Hell no," she says, her body twisting with revulsion. "What kind of person do you think I am? You don't put a price on friendship."

Ah-ha. Now I'm getting somewhere. You can put a price on other things. "Has Mrs. Landon ever said anything about wanting her husband dead?"

Abby tilts her head back in laughter. "Is wishing your husband dead a crime?"

I raise an eyebrow. "In this case, it might be."

I scan her facial expressions and body language as she responds, wanting to see signs of guilt or knowledge. Instead of leaning back from me like Emma, Abby leans forward, lessening the distance between us.

Abby guffaws and spittle flies from her mouth. "You've got to be kidding me! Emma wouldn't hurt a fly. Nate? He's a toxic, narcissistic monster, and so is his nasty group of friends. If somebody killed him, I'd look in Gordon Flynn's direction and leave Emma alone."

"Why Mr. Flynn?"

"The old pervert lives next door." She throws out her arm, flicking a hand toward the property. "Right over there. Nate bought this place from him, bribed Emma with it, and then tried forcing her to be friends with Gordon's wife, Irina."

Emma did tell me about the wedding gift. And she did

express how she thought Nathaniel's friends were a seedy bunch.

"Is Mrs. Landon still friends with Irina?"

"No, she's dead. Died from a drug overdose around five or six years ago." Abby lifts a brow. "Look, Emma couldn't stand Nate's friends. She did her best to avoid them. Don't get me started on Ben and Becks Stark."

And Emma had said the exact same thing. Perhaps she was being more honest than I've been giving her credit for. Then again, there's a trick to telling lies and Emma's tells were obvious. She'd swallowed, freaked out, picked at her cuticles, and didn't meet my eyes. So, she was either embellishing a lie with the truth or telling her version of the truth with lies.

"I see." I click the top of my pen. "A few more questions and then you can leave."

"I'm not leaving without seeing Emma," she says, her eyes blazing. "She's just gone through a very traumatic experience. I have to be here for her."

Funny, Emma's not acting like a woman traumatized by her husband's death. If anything, she's more upset about me questioning her.

"When I'm finished, you can join Mrs. Landon in the living room," I say, and Abby blows out a sigh of relief. She waves a hand, ushering me to carry on. "I'm curious. All those years ago, why didn't Emma take your advice?"

"You'll have to ask her."

OK. That went absolutely nowhere.

"And what was it about Mr. Landon"—I look down at my notes—"that made you hate him on sight?"

Abby ponders this last question for a moment. "I've never met anybody that I despised—not like that. I'm a people person. I usually get along with everybody. But there was something about Nate, the way he carried himself, the way you could tell he thought he was worlds above you. He was sketchy. Something wasn't right. You pick up on things, you know? It's like a gut instinct."

I grunt out a yes while taking notes. I know gut instincts all too well. Abby may not have liked Nate, but she didn't have anything to do with his death. A straight shooter, if anything, she's just an accidental alibi who is overly protective of her friend. I can tell by her expression that something else is on her mind. "Go on."

She sighs. "When Emma first started dating Nate, she began to change."

"How?"

"She lost herself in him. She was putty in his hands and he controlled and manipulated her. Emma ticked all of Nate's boxes—polite, polished, presentable, and, more important, mold-able. She was what he wanted from a wife. He started grooming her—buying her clothes and lingerie, telling her how to wear her hair, what color lipstick to wear—Chanel's Rouge Allure Ink, color choquant. He bribed her—"

"With what exactly?"

"The idea of the perfect life, him—oh, what a fucking catch! —the girls, this house, her own thriving business. But once he'd ensnared her in his world, he went back to being who he really was." Abby pauses, sensing my quizzical expression. "I think Emma explained it best on her call to 911."

"She told you what she said?"

"She really didn't mean to say that," says Abby with a slight snort. "But at least she was being honest."

Lying. Bastard. Cheating. Again, Emma's words ring in my head.

"What about divorce? Did she ever consider leaving him?" I persist.

Abby's throat constricts and she swallows nervously, as if I'm trying to trick her into revealing something she shouldn't.

"She couldn't leave him. Don't you get it? He had trapped her, manipulated and blackmailed her into staying."

Bribery. Blackmail. Manipulation. All motives.

"And now he's dead," I state flatly. "I'm wondering, if he was so awful, if all the warning signs were there, why did Mrs. Landon marry him?"

"Beats the hell out of me." Abby lowers her head, shaking it from side to side. "Again, you'll have to ask her. And, like I said, I really wish she hadn't."

THIRTEEN

EMMA

Then: February 14th, 2008

I raced around Nate's loft, preparing a roast for our first Valentine's Day, wearing an apron over tiny shorts and a T-shirt, my hair in a messy bun on the top of my head. Even with the recipe splayed out before me, I had no clue as to what I was doing. I was knocking ingredients over, the floor was covered in pepper grains. I nicked my thumb while cutting potatoes. I really didn't know my way around a kitchen, but I was an over-achiever and failure wasn't an option.

"We need to talk," Nate said from the doorway.

I looked up from chopping garlic. "About what? The meal? Don't worry, I've got this. It won't be a disaster. It's my mother's recipe."

"No. We need to talk about us," he said and my heart jolted.

He couldn't break up with me on Valentine's Day. Aside from a couple of disastrous meals, I thought our relationship was on the right track. Although I'd tried my best, the first time I cooked for Nate, I burned scrambled eggs. The second time, the pasta was so overcooked the noodles dripped off the fork.

He smiled and held out the small box he'd been hiding behind his back, and I took it.

"What's this?"

He raised a brow. "A Valentine's Day surprise."

I eyed him warily and undid the red bow, letting it fall to the floor. I opened the lid, my eyebrows pinching with confusion. "It's a key—"

"To my place," he said.

A mix of emotions and thoughts played tug of war in my mind. What if the dynamics in our relationship shifted, and not in a good way? "We've discussed this. I don't want to take that leap until we're married or at least engaged—"

"You and your crazy rules," he said with a slight laugh. "We're not going to break them." He pulled out another box from the pocket of his jeans. My throat caught and I couldn't swallow, couldn't say a word. "I know we've only known each other for a short time and this might be too fast for you, but I want to spend the rest of my life with you, have children with you, and grow old with you."

The knife I'd been chopping with clattered on the counter. I opened the box, revealing a sparkling diamond surrounded by sapphires. My hands flew over my mouth.

"Emma Novak, will you do me the honor of marrying me?"

I went completely silent, my chest rising and falling with excitement. "D-d-did you ask my father?"

"Where do you think I went last Saturday after I golfed with Ben and Gordon?"

"Oh my goodness, what did he say?"

"Ben? Or Gordon?" he asked, his eyes lighting up. He clearly enjoyed watching me squirm.

"My dad!" I said with a squeal.

"He said no." My eyes went wide with panic until he chortled out a laugh. "Of course he said yes, Emma. He said he'd be thrilled to welcome me into the family, but mentioned he thought a long engagement would be in order—at least a year."

I nodded, my eyes clouding over with tears.

He clasped onto my hands. "Emma, you haven't answered me."

"Yes," I said, gulping. "Yes! Yes! Yes! I'll marry you, Nathaniel Booth Landon."

Our mouths met and we kissed—deep, hard, and long. I pulled away, steadying myself with my hands on Nate's shoulders.

"You haven't even looked at the ring," he said.

I batted my eyelashes. "Because you haven't gotten down on one knee and put it on my finger."

He did as I instructed. I eyed the diamond glistening on my slender finger. "Wow, this is beautiful. It's enormous."

No plaything, the diamond was 6.5 carats, emerald cut, set with small pavé sapphires on a platinum band.

"I have something else for you." He pulled out an envelope from his briefcase and handed it over. I ripped it open and then frowned at the paper in my hand. "Paid? What? You paid off my student loans? And my tuition for this year? Oh my goodness, Nate, you shouldn't have done this. Why?"

He kissed me on the nose and squeezed my shoulders. "No future wife of mine is going to worry about money. Ever."

I lifted up my chin to meet his eyes. "Honestly, I don't know what to say."

"Say I love you."

"I love you," I squeaked.

"And now you don't have to worry about anything. I was thinking we'd get married next year. Maybe in February?"

My eyes darted to the papers set on the kitchen counter. "What about school? And working at Pearl & Prime?"

"You won't need to go next year. Why would you?" His eyes

met mine. "And I think you should quit working at the restaurant."

Feeling under pressure, at the time, I could only blurt out, "I want to get my masters. My dream has always been to start my own interior architecture firm—"

"I thought I was your dream. And you won't need to work. You'll have everything you need."

What a hypocrite. He was crossing a line. "You work, even though you don't need to—"

"I'm not *just* a trust fund kid or the heir to a massive steel fortune." His eyes glazed over and he looked up to the ceiling, his chin held high. "Holding a heart in my hand, feeling it pulse and beat, fixing it, is like orchestrating life. And I'm excellent at it—a maestro. It's my calling."

My throat tightened. For him, being a surgeon wasn't just about saving lives; it was about asserting control over the very essence of life itself. He'd basically told me he had a God complex. As much as I loved him, I didn't want him controlling me.

"I'm getting my masters," I whispered, my head hanging low. A tear crept down my cheek. "Nate, I'm good at what I do. And *my* beating heart will break if I don't try reaching for the stars."

He went silent for a moment. His hand lightly pulled up my chin. "That's what you want?"

"It is."

He clucked his tongue. "OK, Emma. You'll finish your studies. I'll pay for next year's tuition. We'll get married as soon as you receive your masters. Sound like a good plan?"

"I guess so," I said. "But I don't want to be indebted to you."

"You're going to my wife." He smiled. "And you're quitting your job at Pearl & Prime."

"But—"

"No buts," he said, pulling me in for a hug. "We've come to

an agreement. Now I want to spend every spare moment we have together."

Thick smoke filled the kitchen. I waved a kitchen towel around like a madwoman. "I'm sorry. Ugh! I can't do anything right. I'm so, so sorry—"

"Don't worry, we'll order in." He kissed my fingertips. "We're going to have a beautiful life. And, now that you've said yes, there is something else we need to talk about. It's just a minor legality—"

I parroted him. "Legality?"

"I hate to bring this up now, but I need you to sign a prenup before we make everything official."

My lips curled into a bewildered sneer. "I don't know why we have to be so formal. Our relationship is what it is. I love you. You love me. End of story."

"With my wealth, we need to be careful." He paused. "My attorney is protecting both of our interests. Unless you're only after me for my money?"

My jaw went slack. I hadn't asked Nate to pay off my student loans. I hadn't asked for the clothes or this enormous diamond. "I, uh, Nate, I can't believe you'd say that—"

He stooped down and pulled a file out of his briefcase, placing it on the counter, a pen by its side. "Just sign it and we can start planning out the rest of our lives."

"B-b-but I don't know what I'm signing. Shouldn't I have my own attorney look it over?"

"It's boilerplate. Nothing to worry about. I'd like to trust your intentions. Don't you trust mine?"

I licked my fingers and scanned through the forty-page document, and then I rubbed my forehead. It might as well have been written in Greek. "I don't understand all of this legal jargon—"

"Basically it says, if I divorce you, you get half of my wealth. If you divorce me, you get what you came into the marriage with, unless we have children. I also had the attorney put in an infidelity clause. If one of us cheats, and the other has proof, we'd be ordered to pay a financial penalty—"

My eyes volleyed from the pages to his lips. "I'd never cheat on you. You're the love of my life. Besides, I don't have money to pay for penalties—"

"If I'm the love of your life, we won't have any problems." His gaze met mine and the look in his eyes was so intense it sent chills up my spine. "Is everything clear? Sign it. Then we'll pop open a bottle of champagne and toast the beginning of our perfect life."

With my stomach turning, I picked up the pen and scribbled my name on the signature line. Something in my gut told me that if I didn't, I'd lose Nate. And I didn't want that to happen.

FOURTEEN

EMMA

Then: February 15th, 2008

The day after the proposal, I pushed the prenup fiasco to the back of my mind and raced through the door of what would soon be my former apartment, heading straight to Abby's room. I jumped on her bed, shaking her.

"Tra-la-la, wake up sleepy head. Tra-la-la!"

"Jeez, Emma," she said, opening one eye. "Leave me alone."

"I can't. I have news! Big news! Huge news! The kind of news you're going to die from." I bounced on her bed. "I'm engaged. And when we get married, you, my dear, are going to be the maid of honor."

Abby rubbed her eyes and propped herself up on her elbows. "Come again?"

"He proposed last night." I held my hand in front of her face and wiggled my finger. "Isn't it beautiful?"

"It is," she said, shaking her head, her gaze focusing on my diamond. She sat up straight and latched onto my hand. "Holy shit. It's massive."

"Right? Isn't this incredible?"

"No, wrong. Don't you think you're moving too fast? You barely know the guy. It's only been five months."

I recoiled. Just like Abby to put the pin in my balloon. I felt my previous excitement deflate. *Sisssssssss. Sissssssss.*

"Incredible months," I said with an insulted scoff. "Don't be a Debbie Downer. I know what I need to know and I'm in love."

"With him?" She snorted. "Or the *idea* of him? Come on, get real, girl. You're starting out your relationship on a lie."

I stormed out of her bedroom and she followed me into mine. "Why can't you be happy for me?"

"Because you basically stalked him to bag him."

"I didn't stalk him," I said, crossing my arms over my chest. "I researched him. There's a huge difference."

"Same thing, in my mind. Do I have to remind you about your bizarre obsession with JFK, Jr.? Don't forget, I saw your high school yearbook." She blurted out a caustic laugh. "Come on, whose senior superlative is 'most likely to marry a Kennedy'?"

"What the hell is your problem? Is it with him or with me?" I snarled.

"Maybe both of you. Ever since you met him, you've changed—and they aren't good changes. You're late to work. You preen in the mirror like some kind of diva. You blow everybody off, meaning me, when he calls, and jump right to his side or into his bed—like his beck-and-call girl."

I pointed a shaky finger at her. "You're completely out of line."

"Am I? Does the truth hurt? You have lost all sense of who you are." She shook her head as anger coursed through my veins. "Seriously, since when is *The Talented Mr. Ripley* your favorite movie of all time? Or *American Psycho*? You like romantic comedies. I know because I *used* to watch them with you."

"What can I say? He's introducing me to new things," I said, turning to her, a scowl on my face. "It's called being in a relationship. Maybe you should try having one."

Abby reeled back as if I'd slapped her face. "It's also called life. And, a piece of advice: you need to start living *yours*, not just his."

"I think you're jealous."

"I'm not. I'm being practical." She flopped down on my bed, twiddling her fingers. "Look, I don't want to fight with you, but I'm concerned. If I'm your best friend, why haven't I met him? Don't you think that's weird?"

"No," I said with a triumphant smile. "Because, if you're up for it, you're meeting him tonight."

"What if I have plans?" she asked.

"Do you?"

Abby hadn't been out in months, basically glued to beads and her sewing machine and swimming in fabric. I'd never seen anybody work so hard for what could be a pie-in-the-sky dream and spend every dime she had to catch it.

"No." She eyed the small dining room table that we never ate at, considering her sewing machine took up all the space. "I was planning on working. My interview to be one of Zala's head designers is next week. I have to make sure everything is on point."

"Maybe take a break?"

"Maybe," she said, arching a brow. "It might depend on where we're going—"

I cut her off. "Daniel."

"That super-expensive French restaurant? The one that would cost us one month's rent?"

"The very one."

As she looks toward the ceiling, her hazel eyes spark up. "I've always wanted to eat there."

"I know. I told him."

"His treat?"

"Of course. But you have to promise me you'll be on your best behavior."

She cocked her head to the side, her eyes narrowed. "I'll act however I want to damn act. I'm not a trained monkey. OK, stalker?"

"I'm not a stalker or a monkey."

"But he's training you. For what, I don't know." She eyed my outfit. "You've got the Park Avenue princess look down to a T."

I curtsied. "Thanks."

Nate had a car pick us up at seven as he was running a little late and would be meeting us at the restaurant. This wasn't out of the ordinary; he always sent a car for me. I thought it was sweet; Abby thought otherwise. I mean, if Nate was such a gentleman, he'd be on time.

Maybe this *worlds collide* scenario was a very bad idea. Abby had more opinions than any of the reigning divas—including Madonna—and she wasn't afraid of sharing them. Her snappy, caustic demeanor shifted when we pulled up to the restaurant—a cream-colored limestone building set aglow with golden lights.

"Girl, now this is class," said Abby with a wide grin. "On second thought, maybe I've been a bit too judgmental. I could get used to this."

The driver opened the door to the car and we got out, standing on the sidewalk for a moment. I shot Abby a look of warning. "Be on your best behavior. I mean it."

"OK, Ms. Snooty Pants."

"It's Ms. Sassy Pants," I said with a giggle. "Seriously, he's important to me. Promise."

Abby shrugged. "You are so whipped."

We meandered into the elegant space, lit by magnificent

dome lighting and iron wall sconces, each table dressed in ivory linens. As an interior architect, I was always drawn to spaces, and the nuances—from the crown molding to the arched door-ways to the brass details. We made our way down steps covered in red carpet and I took in our luxurious surroundings with a gasp. One day I'd love to design a restaurant where people gush about the ambiance over the food. I straightened my posture, my eyes landing on the bar, and to my surprise Nate was seated on a stool, Ben by his side.

Abby nudged me. "I really hope this isn't a double date. I don't like the looks of him."

I whispered, "I would never set you up with him. A: He's married. B: You're way too good for a guy like that. C: He's a misogynistic pig. And D: I really hope he isn't eating with us because his manners would send you running for the hills. He chews with his mouth open and his fork scrapes his teeth. Plus, he moans a lot."

"What a catch," said Abby with a laugh. "I'm sold."

"Don't say that." I met her gaze. "Trust me, because he might ask."

I meandered up to Nate and tapped him on the shoulder. "My gorgeous fiancé is already here."

Nate turned and flashed one of his brilliant smiles. "Surgery got out earlier than I thought and I decided to meet up with Benny for a drink," he said, and then shifted his attention to Abby. "Abby, nice to meet you. Emma's told me all about you."

"Only good things, I hope."

"All I see are good things," said Ben with a wiggle of his brows.

"Ben, a pleasure to see you. Are you joining us for dinner? With Becks?" I asked.

Please say no.

"We are." His fat tongue darted out, gliding over his lips.

"And then we're going to a party at Gordon's. The three of you should come—"

My body went stiff. I didn't want to hang out with Ben or Becks. And I didn't want to cross paths with Gordon Flynn ever again.

"That's a hard no," said Nate.

"Hard? Good choice of words." He eyed Abby lasciviously up and down and then kissed my hand—a wet, slobbery smack. "Emma, you look good enough to eat."

I forced a smile, choosing not to respond. As I grabbed a napkin off the bar to wipe off Ben's drool, Abby leaned over and whispered, "That guy seriously gives me all of the cringes."

Me too, I thought, but didn't have time to voice an opinion. Nate put his arm around my waist, pulling me into him. He nuzzled into my neck. "You smell and look delicious. I love the color red on you."

"And I love Chanel." I curtsied. "Thank you, again, for buying me this skirt suit."

"It really does suit you. And it's not a cheap knockoff." He kissed my earlobe, his teeth gently tugging, his hand riding down my spine under the jacket. "You can thank me later. Again."

Thankfully, Abby didn't hear Nate's comment. She coughed dramatically into her hand. "OK, lovebirds, cool it. We're in a public place. What are we drinking?"

"Anything you want," said Nate, looking at his watch. "We have time for one before we're seated."

"I'll have a shot of tequila," said Abby.

Ben flashed her a wicked grin. "Tequila? My kind of gal."

"Tequila? Really?" I said with disapproval. "How about a glass of champagne?"

"I need something stronger," she said, and then whispered in my ear, "to get me through this night."

Nate's eyes said what his lips didn't. I knew he was already judging Abby, and she him. It was obvious they couldn't stand one another.

Much to my chagrin, Nate ordered a round of Gran Patrón Burdeos Anejo with a sangrita chaser—tomato, lime and orange juice, onions, hot sauce, and limes on the side. He winked. "It's one of the best sipping tequilas in the world."

"Cheers," said Abby, grabbing her glass. Nate met her eyes and they clinked glasses. Abby downed her shot.

"I think you were supposed to sip it," I said, shooting her a side-glance.

"I did," she said, raising a brow. "In one sip."

I gave Abby a look of annoyance just as Becks rushed over, her perfume overpowering the aromas in the restaurant. I wished I'd worn a mask and blinders, her tight silver metallic dress highlighting curves in all the wrong places. She kissed me on the cheek, gave Abby the once-over and then clucked her tongue. "Who is our new friend? And what did I miss?"

Becks really needed a lesson from Miss Manners. She broke all the rules of etiquette. Didn't she know that it was rude to stare or talk about people in the third person? Becks ignored Abby as she tried to introduce herself and turned instead toward Nate. "Darling, you look fabulous, as always. You must stop by the gallery. We have a new exhibition—street art, one of those guerrilla artists. I think you'll absolutely adore the pieces. So on the pulse of these times. The colors, the strokes are to die for. The opening is next Friday."

"We'll be there," he said.

No, we won't. "Sorry, I have plans with Abby."

"Who?" asked Becks. "I had a long day. What are we drinking?"

Ben's hand dove into his pocket and then he squeezed Becks's hand. Her eyes lit up. "Hold that thought. I have to go powder my nose." She winked at Nate. "I'll be back in two shakes of a lamb's tail."

Abby's eyes flickered with disgust as Nate called the bartender over with a wave. "Another round of Gran Patrón."

I flipped haphazardly through the bar menu. This tequila ran $125 a shot and Abby had downed two like we were at a college party. Before she did any more damage, the maître d' sauntered over, alerting us that it was time to be seated. We followed him to our table, Nate pulling out my chair, and the maître d' Abby's, which she sank into.

"Where are the menus? I'm starving! I need to drown out the tequila with some sustenance," said Abby as Becks slid into the chair next to mine. "What's good here?"

"I've already ordered for us," said Nate. "Tonight, we're having the seven-course tasting menu with wine pairings, followed by dessert."

Abby tilted her head to the side as the server poured champagne. "What if I wanted something else?"

"Did you want to pick up the bill?" said Ben with a har-har-har.

"I think she'd be spending her rent money, darling," said Becks, loud enough for all of us to hear. Her teeth ground against one another and she dabbed her lips with a napkin.

"Maybe you should go powder your nose again," said Abby, and I nudged her with my foot under the table.

Nate cleared his throat. "Abby, I suppose Emma told you the good news."

"Oh yeah, your engagement. Congratulations." Abby threw back her glass of champagne in one gulp. "Cheers."

Ben and Becks lifted their glasses, shooting Abby amused smirks.

"Not that," said Nate, squeezing my hand. "You didn't tell her?"

"No, not yet. I was waiting for the right time."

Abby's eyes went wide and she raised her chin. "Tell me

what? Are you pregnant? Figures. A quickie turns into a quick engagement—"

"No, nothing as life-changing as that," I said, forcing a laugh. "I'm moving out of our apartment this weekend."

"To where?"

"Obviously, Emma is moving in with me," said Nate.

"I think Emma can speak for herself." Abby slammed her glass down and stared at me. "What about me? The rent? Our mutually purchased things like the TV and the shared bills—"

"Don't worry. We've already discussed this issue," said Nate with a nonchalant shrug. "I'll take care of Emma's portion of the rent until you find a new roommate. As for your things, Emma no longer needs them. It's all yours."

Under Abby's glare, I went silent.

"Emma? What the fuck? Why aren't you saying anything?"

"Because Nate just explained everything," said Becks. "Are you thick in the head?"

Abby's jaw clenched and she raised her glass. "Congratu-fucking-lations." She stood up, her chair nearly toppling over. "Enjoy your meal. I'm leaving."

And just like that, Abby stormed out of the restaurant.

Of course, once the word of our engagement got out, people I knew from my past scurried back into my life. I knew that would happen. Much to Nate's chagrin, in addition to old friends from high school who would become bridesmaids, Abby still agreed to be my maid of honor and my best friend, although I had to bribe her.

"You can design the dresses for the bridesmaids," I'd said.

She'd laughed. "They'll be black because it's your funeral."

FIFTEEN

EMMA

Sunday, May 26th, 2024: 12:23 p.m.

Like drinking a cool lemonade on a hot summer's day, relief washes over me when Abby walks into the living room, plopping herself beside me. She fans her face with her hand. "I just want this day to be over and done with."

"I know," I whisper. "Me too."

Detective Rossi clomps in a few moments later and we both go silent. "Mrs. Landon, until we rule out your house out as a crime scene, you'll have to vacate the premises."

"Crime scene?"

"That's what I said."

"Based on what?"

"The evidence we've been collecting."

"You really think somebody did something to Nate?" Abby asks.

"I do." Rossi narrows her eyes at me. "Do you have anywhere you can go?"

"Yes. Our place in the city—a loft in Tribeca," I say.

"I'm afraid we'll need to process that place too, so I'll need the address and access to it. Anywhere else?"

"Don't you need a warrant?" Abby asks and Detective Rossi shoots her a look. "I watch a lot of Netflix—"

"I could put in a request, but having Mrs. Landon's permission to enter the premises would be easiest on everybody." She locks her gaze on me. "Unless she's hiding something."

"I'm not hiding anything," I snap. At least, nothing she'll find. "I'll give you what you need."

"She can stay with me," says Abby, nodding her head. I grip her hand.

"And where do you live, Ms. Hoffman?"

"Katonah."

"Address?" she asks and Abby blurts it out.

"Noted." Rossi straightens her posture. "Mrs. Landon, please don't cross state lines until we're finished with our investigation."

"Look, I don't know what's going on. A crime scene? You're flipping me out and not letting me digest anything..." I pause, taking in a deep breath. My imagination is now running in overdrive. "Wait. Am I a person of interest?"

"Should you be?"

Is she for real?

"I think *not*. Look, I'm doing my best to cooperate with you. Give me time to process everything."

"That's exactly what I'm doing. Processing. And, just so you're aware, I'll also need access to both of your banking accounts."

"Why?" asks Abby. "Again, I think you need a warrant for that."

Rossi smiles. "Like I said, I'm looking at every angle. And, again, if Mrs. Landon isn't hiding anything, she'll be helping out the investigation."

"You're a real piece of work, you know that?" says Abby.

Rossi shrugs. "I'm just doing my job."

"Noted," I say, my throat pinching. "There are four of them —my business account, his personal account, my account, and our joint account. I'll give you the information." Feeling her eyes on me, I write down the information and hand it over. "Here."

"Any offshore accounts?"

"Not to my knowledge." I clench my fists into tiny balls. "How long do I have stay out of my house?"

"At least twenty-four to forty-eight hours, maybe longer," she says. "Your property is massive."

"Can I go upstairs so I can pack a bag?"

"Of course. I'll have an officer escort you up to your room." She pauses. "Do me a favor, Mrs. Landon, be quick."

"Do *me* a favor, Detective, stop with your sensationalized insinuations." I swallow, trying to keep my anger at bay. "I'm thinking the next time we speak I'd like to have an attorney present."

"That would be wise."

She clicks on her radio, turning her back on me.

Abby kisses my cheek and whispers, "Meet me at my car. I cannot wait to get out of here."

I watch Abby stagger out of the room, and as I wait for the officer to arrive I find myself reviewing all the bad decisions I've made. So stupid. Why didn't I see the signs when they were right in front of me, practically flashing like neon lights? I should have run away from Nate and this life in Bedford as fast as my feet could carry me when I'd had the chance.

SIXTEEN

EMMA

Then: 2008–2009

Nate's housekeeper Luisa's duties included: cleaning, taking care of the groceries, and making sure the plants were watered. After a month of living with Nate, I'd never seen her until I literally bumped into her as she sauntered down the steps. She was younger than I'd expected, maybe my age, with long, shiny hair, big brown eyes, and a cute little figure, from what I could tell. I'd tried to introduce myself, but she'd flashed a hesitant smile, a look of fear in her eyes, and scurried down the street. Which, of course, I thought was beyond odd.

I meandered upstairs and punched in the code for the alarm, then let myself in. After hanging up my coat, I found Nate in the study, reading Bret Easton Ellis's latest tome. He set his book down and tilted his head to the side when I tapped my foot.

"What's wrong? You look like you've seen a ghost."

"I just met Luisa," I muttered. "You didn't tell me she was beautiful. I mean, when you told me you had a maid that did housework and cooked for you, I was picturing somebody completely different in my head."

He lowered his reading glasses to the bridge of his nose, a flash of amusement lighting his eyes. "You're bothered that she's attractive?"

"Wouldn't you be? What if I had some hot tennis pro or pool guy?"

He laughed. "Do you want one of each? That can be arranged after we're married."

"You're not funny."

"And you're cute when you're jealous." He met my gaze, placed his book down on the coffee table, and stepped over to me, his expression tense. "Did Luisa say anything to you?"

"No." My upper lip lifted. "Why, is that a problem? Is there something I should know?"

"We don't fraternize with the staff," he said with a cocky shrug. "She's only here to work."

"So, I can't be nice?"

"You can be nice to me," he said, his hand grazing my waist. "I've been thinking about you all day."

"Wait a second. This conversation isn't over," I said, taking a step backward. "Where does she live?"

"In that back room with the locked door. She has her own entrance."

"I thought it was an emergency exit," I said, wondering why our paths never crossed.

"It's not. It's a tiny studio."

She probably did her work—cleaning and filling up the fridge with home-cooked meals—when I was in my classes at Columbia. Maybe Nate had given her my schedule?

"Where did you find her? Hot Personal Assistants?"

"Something like that. Gordon has a philanthropic heart. He helps people out and finds them jobs." He sighed. "We're giving these girls a chance for a better life."

I winced. I'd met Gordon and I was pretty sure he didn't have a heart. If he did, it wasn't located in his chest. "These girls?" I snap. "Tell me, do they cook and clean wearing hot French maid uniforms, bending over like in Gordon's twisted movies?"

"Don't be ridiculous."

"I'm not. I know what Gordon does for a living—"

"He's a businessman working in a very lucrative domain."

"He peddles sex."

He nestled into my hair, breathing me in, and kissed my neck. "Don't worry about Luisa. She does the things you'll never have to worry about—cooking, cleaning, going to the grocery store, the dry cleaner's—"

"What if I want to do all that?"

"Do you?" He laughed. "You can barely boil water."

Anger flared in my chest. Frustrated, I stomped my foot. "Look, Nate, you've made your point, but I don't need help. I'm smart and I can figure things out, including cooking. Don't forget—I used to clean houses and scrub toilets—"

"I know you're smart. And I definitely don't want you scrubbing toilets." He wrapped his hands around my waist and met my eyes, his so very blue and hypnotizing. "I just want you to focus on me and building your dream, OK?"

"What dream?"

"Wait until you see." Nate handed me an ivory-colored purse.

I snorted. "I already have this bag."

"This is the real deal. It's not a fake."

Oh God, he'd remembered Becks's comment from our first dinner. "Uh-huh," I said with a squint. "Thank you, I love it."

"But it's the inside that matters," he said, and then stooped into an over-the-top bow. "Consider it an early wedding gift, my lady."

My hand automatically dove into the purse and I pulled out

a contract. My eyes scanned the papers: land, in Bedford? I looked up, meeting his satisfied smile. "Wait, let me get this straight: you want to move to horse country? You don't even like horses. You think they smell. You told me that when we watched *Legends of the Fall.*"

"I like horsepower."

"Huh?"

"Cars," he said with a smile. "Just think about our future. You'll build the house of your dreams, and then start your own consulting business."

My lips pinched together. "What about the loft?"

"We'll keep it. We'll still need a place in the city."

"I don't know, Nate. This is a lot to take in." My brows pinched with concern. "While I appreciate the grand gesture, we haven't discussed anything of this magnitude. I mean, moving out of the city? That's a pretty big decision."

"What's there to discuss? It's the right move for when we have kids. I don't want them growing up in the dirty city," he said, and when I visibly flinched, he paused, changing the subject, changing gears. "Plus, this house, the one you build, will be your calling card to start your own firm. You'll take charge of your own life, your career. Not only that, you can use the designs for your final project."

That statement got me—hook, line, and sinker. I walked into the kitchen, Nate following, and grabbed a bottle of water from the refrigerator. As I unscrewed the cap, I asked, "How big is this house you're envisioning?"

"As big as it needs to be."

"Budget?"

"Same."

"And I can design anything I want?"

"Anything. A pool. A pool house. A home gym, offices for both of us, a ten-car garage—"

"Who needs that many cars?"

"I do," he said with a shit-eating grin. "And as long as we're brainstorming, we'll need a guesthouse for the staff."

I felt like I was sucker-punched into an alternate universe. "Staff?"

"Of course. Cleaners. A cook." He grinned. "Nannies for our future kids."

I gulped. "Kids?"

He rubbed his chin. "I'm thinking we'll need six bedrooms, maybe seven..."

I spat out my water. I was only twenty-two and not quite ready for this discussion. Not even close. "You want that many kids?"

"No, two-point-one, of course, including a son to carry on my legacy, my name," he said with a laugh and changed his tone when I flinched again. "Don't worry. We'll wait until after we're married and settled in. The sky is the limit for the new construction. You can do whatever your heart desires. And you're going to be very, very busy," he said, and my eyes went wide. "There's a home in Pound Ridge included in the deal that we can live in until our dream is built. It's not much to look at, but there are four bedrooms, it's clean and full of country charm."

He watched me processing this information. "What about Luisa?"

"Fully finished and furnished basement. She'll live there."

In the cellar? "Does it have windows?"

"It does." His lip curled. "It's nice—nice enough."

"What do we do with this temporary home after ours is built?"

"Sell it or give it to your parents. I think they'll want to be close to their grandkids—" His eyes lit up and then darkened at my stunned expression. "When we have them."

Jesus, he really had all angles covered. Like everything—our whole lives—was planned out. "My mom has her business. Besides, my parents wouldn't accept a house."

He chortled out a laugh. "I didn't say it would be free. They'd have to pay the taxes on it. Good news. They're not too high. Probably cheaper than the rent they pay in Bushwick. Plus, with my recommendations, Dust Busters would be running in Westchester County in no time."

"I, uh, I..." Couldn't think straight.

His expression suddenly became more serious. "There's just one thing..."

"What?"

"I bought the land and the property from Gordon Flynn for a great price, the deal of the century. They'll be our neighbors—and his wife, Irina, really needs a friend."

Although I adored everybody Nate worked with at the hospital, I hated Becks and Ben and constantly made excuses to not see them. And Gordon? I'd hoped to never see him again. "What if I don't like this Irina?"

"You will," he said, grasping my hands. "I can't wait for this next chapter in our lives."

Although the dream of building a home had taken my mind hostage, I wasn't sold on the move just yet. "Can I see the property?"

"Good idea. We'll head out there tomorrow."

Set on twenty-three acres, the land, complete with a magnificent pond, the perimeter of the property surrounded by oleander bursting in reds and bright pink, inspired every design instinct in my brain and excitement took hold of me. I already envisioned the home.

"Glass. Cement. Modern. Set over the pond." I looked toward Nate, eyes wide with enthusiasm. "What do you think?"

"I think it sounds amazing. And I trust your instincts. Just don't forget about the guest house, the garage and a state-of-the-art gym."

I grinned so wide I felt like the Cheshire cat. All my dreams were coming true.

An hour later, our driver pulled up to the Flynn estate and I shivered. Painted red, this monstrosity of a Victorian mansion with its Gothic towers and turrets reminded me of a haunted house, complete with dead ivy clinging to the facade. The woman I assumed to be Irina opened the front door. She wore a tight, sequined dress—gold—and looked like a lady of the night. It was eleven in the morning.

I nudged Nate. "Am I not dressed right for the occasion? I mean, I feel like I should be wearing a ball gown."

Nate laughed and rubbed my thigh. "No, she's always dressed up. You look perfect. I'm glad I bought you that."

I eyed my blue silk Lanvin sheath dress, feeling like a schoolmarm.

As she drew closer, I could see Irina was a knockout. Perfect figure. Long, shiny perfectly styled blond hair. Makeup painted on with flawless perfection, her eyes, a crystal-clear blue like Nate's, but offset with lash extensions and liquid-black eyeliner.

We got out of the car and Irina raced up to us, long legs like a graceful gazelle, kissing Nate on the cheeks. And, if I wasn't mistaken, she added a smack on the lips. Then, she turned her attention on me. "You are the famous Emma," she said. "I am so happy we will be neighbors." She pointed to herself and then to me. "We are going to be great friends." She turned on her mile-high stilettos. "Come, come, come, we have a perfect meal to celebrate."

I nudged Nate and whispered, "I don't think she's my cup of tea. Why on earth would you think I would get along with a woman like that?"

"Emma, play nice," he said. "Give her a chance."

We followed her, me wondering how she managed to walk

in those heels when I was tripping over my two feet. Inside the house, every detail was gold, gold, gold and lots of red velvet. A mental whiplash for my aesthetic senses, it was like somebody vomited out French baroque antiques in every corner of every room, which would be nice if used sparingly as conversational pieces. Gordon may have had boatloads of money, but he had zero taste.

Once seated, Irina poured us all shots of vodka. She raised her glass. "Besides becoming neighbors and great friends, I'm excited for your upcoming marriage. Our tiny trouble maker, Taryn—she's three-and-a half years old—is with the nanny right now. We can raise our children together."

I swallowed. Hard. Then I cleared my throat. "I'm not thinking about having kids just yet."

Her blue eyes flitted from side to side. She pouted. "Oh," she replied. "I was just fantasizing—"

Nate piped in. "We're going to wait until the house is built and we're settled in."

Irina smiled. "I hope it doesn't take too long."

Gordon hobbled into the room, tapping his carved wooden cane, and took his seat at the head of the table. He clapped his hands together. "Now that we're all finally together, I believe this calls for champagne. Chariya! Now! Get your skinny ass in here!"

I glared at Nate, feeling trapped as a petite Asian woman scrambled into the room with a magnum. "Mr. Gordon, the Dom."

"Open it. And pour."

"Yes, Mr. Gordon."

After the woman served us, she bowed and backed out of the room. Gordon lifted his glass. "Cheers to the happy couple and to becoming neighbors," he bellowed.

Irina slammed back her glass of champagne. "Vashe zdorov'ye!"

"Did you tell Emma the other news?" asked Gordon.

"I haven't," said Nate.

What other news? We were leaving and I would never have to see these people again?

"Well, I'll do the honors then, if you don't mind." Nate smiled and Gordon paused dramatically. "You can move to the property in Pound Ridge this weekend. Chariya! Bring in the lobster bisque! Now!" He winked at me. "We're having a five-course lunch. Like the French. Hope you're hungry."

My heart dropped into my stomach.

After another torturous meal with Gordon hacking up a cough every two seconds, sending food flying across the table, finally it was over. Nate and I were in the car heading back to the city.

"I'm not moving there," I said, pushing my visions of building our dream house aside. "Not now. Not ever. Those people scare the life out of me. I mean, did he really order her from a catalog? That doesn't happen. It's an urban myth—"

"There's nothing to worry about. Gordon is like a father figure to me." Nate's voice was so cold I could have turned into a human ice cube. "I paid for the land. And we're moving there, unless you don't want a life with me—a life of big dreams."

A feeling of lightheadedness overtook my brain, followed by a strong sense of dread coiling around my stomach like a python. Talk about being pushed into a situation I didn't want to be in. "Is that an ultimatum?"

"I suppose it is." He crossed his arms over his chest. "Don't you like the property? I do."

I slumped into my seat. "What about school? I still have one year left—"

"I'll hire a driver to take you to the city." He tilted his head to the side. "And don't forget, this design is your final project."

I squeezed my eyes shut, visions flashing in my mind.

Visions of a happy life with Nate. Our future children—when I was ready to take the leap into maternal waters—swimming in the pool, playing on a swing-set.

"I loved the land," I finally replied.

"Then it's settled."

"But I'm not hanging out with Gordon or Irina," I said defiantly. "I have my own friends."

"Friends you should change," he said with a sigh. "Just give Irina a chance."

We moved to Pound Ridge the following week and I threw myself into designing the house, going to school, and making constant excuses to not hang out with Irina, though she stopped by often with Taryn. A good mother, she was kind of growing on me.

Aside from saying hello, I still hadn't really spoken with Luisa as she avoided me like the plague, requesting that I write down anything I needed. I even tried to establish a connection to her by telling her I used to clean homes with my mother. Her bottom lip trembled and she asked, "You don't like the way I clean?"

"No, no, no," I said. "It's amazing. You do a good job. The best! Do you like working here?"

"Bueno. I clean now." She nodded, but didn't answer my question, a hint of fear in her eyes. "Mr. Landon no allow talk. I do my job."

She grabbed a mop and, for the most part, ignored me.

Yes, I thought this was very odd, and when I asked Nate about it, he only shrugged and said, "I was raised that way. We don't talk to the staff. This is the way things work around here."

There were a couple more dinners with Ben and Becks, whom I despised, and a couple of galas at the hospital, which I loved—getting dressed up in elegant gowns and getting my hair and nails done—but most of my time was spent planning the wedding. I took the helm—locking down the church and the estate for the party, wheedling down the guest list from eight hundred to three hundred, choosing my wedding dress—the list went on and on, keeping me busy and distracting me from the seeds Nate had been planting and spreading like destructive weeds.

After graduating from Columbia, masters degree in hand, the marriage and our honeymoon in the Seychelles, I came home from the Bedford site to find most of my clothes—the outfits Abby had made for me—in garbage bags. I was in the midst of getting ready to rail into him when Nate placed a hand on my shoulder and said, "I think you'll like your new wardrobe." He grinned. "Don't you remember what Becks said? We wealthy can always spot a fake. Now that you're my wife, appearances need to be kept up."

My response was to throw up on his shoes. That was the day I'd found out I was pregnant.

SEVENTEEN

EMMA

Sunday, May 26th, 2024: 1:27 p.m.

Abby's sitting in her Tesla, waiting for me with the engine running. I drag my suitcase across the gravel and she rolls down the window. "Damn, Emma." She shakes her head. "Get in."

"I'm taking my car," I say, pointing over to my Range Rover. "But there are two things I need to do first."

"What could be more important than getting the hell out of here?"

"I have to see Luisa and the rest of the staff." I raise an apologetic eyebrow. "And then, before we head to your place, we have to stop by my parents'. They need to hear the news from me."

Her shoulders slump and she brushes a lock of hair out of her eyes. "Fine."

"You can head over to my mom and dad's without me if you want."

"I'm not telling them the news. And you know it would come streaming right out of me. Like verbal diarrhea." She tucks her chin into her neck and raises her shoulders, slinking down into her seat. "I'll wait right here and I'll follow you there. That's our plan, and I'm sticking to it."

Before I pass out from exhaustion, I throw my suitcases into the back of my Range Rover and stumble over to the guest-house, a mini replica of the main house at the far end of the property, passing by the cypress trees I'd had our landscaper plant to give my staff and us privacy. Plus, the trees go with the design aesthetic of our estate.

With a sigh, I knock and Luisa opens the front door. She's wearing a red dress and has makeup on. Her dark brown hair is tied back into a sleek ponytail. Four years older than me, she's been with us for fifteen years, Nate longer. She smiles and draws me in for a hug, kissing both of my cheeks with a loud smack. Jennifer Lopez's "Love Don't Cost a Thing" blares in the background, which, I have to say, I find totally ironic. She grins. "Hola, Emma, you're back from Paris!"

Let's just say that over the years Luisa and I didn't listen to Nate. I did talk to my staff—they were my family, took care of me when Nate wasn't around. And I took care of them.

"I am." I clear my throat. "You look absolutely gorgeous. Big date with Diego?" I ask and she grins.

She's been dating the landscaper for five years. Nate doesn't know. But it's not like it's going to kill him. I'm just happy she has a life outside of this world.

"Gracias, you look, uh, tired—"

My heart pounds so wildly a sense of dizziness sets in. "The cops have been here for hours. Nate's dead." I quickly explain the events of this horrific morning and how I found Nate floating in the pond. Luisa stands in shock, her eyes wide with panic. "You didn't hear the sirens?"

"No," she finally says, pointing to her sound system with a shaky hand. "My music is loud." She swallows and looks toward the sky. Her hands run across her mouth. Her chocolate brown eyes scan my face with worry. "I can't believe he's dead."

"Neither can I," I mumble. "Are the others here?"

"No," she says, gulping. "Homa and Kom went into the city to see a Broadway show. And Alba is taking a cooking class at some French restaurant. She wanted to surprise you with French recipes—" She slaps her hand on her forehead. "And I just ruined the surprise."

Before I can respond, Rossi stomps up the path with Kowalski. Luisa's eyes go wide with fear. Rossi raises a brow. "You're still here, Mrs. Landon?"

"I wanted to speak with my staff before I left for Abby's." I'm wearing sunglasses now so she can't see the glare I'm sending in her direction. "Are they going to be kicked out of their home too?"

Luisa shakes her head defiantly and whispers, "They kicked you out of your home?" and I nod.

Rossi's gaze sweeps the yard, the house. "It's set far enough back from the scene of the crime. I don't think that will be necessary," she says, and Kowalski grunts out an agreement. She turns her head, focusing on Luisa. "And you are the house manager?"

"Si. Luisa." Her body trembles for a second and then she snaps her shoulders back, straight and proud. "I'm also Emma's assistant. I help her manage her design and architecture projects—Atelier Em."

"Good to know," says Rossi. "We'd like to speak with you and the other members of staff. Alone." She turns, focusing her gaze back on me. "Mrs. Landon, I'll be in touch."

I pick up on her not-so-subtle hint.

"Luisa, call or text if you need anything. I'll be staying with Abby," I say, and she pulls me in for hug.

She swallows and places a hand to her throat and blinks once.

"Mrs. Landon?" barks Rossi. "Don't you have somewhere to be?"

I kiss Luisa's cheek. "We'll all talk later."

"Don't worry," she whispers. "I see how this mean detective is looking at you, but everything will be fine."

I'm not so sure about that.

I squeeze Luisa's hand again and turn to walk away, feeling Rossi's eyes directing invisible bullets of suspicion at my back.

I'm sitting in my Range Rover, tapping my fingers on the steering wheel, questioning the best way to tell my mom and dad about Nate's demise. I focus on the first home Nate and I had lived in, the idyllic place where I hold so many memories close to my heart. I'd been so happy and hopeful here. But hope only lasts so long.

Although my parents have done a few renovations and updates, the house hasn't changed much over the years—the same front porch, the blue roof, the white wood-paneled siding. Set back on a winding road, the home sits on five acres, complete with an apple orchard, and a large dog run. A lawn-mower rumbles in the distance—probably my dad on his rider. Abby opens the passenger door.

"Em, you're just sitting here, zoning out," she says.

"I can't do this," I mumble. "They loved Nate and this news is going to send them into a state of shock."

"Nothing shocks me anymore," Abby grunts, throwing her hands into the air. "But, as you said, your parents need to hear this news from you before they hear it from somebody else."

"So do the girls." I pull out my phone and dial. Ava doesn't answer. Grace doesn't answer. Neither does Taryn. "Damn it. They're not picking up."

"Leave another message."

"Saying what?"

"To call you back and that it's important."

So, that's what I do. My phone chimes. It's not a message

from the girls, but an alert reminding me that it's Taryn's birthday. I send her a quick text, keeping it simple, although I'd like to say: Happy Birthday. Nate's dead.

> Happy Birthday, love-bug. Miss you. xox
> Emma-Ma

My mom steps around from the backyard, waving a set of pruning shears. An avid gardener, a floppy straw hat adorns her head and she's wearing a green apron over her practical clothes —a long-sleeved tan top, navy pull-on pants (they're comfortable, she says) and thick rubber boots.

Busted, I amble out of the car, preparing myself. "Hey, Mom."

Her smile lights up her face and reaches her eyes. "Em-Dash! Abby! What a lovely surprise!" An avid reader, she'd named me Emma to honor Jane Austen and nicknamed me Em-Dash for humor. Such a literary twist.

She tilts her head to her clippers. "I was about to take a break from pruning the roses and make a pot of coffee."

"Thank the heavens," says Abby, putting her hands in prayer position and looking toward the sky.

My mom meanders to the front porch and sets her clippers and gloves down on a bench. She kicks off her rubber boots, replacing them with house slippers, and then hangs her hat on an iron hook. Her hair, now silvery gray streaked with white, has always been worn in the same style—a sassy pixie cut bob with a feathered crown, long bangs swept to the side. She shakes out her head, brushes a few rogue strands of hair into place, and then turns to open the screen door. She looks over her shoulder, eyeing me curiously. "What are you waiting for?"

I force a closed-mouth smile. "I'm coming."

We follow her into the house, my steps heavy on the pine flooring, and then Abby and I settle onto chairs in the country kitchen. My mom went slightly overboard with porcelain

chickens and roosters in all different sizes and red-checked gingham. Although our tastes are very different, this does feel like
home. Even some of the art I'd made as a child decorates the
refrigerator like it did in Brooklyn.

The moment we sit down at the kitchen table, three cats—
varying breeds and varying colors—wander into the kitchen and
I sneeze. "How's Dad's animal rescue going?"

My dad had to retire from his veterinary clinic after two
major health scares—both strokes. Although he has a stent in his
heart and a pacemaker, he couldn't abandon his passion for
taking care of animals. So he saves them and finds them new
homes.

"It's good," she says.

A couple of more cats wander into the kitchen, one jumping
on the counter. Mom shoos him or her off with a kitchen towel.

"How many cats live here now?"

Mom shrugs. "I don't know. Maybe twenty? I can't keep
track of them all. They come and they go."

"And Dad? How's he doing?"

Nate had looked over my father's scans and treatments and
told me not to worry, that he'd take care of the bills. But that
doesn't stop me from worrying. My parents refused any more of
his financial help; I think they felt awkward moving into the
house, but they'd done so to be closer to me when the girls were
born.

She smiles. "He's right as rain. Had an excellent check-up
last week."

Mom sets to making coffee, pulling out a tin of Folgers and
scooping the grains into the machine. "It's not the fancy
espresso you drink from that robot of yours," she says with a
shrug. "But we like it."

"I'm just happy for coffee. Any kind. I couldn't get my
machine to work at home."

She laughs. "Sometimes simple is better."

Then why is my life so complicated? I wonder. Grand Complications. I'm now thinking about Nate's watch. While Abby and my mom chat about Paris and Mom's booming business, my mind sifts through the past to the first night my parents met Nate, and how they'd fallen for his charm and charisma as quickly I'd had. I remember my mom calling me up the day after, telling me how much she approved of him, how polite and handsome he was, and how I had excellent taste.

A taste that had left a sourness in my mouth, my life. Like bile. They've never known the real Nate. Come to think of it, neither have I. I wring my hands underneath the table, focusing in on one of Mom's many chickens, thinking I can't chicken out: I have to stop procrastinating and tell her the news. Nate, the son-in law they'd loved, is dead.

Soon, the coffee is percolating, the aroma wrapping me in sweetness. Mom darts around the kitchen, placing milk, sugar, and a plate of blueberry muffins on the table. "I made them this morning. They're your dad's kryptonite." She pats my hand. "Good thing you and Abby are here now, otherwise they'd be gone. Although I have him on a sugar-free diet, he gets one cheat day a month. And today is the day."

I have the urge to laugh. Nate's cheat days? They were whenever he wanted, with somebody younger or sexier than me. And I let him get away with it.

"They look delicious," I say, grabbing a muffin even though I'll only dig into the top, if I can manage to eat at all. "Dad and his sweet tooth."

Finally, she returns to the table with three mugs and sits across from me. I'm having trouble meeting her eyes. After adding a dash of cream, I take a sip of my coffee, letting the warmness coat my throat.

"Tell me about Thailand! And Paris! I'm so glad I can live vicariously through you."

Mom and Dad never traveled too far, only recently

choosing cruises in Europe and the Caribbean. When I was a kid, Florida was the chosen vacation spot to thaw out from the dreary New York winters.

I brace my hands on the table and lower my head. "Mom, it was all work, finding furniture and design elements for a client. Nothing much to say about it."

"What about the food? You must have eaten wonderful meals—"

"Actually, Mom, I'm here to tell you something else." I exhale the breath I've been holding in with a long whoosh. "It's pretty serious."

Mom's hands fly to her heart and she exhales a sharp breath. "Oh my goodness, please don't tell me that something is wrong with you."

"No, I'm fine," I say, twiddling my fingers in my lap.

"The girls?"

"They're fine too."

Mom sniffs the air. "What's that smell? The two of you reek."

"Pond water," says Abby. "And grimy clothes."

Mom shoots Abby a confused look and then her gaze snaps directly onto mine. "What is going on, Emma? And, when you tell me, look me in the eyes. I know when you're lying. I always do."

Oh boy, I'd almost forgotten my teen years, living with mom radar. Me? No, I didn't smoke. Somebody else did. Me? No, I didn't have a drink at the party. OK, maybe just a little sip. Me, no, I'm still a virgin. I swear. After the last white lie, she'd driven me to planned parenting and put me on the pill, not wanting to be a grandmother or, more important, me having kids at the age of nineteen.

I gulp. How do I break the news to her? I'm fidgeting in my chair, trying to find the right words. But there are no right words. So I just blurt them out. "Nate's dead."

Mom's hand flails and she swipes her coffee cup to the ground. "What?"

Nobody moves to clean up the pieces of the shattered ceramic chicken mug or the spill, which is spreading on the floor like murky pond water.

"They think he was murdered." I squeeze my eyes shut. "And I'm pretty sure the detective thinks I had something to do with it."

She sinks into her seat, her mouth agape. "Did you?"

"Of course not," I say.

"Olivia, we were in Paris," says Abby. "We came back this morning and Emma and I found Nate floating face down in the pond. Dead."

Mom clasps her hands over her mouth.

Dad walks into the kitchen, dressed like he's about to head off to play a round of golf—pressed khakis, a polo (green today), Sperry top-siders (tan), and a grosgrain belt. This is his daily summer uniform and it only varies slightly. Like Mom, his hair is gray, maybe even grayer than the last time I'd seen him, but shorter and slightly tousled. He's also skinnier. "Baby girl! You're here! What a nice surprise! And Abby too. I always forget who is Sugar Pie and who is Honey Bunch." When nobody responds, he regards Mom's face, then mine, then Abby's, and then the spilled coffee and shattered mug on the floor. "What's going on? Did somebody die?"

My mom nods solemnly. "Nate. He's dead."

"*What?*" Dad's hands fly to his heart and a sense of panic overtakes me. I jump out of my chair and lead him to the table, rubbing his back.

"Pops," I say with concern. "You might want to sit down."

He takes in a breath and nods. "I'm OK."

Two hours later, after filling my parents in on me wanting to divorce Nate, his serial cheating, hiring the attorney, the private investigator, and discovering Nate's body this morning, my dad doesn't gasp out in shock and my mom doesn't scream or cry.

Complete silence is not the reaction I expected.

"Wasn't I clear? I was going to divorce Nate. I came home to a dead body. Nate's dead body. We had to pull him out of the water. I'm definitely a person of interest and I'm pretty sure the detective made up her mind about me before she'd even met me." My eyes dart between them. "Why aren't you saying anything?"

Mom clears her throat. Dad coughs. I growl. "Seriously?"

"This is real life. This isn't like one of the thrillers we've read. The police always suspect the most obvious suspect in the beginning—especially the wife. And they're usually dead wrong." Mom wrings her hands. "We're more concerned about you, not him."

"But I thought you adored Nate," I say, my jaw unhinged. "I thought you'd be devastated."

"Neither of us liked him very much." Dad lowers his head, not meeting my eyes. "We didn't say anything because you were in love."

"Yep," says Abby.

I shoot Abby the stink eye. "You made your distaste of Nate very clear."

"What can I say? I'm a good friend."

"You are," I say. "You're the best."

"I know," she replies.

"We know you've had problems. We figured you and Nate were working things out," says Dad. "Why rearrange the deck chairs on the *Titanic*?"

Dad and his metaphors and idioms. "The *Titanic* sank."

"It did. That's the point. We couldn't change the outcome even if we tried," continues Mom. She lowers her voice. "Over the years, we saw how Nate changed you. And they weren't good changes."

"Like what?" I ask, not sure if I want to hear what she's going to say.

"He sucked you into his world and, until the girls were born, you put him before anybody else—including yourself. You only live ten minutes away and we rarely see you."

"I was building my dream, designing my life!" I say defensively.

"His dream? Or yours?" asks my dad. "Think about it. Over the years, how many concessions have you had to make? Did you design your life, or attach yourself to his? Did you want to move to Bedford? Have kids so young? Have a staff? A cook? Send the girls to boarding school? And, on that, we are not happy about it."

Abby clears her throat. Her red hair brushes her shoulder blades as she swings her head to the side, avoiding my gaze. She thinks my parents are spot-on with their thoughts. As do I. I know, from the bottom of my soul, they are right. Eyes closed, I lean forward, elbows on the table, thumbs under my chin, and my index fingers pressing the sides of my nose, my dad's questions and guilt hitting me in the gut.

Nate had manipulated all of my dreams into his, making me think they were mine. But they weren't. I'd wanted to live in the city. I didn't want to have kids right away. I'd wanted to establish my career, pave my own path. I didn't want everything handed to me. All the bribes. All his ultimatums. All his threats. And he separated me from my girls. Boarding school? He'd told me I didn't understand the value of having a good education because I'd gone to public school.

"I really wanted to learn how to cook," I sob. "And I tried. I tried—"

My shoulders shake and I can't stop my tears from flowing. I can't remember the last time I've cried, not like this. Because these tears, the sobs I can't contain, are real—raw and cutting. They sting. They rock my entire core. I'd turned into a person I never wanted to be. Worse, I'd let it happen. I could blame Nate, but this is all on me.

"I'm so, so sorry," I say, my words a garbled mess. "Earlier, I told Abby I was a horrible person. And I am one."

Through this volcanic eruption of tears, I don't feel the hands rubbing my back until my dad squeezes my shoulder and my mom yells, "Enough with the pity party. Stop ugly crying! You're not a horrible person! You were brainwashed by a pompous asshole!"

Well, that snapped me to attention. I slap my hands to my head and rub my eyes with my palms. Abby hands me a tissue. "Blow your nose," she demands, and I do.

When I look up, my mom says, "It's good to have our Emma back." Her lips pinch together. "Nate's death, although horrible, is really a blessing in disguise."

"Another positive," says my dad. "Now you don't have to go through a messy divorce."

"That's what I said," says Abby. "Ain't karma a bitch?"

For the thousandth time today, I'm rendered speechless.

"Now get yourself together." Mom places her hands on her hips and then points. "Go wash your face, then we'll figure out this situation."

A bit numb, I shuffle to the powder room, facing my reflection. Not only did my mom swear, which she never does, she accused me of ugly crying—and she was right; my eyes are bloodshot and puffy, my nose is Rudolph red, and my cheeks look like somebody took a rake to them. Turning on the sink, I splash cold water on my face. I don't look much better, but does it matter? After dabbing my face dry with a fluffy yellow hand towel shaped like a chicken, I rejoin my parents and Abby in the kitchen.

"Sorry if we were hard on you," says my mom, worry creasing her brow. "We just want what's best for you."

"The truth hurt but it really felt good to cry. I think I've kept all my feelings locked up for so long, they really needed to get out," I stammer, taking my seat. "And, honestly, I've had the same thoughts, but I think I needed to hear them from somebody else."

My dad leans over and places a hand on my shoulder. "We all love you. I hope you know that."

"I do." My lips curve into a melancholy smile. "And, even if I haven't been the best at showing it, I love you too."

"We know." Mom pats my hand. "So, let's get back to the subject at hand. Your house is a crime scene? Where are you staying?"

"With me," says Abby.

Mom shakes her head. "Don't be silly, Em-Dash, you're staying here."

"Are you sure?" I ask.

"No question about it. This is your home. Literally," replies my mom with vigor, and Abby blows out a long sigh of relief. I don't blame her. After what we've been through this morning, I'd want to get as far away from me as I possibly could.

And now I'm wondering if my parents resent me for having them move here. My mom answers me before I can ask my question. "This is our home. This is your home. We love it here. Really."

"I have to text Rossi and let her know. Wouldn't want to end up on *America's Most Wanted*." I snort at my own joke. Nobody else does.

I pull out my phone and her card, tapping away. Whoosh. Off my message goes. I'm not expecting a quick response but one immediately comes in.

Noted. Surprised that you informed me.

I stare at her reply with my eyebrows raised. Even six words seem to carry suspicion. This woman has it in for me. I feel it in my bones.

"Do the girls know yet?" asks Dad, bringing me back to the present.

"I haven't been able to reach them. I've been trying all morning, but they haven't gotten back to me." Shaking the thought off, I take a sip of my coffee. It's so flavorless and weak. "I think I need something stronger."

"Tequila?" asks my mom.

"Definitely," Abby and I say at the same time, even though I'd meant a stronger roast.

Mom grins. "Why don't we all get comfortable in the living room? These kitchen chairs hurt my back. Grab your coffees and I'll grab the bottle."

"Don't forget the cocoa, the chili flakes, brown sugar, and whipped cream," says my dad, and I shoot him a look. "We had that Mexican coffee on our cruise and I love it."

Abby nudges me in the ribs and then indicates her body and clothes. *Got it.* "Mom, Dad, Abby and I really need to shower and change. We... uh... pulled—"

"Not another word." She steps over and kisses my cheek. "Dad will help you with your things while I put another pot of coffee on."

An hour later, we settle in the living room, clean and scrubbed, spiked coffee in hand. Like Dorothy said in *The Wizard of Oz,* "There's no place like home." Everything about this place is familiar and comfortable—the red-and-white gingham curtains, the shabby chic furniture adorned with matching throw pillows, and the lithographs of plants hanging on the walls. Nostalgia has wrapped me in a warm embrace and, for a few moments, I'm not thinking about Nate, the pond, or the detective. It's like I can breathe again.

Dad lounges back in his recliner and turns on the television. Words flash across the screen:

BREAKING NEWS: Billionaire Nathaniel Booth Landon FOUND dead. STAY TUNED FOR LIVE AT FIVE

Mom lets out a horrified gasp. "Get ready for a media storm. Emma, they're going to come after you like vultures."

Just when I'm finding an ounce of inner peace, my heart rate speeds up again. I squeeze my eyes shut. When I'd first married Nate, we had to sneak around, avoiding the paparazzi. But they always caught up to us, captured us. Nate's death is a huge story. Me? The billionaire's widow? I'm an even bigger one. All of the lunatics are going to crawl out of the sewers like rats, targeting me.

I get up, pouring more tequila into my cup. No coffee needed. "How much is one person supposed to take? What am I going to do?"

"I wouldn't leave the house," says Abby with a grunt. "And you've already had more than one."

I shoot her a look. "I need it."

I jolt as my cell rings and grab it, looking at caller ID before picking up. The sigh of relief escaping my lips is palpable, releasing some of the tension threatening to pull me down. "Thank God, it's the girls."

Mom scooches closer to me as I click the line open. "Ava? Finally! I've been trying to get a hold of you all day."

"Mom, you're on speaker. Say hi, Grace."

"Hi, Mom!" She hiccups. "Taylor Swift is so awesome! We met her and wow! She's performing again tomorrow night. Anyway, why have you been texting and calling us like a stalker? We're celebrating Taryn's birthday. She got your text. She was so happy you remembered. Is something wrong?"

I go silent for a moment, the lyrics to Taylor Swift's "I Knew You Were Trouble" floating around in my brain. Shame on me. I'm glad my girls are having fun. And I'm glad our trouble—meaning Nate—is lying on a cold, hard slab in the morgue. I shake my head to clear it. I can't tell the girls that.

"You could say something is wrong." I take in a steadying breath and let it out. "I'm so sorry to tell you this over the phone, but I don't want you to learn about it online. I have some really bad news. It's really bad. Devastating." I swallow before continuing. "Your father passed away."

Silence.

"Ha-ha. Good one. You almost got us," says Ava. "When's the funeral?"

I don't know why they think I'm joking when I don't have the kind of macabre sense of humor Abby does. I'm also not thinking about his funeral. No, he'd be better off being cremated, his ashes scattered in every corner of the earth.

"Girls, I'm serious. I came back home this morning and found him in the pond—"

"Sleeping with the fishes?"

"Would you two stop it! I'm not joking. The house is a crime scene and I'm staying with your grandparents," I start, sick and tired of repeating myself. "And the detective thinks I had something to do with it."

Heavy breaths punctuate a long silence.

"You're serious?"

"I am." My mom squeezes my leg and edges closer to me. "And, girls, I'm sorry to drop this news on you like this."

Silence. More breathing.

"Wait a second. Why aren't you saying anything?" I ask, my tone more snappish than I'd intended. I figured they'd flip out or burst into tears. Then again, I didn't react that way either. Maybe my girls are more like me? "Are you OK?"

"I think we need some time to think." Grace gulps. "It's like it doesn't seem real. And, well, we're not there."

I'm reminded that the twins always speak for one another, as if they share the same brain, the same thoughts. There is no *I* in team and they're always a *we*. But I can always tell them apart. Grace's voice is softer than Ava's. So far, Ava hasn't said anything. I do not want my girls coming back home to their mom being investigated. And I know it's going to get worse. "I think you should stay in France until things settle down."

"What? No. We should be there," says Grace, her voice quivering. "And what about the funeral?"

The funeral. Right. "I haven't even planned anything yet. I'll let you know when I do. Believe me, I'm fine," I lie. "I have Abby and my parents. Please, stay in France."

"Are you sure?" Ava asks.

"I am."

"Mom, there are a lot of people around," says Grace. "Can we call you later?"

"Of course."

"Love you—" they say, voices overlapping.

"L-l—" The line goes dead.

"That was an odd conversation." My mother tilts her head to the side. "How did the girls feel about Nate?"

"They hated him." I take in a shaky breath. "They were the reason I stayed in the marriage. And they were the ones who urged me to divorce him."

I don't tell my mom I'd stayed in the marriage for her and Dad too. They might not have accepted Nate's offer to help with my dad's medical bills. But they did accept my money.

EIGHTEEN
DETECTIVE ROSSI

Sunday, May 26th, 2024: 1:35 p.m.

Luisa ushers Kowalski and me into the guesthouse—the staff's house. It's bigger and more beautiful than I ever imagined. God, if I wasn't a detective, I'd become a maid or a house manager or whatever to live like this. She leads us into the living room. "Alexa! Off."

Selena's "Bidi Bidi Bom Bom" dims to a beep. I know the song well. My mother used to sing and dance to the beats while cooking in the kitchen. Something Emma Landon, apparently, doesn't do.

Luisa turns on a couple of lamps and waves a hand toward a white couch, almost identical to the one in the Landon residence. "Please, sit."

Kowalski clears his throat. "Mrs. Landon—"

"It's Emma to me," says Luisa, taking a seat in a bolstered chair across from us.

"Why did Emma stop by?"

"She wanted to tell me about Mr. Landon." She performs

the sign of the cross. "I was sorry to hear about it. But life is life and death is death, and only one of these we can control."

I'm assuming she's talking about life.

"Did she instruct you to do anything?" I ask. "Hide something, perhaps?"

Luisa looks at me as if I'm crazy. She snorts. "Like what? A knife? She told me he fell into the pond. Is this not true? Was he stabbed?"

"No," I say, already knowing where this conversation is headed before it even begins. She's not too concerned Nate died and probably doesn't care. "Where are the other members of the staff?"

"They are enjoying their day off."

She's dressed up and her eyes say what her lips aren't. *Like I should be.*

"Can you call them in?"

Her eyes narrow. "Si, I can, but they won't be happy. They are headed for the city, so it could take a while."

"We've got time," says Kowalski as Luisa pulls out her phone.

As she speaks rapid-fire Spanish, my eyes sweep the living room, landing on the two intricately carved and beautiful lamps, inlaid with jewels, and shining a kaleidoscope of fractured colors on the walls. I kind of love them. I'm wondering how much they cost and figure they must be a gift from Emma.

"They're turning around," says Luisa.

Although she speaks English fluently and quite well, there is a trace of an accent.

"Where are you from?" I ask.

"Here," she says with a dramatic eye roll.

"Originally?"

"Just outside of Puerto Vallarta, Mexico. And if you ask me if I'm legal, I am. Also, I'm not talking to you until the others arrive.

I have a feeling we will all be repeating ourselves." She straightens her posture and stands up. "It's hot outside. Would you like a chilled aguas fresca while we wait? I just made guava and lemon."

Kowalski nods his head and licks his lips. I glare at him. "What? It's hot and I'm thirsty."

"So, you make natural drinks?" I ask Luisa.

"Stop it with that theory," Kowalski hisses in my ear.

Luisa turns to face me. "I do. Very healthy. No sugar. I use honey to sweeten. I'll grab some glasses now."

Luisa heads into the kitchen and my gaze is drawn to an intricately carved silver bowl with potpourri set on the coffee table. Next to the bowl, three small monkeys, also carved in silver, one covering its eyes, one covering its ears, and the last one covering its mouth. See no evil. Hear no evil. Speak no evil.

I'm about to nudge Kowalski, but Luisa returns with a tray, setting it down. She ushers us to take a glass and so we do. Admittedly, the taste is refreshing and phenomenal. "This is delicious," I say. "Thank you."

"Can you taste my secret ingredient?" she asks, and my stomach lurches. "It's ginger. Good, yes?"

"It is." Kowalski guzzles his glass and Luisa pours him more. Kowalski shoots me another one of his "stop being paranoid" looks—a scowl, followed by a sneer.

Ignoring him, my gaze shoots to the butterfly lithographs on the far wall—a series of three prints, strikingly vibrant in deep magnificent blues with intricately detailed wings, and framed in what looks like platinum. I clear my throat and point. "Luisa, those are beautiful. Did Mrs. Landon give you those? Or do you like butterflies too?"

She looks at me like I'm crazy. "Who doesn't like butter-flies? What they symbolize? Freedom. Transformation. Meta-morphosis." She raises a brow. "Those are blue morphos—the most magnificent, maybe the biggest in the world. And, no, Emma did not give me those prints. I bought them myself when we were working on a project—Amazon chic." She grins. "I got a good trade discount, thanks to Emma's company."

"Oh," says Kowalski, eyeing me. "That's great. How long have you been her assistant?"

She scratches her chin. "I think I changed roles when she became pregnant. The girls will be turning fifteen in December. So almost sixteen years."

We sit in awkward silence for a moment. Finally, I speak up. "I love the bowl and the monkeys."

Luisa smiles. "Oh, yes. Emma brought those back from her trip."

"From Paris?"

"No, Thailand."

"When did she go there?" I ask, my curiosity piqued.

"Oh, we're designing a house in the Hamptons for JenX, the singer—the concept, exotic chic." She taps her chin. "I believe she returned last Saturday—so eight days ago."

I take notes, putting her timeline together. Maybe she'd done some side business while she was away, purchasing something a bit more lethal than silver monkeys.

Twenty minutes later, Homa, Kom, and Alba meander into the house. The women introduce themselves and sit across from us, hands clasped in their laps. It dawns on me. All of these women are beautiful and stylish. Since when do household staff wear designer clothes and look like they've just walked out of Drybar with perfectly styled hair and manicured nails? Me? My hair is matted with sweat and my nails look like somebody took a hacksaw to them.

"That was quick," I say, once I find my voice.

Homa glares at Kom. She snaps something in another language and then meets my eyes. "We turned the car around and got back here as quickly as we could." She shakes her head from side to side, her lips pinched into a frown. "It's true. Mr. Landon is dead?"

"He is. And I'm sorry."

Not one tear falls. Not one sound. No sniffles. They all just nod solemnly.

"Is Emma OK?" asks Homa with concern.

The staff call Emma by her first name and refer to Nathaniel as Mr. Landon. Very formal. Homa and Kom—Asian, appear to be in their early to mid-thirties. Alba, Hispanic, around the same age. None of them have an emotional reaction to Nathaniel's death, but they are worried about Emma.

"Emma is fine," Kowalski responds when I don't.

"Thank the stars," says Kom.

"Did you notice anything unusual while Mrs. Landon was out of town in Paris or Thailand? Maybe somebody skulking around the property?" I ask.

Luisa shrugs. "We'd like to answer you, but we can't because we weren't here when she was in Paris. Emma gave us the week off, so we decided to go to Atlantic City for a little fun. The Resorts Casino."

"You all went together?" Kowalski asks, and they mumble out yes.

"What about Mr. Landon? Wouldn't he have needed your help?"

"He was supposed to be staying at the loft in the city," says Luisa. "And he also stayed there when Emma was in Thailand. The girls were still in school."

Interesting. Now I'm wondering what he'd been up to.

"When did you get back from Atlantic City?"

"Late Friday night," says Luisa.

"You didn't notice anything upon your return?"

"No, our home is set back from the main house and we have

our own entry." She waves her hand toward the back of the house. "Mr. Landon likes his privacy."

"What about noise? No music playing? No laughter? The chatter of people?"

"No," says Kom, dreamily. "It was very quiet. Very beautiful. So many stars. And the moon was full."

"And how do you know this?" I ask.

"I'm not allowed to smoke in the house or in the car, so I had a cigarette outside." She looks toward the porch and I'm thinking she probably wants a nicotine fix right about now.

Kowalski leans forward. "We'll need proof of your trip to Atlantic City—the casino you stayed in, gas and toll receipts, expenditures—"

"Why?" asks Alba.

"Protocol," says Kowalski, and she nods.

"I'll go get them. They're stuffed in a bag in the car."

"You kept everything?" I ask.

"Of course," says Alba, looking over her shoulder. "Our credit cards are linked to Emma's. She likes to look over the receipts for her tax files—"

It's almost as if Emma basically paid her staff to get out of town so they wouldn't be here to witness anything. I eye the monkeys. See no evil. Speak no evil. Hear no evil.

"And Mr. Landon? Was he aware of this?"

"No, probably not. She pays us our bonuses from her own account. Emma is a kind, beautiful woman. She treats us with respect," says Homa, and the other women nod their heads with furious agreement.

"She paid for private tutors to help us with our English—"

"Taught us to drive, paid for our driving lessons. Bought us cars. She makes sure we have everything that we need, that we're happy."

Now this is interesting.

"Have you ever suspected she might be bribing you for your loyalty?" I ask, leaning forward.

"No," says Luisa with force. "And I saw the way you were looking at her."

"I'm sorry? I don't understand."

"I think you do," Luisa says flatly. "If something happened to Mr. Landon, Emma had nothing to do with it. She never bribed us—"

"She repaid us for our kindness *to* her. In addition to cleaning, Kom and I help to raise the girls, Ava and Grace," interjects Homa, "and we all took care of Emma before their birth, when she was on bed rest. And after."

"She had problems?"

The women speak over one another, finishing each other's sentences.

"Bad birth. Almost died. Had to have a life-saving hysterectomy."

"Severe postpartum depression. Couldn't leave her bed for months."

"Mr. Landon was never around. We all—all of us—took care of her and the girls."

Maybe this explained the change in the photos I'd seen online. Maybe she blamed him for her problems. Then he started having affairs, which I'm certain of. Maybe this is why she's an emotional wreck and slightly out of kilter. Deep in thought, I chew on the top of my pen. A small drip of saliva runs down my chin and I wipe it off with the sleeve of my blazer.

"Did any of you go by the main house yesterday?" asks Kowalski.

"No, we always have the weekends off," says Luisa. "Alba wanted to surprise Emma. She was taking a French cooking course—"

"Alba, where are you from? Originally?" I ask.

"Placencia, Belize."

"Homa, Kom?"

"Thailand. Near Chiang Mai. Both of us." Homa points to the monkeys. "That's where Emma bought our gifts."

Luisa suddenly stands up and smacks her fists to her sides. "Why do you keep asking where we are from? Should I ask you where you are from?"

"I'm from the Bronx," I say, a bit taken aback by her snappish tone, the insulted look her in eyes.

"But from where, *originally*?"

"I'm Italian. And I get it. It's a rude question." I hold my hands up. "Look, I'm just doing my job." I pause. "How did you feel about Mr. Landon?"

Luisa sits back down and takes a deep breath. "Mr. Landon treated us like servants. In case you're wondering, that's why none of us are crying our eyes out. We're a bit sad, maybe a little shocked, but not distressed. But if something happened to Emma, that would be a different story. She and the girls are our family." Her right hand launches into the sign of the cross again —forehead, heart, left shoulder, right shoulder. "May Mr. Landon rest in peace. Wherever he is."

Kowalski nudges my side and mouths, "I think it's time to hit it."

He's right. Luisa's eyes are boring into me. Regardless of what I think about Emma, her staff are ferociously protective of her. I'm not getting anywhere with them. I stand up. "Ladies, thank you for your time and for the delicious drink. We'll be in touch if we have any more questions."

Luisa walks us to the front door, practically pushing us onto the front porch.

On the walk back to the main house, I turn to Kowalski. "I don't get it. Everybody I've spoken to has expressed clear hate for Nathaniel and makes Emma out to be a saint or some kind of victim."

"Maybe she is. And maybe he is that much of an asshole," he says with a shrug. "Maybe his past caught up with him. I'd start looking elsewhere. Stop focusing on Emma." He scratches his chin. "My bet is on Luisa, the house manager. In the study. With a candlestick."

I push his shoulder. "Very funny," I say as he snorts in his hand. "But there's something completely shady about Emma. She's still a person of interest."

"Whatever," he mumbles. "I think you're spinning your wheels."

We're almost back at the main house when Kowalski nudges me and then points. Emma has left the garage door open. He walks over, peeking his head in, and I follow his lead. He slaps his hand over his heart and whistles through his teeth. "Holy shit! I think I've died and gone to gear-head heaven."

My nose pinches with revulsion as I eye the cars—an electric blue McLaren, a bronze Bugatti, a Bentley Continental GT, a Rolls-Royce Phantom, a Dodge Viper, and a 1962 Jaguar E-type, among other extravagances like Ducati and Indian motorcycles. "Such a disgusting display of wealth."

"That motorcycle is the farthest thing from disgusting." He points and then walks over to the red-chassised beast, running his hand across the tan leather seat. His voice raises with childlike excitement. "It's a piece of history! A 1915 Indian 8-valve! I can't believe it!"

I slap his hand. "Have the forensic team processed the garage yet?"

He pulls his hand back. "I don't think so. Not yet."

There's one car missing—a black Range Rover. Shit. I didn't tell Emma she couldn't take her car and she could be hiding something in it from one of her trips. This mistake is on me and I'll need a warrant.

Twenty minutes later, I'm about to head back to the station

when Officer Roberts hands over the coroner's initial report. "That was quick," I say.

"Well, he was a billionaire and kind of a celebrity. You know they named him the new prince of New York—"

"Yeah, I know." My eyes scan the page and I groan. This can't be right. "A heart attack? That's what killed him?"

"Explains the vomit."

"Mmm-hmm," I mutter. "What about the rash?"

"A wasp sting, but that's not what killed him. A heart attack did."

And there goes another one of my theories. Nobody poked the hornets' nest.

How could a man in peak physical shape, a man whose life revolved around *saving* hearts, have a heart attack? Granted, nobody including Emma seemed to like the man, but nothing else is adding up. Who else, besides her, would profit from his death? Right about now, I'm thinking somebody paid the coroner off—somebody with deep pockets, like his wife, Emma Landon. I heard her call to the station. I met her, interviewed her, saw the coldness in her eyes. She'd even asked if she needed a lawyer when I questioned her. Something isn't sitting right.

"Did we get his phone up and running?"

"Yeah," he says. "But what's the point? CD says the investigation is over. Case closed. We're packing up our gear now."

"I'd like to see the phone."

Officer Roberts rolls his eyes and pulls out his radio. I know he'd rather bolt out of here and grab a beer. I'm thinking the same thing myself. He huffs into the receiver, "Rossi wants Landon's iPhone." Then he turns and stomps toward one of the vans, glaring at me over his shoulder. He has a bad attitude and an even bigger drinking problem. Oh, snowflake, so sorry for ruining your plans.

While I wait for his return, I hop in the car and turn on the AC, rolling over the facts in my head, my eyes locking onto the oleander. Dead billionaire. Heart attack. Wife gets everything. Hired killer? Her? Or somebody else? Abby mentioned Gordon Flynn. And Emma mentioned David Clark. A couple of minutes later, Roberts taps on my window and I roll it down. He hands the phone over.

"Everything unblocked?"

"Of course," he sneers.

I open up Nathaniel's texts and the name ThornInMySide immediately catches my eye. Obviously, it's the kind of tongue-in-cheek name a husband would give to his wife and I wonder what her ringtone is. Shaking the thought off, I blink as I click on a recent message.

THORNINMYSIDE:

I'm going to kill you.

I slap my free hand on the dashboard and whoop, before scrolling down:

THORNINMYSIDE:

I'm going to kill you. I asked you to do one thing while I was away. One!

HEARTDOC:

What are you going on about?

THORNINMYSIDE:

The pump for the pond! The fish are dying!

I've got intent. Not one, but two death threats. Regardless of him not taking care of the fish, or if Emma was texting in anger, I know Emma and her girls will profit greatly from his passing. The motive? Loot and loathing. I shake with excitement.

Before I close out of his phone, I flip through the application screens, and a button marked HUSH catches my attention. I click on it, a photo gallery pops open, and I jolt backward as my brain realizes what I'm looking at. The images are of women—

and not just one—at least twenty—in very comprising sexual positions. The male's face isn't featured in any of them, but there's a birthmark on the left thigh shaped like a dog. Just like Mr. Landon's.

Emma's frantic call to Dispatch echoes in my mind.

Yes—and I pulled the lying cheating bastard son of a bitch out of the goddamn water—

These pictures would certainly drive an obsessive woman to the brink of insanity. She must have known. My hands tremble as I radio CD. "Chief!"

"Rossi? Didn't you hear, we're shutting down the investigation. Go home, have a beer, put your feet up—"

"CD, you can't close this case until I get the tox report in and we process the evidence."

"You're wasting my time and yours."

"But I'm not," I say, explaining what I found.

"You're the thorn in my side," he growls. "I'm giving you two weeks. No more, no less."

"A team?"

"Kowalski, Roberts, and Brenner," he says, and I almost plead to trade in Roberts, but don't want to push my luck. But I still have one more question. And he answers me before I can ask it. "Yes, forensics will process everything they've found."

Excitement courses through my veins. I pull out my phone and tap at the keys like a caffeinated woodpecker.

Need full toxicology screening re: Nathaniel Booth Landon specifically toxic cardiac glycosides.

DRC:

??? Drug screen clear. Heart attack. Case open/shut.

Not in my mind. A hunch. Landon house is surrounded by oleander.

DRC:

Wife

Def. a person of interest.

DRC:

Got it. Tox will take a couple of weeks, maybe longer. Backlog at labs.

Faster?

DRC:

Will try. I'll call in a favor.

You're the best.

DRC:

I know. 😊

I close out of the chat and place my phone on the magnetic strip on my dash with a shit-eating grin. Kowalski slinks into the passenger seat. "Happy for beer o'clock?"

"Nope, we're heading to the Clark residence and then to the hospital and the loft."

His nose scrunches with confusion. "Why? CD closed the investigation down."

"And I reopened it."

"You found something, didn't you?"

I turn the key in the ignition, put the car in drive, and press down on the accelerator. "I sure as hell did. And you're on my team."

"Aw, damn it," he says with a long beleaguered sigh. "I was really looking forward to a beer."

We're standing outside the Clark estate and the sounds of splashing and children laughing resonate in the air. The house is a lot more modest than the Landon residence, but expensive as hell all the same. Probably around six thousand square feet, set on the minimum of four acres of land that houses are required to have in Bedford. I tilt my head. "Let's head around back."

"Can we jump into the pool too?" Kowalski asks.

"No, you big lug."

A man tending to a barbecue looks up as we round the corner. He's holding a beer, the condensation bubbling on the bottle, and Kowalski is practically salivating. The man's *The Grillfather* apron makes me cringe. As an Italian, I really hate puns like that, especially when they relate to mobsters. He looks up when he notices our presence and clears his throat. "Can I help you, officers?"

"Are you David Clark?" I ask.

"I am," he says, his free hand fidgeting with the strings of his stupid apron. "What's going on?"

"We'd like to talk to you and your wife about Nathaniel Landon."

A woman, whom I'm assuming to be Audrey Clark, steps onto the pool terrace, a glass of rosé in her hand. Another Bedford wife, or as I like to call them, Stepford wives, although Emma Landon breaks the mold with the icy-cold look in her eyes and super-rigid posture. I survey Audrey, trying to find any distinguishing traits. But these types of women all blend into the same person for me—the same manicured nails and perfectly plucked eyebrows and collagen-puffed lips. "What about Nathaniel?" she asks.

"He's dead. Foul play is suspected," I say matter-of-factly. "And we're here because, during our questioning, Emma Landon mentioned the two of you."

David's barbecue tongs thud onto the terrace. He waves his arms frantically to the three towheaded kids—probably ages ten to eighteen—dunking one another in the water. "Boys, out of the pool and into the house."

"But, Dad—" the youngest begins to whine.

"What are the cops doing here?" asks the oldest.

"Do what your father tells you to do!" screams Audrey. She stomps her foot with motherly force. "I mean it. Now!"

The kids scramble out of the pool, grabbing towels off loungers, and start to skulk into the house. The oldest one stops, eyeing Kowalski and me with fear. "Is this about me?"

"Why on earth would this be about you, Kyle?" Audrey snaps, shooting him the dirtiest of looks.

"Just checking." Kyle raises his hands up in surrender, blows out a sigh of relief, and heads into the house.

I watch him as he disappears through the sliding doors. Another rich Bedford kid. Probably his brand-new BMW in the driveway. Confident swagger. Big allowance. He doesn't give off the drug dealer vibe, but no doubt smokes the occasional joint. Then again, I'd busted a ring a couple of years ago and the kid looked just like him and I shouldn't jump to conclusions. It's always the ones you don't suspect—like Emma Landon.

Audrey and David usher us over to an iron and glass dining table on the patio. "Please have a seat," says Audrey. "Can I get you anything? Water? An iced tea? A beer?"

Kowalski's eyes light up and then dim when I say, "A water would be great. We can't drink on the job."

"Sparkling or still?"

"Just regular water," I say.

Audrey scurries away and David leans forward, his elbows on the table, his fingers pressed to his temples. "I can't believe Nate's dead." He looks up. "How did it happen? Do they know who did it?"

"We're trying to figure that out."

He nods. "And Emma mentioned us? Why?"

"Mrs. Landon told me that you recently moved back to town, but that you and Mr. Landon had problems in the past." I pull out my pen and my pad, placing it on the table. "Can you tell me what that was all about?"

Audrey returns with a tray holding two water glasses and a refill of her rosé. She sets the platter down. Once she takes her seat, David says, "You may want to ask my wife that question."

I turn to Audrey. "What was your relationship to Emma and Nathaniel Landon?"

She blinks. Repeatedly. Then she launches into a coughing fit.

"She didn't have one with her, not after her affair with Nate," explains David with a frown.

Now composed, Audrey wipes her mouth with a napkin. "But that was so many years ago."

"How many?" asks Kowalski.

"Six," says David, scowling at Audrey. "The year is etched into my memory."

"And Emma knew about the affair?"

"She did," says Audrey, swallowing. "David was the one who told her about it."

"I may have used some words I shouldn't have, and I shouldn't have threatened Nate, but I only said what I said in anger."

"Do you remember what you said to her?"

"Not exactly. Something about if Nate doesn't stop fucking my wife, I'm going to kill him." He shakes his head. "Not my proudest moment."

"Or mine either." Audrey nervously tugs at her bottom lip. "The affair ended, David and I worked out everything in couples' therapy, and we moved to Malibu for a fresh start." She takes a huge sip of her wine, glossy pink fingernails tapping the glass. "We moved back to Bedford a couple of months ago, and when Emma saw us at the party, she went bat-shit crazy. I think she might have some severe mental issues."

"What party?"

"At Gordon Flynn's. The Saturday before last." Audrey picks up her phone. "Becks Stark took a video of her outburst and posted it on her Instagram. I can show it to you if you want?"

Abby had told me that Emma despised Gordon Flynn and Nathaniel's friends, tried to avoid them at all costs. But she went to a party at Flynn's house? More of Emma's lies scattering around like cockroaches when the lights are turned on.

I nod my head yes and we peer at the screen. Emma looks like a complete madwoman. Her eyes have a wild look in them. Her hair is out of place. Spittle flies from her mouth.

Kowalski stifles a laugh and snorts. "She's stabbing the air. What the hell is she doing?"

"She's doing some form of charades," says Audrey. "Acting out *A Perfect Murder*."

There's a heat in my chest, a burn of excitement when I realize my intuition is right.

"I think she was threatening me." Audrey's eyes go wide. "Or maybe Nate."

Kowalski's shoulders raise up and down; he's still trying to keep it together. Admittedly, the video is disturbingly funny. But, like he'd said earlier, there is no such thing as the perfect murder. I tap my pen on the table. Emma clearly has a reason to hate these people and, by giving me their names, she was trying to set them up. Crafty little murderess. Still, I have to ask. "When was the last time you saw either of them?"

"Not since the party," says Audrey. "She scared the life out of me and we've been keeping a low profile."

"Thank you for your time. We'll get back to you if we have any other questions." I stand up and hand David my card. "Call me if you think of anything else."

Audrey doesn't say anything. She gulps back the rest of her wine, wide-eyed. "Of course," says David, glancing at my card, "Detective."

NINETEEN

EMMA

Sunday, May 26th, 2024: 3:34 p.m.

Before she takes off, I walk Abby to her car to grab my other suitcases from her trunk. My dad and mom step onto the front porch. "Are you moving back home?" asks my dad.

"No," I say with a hesitant laugh. "These are the bags I took with me to Paris."

I'm wondering why Rossi didn't ask to burrow through them while she was upending my life. Pushing the thought to one side, I step in to give Abby the strongest of hugs. "Are you sure you can't stay for dinner? Mom's making her famous chicken chili."

She shakes her head. "Emma, I really need to get home and crash in my own bed. Unlike you, I'm not my own boss. I have to head into work tomorrow."

"Quit," I say. "Start your own label. I'll invest in you."

"We've had this conversation before—"

"I know. I know. Friends and money don't mix." I shrug. "Thought I'd try anyway. After today, I owe you the world."

She yawns. Loudly. Then rubs her eyes. "You don't owe me anything, Honey Bunch."

"But I do, Sugar Pie." I scan her face. She's as spent as I am. "You sure you're OK to drive?"

"The Beastie Boys will keep me awake. No! Sleep. Till. Katonah! Or I'll let Casper do the driving. He knows the way." She taps the hood of her Tesla, grins and pulls me in for another tight hug. "Call me if you need anything. I'm your red phone girl."

"Call *me* or text when you get home."

"Will do."

She salutes and gets in her car. The engine starts and I watch her turn out of the driveway, her music blaring. My dad steps down from the front porch and grabs my suitcases.

"I can manage," I say.

"No, Emma, you need to get some rest—"

As he says this, two cars whip around the corner, pulling up in front of the house. It happens so quickly, I'm wondering if it's the cops and they've come to take me away, until a man shoves a microphone in my face. "Emma Landon? Did you kill your husband?"

"How does it feel to be the richest woman in Bedford?"

"Why did you do it?"

I now know how a deer caught in the headlights feels. I'm completely frozen. My mom grabs me by the wrist, screaming, "NO COMMENT!" and she pulls me into the house, my dad following with my suitcases. He slams the door shut. My mother races around, closing all the blinds and curtains. "The storm has started. Go, sit in the living room and hunker down. Stay away from the windows."

I can only mumble, "How do they know I'm here?"

Mom pulls the last curtain closed and sits down next to me, breathless. "We saw the headlines on the television. Somebody obviously leaked the news about Nate's death. With a person as well known and as wealthy as him, it happens. And you were probably followed."

I hunch over, guilt gripping me in a vice. Abby's involved. My parents are involved. I feel terrible. Divorce would have been so much easier. But that's not an option now.

"I'm so sorry, Mom," I say, letting out a long sigh. "This is a nightmare."

Mom wraps her arm around me and pulls me toward her. "This situation is not your fault. It's Nate's. He was a pain in the ass when he was alive and he's an even bigger one now that he's dead."

My phone rings. I don't move. I can't. My mom gets up and grabs it, looking at caller ID. "It's somebody named Hedra."

"Thank the heavens. It's my divorce attorney. I need to take this," I say jumping up, and Mom's lips pinch with confusion as she hands my phone over. "I need a referral to another kind of attorney."

My dad comes into the living room and I'm now sand-wiched in between my parents. After updating Hedra, and three-way calling the other attorney, I hang up the phone and my rigid spine loosens with relief. "She'll be here in an hour."

"Who?" my parents say over one another, sounding like stressed-out owls.

"Your divorce attorney? I don't understand—" my mom begins.

"No, Dina Fadel, one of the partners at Hedra's firm—Siegel, Fadel, and McKenzie." I tuck my chin into my neck. "She's a criminal attorney. And she's supposed to be one of the best. Judging by the way the detective eyed me and insinuated I had something to do with his death, I need the best."

"Oh, honey," my mom says, rubbing my back. "You'll get through this."

I'm not so sure about that.

My dad peers through the blinds. "The reporters. There are

more of them. They're on the porch. In trees. Swarming like rabid monkeys." He swallows, his Adam's apple bobbing up and down. "It's a zoo out there."

An hour later, I receive a text:

DINAF:

I'm here.

The doorbell rings and my mom peeks out the window. "It's OK, Mom, it's the attorney. Let her in."

I'd already googled her. She has the same reputation as O. J. Simpson's lawyer, Johnnie Cochran. If the glove doesn't fit, you must acquit. Although in my mind the only thing I'm truly guilty of is marrying Nate, I'm glad to have her on my side because I don't know what's waiting for me around the bend and I need to be prepared for anything.

Hesitantly, my mom opens the door and in walks Dina Fadel. She's dressed in black slacks, a silk blouse with a green print, and kitten heels, her long hair tied back into a slick pony-tail. Her makeup is minimal, offset by dark lips. "I got rid of the reporters as best I could. The maggots are still on the street, where they will stay," she says, her voice low. "Nobody likes to be threatened with trespassing or the destruction of private property."

I hop off the couch. "Thank you for coming over on a Sunday, Dina."

"No, thank you, Emma," she says with a wink. "You got me out of the most boring luncheon I've ever attended."

I point toward the living room. "Should we sit?"

A couple of cats traipse by, one of them stopping. Dina's gaze darts to the kitchen, to the living room.

She nods and then whispers, "Why are there so many cats here? Is your mom a crazy cat lady?"

"No, my dad is. He saves animals, finds them new homes."

Dina grins and points to the tabby snaking around her ankles. She scooches down and pets the cat's head. "I may take this one home with me. Adorable." She looks up at me and winks. "But enough about my love for furry cuties. You were right to bring me in," she says with a nod. She sashays to the couch, taking a seat. She pats the place next to her for me. So I sit. My parents saunter over, my dad splaying out in his sapphire blue La-Z-Boy, my mom in a chair I'd designed for her —also sapphire blue. "OK, first things first. Detective Rossi should never have questioned you. Not like that."

She slaps a file down on the coffee table and then places both hands on it, fingernails sharpened, ready to attack. I like her already.

"I shouldn't have answered her," I say. "And I shouldn't have given her my bank information or access to the loft."

"No," she says. "But you didn't say anything incriminating, did you?"

"Just what I said on the phone call."

"So, you called your husband a lying cheating bastard son of a bitch? Big deal. I've said worse to my own." She laughs and then her expression turns serious. "Her next move will be calling you down to the station. If that happens, I'll be there, fielding any questions or issues. So, I need to know, are there any issues?"

"I don't know. I didn't tell her about my plans to divorce Nate. Or about hiring the private investigator while I was in Paris."

"Not her business."

"She asked me if he was cheating—and I refused to respond."

"Again, none of her business." She leans forward. "Anything else?"

"Did Hedra tell you about the video Becks Stark posted?"

"I saw it."

My mom chimes in. "What video?"

"It's nothing, Mom. I was drunk and I may have snapped during a party at Gordon Flynn's."

"Why?"

"Because David and Audrey Clark were there. And Audrey had an affair with Nate."

"No," says my mom flatly. "Why were you at Gordon Flynn's? You can't stand him."

"Mom, I'll tell you later," I say, and she nods. I turn to face Dina. "Sorry."

"No worries. I have parents too," she says. "The good news is, I have Stella's video, should we need to use it. It proves Nate to be a very seedy character with very seedy friends. I'd highly suggest against viewing it right now." She tilts her head toward my parents. "Pretty disturbing stuff on it."

"Who is Stella?" asks my dad.

"The private investigator I hired," I say. "And the video might point Rossi in another direction and she'll leave me alone."

That's my hope.

Dina smiles again. "I think I'm all caught up on everything I need to know. And"—she looks at her watch—"right about now, I think we should turn on the news. Mr. Novak? Channel Five, please."

My dad grabs the remote and anchorwoman Maggie Pressly's image fills the screen.

"The Bedford Police Department has just confirmed the death of billionaire Nathaniel Booth Landon. Live at the scene is Rick Meyers. Rick, what can you tell us?"

Dina sinks back into the couch, crossing her legs at the ankles, as I lean forward, bracing my hands on my knees. All of us sit in silence as my house—or at least the front gates—comes into view.

"Maggie, as you can see from the activity behind me, the press, unfortunately, are prohibited from entering the gates of this sprawling estate known as the Glass House on the Pond in Bedford, Westchester County. For now, what we do know is that paramedics took Nathaniel Landon's body to the coroner's facilities earlier this morning—

"Just one moment. I see movement. Detective Rossi is leaving the scene. Detective Rossi? Detective Rossi? Why are you here? Was there a crime committed? Do you suspect foul play?"

"At this moment in time, we're looking at all angles."

"From what we've uncovered, Mrs. Landon arrived home from Paris earlier this morning to find Nathaniel Landon floating face down in the pond and she called 911. For a detective to be called to a scene of the crime, something suspicious, a red flag, must have been discovered. What was it?"

"Look, you know that if I told you anything I'd be hampering my investigation."

"So, there's an investigation into Mr. Landon's death?"

"I think I've already answered your question."

"Is Emma Landon a person of interest?"

"No comment. Now, get that damn microphone out of my face so I can do my job."

"Apparently, the circumstances behind Nathaniel Booth Landon's unfortunate passing are undetermined at this time, the police allegedly suspecting foul play. Back to you, Maggie."

"This is quite the story. Frankly, I'm shocked. Were Nathaniel and Emma Landon's enviable lives truly a fairytale or was something more sinister going on behind the scenes? I'm Maggie Pressly and this is New York Live at Five, where we bring you, our faithful viewers, all of the breaking news first."

My heart races. I turn to my parents. "Mom, Dad, can I have a moment with Dina alone? In private."

"We'll be upstairs if you need us," says my mom. She gets

up from her chair, straightens out her pull-on pants, and eyes my father. "Mark, you coming? Or do I have to drag you off your recliner with a crane?"

My dad grunts. "I'm coming, you bossy woman."

After they leave the living room, Dina says, "I take it there's something you want to tell me, something you don't want them to hear."

I take in a deep breath and nod. "Attorney–client privilege, right?"

"Of course."

I swallow down the lump of dread forming in my throat. "I'm going to tell you everything about Nate. And it's bad. Really bad," I say, the level of my voice in a low whisper.

"Hold that thought." Dina eyes her watch. "And five, four, three, two, one—"

My cell rings. I look at caller ID and then to Dina. "It's Rossi. How did you know?"

She raises a brow and taps her temple twice. "Oh, one more one thing: before you answer, she'll insist on having a cruiser pick you up. Say no, thank you for that very kind offer, but you can manage." She winks. "I've got you covered. And, after you speak with her, I'll need to know everything."

TWENTY
DETECTIVE ROSSI

Sunday, May 26th, 2024: 5:42 p.m.

Emma's agreed to an 8 a.m. interview down at the station, but she's refused to have a police cruiser pick her up, even when I insisted she'd be safer from all of the press surrounding her parents' home. Which means she's engaged counsel.

We're on the way to the hospital where Nate worked when Chief radios in. "Rossi! Who the fuck leaked the news of the Landon death?"

"I don't know," I say.

"Why did I see you on the five o'clock news?"

"Because somebody leaked the story. And it wasn't me."

It was. I wanted to ruffle Emma's feathers, put some more pressure on her.

"Damn it, you implied she's a person of interest."

"She is. And she'll be at the station tomorrow morning," I say.

"I'm sitting in on the interview. Over and fucking out."

Kowalski nudges me in the ribs. "He's pissed."

"He'll get over it."

"You're like a dog with a bone," he says. "You're really gunning for this woman. Hard. I've never seen you like this."

"Meatball thinks I'm more of a cat person," I say, referring to my gigantic furball of a feline.

Kowalski growls with exasperation.

We pull up to the hospital and jump out of the cruiser, following the signs to the Coronary Care Unit/Cardiology Ward. Nurses walk down the hall, sniffling, their eyes red from crying. Finally, people who care this man is dead.

I walk up to the nurses' station. A woman, nametag Catherine, blows her nose and looks up.

"Officers? Is this about Dr. Landon?" she asks, a knowing look in her eyes, and I nod. "As you can see, the news of his death has hit us all pretty hard. We're trying to keep it together. Dr. Landon was a wonderful man, a brilliant and caring doctor. We're all going to miss him very much."

"I understand," I say as she chokes back a sob. "And I'm sorry to trouble you. But was there anybody who wasn't fond of him?"

"Not really. Oh, I don't know." Her brows pinch together. "Maybe Jane Carter? He had me transfer her to geriatrics a few days ago. She wasn't very happy about it."

Kowalski clears his throat as I scribble the name down. "And Mrs. Landon? How did you feel about her?"

"Oh, Emma! Everybody loved her! She was so kind and sweet. Every time she visited, she'd bring the staff decadent treats." She blinks rapidly. "I saw the news. A person of interest? Between you and me, I don't think she had anything to do with this. It was probably a freak accident."

Emma, the ass kisser.

"Thank you for your time, Catherine," I say. "Before we leave, do you mind if we take a look around his office?"

She steps around the corner of her desk. "I'll unlock it for you."

We follow her down the hall and she puts the key in the knob, twisting the door open. "Let me know if you need anything. I'll be at my station."

As Catherine's shoes squeak down the sterile corridor, we put gloves on. I scan the space. The sleek, wooden desk is modern and organized—a computer, a brown leather paper tray with matching desk pad blotter and pen holder, and a beautiful carved silver lamp—the latter two both Moroccan in style. Emma obviously had a hand in warming up his office. The only sign of anything personal is a photo of the family. It's of Emma, the girls, and Nathaniel standing in front of a yacht, palm trees in the background. She and the twins, then very young, wear matching dresses—navy blue for her, sky blue for the girls, their hair blowing in the wind. He's wearing a navy polo and khaki shorts. They look like they've been ripped out of a Neiman Marcus catalog, smiling and happy with no troubles in the world. It must have been taken eons ago.

Two leather chairs face the desk, in addition to the one behind it. On the back wall, an iron and glass bookshelf, standing to the left of the window, the blinds pulled halfway open. Nothing to note here, save for design elements like a small silver airplane, a pendulum swing, an antique clock, and of course, books.

We open drawers—nothing but patient files, no hidden traps.

"This is a waste of time," says Kowalski.

"You're right," I say. "But at least we learned that Nathaniel was loved here, instead of hated."

"Don't forget. So was Emma."

"I'm looking at both sides," I say. "Let's go find this Jane and then we'll head to the loft."

"You're a bossy detective," he says. "I need a break and I'm grabbing a coffee. I'll be waiting in the Impala."

. . .

The moment I walk into the ward, I recognize Jane. She's the girl from the last few photos on Nathaniel's phone. Plump lips. Curvy figure. Black hair. I pull out Nathaniel's cell from the pocket in my blazer, bringing up her image, and I walk straight up to her. "Jane Carter?"

"Yes, that's me," she says, her voice hitching. "Can I help you?"

I hold out Nathaniel's phone and when her gaze locks onto the screen her shoulders tremble. She takes a step back and grips her hair. "The bastard sent my photos out? He told me he wouldn't if I kept quiet. What if my parents see them?"

She bursts into tears. I feel bad for her.

"He didn't send them out, not to anyone. I'm a detective and we found his phone this morning," I say, and she looks up. "He died and I'm investigating his death."

She rubs her eyes. "He died? How?"

"Heart attack," I say, and her lips curve into the subtlest of grins. "Let me get this straight, he blackmailed you? With photos?"

She clenches her fists. "He did. And I'm sure there were others."

"How can you be so sure?"

"By the way he treated me. Like garbage. Just threw me away. I also heard rumors from a few other nurses." She blows out an angry breath. "Can you delete my pictures, please?"

"I can't. It's evidence. But don't worry, the photos won't be released to anybody."

"Then I'm happy to hear he's dead and I have absolutely nothing else to say to you. Excuse me, I have patients with kind hearts that need attending to. Dr. Landon didn't have one." She wipes away her tears, turns on her heel, and stomps down the hall, muttering "bastard" under her breath.

Speechless, I'm now left wondering how many people hated Nathaniel Landon. Because, the more I learn about him, the more I realize what an absolute monster he was. Treating his staff like shit. Blackmailing nurses after he's used them. Cheating on his wife. Part of me doesn't blame Emma if she'd had him bumped off or did it herself. To think I used to crush on him hard! I am so lucky I stuck to my own kind—even though Kowalski snores like a growling bear, gurgles and snorts included, and he hogs the blankets. I'm dating an animal. I hop into the Impala and nudge him with my toe. "Wake up, you beast. We're heading to the last stop. And I'll need your help."

He groans.

Although the hospital shed some light on the case, my discoveries at the loft shine neon directional lights right onto Emma Landon—practically blinking with the words *you've found his killer*.

"Nathaniel Landon was planning on divorcing Emma," says Kowalski, picking up a thick file and handing it to me.

"And I bet she knew that too."

We peer into the master bedroom, Alex shining his flashlight. He leans over, his ass in the air, as he looks under the bed.

"Find anything?"

He hands over an iPad mini. "This."

I sit cross-legged and power the iPad on. Butterflies fly across the screen, flashes of an orgy, and then a message pops up:

Thank you, Mr. Landon,

Your wire of 150,000 dollars has been well received. As luck would have it, all of your guests for the private party you've requested have paid their initiation fees. The Sanctuary looks forward to making all your wild fantasies come true on Thursday night. You have ordered six butterflies and two dragonflies. Should your preferences change, please let us know at your earliest convenience.

Here's to sexy days and hedonistic nights.

xox, Madame Butterfly

The screen goes black.

"Damn it! Damn it!" I scream. I'm pressing buttons, but the stupid thing won't power on again.

"Besides freaking bizarre, what the hell was that?" asks Kowalski as he looks over my shoulder.

"Something connecting Emma to the crime, I'm sure of it."

Emma Landon is obsessed with butterflies. Emma Landon has a butterfly tattoo on her neck. Her garden. The art on her walls. On impulse, I pull out my phone and send her a text.

> See you at the station, Madame Butterfly.

Three dots.

EMMA:
> I have absolutely no idea what you're talking about.

Kowalski grabs my phone and looks at the message, scowling. "For fuck's sake, Gabby, you really crossed the line with this one. Not cool. And you know it."

I swallow. My ego got in the way and he's right. Sometimes I get a little too overzealous. I can't help it. It's the way I'm wired. I've been this way since I was a kid—fighting for what I believe in. Just like when I'd tipped off the media, I'd wanted her to know I was on to her.

I shrug. "Yeah, it wasn't cool. But it's not wrong either. Besides, I can't take back a text I already sent."

I also know I'm right. The sirens in my head are spinning, landing on guilty. The way she fidgeted, couldn't meet my eyes, not to mention the vodka.

Liars come in all shapes and sizes—compulsive, frequent, sociopathic, narcissistic, and exaggerators. What kind of liar is Emma Landon? Tomorrow, I'm going to find out. And I'm looking forward to seeing her squirm.

TWENTY-ONE
EMMA

Monday, May 27th, 2024: 6:00 a.m.

My alarm chimes at six in the morning and it's still dark as a bat's wing outside. Waking up in my childhood bed is strange, but familiar. When my parents moved from Brooklyn, they wanted to keep all of the nostalgia, the things they'd worked hard to pay for. Lop-lop, my favorite stuffed bunny missing one eye, looks the worse for wear. And I think Mom sprayed my pillow with tea rose perfume.

Although I'd found my emergency Xanax prescription in my suitcase, I didn't sleep at all, tossing and turning all night long. Every few minutes, my eyes would pop open and my skin was cold and clammy—feverish. It felt like somebody was pricking my body, my brain, with little pins. Hoping to have heard more from the girls, I'd made the mistake of checking my phone.

STELLA:

> Attorney has video. Thought you might want to prepare yourself.

Let's just say, the images she'd attached definitely gave me nightmares and I'm wondering how many days somebody can survive without sleep and shutting down completely. I don't want to, but I have to get up—shower, brush my teeth. What does a person of interest wear to a police station? I decide it doesn't matter and hastily choose an olive green dress.

Mom is in the kitchen when I head downstairs. She smiles and hands me a glass of freshly squeezed orange juice. She kisses me on the cheek. "Sit down. You need to eat something."

I don't know if I can. When she's not looking, I swallow a pill. A few minutes later, she sets a plate of toast and strawberry jam in front of me. I just stare at it. Dad shuffles into the kitchen wearing his cotton pajamas and slippers. He places a hand on my shoulder. "Don't worry, Em-Dash. Everything will work out."

I can only nod. I get up and peek through the blinds. The press is still camped out in front of the house. Even though they can't see me and although I'm wearing clothes, I feel naked, violated. Exposed.

A black car with tinted windows picks me up at 7:20 a.m. Two armed bodyguards knock on the front door, shield me from the glare of cameras with a coat, and I'm pushed into the back seat with Dina.

"They're ex-military. We'll get through the maze of reporters," she says, snapping her fingers. "Easy."

I'm already sweating bullets.

Some of the reporters bang on the hood while screaming out my name, but we leave them in a trail of dust. The driver doesn't slow down; doesn't stop, just guns the engine through the crowd.

Dina pats my leg. "Get any sleep last night?"

"A little," I say, wondering if ten minutes counts. "Any last-minute advice?"

"Let me do all the talking."

Good, because right now I can't talk. It takes an effort to blink, to move my lips, to move at all. The car pulls up to the police station and one of the bodyguards jumps out, opening the car door. Dina steps out first. She turns back to me and holds out a hand in the stop position. "More reporters. Let Tony clear a path. Frank will take you in."

The man I assume to be Frank holds out his hand and then throws a black coat over my head. As he guides me up the steps, shouts echo in my ears.

Dina Fadel! Are you representing Emma Landon? Did she murder her husband? What charges is she facing? Has she been charged? Emma, care to comment?

Their voices ring in my ears, blurring into a massive taunt from the nastiest of bullies. Frank gently steers me through the front door. My heart dances with fear. My lungs feel like they're going to explode. Somebody whips the coat off my head. I hunch over and Dina places a hand on my back. "Breathe in through your nose, out through your mouth. It'll pass."

Once my breathing returns to a normal level, an officer escorts us to a conference room, where Detective Rossi and a distinguished older man sit. He stands up, holds out his hand to Dina. "Attorney Fadel, always a pleasure to see you, regardless of the circumstances."

Rossi grins and I swear she whispers under her breath, "She's breaking out the big guns," but I can't be sure.

"Chief Davis, same to you," she says with a tight smile. "And it's Dina."

"Dina, Mrs. Landon, have a seat," he instructs, and we do. "Coffee? Water?"

"Nothing for me," Dina replies. "Emma?"

I shake my head no.

"Shall we begin?" asks Dina. "I'd like to know: is my client being charged with anything?"

"Not at the moment," says Chief Davis. "This is more of a fact-finding interview. We'll see how it goes."

"Then let's not waste time. Let's get on with it."

Detective Rossi lowers the lights and then pulls up an image on a monitor. "Can you explain this text you sent to Mr. Landon the morning he died?"

I read the words: *I'm going to kill you.*

I swallow three times.

"What's the time stamp?" Dina demands.

"Sunday, 9:12 a.m.—" Rossi begins.

"I understand Mrs. Landon walked into a catastrophe in her kitchen." Dina laughs. "Haven't we all used that threat when our spouses or partners do something to piss us off? What's your point?"

"It shows intent."

"To what? Kill him again after he's already dead?" She pauses. "He died the day before. Around 10 a.m.? Isn't that what the coroner's report said? Get serious."

Rossi blinks and flips to another screen, bringing up a new message.

> I'm going to kill you. I asked you to do one thing while I was away. One!

NATE:

> What are you going on about?

> The pump for the pond! The fish are dying!

"Mrs. Landon sent this to Mr. Landon eight days before his death," says Rossi. "Odd coincidence. Another death threat. The pond."

I'd forgotten about my anger that day. I'd forgotten about the text. Dina turns and ushers for me to whisper in her ear. "I'd just returned home from a trip to Thailand. And I was angry he didn't call Diego, our pond guy. My fish were dying."

"I could charge Mrs. Landon with a criminal threat and intent," says Rossi.

"But you can't," says Dina, cutting her off. "And if you did, I'd have her out in ten minutes." She turns to Chief Davis. "This is ridiculous."

He shrugs as Rossi clicks to another screen. She cocks her head to the side, smirking. "Is it?"

> Taking the girls to Paris. Staying at the house. Leaving tomorrow night. Back on Sunday. Using the black card. #points 😶😶😶

> Giving staff the week off. Ryan boarding dogs at his farm. He'll drop them off on Sunday afternoon.

> I need some time to clear my head. I think you do too.

"And?" huffs Dina. "I'm not seeing the connection."

"You will," says Rossi. She presses a button on the remote. "That message was sent to Nathaniel a couple of days after this."

She brings up a video. It's of me, the night of the party, and I look absolutely insane. I hate Becks Stark for posting this. I lower my head, anger boiling underneath the composure I'm trying to retain. "Can you explain what you're doing here?"

"I can," says Dina. "She's doing charades, acting out *A Perfect Murder*, because she was hammered at a party she didn't want to be at."

"Did anybody else do charades at the party?" Rossi asks.

"How would she know? She stumbled home drunk right after, what I think, was a great performance." Dina grips my hand. "Again, where are you going with this? Did anybody die that night?"

"No, but Audrey and David Clark were at the party," Rossi says, clucking her tongue. "And Mrs. Landon is fully aware Mr. Landon had an affair with Audrey. Weren't you, Mrs. Landon?"

I whisper to Dina again. Dina clears her throat. "Which is the reason Emma snapped at the party. How would you feel when coming face-to-face with your husband's ex-lover?"

"She could have told me about his cheating when I questioned her, that might have explained her call to 911—"

Dina taps her hand on the table. "His cheating, something that upsets her, is none of your business."

"But it is. Because Nathaniel Landon died a week later." Rossi walks over and places an iPad mini in front of me. "Care to explain this, Madame Butterfly?"

I look up. "I don't know what you're talking about. I've never seen this before in my life."

"It's an invitation to a private sex club, one that you orchestrated."

"She designs exclusive homes, not parties," says Dina. "And why on earth would you think she had anything to do with a sex club?"

Rossi clears her throat. "Because Mrs. Landon is more than obsessed with butterflies." She meets my eyes. "Aren't you?"

"I am," I say and Dina cuts me off.

"What's your point, Detective?"

"The invitation was sent out by somebody calling themselves Madame Butterfly." She wags a finger in my direction. "And I'm looking at her."

Dina spits out a laugh. "Oh, are you? With what proof? A name? What's in a name? That's Shakespeare, if you didn't know. And *Madame Butterfly* is a very famous opera. Let's move on." Dina shakes her head and rolls her eyes. "Stop wasting our time."

Rossi nods. She slaps a file in front of me, the sound reverberating in my ears. "Were you aware that Mr. Landon was planning on divorcing you?"

I flip through the file, locking onto the words *harmful actions* and *opioid addiction*, before landing on two single pages: one a form to have me committed to a psychiatric ward, already signed by Weiner, one of the many judges in his back pocket, the other a form to get custody of the girls. I launch out of my seat, the chair toppling over, and bang my fist on the table. Rossi flinches. Dina and Chief Davis share a startled look. Dina's shoulders go rigid.

I don't care if I'm making a scene.

"What the hell? He was going to divorce *me*? He was going to have *me* committed? He was going to take the girls away from me? And take care of them. What a fucking joke." I hit my thighs with my hands. "I was planning on divorcing him. That conniving bastard! That sick, twisted monster!" My body shakes uncontrollably. "I'm glad he's dead! He deserved to die! There I said it. Get what you want, Detective?" I stomp my foot. "And if you knew what I knew, you'd be happy he's dead too."

I hunch over, placing my hands on my thighs, my whole body radiating with so much anger I think I'll spontaneously combust.

Dina grabs my hand and mouths for me to find my breath. "By my client's reaction, I think it's quite obvious that Emma wasn't aware of Nathaniel's plans."

"Humph." Rossi scoffs, smirking. "Divorcing him? Would have been nice if you mentioned that yesterday."

I am tempted to slap the smug grin right off her face, but refrain. Chief Davis gets up and picks up my chair, ushering me to sit down. My nostrils flare and I breathe in and out through my nose like an angry bull.

"Would it have been?" interjects Dina. "Not really. Because

it's none of your goddamn business. It's extremely personal. But we're getting everything out in the open now."

Rossi scowls. "And the divorce attorney?"

"Hedra Siegel, a partner in my firm. It's how I connected with Emma. Nate was a serial cheater," says Dina, giving me a look as if to say calm down and sit down. "And the only way for Emma to get out of her marriage and keep her lifestyle intact was to negate the ironclad prenup she signed." She pulls a thumb drive out of her purse. "Stella Kincaid, the private investigator she'd hired, filmed this video using hidden cameras, with Emma's approval, at their home. If you're looking for a killer"—she taps the drive—"I'd start here. She's already told you about Gordon Flynn and Ben and Becks Stark. Is there's anything else, Detective?"

Chief Davis clears his throat. "Until we look at the video, nothing from me. You can go. Sorry to have troubled you—"

Detective Rossi steps forward. "Wait. I do have a question."

"Rossi!" snaps Chief Davis. "Back off."

Her face blanches ever so slightly. After the way she tortured me yesterday, I like seeing her squirm. "My question may help find whoever is responsible for his death."

"You really think somebody murdered Nate?" I ask, and she nods. Curiosity gets the better of me. "What's your question?"

"It's more of an umbrella question with many prongs," she says. "What happened one week prior to Mr. Landon's death?"

"The full week? Leading up to her taking action to divorce?" asks Dina, and Rossi nods yes. "Emma, are you OK with this?"

"Yes," I say, wanting to share my side of the story. Share what I know about the monster that was my husband.

Rossi grunts. "Before we start, Chief Davis and I need to look at whatever's on the video." She locks her gaze on me. "Do you want to see it?"

Dina growls. "Emma has been through enough." She grips

my hand and shakes her head. "Believe me, the video will give you nightmares, mess you up."

"CD?" says Rossi. She picks up the thumb drive. "You coming?"

Chief Davis blinks with annoyance. "Clearly."

After Rossi clomps out of the room, Chief Davis shuffling behind her, I whisper to Dina, "I don't need to see the video. Stella sent me screenshots."

TWENTY-TWO

DETECTIVE ROSSI

Monday, May 27th, 2024: 8:26 a.m.

I follow CD into his office and he plugs the thumb drive into his computer. The timestamp on the video flashes 8:45 p.m. Nathaniel sits in a chair, an iced drink in hand, a bottle of Glenfiddich Grande Couronne set on the table beside him. Two firepits spit out flames of orange and red. Enigma's "Mea Culpa" plays softly in the background.

"We have sound?" CD says incredulously.

"Apparently," I respond. "Guess this Kinkaid has good equipment."

Nate sets his drink down and lights up the tiki torches surrounding the pool, the latter reflecting the flames and the full moon. In the distance, fireflies spark up the sky.

"He's just hanging out by himself with a bottle of really expensive Scotch," says CD. "I don't know what Dina was going on about."

I lean over, fast-forwarding until an older man with a cane joins Nate on the terrace. I recognize him: Gordon Flynn. "Now, it's getting interesting," I say.

"Where's that crazy wife of yours?" asks Gordon.

"You mean the one I'm finally getting rid of?" Nathaniel lets out a hard laugh. "She took the twins to Paris. Needs some space to clear her head. Little does she know what I have planned for her return."

The clink of ice cubes. Nate pours Gordon a Scotch.

"To new beginnings—and happier endings," says Gordon.

They raise glasses, toast, and settle back in their chairs, flames flickering on their faces.

Nate shakes his head and looks up to the sky. "When you sold off most of your businesses, I thought parties like this were days in the past. I'm glad you're bringing the excitement back."

"I don't know what you're talking about, Nate," says Gordon. "I'm just scoping out what the competition is up to. So I can crush them. I still own stock in my companies and 25k was a drop in the bucket."

"You didn't put this together?"

"I didn't." Gordon takes a sip of his drink. "But it seems like somebody wants to dethrone the king." He throws his head back, laughs with a hack. "I was thinking about the first time I met you, when your father brought you to one of my parties. How old were you the night you became a man?"

Nate leans back in his chair. "Thirteen." He closes his eyes and grins. "Not many guys can say they lost their virginity to a porn star. And I learned tricks beyond my years."

Gordon hacks again and then lights up a cigar. "Those were the days. I miss Peter. A good man. Like you."

"I miss him too," says Nate, and they toast again. "To Peter."

"To Peter."

"Well, that's one messed-up conversation, but nothing is really happening," I mutter, pressing fast-forward again.

Within minutes, one by one, more people saunter onto the pool deck. CD points at the screen. "I know who those people are. Jeff Cox, Harold Katz, Becks and Ben Stark—" He takes in a deep breath, letting it out. "Why the hell is Congresswoman Claire Woodbridge hanging out with these people?"

"Your guess is as good as mine," I say. "I guess we're going to find out."

Ben leans forward. "What time are they getting here?"

"Antsy?" asks Nate.

"Yes. How many did you order?" asks Becks.

"Two dragonflies." Nate nods his head to Harold and he rubs his hands together, grinning. "Six butterflies."

Claire snickers. "You should have ordered more butterflies because I'm a very greedy woman and I'm claiming two."

"Not afraid of a political scandal?" asks Nate.

"Hey, we're among friends." Claire taps her head and then her chest. "And if the polls are on point, you're looking at New York's next governor."

"Thanks to our money," says Gordon. "And the strings we pull."

"True," says Claire with a curtsy. She winks. "Thank you, you dirty bastard. And I've got your back."

CD slams a hand over one eye. "Oh God. I voted for her." I shudder. "So did I."

Becks stands up. "Nate? Where's the wine? The vodka? The champagne? All I see is Scotch. I'm going to raid your cellar—"

"You know where it is," he says. "I put some of the good stuff in the pantry. Even that fancy vodka you like. Be a good girl."

"I'm always good." She pauses. "Those beasts aren't in the house?"

"Nah, our dog walker has them at his farm."

"Thank the heavens. I don't know why you have such big animals."

"You have one," says Nate and Ben growls.

Becks walks away. A light brightens the kitchen.

"Fast-forward again, Rossi," instructs CD. So I do. "Stop."

An intercom buzzes.

"They're here," says Nate. He presses some buttons on his phone. "Have your driver park to the side of the garage. We're around back by the pool."

Ben is cutting up cocaine on the glass coffee table. He looks up to Nate. "What? I brought some party favors?"

Claire steps over and snorts a line, followed by Becks.

Becks looks up. "Your little hoity-toity Madame Butterfly would die."

Nate laughs and eyes the stars in the sky. "One can dream."

A woman walks onto the pool deck. Glimmering white butterfly wings adorn her back like a Victoria's Secret model. Along with the tiki torches, the moon and the starry sky light up her body, highlighting every curve. She cracks a whip.

"Out of this wood do not desire to go;
Thou shalt remain here whether thou wilt or no.
I am a spirit of no common rate,
The summer still doth tend upon my state;
And I do love thee: therefore, go with me,
I'll give thee fairies to attend on thee;
And they shall fetch thee jewels from the deep,
And sing, while thou on pressed flowers dost sleep:
And I will purge thy mortal grossness so
That thou shalt like an airy spirit go.

"Welcome to this Midsummer Night's Dream." She pauses, raises an arm, and cracks the whip on the terrace. *Snap*. "Peaseblossom! Cobweb! Moth! Mustardseed! Butterflies and dragonflies, now is the time to fulfill wild fantasies."

Becks lets out a soft whoop. "This is amazing."

Ben slaps Jeff on the back. "Thanks for the invite, man."

Jeff's grin fades into a bewildered smirk. "You invited me. What are you talking about?"

"The invitation you sent me on the iPad mini. I sent one on to Nate."

"Benny, I didn't send you the iPad. You sent one to me."

All eyes shoot to Gordon. He shrugs. "Wasn't me."

A group of six beautiful women and two men wearing wings emerge from the darkness, swaying their bodies rhythmically, every muscle of those perfect bodies coming to life like a painting in the moonlight. They're bending and twisting and turning—real Cirque du Soleil movements.

"Who the hell cares who sent the invite?" screeches Becks with a howl. She tilts her head back, baring her fang-like teeth. "I'm really looking forward to tonight."

Claire leans over and kisses Becks, running her fingers across her chest and down her stomach. "Me too."

Becks licks her lips. "Let a night of hedonistic debauchery begin."

As Gordon settles back in his chair, Claire eyes him curiously. "What?" says Gordon. "I just like to watch."

"So do I." Becks winks and then she eyes Nathaniel. "But since Nate is here, I think I'll join in."

"Are you obsessed with me?" asks Nathaniel.

Becks grins. "You know I am."

The woman with the whip beckons to Nate with a manicured finger. He steps over and she wraps the cord around his neck. He smiles and the rest join in. As clothes are ripped off, tumbling onto the pool deck, the video just gets more twisted and graphic and horrible from this point on.

My mind is spinning. This is the invitation I'd seen on the iPad mini brought to life, but a hell of a lot more graphic. I can't take it anymore.

"What the hell am I watching? The photos on his phone were bad enough! Turn this sick, orgy shit off!" I scream.

TWENTY-THREE

EMMA

Monday, May 27th, 2024: 8:57 a.m.

While Dina and I wait for Rossi's return, I check my phone, hoping to have heard something from one of my girls.

AVA:

> All flights are full. Flying private with M.V. She wants to come to NY anyway.

I'm about to respond when Kowalski walks into the room, handing over blueberry muffins and lattes from my favorite café in Katonah. I set my phone down on the table with a sigh. I'll get back to my girls after this nightmare of a morning is over.

"I thought we were going to be here for a while." Dina winks. "I handed him a fifty, told him to get what he wants. A little bribery goes a long way."

My hands tremble. "I wish it was vodka or tequila."

"Me too," she says, her grin changing into a snigger when we hear Rossi scream from somewhere inside the station.

Rossi stomps into the room. She paces back and forth, breathless, like she's trying to figure out what to say. Her eyes finally meet mine and she waggles a finger. "Your late husband and his friends are severely twisted!"

She's only stating what I'd told her with different words. It takes extreme self-discipline to keep myself from saying, *I told you so. You just wouldn't listen.* Instead, I raise an eyebrow.

"She knows," says Dina. "That's why *she* was going to divorce *him.*"

"I had one of our techs print out a couple of screenshots... of their, um, faces." Rossi places a stack of photo-grade paper in front of me. "Can you identify these people?"

One by one, I flip through blurry images, slapping each page down and spreading them in front of me. "I can," I say, tapping with my index finder. "Nate. Ben Stark. Becks Stark. Gordon Flynn. Claire Woodbridge. Harold Katz. And Jeff Cox." I meet her gaze. "I have no clue who the others are. But at least now you have an explanation for the feathers and the masks."

My eyes say what my lips don't: *The nerve of you to ask me that question the other day. You should be thankful that I'd cooperated with you then like I'm cooperating with you now.* I lift up my chin, waiting for an apology that doesn't come. I could stand up and leave, but I don't. I want everybody to know what a monster Nate is.

As Chief Davis takes his seat, he shoots me a sympathetic smile.

"The video was taken last Thursday." Rossi rubs her forehead and slumps into a chair, defeat written on her face. "Are you ready to take me back to the party that Saturday night, to the party you snapped at? I believe everybody you've just mentioned was there. I'll try to put the pieces together and we'll move on, putting the timeline together until yesterday?"

"I'm ready," I say with a fierce nod. "And I'll tell you everything I know. But I can only speak for myself, not Nate."

Detective Rossi swallows. "With what I now know about

your husband, I think I'll be able to fill in the details. Let's go over everything you remember."

What Detective Rossi doesn't know won't kill her and I will share most of the truth. And, like she'd done with me, she'll jump to her own conclusions about my late husband and his so-called friends.

ACT TWO: ONE WEEK PRIOR
BAITING A WASP WITH A SUGAR TRAP

*Well, I must endure the presence of a few caterpillars
if I wish to become acquainted with the butterflies.*

—Antoine de Saint-Exupéry, *The Little Prince*

FACT: Wasps are attracted to bright colors, flowering plants,
and the scents of sweet drinks, perfumes, and fruits. The best
bait to use for trapping a wasp is a sugary substance. Never
spray a wasp with vinegar; it will put them in defense mode.
Instead of drawing them into a trap, this action will cause them
to fly toward you and attack, stingers out.

TWENTY-FOUR

EMMA

Saturday, May 18th, 2024

I'm pacing, looking at my watch. Nate isn't at the airport like he'd said he was going to be. I've been waiting outside of arrivals for fifteen minutes, all of my calls going straight to voicemail. So I text him.

> Where are you?
>
> Damn it, Nate. Respond.
>
> I can't believe you.
>
> Thanks for nothing.

Steaming with anger, I tap the app on my phone and my Uber shows up within five minutes. Without a word, I slump into the back seat as the driver loads my suitcases into the trunk. I am beyond livid. If Nate had picked me up, or at least called, he might have had a chance. He might have changed my mind.

I'd just arrived at JFK from Thailand, after an eight-day mission to curate some exotic pieces for one of my clients. At least, while I was there I picked up a few things for myself and for my staff. But, great buys aside, I'm more than ticked off; I feel deeply betrayed and disillusioned. However much I want to, I don't send any of the following texts and clear the messages one by one.

> You're a bastard.

> You're the perfect husband.

> And we have a perfect marriage. A perfect life.

> That's a joke.

> You'd be better off dead.

I know it's time to change everything—to set my plan into motion.

I scroll through my messages, catching up on recent texts sent while I was on my flight.

AVA:

> Stayed the night at Taryn's. Dad said OK. C U later. Back around dinner. 😊

I clench my teeth. Damn Nate. I want to see my girls. It's almost as if he purposefully keeps them away from me. Sending them to boarding school when they were twelve? Not my idea. Another argument that I lost. Sending them to summer camp too? He'd said that I worked too much, drank too much, was a hot mess. He wasn't entirely wrong, but I've always made time for my girls. And I'm always sober around them. It takes liquid courage to face him, to look him in the eyes. Becks had been right all those years ago when she'd said my tastes in alcohol would change when hanging out with Nate and his messed-up club. Sauvignon Blanc? No, thank you. I'm already thinking about vodka or tequila.

An hour later, the driver pulls up to our estate and I open

the gates using the code on my phone. In the rearview mirror, I see the driver's eyes go wide and her jaw drops open. She pulls the car to the front of the house and looks over her shoulder. "I'm only supposed to take the bags out of the trunk. But do you need help carrying them up to the house?"

"I do," I say. "And I'll give you a good tip. Cash."

She grins. "Maybe your rating will go up."

I rub my eyes. "Passengers get rated by the drivers?"

"They do. And yours is pretty bad. I almost didn't pick you up until I looked at your name." She sighs, eyeing my estate. "Such a dream life. Married to Nathaniel Landon. You're one lucky woman."

I hold back my laughter. "Along with a big tip, I'll throw in my husband. You can have him."

"Ha-ha," she says with a snort. "You're funny, Mrs. Landon."

I'm not joking.

I force a tight smile as she hops out of the car to grab my bags. She wheels them up the steps to the front entry and I hand her two crisp hundred-dollar bills. Stunned, she looks at the money. "Your rating is definitely going up."

"Thank you, uh—"

"Marie."

"Thank you, Marie."

She bounces off back to her Toyota Camry with a smile. "No, thank *you*, Mrs. Landon."

I punch in the code for the front door, leaving my suitcases outside on the front stoop. Nate can take them in later. After the Uber leaves, I close the front gates and look at my phone. Not one text. Not one message. The bastard.

I sigh. I'm overtired and under-stimulated. Jet lag combined with a grueling twenty-plus-hour travel day and no sleep has sucked the life out of me.

I need coffee like I need air to breathe.

Coffee! Give me coffee!

I walk down the long hallway, my shoes clicking on the marble floor, heading to the kitchen. I stop mid-step, my jaw clenched. A strange green hue bathes the glass atrium in an unnatural light and, as I look out the window, the source of the glow makes my heart stutter.

A green murk covers the pond in a thick veil of grotesqueness. Although a couple of hot pink buds from the water lilies brighten the blackness, the view from the kitchen is right out of a horror film and I can't help myself but wonder what else lurks beneath the surface. Surely, one of the twins' long-lost Barbie Dolls, a Mary Jane shoe or ten, old bones (not human, but from T-bones, thanks to the monster-sized dogs), and, more likely than not, a couple of the dishes I'd thrown at Nate during one of my severe postpartum tantrums when they were born—the girls, not the dogs.

Granted, it was my idea to build the house over the pond, adding the cascading waterfall—two architectural elements I'm supremely proud of. And, sure, I'm the one who always checks the filtration system, the one who regularly tests the PH levels of the water, so it should come as no surprise that I'm the one who notices that one of our koi fish is floating on its side, his white-spotted scales glimmering in the sunlight. He's not moving—not one flip of a fin, not one burble of a bubble. Damn it. I'd told Nate to get somebody in to fix the pump while I was traveling. He'd told me he was on it. But the evidence is clear; he didn't, because a few of my prized koi fish, the ones reminding me of leopards, are dead.

Leopards. Spots.

Spots. Leopards.

Liars. Cheaters.

One can't change their essential nature. Or can they? Over the years, I know I've changed. But Nate has not. He might have hidden his true nature better before, but he's always been the same control freak who thinks he can get away with anything. Narcissists have a way of pulling strings, making you believe in all of their lies. And, over the years, I've let him get away with it. Not anymore. My strings have snapped. The vein in my neck pulses with anger. I pull out my phone from my purse and text Nate. Again.

> I'm going to kill you. I asked you to do one thing while I was away. One!

NATE

> What are you going on about?

I laugh. I send him a death threat and now he gets back to me? I angrily tap out my message.

> The pump for the pond! The fish are dying!

Three dots. I wait. Then nothing.

I slam my phone down on the counter and glare at the Elektra Belle Epoque Riforma, the 17k-dollar machine looking more like R2D2's sexy Italian chrome and copper robot girlfriend than a coffee maker. "It's the best in the world! A real conversation piece!" Nate had exclaimed, and then he'd thrown the De'Longhi in the trash. (I'd pulled it out and donated it to a local church.)

Seriously, unless you're running a restaurant, who spends that kind of money on a coffee maker? My husband, that's who.

Nate's tastes edge toward the unconventional, and he likes to collect beautiful things. I suppose I used to be one of Nate's beautiful things and, back in the day, he'd called me priceless. But fifteen years of marriage later I'm just a collector's item, and instead of getting more valuable with age, my worth has depreciated. I'm surprised Nate hasn't tried to throw me into a dumpster.

Where did the time go? And how do I work this damn machine? I'm pressing buttons and nothing is happening. I'm useless. Our house staff get the weekends off and I'm tempted to call one of them in, but my need for caffeine is not an emergency.

"Alexa!" I yell into the air, my head thrown back in frustration. "How do I work an Elektra Belle Epoque?"

The computerized voice fades in, becoming louder. "Here's what I found. The Belle Époque is a period of—"

I cut her off before she rambles on giving me a lesson in French history. "I'm talking about the coffee maker."

"I don't understand 'I'm talking about the coffee maker.' But I can search the web for it."

"Gah! I just need coffee!"

"Coffee drinks are made by brewing water with ground coffee beans. The brewing is either done slowly by drip—"

My fingers shoot to my throbbing temples. "Alexa, shut up! Just shut the hell up!"

Alexa ends our not-so-helpful chat with three long beeps. I thought I'd designed a smart house—speakers, lights, thermostats, our refrigerator, and, after the birth of the girls, despite Nate's aversion of being monitored, even Nest video, in addition to the surveillance cameras on every corner of the property. Yet here I am, the salutatorian of my high school class with magna cum laude accolades for architectural design, feeling like a world-class idiot.

"Damn it, Alexa! Where did I go wrong? Change my life," I yell, raising my arms up in defeat.

"I didn't get that. Could you try again?"

Oh boy, now that's a loaded question, one that sends chills up my spine.

My phone vibrates on the counter. Before it shimmies to the floor, I look at caller ID and answer. "What?"

"Emma, my darling," says Nate, "I've missed you."

"Funny way of showing it," I hiss. "I must have called you five times and texted you at least twenty—"

"I was in surgery. A triple bypass. You made it home OK?"

I'm wondering if the patient is scarred like I am—my scars emotional. I think he gets off on torturing me.

"I did, no thanks to you and your army of cars."

The man has a Bugatti, a Bentley Continental GT, a Rolls-Royce Phantom, a Dodge Viper, a 1962 Jaguar E-type, and a 1968 Mustang Bullitt, the latter purchased because it was made famous by Steve McQueen, not to mention his collection of Indian and Ducati motorcycles. And he couldn't pick me up in one of them.

I'd like to remind him that I'm the one who designed his air-conditioned garage, but instead, I sigh and change my tone. Being passive-aggressive doesn't work with Nate. "Where are Harry and Potter?"

"The boys are with Ryan. You know, our dog walker." He pauses when I huff. Like I don't know who walks the dogs? Or orders their special food—real beef—that, in one day, could feed a starving village for a week.

When Nate brought the puppies home (surprise!), Ava and Grace instantly fell in love with the furry duo, naming them after their favorite book series. It was yet another battle won by Nate. What was I supposed to do? Tell the girls we couldn't keep the puppies? Become the bad, evil mom? No, as usual, I'd caved in like a molten lava cake, oozing into a puddle of sticky compliance to avoid a tear-infused nuclear war.

Eight years later, I've grown to love the gigantic beasts, surviving clumps of hair that appear in every corner of the house and their non-stop, fountain-like drool. In fact, I love the dogs more than I love Nate. Loyal and protective, they don't lie.

Nate continues, "I'm so sorry, honey, my secretary must have misread the time. I thought you were coming back at five tonight."

"Nope, my flight got in at five a.m.," I manage to spit out.

We both go silent, me listening to his ragged breath.

"For crying out loud, Emma, I was meeting with the anesthesiologist. Big surgery this morning."

And now I'm the bad guy. *No, Nate, you can't put this on me.*

"Before I left, I told you that I'd forgotten to tell Luisa to get somebody over to fix the pump in the pond. I asked you to handle it and you said you would. But, clearly, you didn't. The fish are dying—"

"I know. I read your angry texts."

"You'd be ticked off too."

"People are more important than fish," he says with a soft laugh. "Don't you think?"

This is the problem with being married to a cardiothoracic surgeon. My job, my life, seems infinitely unimportant when compared to his. I design houses; he saves lives. I'll never win this argument. "Fine," I say with a guttural growl. "But I'm *not* happy."

"You're never happy and you'll get over it, or maybe you never will," he mumbles. "Don't forget we have that cocktail party over at Gordon's tonight—an introduction to our governor-to-be."

I did forget and would rather stick knives into my tired eyes than deal with *those* people, each one worse than the other and topped off by their unscrupulous grand master Gordon Flynn. "You cannot be serious. I just got back. Can't we cancel?"

"You canceled last time, so no. Plus, you promised you'd make your yearly appearance," he says, and an overly-dramatic groan erupts from my throat. "Emma, you have all day to recuperate and I don't ask much of you. You'll be fine."

"I'm not going," I snap.

"We'll stay home then. Maybe you could prepare some koi sushi?" He snorts, laughing at his own joke.

"That's not funny."

"But it is. Look, I'll call Diego about the pond. The party starts at eight. Get some rest." He clears his throat. "Isn't every marriage based on compromise?"

I go silent. He's using my words against me.

"It's settled then," he says and the discussion is over.

We hang up and I head over to the coffee maker, steaming with anger. I thought I had a backbone made of steel. And I do when it comes to my work. But I don't with Nate. I cave in every time as if he has some kind of hold over me, like I've been brainwashed. I really need to snap out of it.

I want coffee. I need coffee.

I tap a few buttons. Nothing but an error message, followed by a long hiss. I make a mental note to buy a new machine—one I know how to use.

The pages of a recent *Vanity Fair* exposé with airbrushed photos of me and my *perfect* life flutter on the marble counter, taunting me with its fake and styled reality. My stomach lurches and I place my hands on my knees. I only have one person to yell at now—myself.

"Excellent! So excellent! My entire life is one stinking big fat lie! All lies!"

Alexa's voice clicks on and I almost jump out of my skin. "Here's what I found. 'Lies' by the Thompson Twins. Released in 1983."

In seconds, the kitchen booms and rattles with 'Lies' and I'm wondering if Alexa's having an identity crisis like I am. I listen to the lyrics, looking at the slightly iridescent white walls of my pristine kitchen, thinking how it needs to be repainted, the sparkles fading. As the chorus blares through the speakers, my thoughts snap from this house I've designed, chose every element of, every color of every wall, to the color of lies—from white ones to red ones: white (the little ones, slightly altruistic, the ones we tell to protect others or ourselves); gray (a bit shadier than white, depending on the balance of helping or harm); black—very callous and damaging; and, the worst of them all—red, carved in blood and all about betrayal.

I place my head in my hands and sob. "Alexa! Off!"

Silence—except for the truth ringing in my ears. I stare blankly out the window. It could be my imagination, but the water in the pond seems be turning black. Like rigor mortis. Like death. Like my marriage. The truth, as they say, always rises to the surface.

When I'd first met him seventeen years ago, I'd convinced myself that Nate was the perfect man and we'd build a dream life together. As much as I want to believe in the concept, I now know that there is no such thing as perfection.

My gaze shoots to my butterfly garden. One day, and soon, I'm going to fly free from Nate's web of lies. I've been planning my escape for two years. Everything is set. I'm just waiting for the perfect time to spread my wings. And that time is now.

TWENTY-FIVE

NATE

Saturday, May 18th, 2024

After hanging up with Emma, I want to punch the wall in my office.

I give the woman carte blanche to do and spend whatever she wants and it's never enough. I've given her everything—the house of her dreams, the twins, all the first-class family vacations, the private planes to exotic locales around the world. Everything. She's acting like a spoiled brat. Isn't her $50,000-a-month allowance enough? What more does the woman want from me?

Harping on me about the damn pond? She'd wanted to build the house over the water to establish her career and I'd paid over ten million to do it, not including the land and what I had to do to get it. Not that I'd minded. The memory brings a smile to my face.

TWENTY-SIX

NATE

Then: August 16th, 2003

When Gordon Flynn talked, like E. F. Hutton, people listened.

"Nate," he said. "I have the deal of a lifetime for you. It's... how do you say it: an investment that will benefit both of us."

"Go on."

"I'm selling the property adjacent to mine and I'm going to offer it to you at below market value, but..."

I knew Gordon. "But there's a catch."

He puffed out a hearty breath. "Of course there is."

"And...?"

He hacked a phlegmy cough and cleared his throat. "Irina needs friends. She's sick and tired of being snubbed by everybody in Westchester. And by everybody, I mean everybody. The woman can't even get her nails done at the local salon without ending up tears."

"I get it. You need someone to look out for her."

He sighed. "I do. I'm figuring you'll find a nice girl, get

married, have kids, and settle down soon. When you do, you'll move here. Understood?"

"How much are we talking about?" I asked. "For the property."

"Don't worry. You can afford it. Harold's already drawn up the paperwork and we'll seal the deal in an hour. A car will be picking you up in twenty minutes."

The line went dead.

After showering, dressing in a white polo and khakis, and making a smoothie, I waited for the driver out front, pacing. A black limousine pulled up and the driver stepped out.

"Dr. Landon?" he asked.

"The one and only."

"I'm Ahn. Mr. Flynn sent me to pick you up." He opened the door. "Do you need anything?" he asked, pointing to the bar. "There's fruit and coffee. Bourbon. Scotch—"

"No, thank you. I'm good," I said, holding up my smoothie as I climbed in the back.

Forty-five minutes later, we exited the highway, rumbling down a road in picturesque Bedford—horse country. Before reaching Gordon's estate, a sign caught my eye; land for sale. Twenty-three acres on a pond. Land that might soon be mine.

A petite Asian woman—I forget her name—opened the door and led me into the living room. Gordon sat in a winged-back leather chair, still in his silk pajamas, looking like the wealthy man of leisure that he is. "Am I early?"

"Right on time. Coffee? A scone? Fruit?" he asked, pointing to a spread on the table.

"Thanks, but I already ate." I took the seat across from him. "The property adjacent to yours?" I asked, and he nodded. "I saw it on the drive over and I am definitely interested."

"Good. I'm throwing in a house in Pound Ridge as part of the deal. About ten minutes from here," he said with a shrug. "You'll need somewhere to stay once everything is set in motion.

You can rent it out until then. I know you're still a city boy." He flashed a wicked grin. "As for the land, I think you'll like the deal I'm about to propose and the perks that come along with it."

His wife, Irina, sauntered into the room carrying a bottle of champagne. Even at this early hour, she wore full makeup, a tight dress highlighting her luscious curves, and heels. Twenty-six years old, her entire being screamed sex, from the pouty lips to her straight perfectly coiffed blond hair, right down to her perfectly manicured nails. A "model" Gordon discovered in Russia, she was beyond hot—the kind of woman I definitely wouldn't marry, but would keep on the side.

I stood up and kissed her cheeks the European way. "Always a pleasure to see you."

"Pleasure is mine," she said, and then she looked at Gordon. "We celebrate the deal?"

"I have to see the land first," I said.

"I show you," she said with a nod.

Gordon shrugged and glanced at Irina. "I'll leave the two of you to get better acquainted." Before exiting the room, he focused on me and said, "I'm not the young man I used to be."

"I don't understand," I said.

"You will."

"I drive you in the new car. Bugatti," said Irina, turning before I could respond.

She led me out the front door to the garage and I couldn't stop my gaze from landing on her shapely ass. I wondered what moves she had. And I'd soon find out because she was making one on me. She stepped closer as I checked out the car, her hand caressing my crotch, and I was instantly hard.

"Beautiful? Yes?"

She hiked up her dress and bent over the car, placing one elbow on the hood, then looked over her shoulder. "I'm part of the deal."

. . .

"What did you think of the land?" asked Gordon.

"It's gorgeous," I said. "I just don't know if I'm ready to move from the city to horse country any time soon—"

"It's what I want. What Irina wants." He cleared his throat. "I'm not saying you have to move here tomorrow. I know you're young, still have wild oats to sow. I'm giving you five years. And if you don't pull through, I'll post the video of you in the garage fucking my wife on one of my sites." He cackled. "Wouldn't want to tarnish your stellar reputation. Don't you have aspirations to become the medical director? Then, again, the hospital board might be impressed. You've got some moves."

I slapped my hand to my forehead. My jaw went slack. "You taped us?"

"Of course. I like to watch."

I went silent for a moment. Gordon had blackmail down to a science. Oddly, this made me appreciate him even more—the savvy fox.

"Why me? Why not Ben?"

"Because Irina likes you, thinks you're handsome—and that Ben is a disgusting prick who looks like the Pillsbury Dough-boy." He coughed and, after slapping me on the back, placed the land deed on the table. "I don't believe we're negotiating, son." He tapped the paper. "Sign here. If you don't, I'll leak the news to the hospital about our little side deal. And I'm not talking about Irina."

I knew exactly where this conversation was headed.

"I didn't buy Luisa—"

"But you knew your father purchased her, yes?" he asked, and I shrugged. "Your little graduation gift, along with the loft he bought you when you got into med school."

"I see where this is going," I said, shaking my head.

"I never go back on my word, son."

I swallowed.

This was, as Gordon said, the deal of a lifetime, and it did come with perks, so I signed my name on the dotted line. Now, it was only a matter of finding a nice girl to settle down with, somebody I could take to all the hospital functions and charity events. None of the women I'd been seeing were marriage material; they were only good for one thing. I closed my eyes for a brief moment and came up with a plan. I could make this work. I handed Gordon the file.

"Pleasure doing business with you," said Gordon with a wink. "I'm looking forward to welcoming you to the neighborhood." He shot his hand out, shaking mine with a forceful pump. "Ahn will take you back to the city. Wire the funds today."

TWENTY-SEVEN

NATE

Saturday, May 18th, 2024

A photo on my desk catches my attention. It's of Emma, the girls and me in the Bahamas standing in front of the yacht I'd chartered, palm trees in the background. I tap her face and hiss, "I've given you the ideal life, the perfect life. Most women in your position would kill for what you have."

But she doesn't care. And she can't hear me.

One of the few things Emma can still claim is that she knows how to rub shoulders with the right people and has impeccable taste. I do love her place in my world when she's acting the way she should. Approaching forty, she's still gorgeous, although a bit worn around the edges and softer in the middle. She's smart. She's a fantastic mother. But she overlooks my needs.

After we got married, instead of dragging me by the tie into a dark alley in the city and unzipping my pants like she used to, she'd drag me to showrooms so we could build *her* dream house, the one I bankrolled. Our sex life dwindled until it became non-existent after the twins were born. I think she blames me for the emergency hysterectomy she had to have. Like it was my fault they couldn't control the bleeding. Doesn't she realize that surgery crushed my dreams too? I'd wanted a son to carry on my legacy, my name.

I pull up a photo of my latest baby, a sleek and sexy McLaren—exposed blue carbon fiber and silver, delivered to the house a couple of days ago. Ah, what a dream: 0–100 in 2.9 seconds.

I collect beautiful things like my cars. So sue me. There are far too many temptations in this world, including women.

The new clinical nurse on my rotation—Jane? Joan? Janet? —sidles up to me as I look over a patient's chart. She's been at the hospital for a couple of weeks, always eager to please, do what anybody tells her to do, like cleaning the bedpans. Today, she smells of cheap vanilla perfume, probably purchased at the local CVS. Doesn't she realize a woman's scent is her calling card? More importantly, she shouldn't wear fragrances while working—asthma, allergies, and airway issues could wreak havoc in the ward and it's completely against protocol. I'm about to reprimand her for her blunder when her full breasts press into my arm and she whispers hotly in my ear. "How's it hanging, Dr. Landon?"

"A little to the left," I respond out of habit.

She chokes back a laugh.

"I'm sorry," I say, taking a step back, assessing her. "That's an inside joke with another colleague. And completely inappropriate."

"No worries," she replies with a snort. "It was funny. Don't stress."

"I'm always stressed, Joan."

"It's Jane," she says, gingerly touching my hand. "Maybe you just need to unwind. You know, relax, take a load off."

Load off. She's speaking my language. By the way she smiles at me with those come-hither blue eyes and batting her lashes, she's definitely flirting. I know her type—probably got into nursing with the hopes of bagging a rich doctor, stealing him away from one of their uptight wives.

She's got great, full tits and, as I look over my shoulder, a luscious ass. Her eyes are a little too wide set for my tastes, but her skin is smooth, taut, and I can't help but imagine what she can do with those plump lips.

"I've got my ways of releasing stress," I say, not breaking eye contact.

Jane clears her throat and tilts her head to the side, a piece of silky black hair falling over her eyes. "I'm sure you do."

I take a step back. "Can you handle it?"

She bites down on her plump bottom lip again, her blue eyes glimmering. "I-I..." she stutters and then quickly gathers herself together. "Handle what?"

By the way she squirms, and adjusts her weight from one foot to the other, I know she's picked up on my innuendo. But I'm going to throw her off the little game of flirtation she's playing. I've got years of experience and I'm better at it.

"The stress of surgery," I say, pointing down the hall. "Theater 8. Twenty minutes. We have a cabbage."

She blinks with confusion. "A what?"

"A CABG—coronary artery bypass graft."

"Right, right. I knew that," she says, a blush creeping across her cheeks. "I'll get everything sanitized and set up."

"While you're at it, sanitize yourself. Fragrances are prohibited in the hospital. You should know that."

"I did know. I do know. I'm sorry," she says.

"Good. I'll see you in twenty."

Three hours later, the CABG is going by without any glitches—two grafts, the cut down the middle of the chest, the breastbone divided to access the heart, which I now stop, giving me thirty to ninety minutes to perform my magic.

Jane wipes my forehead. I nod and continue, my hands steady. So far so good. Forty minutes later, I attach the grafts and then start up the heart using controlled electrical shocks.

"Time to finish up," I say with a nod.

After reconnecting the breastbone with permanent metal wires, I suture the skin on the patient's chest with dissolvable stitches. I clap my hands together. "We're done here. Thank you all. Great work today."

"Amazing doctor. He's like a god," says Jane, which raises a few eyebrows, including mine.

The staff scatter to clean up the room. I discard my gloves and wash my hands as one of the nurses rolls the patient on a gurney to the recovery ward.

"Your next consultation is in two hours," says Catherine, the head nurse on my rotation. "We finished earlier than I thought."

"Any family members waiting in the lounge?"

"Nope," she replies. "They'll be back in a couple of hours."

"Any patients need checking in on?"

"We're in the clear."

"Fantastic." I grin. "For once, I have time to grab something healthy to eat."

Per my usual post-op habits, I head to my office to check my phone—three more calls from Emma and a couple of others. Nothing urgent. I fill out the paperwork for the CABG and then check my emails.

My cell vibrates on my desk and the ringtone from the chorus of Kenny Loggins's 'Danger Zone' alerts me that it's Emma calling again. She's probably going to try to wiggle out of going to Gordon's tonight or harp on at me again about the pond. This time, instead of ignoring her call, I pick up and cut her off before she goes on one of her manic tirades. "I already called Diego. He'll be over tomorrow."

"On a Sunday?"

"I'm paying him double," I say. "He's bringing some new fish, too."

"Thank you," she says. "The spotted ones?"

I have no clue. "Yes."

"Great. Anyway, that's not why I'm calling. My personal shopper from Saks is coming over at six..." She pauses. "I need something to wear tonight. Flynn's party. Your very bad idea."

"You can't find something from that gigantic walk-in closet of yours?"

She tsks. "And wear the same thing around Becks? And Mitzi. And Babs? What stupid names, by the way. Nope. You know how *they* are. Besides, a new dress is calling my name. Emma-aaaaa—"

"You win," I cut her off, needing to mollify the ingrate. Just listening to her whiny voice has me flinching with irritation and I'd rather put firecrackers in my ears. She's like an emotional dog—one of the little ones like a Chihuahua—and she won't stop yapping until she's pacified. "I've got this. Use the black card. Points."

"Right, points. On that, can I do a little more damage? Maybe a new pair of shoes? Or two? Or three?"

I roll my eyes. "My baby can always buy a new pair of shoes —even if she already has a thousand pairs of Jimmy Choos."

"Funny," she says. "And true. But you know how *those* people are."

"Aren't we those people?"

"I should hope not."

"You're right. We're better," I say.

"Just so you know, I'm doing this for you. I'm not looking forward to this."

I sigh. "I know, Emma."

A hesitant knock sounds on my door. "Come in."

Jane stands in the doorway.

"I'll see you tonight," I say, click the line to a close, and survey Jane. "Did you need something?"

"Hi," she says, tapping her feet nervously. She visibly exhales. "You were great today. Incredible really. The way your hands move. I don't know how you stay so calm."

"Goes with the job," I say with a lift of my shoulders.

"It's almost two. I overheard you mentioning that you were getting a bite to eat. I was thinking I could pick something up for you, bring it back. Something healthy, right?"

"I am hungry, but I don't want anything from the cafeteria. What were you thinking?"

She takes a bold step forward and runs her tongue across her top lip, raises a seductive brow. I'll give credit where credit is due, she's a ballsy little minx. I turn my chair to face her. She's locked the door and is down on her knees before I can say coronary artery bypass graft. I lean back in my chair, my hands behind my neck, and Emma's annoying voice stops ringing in my ears. And, yes, I'm feeling a whole lot less stressed.

TWENTY-EIGHT

EMMA

Saturday, May 18th, 2024

I hang up with Nate, stumble upstairs and plop myself up with plush pillows on our king-sized bed, ordering a new coffee maker that I know how to use from Amazon. I'm in the midst of clicking purchase when FaceTime buzzes. I smile: my girls, the lights of my life.

"Mom! You're back!" my mini-mes say in unison, their almost identical faces fighting for the best position on screen. Ava has freckles smattering her nose like a dot-to-dot pattern. Grace does not. When the girls were five, she'd tried connecting the dots on her twin's face with a Sharpie. It took me hours to clean Ava's face.

I laugh softly at the memory. "I am. You're at Taryn's?"

"Dad said it was OK. We'll be back a little later, after dinner. Taryn's coming too, 'K? Can't wait to hear about your trip."

"Your dad and I have to go to a party at Gordon's tonight," I say with a shudder.

Grace huffs. "Ugh. Fake an illness."

"Wish I could. But I promised your dad I'd make my yearly appearance, and he'd know I was faking." Damn it. I want to see my girls, smother them with sloppy kisses. "But I'll see you in the morning."

"You can count on that," says Ava.

"Tell Taryn I say hi."

"Tell her yourself."

Taryn's face pops onto the screen. She blows me a kiss and I pretend to catch it. "Emma-ma! I've missed you."

I chuckle at her pet name for me. "Missed you too, love-bug."

"Sorry you have to go to the palace of horrors," she says.

"I wish I didn't have to. But I'll put my big girl panties on and get through the evening."

"Good luck with that," says Taryn. "He might try and take them off."

"I'm your almost-mother. Don't talk to me like that."

The three girls roll around laughing at this.

"Hey, quick q, before we bolt. Did you get your results back from AncestorsUnite?" asks Ava, eyeing me from an upside-down angle, her ponytail hanging over the side of the bed.

"I haven't looked yet."

"Well, look," says Grace, her brows raised. "Did Dad do one?"

"I asked him to when I sent mine in. He refused."

"Well, convince him," says Ava. "It's our summer project for school—a closer look at the DNA of twins. Don't forget, it was your idea."

"Oh, they just want to be sure they aren't the postman's daughters," says Taryn with a snort.

I blurt out a laugh. "You are such a brat. Anyway, we have a postwoman." My eyelids flicker. "Girls, can't wait to see you tomorrow morning, but, right now, I need to get some sleep."

"Get some rest, Mom," says Grace.

"Love you," says Ava.

"Emma-ma, you're the best."

"Stay out of my closet," I say with a raise of an eyebrow. "And don't let the dogs upstairs or go into the living room. Their place is in the kitchen."

The line clicks to a close and the girls' laughter fades.

Before I pass out from exhaustion, I grab a bag from my suitcase and stumble over to the guesthouse on the far end of the property. With a sigh, I knock, but nobody from my staff answers the door. And then I remember it's Saturday and they get the weekends off. I open the door and grab a piece of paper, a pen, and tape from the drawer in the side console, and scribble: *With love from Thailand, Em.*

After leaving the gift on a chair in the living room, I stumble back home, my legs feeling like overcooked spaghetti as I trudge along the path to the main house, thinking about my girls and Taryn. Yes, the poor girl has lived a messed-up life, but she has the twins and me, her stand-in mom. I can't believe she's turning twenty in a week. It feels like only yesterday I was in her shoes —young, hopeful, and full of big ideas. Thought I had life all figured out. All of the possibilities seemed endless. And then I'd met Nate and, one stitch at a time, all of my dreams began to unravel, leaving me tangled in a twisted mess. I should have paid closer attention to Irina's warning.

TWENTY-NINE

EMMA

Then: 2009–2019

I tried to avoid Gordon like the plague, but Irina stopped by often.

One day, I took her for a coffee in the neighboring town of Katonah, but the whispers following our every step made me never want to be seen with her in public again. With the way she dressed and carried herself, going unnoticed would never happen. Instead, people steered clear of us and gossiped behind our backs.

Isn't that the whore wife of that porn king?
I heard she's like Skippy—spread and ready.
What's Emma Landon doing with her?
I think they're both wasted. Look at them stumbling.

Although the ladies who lunched sucked up to me at the charity functions I attended, what they said behind my back wasn't much better.

Emma Landon, the little gold digger.
How long do you think her marriage will last?
Why'd he marry her anyway?

While at first I thought there would never be a real connection between us, I soon realized Irina and I had more in common than I'd initially thought. And I liked her. So I'd befriended her privately—meeting up at the house in Pound Ridge at least once a week. Taryn was four, often accompanied by her nanny, Chariya, and driver Ahn. Irina and I would commiserate and laugh, usually over a liquid lunch, namely white wine for me and hard alcohol for her.

"Why'd you marry Gordon?" I'd asked her one day.

She'd frowned, her bright blue eyes losing their luster. "I know he's disgusting. But I didn't have a choice."

"Is it true? Did he—"

"Buy me? Yes. I'll tell you the whole story—but after I'm finished, I don't want to talk about it ever again."

She took in a breath and I motioned for her to carry on.

"One night," she said, a light sparking her eyes, then dimming, "a photographer came into Night Flight, the club in Moscow where I worked as a dancer, and asked to take my picture." She paused. "He told me I could make a lot of money. Be rich. Move to America. Become a star."

She took a swig from her vodka tonic. "He put me in a catalog. And I ended up here, living this wonderful life."

My eyes shot to the side. I heard the sarcasm, the weight her words carried. I was rendered silent for a moment, letting her story sink in. "Why don't you leave him?"

Her eyes flashed with a fear so palpable I could feel it zapping through my bones. "Because he said the only way I'd ever leave him would be in a box. He's a very powerful man. He could do it."

My entire body jolted. "You have to report him."

"I don't think you understand," she said, frowning. She slammed back her drink and shrugged. "Now, show me the plans for your house."

I tried pressing her for more information, but she glared at me. "I've already said enough."

The conversation was over and, true to her word, she never brought it up again. Months later, she was so excited when she learned I was pregnant. "Taryn will have a little sister or brother!"

But I wasn't happy and, by my expression, she knew it.

"What's wrong?" she asked.

"I take birth control pills. I don't know how this happened."

"Nothing is ever 100 percent certain." She shrugged and then winked. "Get ready for your entire world to change."

A thought hit me. Nate knew I wasn't ready to have children. I'd wanted to wait until the house was built, wait until we were more settled in. Supposedly 99 percent effective in preventing pregnancies, I'd been religiously taking the pill, never missing one day. My doctor told me that I fell into that rare 1 percent.

But Nate wanted kids right away. His timeline, his demands, and his needs. It was like I had no control over anything.

Irina almost fainted when I told her I was having twins.

After I found out I was pregnant, I also became closer to Luisa. At first, she was hesitant. It was like trying to approach a feral cat, it took time and patience. Then one day I pulled her to the side.

"He's not here. You can talk to me! I want to talk to you. I can't take this silence anymore."

She cowered and pointed to the ceiling. "What if camera?"

I laughed. "He's against them. Feels like he's being spied on."

A grin spread across her face. She pulled me in for a hug. "I'm so excited for baby." Then, she looked around nervously. "You sure, OK?"

"What Nate doesn't know won't kill him. It's our secret." I

laughed again. "Come with me. I'd like to show you the designs for the guesthouse. Get your input."

And that was the day Luisa became my personal assistant. It gave us a pretext to continue our forbidden friendship. But Luisa always clammed up when I asked her if she liked working for Nate; she'd quickly change the subject, saying she liked working with me. She also didn't believe me when I told her I used to be a maid. In fact, she rolled on the ground in laughter until tears streamed down her cheeks. I never asked her why she found it so funny.

For years, Irina and I kept up our weekly meetings, usually on Saturdays, when I wasn't working. She came to the house party we held when it was finally completed. She took special care of the girls and didn't drink around them. When the twins were old enough, Ava, Grace and Taryn attended extracurricular activities together: riding, tennis, and gymnastics. Irina and I always went along to cheer them on, learning to ignore the whispers behind our backs.

But then our meetings became more sporadic and she stopped coming by the house as often, letting Chariya bring Taryn over. I didn't think much of it at the time because I'd been so busy building my business. And then one day I got the news she would never show up again.

Taryn was fifteen when Irina died from a drug overdose. She'd rung our doorbell in complete hysterics at six in the morning. Nate had told me not to let her in, but I opened the gates anyway and sprinted downstairs. When I opened the front door, I watched her tear down the driveway like a wild horse, her blond hair blowing in the wind. She'd given me a long hug and then brushed past me. "I need to see Ava and Grace. Now. Gordon is sending me to boarding school in Switzerland. I don't have much time. And I have to say goodbye to them."

Stunned, I watched her race up the steps to the girls' rooms. I stood immobile. Ten minutes later, she ran out of the house.

She'd turned at the front gates and looked at me with tears streaming down her cheeks. "Never forget, I love you, Emma-ma."

The girls and I were devastated with the news of Irina's death and Gordon's treatment of Taryn, just shipping her off. Ava and Grace wrote Taryn letters every week. I would receive the occasional postcard from various European cities.

Greetings from Paris! I miss you, Emma-ma! Can't wait to see you!

About a year after Irina died, Chariya, who, like Luisa, had become one of my forbidden confidantes, came over to the house. I couldn't remember the last time I'd seen her. As usual, she wore her crisp uniform, her black hair tied up. "It's so nice to see you."

"I miss you and the girls too." Her lips curved into a smile. Then, she handed over an envelope marked *Emma*. "I'm so sorry," she said, her head hung low. "Mr. Gordon had me clearing out Irina's things and I just found it. I think you should read it alone."

Without another word, she turned away. I watched as she walked down the gravel driveway, then, shaking my head with confusion, I opened the envelope and read the tear-stained letter.

Dear Emma,

He watches. He makes me do things, things against my will. He said he could do whatever he wanted with me because he bought me. But I have the last word. He can't take my dignity, my pride. Not anymore. I will not live in shame.

He will tell you that I died from a drug overdose. But that's not true. I am going to eat a seed I ordered online. I have to get away from him, get away from all of them. They are monsters.

One day, Taryn will learn the true identity of her father. Please don't tell her. I'm so, so sorry. I didn't know you then. Gordon made me have sex with him. He said if I refused, he'd send me back to Russia in a box. Tell Taryn I love her. What I'm doing isn't her fault. And please keep her safe from the monsters. Keep yourself safe too. Promise me.

Much love,

Irina

I've never shared the letter or what I'd learned in it with Nate, keeping it hidden in a place nobody would look—in one of my antique butterfly books. Although occasionally I'd drop hints like, "Taryn looks a lot like you. It's the eyes," and Nate would force out a laugh, telling me I was nuts and needed to get my head checked out.

Looking back, I should have paid closer attention to Irina's warning, to her words.

But I didn't.

Over the next few years, I lied to myself and it became second nature. I told myself that if Nate was Taryn's father, he'd had relations with Irina long before he'd met me. I told myself that Nate wasn't a monster. Until, one day, I saw him for who *he* really was. I realized he'd been gaslighting me for so long I'd lost all sense of myself. But there were leaks in his system. Boom. Fire and gasoline. It was time to light the match and reclaim my life.

THIRTY

EMMA

Saturday, May 18th, 2024: 7:45 p.m.

I eye the security camera on my phone, waiting for Nate's car to drive up. My hair is tied back in a French twist. I'm wearing a touch of makeup and a sexy midnight blue—his favorite color—dress, paired with one of the many diamond necklaces he'd given me with matching earrings and bracelets, and metallic pumps. Candles are lit. I listen for the front door to open, the sounds of heavy footsteps. I remain silent.

"Emma? I'm home," he calls out, his voice gravelly. "Where are you?"

"Upstairs. In the bedroom," I respond.

His designer pants—Incotex khakis—rustle as he makes his approach. He tilts his head to the side, noticing me, the candles. "What's going on?"

"I just missed you. I miss us." I sashay toward him. "When I was gone, I got to thinking about everything. You're my life, my husband, the father of my children—"

I really hope I'm not laying it on too thick. Although Nate

thinks with his penis, he's perceptive. I'm hoping I've tapped into his other brain.

He cradles my neck with his hands, looks me in the eyes. "What did you do today?"

"I napped." I slide my hands down his back. "But I'm awake now."

He groans. "Is my Emma back?"

"She's never gone anywhere. I've always been right here."

"You're an amazing woman, Emma."

"Glad you remember."

His hands slide down my back to my bottom. "I never forgot. Are you thinking what I'm thinking?"

I'm not. I'd rather stab knives into my eyes. But I have to play along. I need something from him, something called unde-niable proof. "Maybe," I whisper. "But, first, the twins were wondering if you'd do your DNA test."

"I knew you were up to something." He takes a step back, a scowl twisting his mouth. He slams the dresser with his fist. My perfume bottles rattle. "You know I'm adamantly against that idea."

"It's for the girls. Their idea, not mine. The DNA of twins. Their summer project." I reach for the kit, strategically placed on the nightstand, and hand it over. "All you have to do is put your lips together and blow. Well, and spit, that is."

"I know who my parents are. I know I'm of Northern European descent, my mother French and German, my father English and Scottish. I'm their father. My dad died from a heart attack. My mom suffered from dementia after the death of my brother. There is absolutely nothing else we need to know."

I remind myself to play it cool. When I want to scream, *Liar, liar! Pants on fire!*

"Maybe. Maybe not," I say, holding out the glass tube. "Just get it over with. Spit."

He grabs the kit from my hand and throws it across the

room, his face turning red. "I'm not doing the damn test. I don't like all the data they keep. Who knows what they'd do with it? With our wealth, we have to be careful."

The glower I'm sending in his direction conveys the meaning my lips are not saying: *if you're so unwilling to take the test, you are hiding something.* But I'm not going to push my luck; I know how Nate's mind works.

"On the subject of being careful, I received a disturbing text message today from an unknown caller. They wrote: *You don't know who your husband is and what he's done.*"

His face blanches. "I hope you didn't respond."

"I couldn't. It came from a blocked number and the text vanished."

His eyebrows raise and he scratches his neck. "Best to ignore it, then. With wealth like ours, we attract all kinds of attention. Just another crazy person trying to get us riled up."

I shake my head from side to side. "Probably."

"And another reason *not* to do a DNA test."

Time to move back into seduction mode: his kryptonite. I twirl and then stop, lifting the dress up a bit so he can see the seams of my thigh-highs and the shape of my legs, which I have Pilates to thank for. "OK, enough about DNA and crazy people. You're right. So, what do you think? Tiffany from Saks brought a couple over this afternoon and I chose this one."

He gives me an appreciative whistle. "You made the right choice. You look stunning."

"This old thing?" I say and his mouth twists into a grin. Such a tool.

"How much damage did you do?"

"The dress? Hervé Léger, I think fifteen hundred." I wiggle my foot. "But, the shoes, oh the shoes. Balenciaga, snake embossed leather. When I saw them, I had to have them."

"And?"

"A little over a thousand." I wink. "I used the black card. Points."

"Right, points." His eyes crinkle into a faint smile. "And worth every penny."

"I may have bought a few things for you." I bat my eyelashes. "I'll give you a hint. Your gift is under my dress. So you'll just have to wait until later."

"I'm already imagining what we'll be doing after the party."

Me too. I know what I'll be doing: sleeping, passed out from exhaustion. "Let's get this night over with so we can get to bed. It's a nice night out and I need some air. After being cooped up on the plane and in the house all day, I thought we'd walk—"

He lightly slaps my ass. "We're taking the McLaren."

I touch up my lipstick and meet his eyes in the mirror. "McLaren?"

"The one delivered to the house while you were gone."

My brows knit together in stunned disbelief. "You bought another car?"

"Wait until you see her, she's a real beauty."

I turn and shoot him a death glare. "Let me get this straight. You could take the time away from your busy life-saving schedule and be here for a delivery but you couldn't pick me up? And you couldn't call Diego to deal with the pond?"

I'm trying to keep my tone level, but my voice comes out like a high-pitched whine and Nate cringes.

"Look, Emma, Diego will be here tomorrow. The fish. The pump. Everything is replaceable."

He just had to say that. Of course, I know exactly what he's getting at.

"Not everything." I smack my lips. "I'm too expensive to replace."

He goes silent for a moment, knowing the prenup he'd manipulated me into signing has screwed both of us over. Unless he wants to lose half of his fortune, he won't divorce me.

And I won't leave him because I'd be left with what I came into the marriage with—practically nothing—and I have the feelings of the girls to consider, because he's threatened to take them from me in the past. And I'm not leaving them with him. I'm sick and tired of dancing this tango. Something's got to give.

His gaze shoots to my gold-heeled feet and he raises a brow. "We're driving. Gravel driveways and stilettos don't mix."

"Fine. We'll take your new toy to Flynn's. Good idea. But this party isn't."

He glances at his watch. "We're already fashionably late."

Like me, Nate has his own custom walk-in closet off the master bedroom, complete with a glass display for his vast collection of watches.

"Which one are you wearing?"

"The Patek Philippe—Grand Complications."

"Fitting," I say.

He sighs. "Life is really simple, so don't insist on making it complicated—"

"OK, Confucius, I need five more minutes," I say, shuffling to the bathroom. "Just a couple of finishing touches."

Nate watches me as I fumble through the cabinets, finding what I need to get me through the night. I open the bottle of Xanax, placing the little balm for my nervous system in my hand. As I swallow the pill down, I think about his refusal to take the DNA test, the way he paled. I'm thinking about everything.

I paste on a smile, pulling on a pair of elbow-length gloves that match my dress. "I just need to grab my purse. Let's get this night over with."

Gordon's party is in full swing when we arrive. Servers pass cocktails on trays, a buffet is set up with the works—lobster, crab, and shrimp, among other offerings. A string quartet in the corner of the great room plays Rachmaninoff's Number 2. You'd think Gordon Flynn had an ounce of class. Even though tonight is an introduction to Congresswoman Claire Woodbridge, who just announced her candidacy for governor, I know better.

"I see he hasn't redecorated," I whisper to Nate. "I still love all the gold."

"Be nice," says Nate. "I know you hate the gold."

I lift my hand to wave to Chariya and Ahn. Honestly, it's nice to see two friendly faces in this sea of social sycophants. I want to tell them about my trip.

"We're not here to fraternize with the servants." Nate glowers and latches onto my wrist.

"Servants? Chariya is a house manager."

"Same thing," he says.

As he leads me away, I shoot Chariya an apologetic look.

Ben and Becks make a beeline in our direction and I don't bother masking the very audible groan of abhorrence escaping my throat. Becks is wearing a flowing leopard-print dress in hues of brown, black and white that would look fabulous on somebody much younger, considering the cutouts below her breasts and the waist.

"Somebody needs a stylist," I mumble.

"Jesus, Emma. Couldn't you have checked your bad attitude at the front door? Let's enjoy this evening."

"Oh, I will," I say, smirking. "And I'm looking forward to it."

By his stance, I know my words give him pause. Or maybe it's the look in my eyes.

Ben gives Nate a friendly punch on the shoulder. "Glad you could make it, buddy."

"As if I'd miss free cocktails and food!"

"Har-har-har."

Becks kisses us both on the cheeks. "Tonight Flynn's hosting an apéro dînatoire. These kind of cocktail parties are all the rage in France."

"How sophisticated," I say with a slight lift of my brows. Nate jabs me in the side with his elbow.

He whispers, "Why can't you behave?"

Becks locks her gaze onto mine. "We haven't seen you in forever—"

"I believe we saw each other at the Met Gala," I say. "Just last year."

"But not at the Concorso d'Eleganza Villa d'Este. Plus, you've declined our invites to go out to dinner or come over to our house when we're practically neighbors. I mean, Katonah isn't that far away and you wouldn't be slumming it," says Becks with a caustic huff. "I was beginning to think you thought you were too good for us."

You think?

"Oh, don't be silly." My smile is so plastered on it might crack. "I've been busy with all the fundraisers for the hospital, a bit of charity work, my business, and raising the girls. You know how it is."

"Aren't Ava and Grace turning fifteen in December?" asks Becks, her chin lifted, an eyebrow raised.

"They are," I say, squaring my shoulders. "But a mother's work is never done."

"I wouldn't know," says Becks. "Ah, but there is more to life than kids, and we're enjoying every moment of it." I meet Becks's satisfied grin and she continues, "What's it like being a helicopter mom?"

Touché, Becks.

"What can I say? There's always a flight to catch."

"Well, I'm glad I fly private. Apparently, we missed you when we were in Thailand. Although we couldn't take you back, we offered to take you there. I mean, flying with the masses, even in first class, isn't all that classy, is it?"

I tilt my head to the side. Like I want to spend time with

them? No thank you. "I was traveling for work and needed the write-off for my business."

Ben nudges Nate in the side with his elbow. "Interesting standoff," he says.

"No wonder we don't do dinners," Nate says, watching me like a hawk.

"How's the gallery doing?" I ask, and Nate seems to relax with the change of subject.

"Oh, the 44," says Becks with a slight lift of her shoulders. "I closed it down last year, diversified my offerings. Like you, I only work with private clients now, some of them celebrities too."

Just then, Gordon Flynn, the man of the hour, hobbles over, his cane tapping the floor. He slaps Ben and Nate on the back. "Ladies, gentlemen, glad you could come tonight." He winks and then focuses on me. "Nice to see you, my dear. For once."

Becks eyes Ben. "Why don't you and I head to the buffet?"

As they saunter into the crowd, Nate places his hand on my back and I shake it off. "I spoke with Taryn tonight," I say.

Gordon's posture straightens. "I haven't spoken to that ungrateful brat in years."

"What a great relationship you have with your daughter," I mumble, rolling my eyes.

"For fuck's sake, Emma," Nate hisses.

He really should have left me home instead of worrying about keeping up appearances.

"Oh, Emma, all she cares about is money. She took her trust fund and ran. She cut me out of her life," says Gordon with a hacking laugh. "So I cut her out."

A young woman wearing a gold sequined dress rounds the corner. For a second, she meets my eyes, shares an odd look as if we know one another, and then she sashays to the buffet. She's breathtaking—tall with long, silky blond hair and curves in all the right places. Irina 2.0. Nate's practically drooling, eyes bugging out like that wolf in the cartoon. Simmer down, boy.

I face Gordon and snort. "Taryn has a sister?"

Gordon coughs out a laugh. "No, silly woman; Veronyka and I are getting married in a couple of weeks."

Even if I could say anything, I don't get a chance to because Claire Woodbridge joins our little group. "Claire, this is Emma Landon. I believe I told you about her," he says, narrowing his eyes.

Claire juts out her chin, shooting Gordon a look I can't quite fathom. "Oh, yes, Emma. I've been looking forward to meeting you. I just started a book club to keep my mind off of politics. I've heard you're a reader—I was hoping you'd like to join. We're reading *White Oleander* by Janet Fitch now. Have you read it?"

I have no clue where this conversation is headed, but I decide to roll with it.

"I have—years ago when it came it out in 1999," I say, knowing my tone edges on superiority. "One of the benefits of having a mom who insisted I read a book a week from the age of thirteen was being forced to go to the library." I laugh softly with remembrance. Nate blows out a sigh of relief until I open my mouth again. "My true awakening came when I read Margaret Atwood's *The Handmaid's Tale* and its core message revolving around the expectations for women to be subservient and voiceless to men of power—"

"Nothing wrong with men in power," begins Gordon.

Nate cuts me off before I can throw in one of my cutting quips. "She's always been an avid reader."

"I am. And I can speak for myself," I say, gripping his hand tightly, my nails slightly digging into the flesh of his palm. "I tend to be drawn to flawed characters—"

By his expression, Nate knows I'm referring to him.

"Which is the reason why I bought Emma a signed first

edition of *The Fountainhead*." He laughs. "A bargain, and in mint condition, it only set me back five thousand dollars—"

"I loved that book," says Claire. "There are those who think for themselves and those who allow others to dominate their lives—one of the themes Ayn Rand explored in her controversial novel, yes?"

I lock my gaze onto Nate's. "Yes. Also conformity, how others desire prestige and approval from others."

Nate's spine goes rigid and he clenches his jaw.

"You should really come to our next meeting," says Claire. "I think you'd enjoy the discussion. It's at my house in Scarsdale."

My eyes dart back and forth, trying to figure out how to get out of this evening, let alone a book club invitation. "I'm sorry, but I don't think I'll have time. I'm working on a really big project, but thanks for asking."

At least I wasn't rude. Score for Emma—the first of the night.

Claire smiles. "I understand. I saw the article about you in *Hamptons Life*. Very impressive."

"Thank you."

"I'd really like your advice on something I want to do with my kitchen."

I give a fake laugh as Claire ushers me away, looking over my shoulder and shooting Nate a death glare. Gordon leads Nate onto the terrace, grabbing a couple of their crew along the way—Nate, the doctor, Harold Katz the lawyer, and Jeff Cox, the owner of a tech company, who, after a legal battle, had to change the name of his hockey team from the Tomahawks to the Sentinels. They still call him Chief and Nate's always been jealous of his last name. Ben and Becks meander outside to join them.

I stop mid-step, wondering what this crew is up to—probably no good. "Claire, I'm sorry. I just got back from Thailand

and I really don't have the mental bandwidth to talk about work tonight."

"I understand." She takes a sip of her champagne. "This is a party for me and I should mingle with the guests. I'll get your contact information from Gordon."

My eyes shoot to the terrace. "Perfect," I respond, shifting my weight. "I'm sure our paths will cross again."

"Oh, they will. I've got a big project for you. Big budget too." She winks and turns on a heel to sashay into the crowd.

I watch her meander into the dining room and I slip back into the party to eavesdrop on Nate's conversation. I position myself, hiding between the folds of a horrendous red velvet curtain in front of an open window—no sudden movements, just listening. Watching.

Nate whistles through his teeth. "Congratulations on your upcoming nuptials."

Gordon takes a healthy swig of his drink and swallows. "Veronyka is not my fiancée. I saw how your wife was looking at me with disgust. I only said that to get under Emma's skin."

I can feel my anger rising. I'm so over the mind games these people play.

"You dirty bastard." Nate chuckles. "She reminds me of Irina. Who is she?"

Gordon shrugs. "Hired help. Ben and Becks met her at one of those parties they go to in the city. Her mother used to work for me—I brought her over from Russia a few years after Irina. She's dead now. A junkie, died from a heroin overdose on set. I forget her name." He licks his fat lips. "But Veronyka is still alive and kicking. And she puts on a good show."

"That she does," says Becks with a sigh. "But she won't let anybody touch her. And she won't do her act live."

"She's a webcam girl," says Ben.

Nate scratches his chin. "I'm not complaining, but why is she here tonight?"

"Ahhh, a little eye candy never hurt anybody." Gordon hacks. "And people expect surprises from me."

Chariya steps onto the deck with a silver tray. "Chocolate truffle from Belgium?" she asks. "Mr. Gordon ordered the very best."

Save for Becks and Nate, they all take one. "I'm allergic to chocolate," says Becks, holding up a dismissive hand.

Ben palms two with one hand, patting his belly with the other. "I'm not."

Chariya bows her head and leaves through the glass doors, noticing me. I raise my index finger to my lips. She winks and heads into the crowd.

"Gents, lady," Flynn begins, handing out cigars. "As you know, I sold off most of my businesses a few years ago, but I've been working on bringing one of them back to life—a resuscitation of sorts." He pulls out an 18-karat white gold S. T. Dupont lighter encrusted with diamonds from his pocket and sets the tips of the cigars ablaze. "You'll all want in."

"A seventy-thousand-dollar lighter isn't the best investment," says Jeff, blowing out a puff of smoke.

A thick cloud of swirling gray plumes floats in my direction and I have to hold both hands over my mouth to keep from coughing.

"More like eighty, but who cares about a few thousand, Chief, when you're as rich as us?" He puffs on his cigar, blowing out smoke rings. He winks. "You know what I'm talking about. In with the new, out with the old."

"I don't know," says Nate. "Emma received a cryptic text today. Could be a risk."

"What did it say?" asks Becks.

"You don't know who your husband is and what he's done."

Ben guffaws. "There's nothing to worry about. Somebody is fucking with you."

"Still," says Nate. "Maybe we should lie low for now."

Gordon pipes in. "No, Nate, Ben's right. Somebody is fucking with you and we'll find out who it is, although it doesn't matter. We're untouchable." He clears his throat. "It's all set. The little beasts Becks has been collecting are being stored in the warehouse—some really beautiful cats from India and Thailand." He hacks up a cough. "We'll meet in the grotto on Friday night. You all get first choice." Gordon shakes his head with a perfunctory nod. "This is a solid investment and we'll all benefit from it—"

It's then that I decide to round the corner.

Gordon goes quiet as I tap Nate on the back. He looks over his shoulder, startled. "Emma! For crying out loud, you're like a ninja, the way you're always sneaking up on me—"

By the look in his eyes, he's wondering how much of the conversation I've overheard. I'm just going to play it cool. I know enough.

"There you are," I say nonchalantly, to throw him off. "What are you investing in?"

He blinks. "Horses."

Liar. In my gut, I know whatever they're investing in isn't legal—each one of them shadier than the next. My bet would have been placed on tigers or maybe leopards. The idiots. I know Nate big-game hunts with his crew of derelicts. The pictures of them standing over their "trophies"—lions, rhinos, buffalo, and elephants—hang on the paneled walls in Nate's study and make me sick. Murdering scum, they'd stayed in a luxury resort, paid a fortune to kill animals who were basically brought out to them while they smoked cigars and drank bourbon, and then had their picture taken after they'd shot them at point-blank range. They have zero respect for life, Becks included. Maybe Nate will get arrested? Or maybe a leopard will claw Becks's eyes out, thinking she's a predator in her ill-fitting dress? These thoughts curve my mouth into a wicked smile and then I frown. Because I don't gamble. And they were not talking about cats or horses.

I spit out a laugh. "You don't like horses. Bad investment."

"Not if you pick the winning breeders," says Ben with a shrug.

My disgusted gaze snaps from Ben, to Nate, and then to the dining room. My eyes widen with horror. I point, my entire body trembling, the past just sucker-punching me in the gut. "What the hell are they doing here?"

"Who?" asks Ben.

"The Clarks," I spit out, slamming back my glass of champagne.

"I invited them," says Gordon. "Just moved back to town a couple of months ago." He puffs on his cigar, blows the smoke in my face. His eyes twinkle. "Why? Do you have an issue with them?"

By the expression on my face, he knows I do. He and Nate probably planned this onslaught to drive me to the brink of insanity. Well, it worked. I can't keep my cool. My vision goes hazy. I throw my now empty glass of champagne over the terrace.

I clench my fists. "Yes, I have a huge issue with them."

"Don't cause a scene," says Nate as I snag another glass of champagne from one of the hired servers, downing it.

I don't respond to Nate, just move forward like a feral cat about to pounce on their prey, the past hitting me in the stomach like a sledgehammer, visions coming at me in waves.

THIRTY-ONE

EMMA

Then: August 22nd, 2018

The twins were nearly nine years old.

Taryn, as she'd been prone to do, had slept over and I was in the midst of preparing blueberry pancakes—the only meal I know how to cook without it ending in disaster—when somebody called the house. With my hands covered in batter, I'd put the call on speakerphone, not bothering to look at caller ID. "Landon residence."

"Emma? It's David Clark," he'd hissed, his voice cold and stony.

Odd. Audrey, his wife, was my connection to his family and a good friend. David had never called me, only Nate, mostly to plan golf outings at the club.

"Oh, hiya, neighbor. Can I ring you right back? I'm making the girls break—"

"This won't take long," he said, and then he screamed, "Tell your goddamn bastard of a husband to stop fucking my wife."

"I don't know what you're talking about," I replied, and then dropped the bowl of batter on the floor, the glass shattering.

Quick as lightning striking, I picked up the receiver and took the call off speaker so the girls couldn't hear any more. In the process, I stepped on a shard of glass, cutting my foot.

"They've been having an affair for months. I caught him sneaking out of the pool house last night. I suggest you deal with Nate before I kill him."

Click. The line went dead. I dropped to the floor, panting. As I picked the spiky shard out of my heel, the blood oozing between my fingers, Taryn stooped down next to me, a serious expression on her face. "That looks bad. Do you have a first aid kit?"

Not one for my heart.

"Under the sink," I said, and Taryn nodded.

After grabbing the kit and handing it over to me, Taryn grabbed a broom and dustpan to clean up the mess.

"I guess we're having cereal," she'd said with a shrug. "I don't mind."

"What's fucking?" asked Ava.

"You know, that birds and the bees stuff they're teaching you at school," said Taryn. She placed a box of Cheerios on the table. "The sex stuff. How a man and a woman make babies—"

"Oh," said Ava.

My heart almost stopped. "Don't you dare tell them anything more," I said, pointing a shaky finger at Taryn.

"Ew, gross," said Grace. "Why would Daddy want a baby with *her*?"

Taryn shrugged. "Sometimes people have sex because it feels good."

My hands flew to my face. "Taryn Elizabeth Flynn! Not another word! I mean it!"

I remembered all the times we'd had the Clarks over for dinner, or when we went to their place, drinking champagne and eating decadent meals or playing card games. The last time we'd seen them was a couple of months ago. I should have picked up on the affair, the sexual tension, the way she would lean over squeezing her breasts together, the way she'd laugh and touch Nate's hand, the way she'd drop something, bend over, and wink.

All the signs were there. I just hadn't picked up on these not-so-silent flirtations.

Anger raged inside of me. A raw nerve snapped. I threw on my rubber boots and raced out the front door in my silk pajamas, tearing down the driveway straight to the Clark house. When I banged on the door, Audrey opened it, her eyes red. "I guess he really did call you," she said with a sniff.

I clenched my teeth so hard my jaw hurt. "He did."

"I-I-It didn't mean anything," she stuttered. "It was just sex. I'm sorry. I'm so, so sorry."

"Sex with *my* husband," I hissed. "I thought you were my friend."

How many times had she popped over after the surgery, the birth of the girls, bringing me prepared meals or asking if I needed anything? How long had I been blind? Was I always blind?

"I am. I was," she began.

"Some friend." I slapped her. Hard. Damn, did it feel good. "Stay away from him. Stay away from me."

She recoiled. "Don't worry about that. David and I are going to try to work things out. We're talking about moving—for a fresh start."

"I hope you find a nice spot in hell," I spat. "Where you belong."

I didn't realize until I turned around ready to storm back home that the girls had followed me. Ava, Grace, and Taryn stood on the gravel drive with their mouths agape. The twins linked their arms into mine and we stomped down the road, none of us saying a word.

After sending Taryn back to her place and the girls to their rooms, I called Nate. "I know about Audrey. Don't bother coming home," I hissed.

"Let me explain—"

"There's nothing to explain."

"Emma, I was weak. I gave in to temptation. You ignore me. We haven't had sex in over six months." His voice was cool and calm. "It's over with her."

"And it's over with us. I want a divorce," I said breathlessly.

"We can get through this. You can't just throw ten years of marriage down the drain without trying to work things out—"

But I could. I'd never trust him again.

"Don't you dare put this on me."

"Don't forget," he said, spitting out the words. "You signed a very detailed prenuptial agreement."

"Don't forget about the cheating clause—"

"It would be my word against yours."

"David Clark—"

"Would never go against me," he said with a chilling laugh. "I have something on him—something he would never want revealed. You'd lose everything, Emma, including the girls. After all, you didn't come into this marriage with them—"

"Then divorce me!"

"And give you eight million? And the house? I don't think so." He snarled. "Think about it, Emma."

My breath grew ragged. I could feel the blood drain from my face.

"Don't come home tonight. Stay at the loft."

"Call me when you get your head together," he said.

A migraine set in. Sure, my design business was doing well enough, but what about the girls? How would this affect them? Nate would deliver on the promise of taking them away from me—not because he wanted to take care of them but because he needed to win. Plus, I had my parents to consider—their house, my dad's medical bills, not to mention my staff.

He came back home three days later, smelling of cheap perfume. "Ready to divorce me?" he asked. "Or do you need some time to think about it?"

I clenched my teeth and glared at him. No, I needed time to come up with a plan to leave him. For now, I had to play the role of the doting wife. I tilted my head to the side and smiled. "Divorce? Don't be silly. I'm sorry I overreacted. To everything. I understand."

He grinned, nodded. "I'm glad you know your place. Let's head upstairs."

I knew his place; he belonged in prison.

THIRTY-TWO

EMMA

Saturday, May 18th, 2024

I swerve through the crowd, stumble up to the bar and order a double vodka—straight up, no ice. My blood is running cold enough to chill every drink in the room. Looking over my shoulder, I slam back the shot, meeting Nate's angry glare. He storms up behind me, his breath ragged.

"Stop acting crazy," he hisses and clasps his hand onto my wrist.

"Crazy? Oh, oh, oh, that's a good one. You calling me crazy. You had an affair with that woman. A friend of mine! And the girls know about it." I break from his grip and point toward Audrey and then make the crazy motion, circling my finger at the side of my head. "Now that's beyond insane!"

Nate stands in stunned silence, clenching his fists. I turn my back on him and wave the bartender over. "Hey there, I need something stronger than vodka. What else have you got?"

"Tequila?" he says. "Patrón."

"Make it a triple," I growl with a wicked smile.

Nate tries to take the drink from my hand, but before he

can, I chug the tequila in one gulp and then race over to the string quartet, telling them to cut the music. More than a couple of people share supremely confused glances.

"It's time for a little fun. Who's up for charades!" I exclaim.

Nate meets my eyes in challenge. He mouths, "Stop causing a fucking scene."

Becks says, "Fantastic idea to liven up the night! You know we all love games, don't we? Ladies and gentlemen, our dear friend, Emma Landon."

Applause.

I jump up onto the coffee table before anyone can stop me and lift up one hand, cranking the other one.

"Movie," echoes from every corner of the room.

I nod vigorously while holding three fingers up.

"Three words."

A thumbs up. I let out a loud woot and continue, holding up one finger, and then pinching my thumb and index finger together. I squint as the guesses roll in. Getting a little overly-excited with my performance, I stumble, almost falling off the table. Thankfully, it's wood, not glass.

"First word."

"Little word."

"The."

"By."

"A."

I woot even louder. "Yes! You're getting there!" Nate covers his eyes with one hand. This is so on. I hold up three fingers, then two.

"Third word. Two syllables."

I nod like a maniac and stab the air.

"Slasher."

I shake my head no, my lips in a pout, and continue stab-bing, shifting my gaze onto Nate and Audrey's eyes.

"Murder."

"*A Perfect Murder*," somebody yells.

My lips curve into a wicked smile. "You got it and I want to go again."

Becks hunches over in laughter. "Why not? You're excellent at this."

I meet Nate's eyes. He's clenching his jaw and shaking his head with anger as I go through the motions again. Another movie. Three words. I blink, squeeze my eyes shut, cover my face with my hands, and bring my arms down to my sides, repeating the sequence. Nate knows the film; it's one of his favorites. He races over to me as somebody in the crowd proclaims, "*Eyes Wide Shut.*"

"Good call," I say with another wicked grin.

Applause.

Nate grabs my arm, pulling me down from the coffee table, latching tight, "Great performance."

"And, funny, because my eyes are finally wide open now."

"Watch your step."

"Watch yours," I say. "I'm going home. Have fun with your twisted friends."

I rip my arm from his grip and pick up my pace, slamming hard into Audrey on the way out. Audrey blinks and rubs her arm, her expression horrified.

When I wake up in the morning, I realize Nate's side of the bed hasn't been slept in. Although we don't have sex, he prefers the master bedroom. Or maybe the hope I'll cave in to his needs. He's probably taken cover in one of the guest rooms or maybe he stayed out all night. But no matter what he's dealing with—even me—he has his morning routine:

- Make a wheatgrass smoothie. Put it in the fridge. Clean up.

- Feed the dogs/let the dogs out in their run.
- Swim for a half an hour (pool heated to 80 degrees, year-round).
- Top his now perfectly cold smoothie with granola and chia seeds and eat.
- Workout in the state-of-the-art gym.
- Walk/run the beasts.
- Shower.

He's getting out of the shower when I wander into the bathroom, passing by the mirror. A fake eyelash sticks to my cheek. Smudged eyeliner surrounds my eyes like a psychotic raccoon. My hair is snarled and matted. Whatever. I'll clean myself up later. I lift up my nightgown, sit on the toilet and pee. Nate towels off and grimaces. "What?" I huff. "We've been married for fifteen years, you've seen and heard worse."

"I'm glad you're just peeing," he says and then mumbles, "Disgusting."

I wipe and then flush. Nate takes a step back and heads into the closet, grabbing one of his many overnight bags. I stand in the doorway. "Where are you going?"

"Do you know what you did last night?"

I lift my shoulders into a shrug. "I went to a party I didn't want to be at and then I went home."

"That's not all you did," he growls, and I flinch. "I don't want to talk to you. In fact, I can't even look at you. I'm staying at the loft."

"Good for you," I say with a grunt and flop back onto my bed.

Before he leaves, he says, "You're not right in the head. I'm thinking of having you committed. And you know I can do it."

I stare at the ceiling and huff out a caustic laugh. "Is that a threat?"

"No, it's a promise."

He stomps out of the bedroom, and the door slams behind him.

THIRTY-THREE

EMMA

Sunday, May 19th, 2024

My hangover beats me on the head with an iron pan. Hair of the dog? Why, yes please and thank you very much. I stumble downstairs to the kitchen and set to making a Bloody Mary with all of the fixings—celery, hot peppers, cornichons, bar onions, and lots of spices. I'm also in the mood for something else.

"Alexa! Bloody Mary! Lady Gaga."

"Bloody Mary. Lady Gaga," Alexa voice chimes in and the song clicks on.

Finally, she gets something right. As I chop, chop, chop, in my head, head, head, I'm wishing my monster of a husband dead, dead, dead. And I'm really in a zone until I hear their voices.

"Mommy!"

"What in the world are you doing?"

"Uh, chopping," I say with a grimace. "Alexa! Off!"

I turn to face Grace and Ava, in matching silk shorty-pajamas, black with roses on them, and hoodies, their chestnut hair piled on top of their heads in messy buns, and

Taryn, dressed the same way, but looking like she's just stepped out of a Drybar salon, her long, blond hair sleek and smooth.

It isn't fair for people to just wake up like that.

"You spent the night?" I ask, smoothing out my hair.

"Uh, yeah, the girls told you I was and that I was bringing them back home." She grimaces. "You look a bit rough around the edges."

A wave of nausea rolls into my gut like high tide. I wipe the muck from the corners of my mouth. "Feeling it too."

The girls wrap me in hugs smelling of expensive perfume, Tom Ford Fucking Fabulous (mine) and these girls have seemingly bathed in it. Taryn also reeks of stale cigarettes (definitely not mine). Or is it pot? My nose twitches. I take a step back. "Have you been smoking?"

Taryn lifts her shoulders. "I picked up the habit in Europe. Don't worry. I didn't smoke in the house." She eyes the twins. "Or in front of them. I'm a very good influence."

"A good influence?" I begin, ready to lay into her, but the dogs barrel into the kitchen, nearly knocking me over. I rub my throbbing temples and turn to open the doors to the terrace, letting the two enormous furballs outside. Their barks resound with excitement as they race down the steps, as if to say *free at last*. They better steer clear of my garden.

"Tell me they didn't sleep upstairs—"

My answer comes with three guilty smirks and this is when I notice the girls are wearing my signature shade of lipstick, Rouge Allure Ink, color choquant. I tap my lips and then point to the smudged glasses in the kitchen sink. "Busted. The color lasts for eight hours."

"You're our idol—stylish and sophisticated," says Taryn, batting her eyelashes.

"That's a lie if ever I've heard one," I snort.

"How was Thailand?" asks Ava, changing the subject.

My head spins. I point to the Bloody Mary mix. "Can I get myself sorted out first?"

"You shouldn't do that," says Taryn.

"What? Drink in the morning? Or drink in front of the girls. Rough night. I'm really hurting—"

"No, frown." Taryn rubs her index and middle fingers between her eyes. "You're getting deep crevices. Number eleven. Botox," says Taryn with a perfunctory nod. "I'm a huge fan."

"You're only nineteen," I say.

"It's preventative," says Taryn with a shrug. "And girls my age, especially in my business, start early—"

"Well, I guess I'm a lost cause."

"You're gorgeous, Emma-*ma*," she replies, enunciating the ma, her pet name for me, "but it's never too late for a little help." She pinches her fingers together. "Just a little bit."

Honest young girls can be so brutal sometimes.

I glare at her. "The only help I need right now is a hangover cure."

"On it," says Taryn with a wink, and I shoot her a chiding look, one eyebrow raised. "What? The drinking age in Europe is eighteen. And I'm turning twenty in a week. I'm almost legal."

"We're in America," I say.

She shrugs. "I'm not having one. I'm making one for you." She turns and sets to mixing my drink. "But you only get one, right? It's vodka."

My eyes go wide. How does she know this?

"Abby told me all about your intolerance to hard alcohol. That karaoke night? Hilarious."

I make a mental note to talk to my friend about what she shares about me. A few minutes later and with a perfectly spiced drink in my hand, the girls join me at the table in the atrium.

"Tell us about your trip," says Grace.

I open up my iPad and flick through pictures, landing on a carved wooden day bed with silk cushions. "Just look at the craftsmanship. Isn't this beautiful!"

I tap the screen.

"Boring," says Grace with an exaggerated yawn. "It's furniture. Where are the elephants? The monkeys? The beaches?"

"It was a work trip, not a vacation—"

"Did JenX go with you?" asks Ava.

"No, she's on tour. I sent her photos of my finds."

"Can we get tickets to her next concert? Backstage?"

"I'll see what I can do."

"You said you could and you would." Grace pouts. "Plus, you also promised to take us somewhere for our break in March. And you didn't."

"Sorry, I forget a lot of things lately. Must be my *old* age."

"Old is a state of mind," says Taryn with a pop of her lips. "And you look like you're in early thirties—not approaching the big four-uh-oh."

"Gee, thanks," I say with a mock glare, and then I remember Taryn was really excited I'd be in Thailand. She was traveling to Kerala, India and then on to Phuket but it was too difficult to meet up due to scheduling conflicts. "How was your shoot?"

She grins, flashing her award-winning smile. "Amazing! They think I might get the cover."

"As you should," I say. "I'm proud of you."

"Should we tell her now or later?" Grace whispers to Ava.

"I don't know. She may flip out," says Ava.

Motherly worry courses through my veins. Neither Grace nor Ava will meet my eyes. "Tell me what?"

Grace holds up her phone. "Mom, you've gone viral on Instagram and TikTok."

My eyes lock onto the screen. I'm doing some strange kind of movement, stabbing the air and look like a deranged psychopath. I squeeze my eyes shut and flashes of the evening come back to me, but I can't remember everything. With dread, I look back at the screen. The original poster is Becks Stark and the vindictive hag tagged me: *Perfectly Poised Emma Landon Has Lost Her Shit*. This is so not good for business. I scroll through some of the comments.

Too bad she didn't have a real knife.
Ha! She's acting out A Perfect Murder!
Emma Landon is headed for the loony bin.

"It'll blow over and the comments aren't that bad," says Taryn. "Don't worry about it."

"But I am worried."

"Do you know how you got home?" asks Taryn.

"I guess I walked—"

"No, Chariya called me this morning. Ahn saw you stumbling and he drove you."

I sigh and hand Grace her phone back. "Please tell Ahn thanks the next time you speak to him."

"What made you snap like that?" asks Taryn.

I probably shouldn't tell the girls, but they know what happened because they were witnesses to my meltdown. "The Clarks were at the party last night and I got a little bit out of control." I take a swig from my drink. "Hence, the hangover remedy. Your father is furious with me."

My statement is followed by a long silence.

"Are you girls mad at me too?"

"No," says Grace. "It's not that." She lifts her chin up, meeting my eyes. "It's Dad. We all think you need to divorce him. We've felt that way since we were nine. We saw what his affair did to you, not to mention what it did to us."

Ava stands up and slams her fists on her thighs like I do when I'm angry. "Why didn't you leave him?"

I press my fingers to my temples. "I wanted to, but I couldn't."

"Why?"

I'm not going to make my girls feel guilty, telling them I'd stayed married to a monster for them. "It's complicated."

Grace exhales a deep breath. "There's something else we need to tell you. It's pretty shocking."

I set my glass down and raise my hands in the air. "Nothing can shock me anymore."

Ava stomps her foot. "We hate Dad."

"We do," says Grace.

I look up, my jaw clenched. "Really? You hate him? Your own father?"

"It's not such a far-fetched concept," says Taryn, tilting her head to the side.

I shudder. "Girls, tell me what's on your mind."

"We know he always wanted a son to carry on his legacy. We overheard him saying that to Ben on the phone," Grace mumbles, her forehead creasing. "He said he was disappointed in his girls, that we were little spoiled brats and he couldn't wait to marry us off to the highest bidder when we were older. Something about Saudi princes."

"And then he laughed," spits out Ava. "Yeah, very funny, Dad."

My girls must have been destroyed. I can't believe Nate would even make a joke like that. Something is seriously wrong with his wiring. Panic blooms in my chest and I can feel it spreading to my heart and my chest like a deadly virus.

"I would never let that happen," I hiss. "Over my dead body."

The doorbell chimes, startling all of us. I almost drop my glass. "Sugar. I completely forgot Diego was coming today. He's fixing the pump for the pond and bringing new koi. The spotted ones—"

"We'll deal with Diego," says Taryn, raising a brow. "You should really get yourself cleaned up, maybe come up with a plan?"

"Yeah, Mom," says Ava. "You've got to get away from him."

What a role reversal. Over the years, I'm usually the one wiping away the girls' tears—all the scraped knees and bumps and bruises. The girls leave the kitchen and for a moment, I sit immobile, staring blankly at the pond.

Leopards. Spots.

Liars. Cheaters.

Monsters. Fiends.

Funny how life works. Now, that I know the girls despise their father I'm ready to attack, without one ounce of regret.

THIRTY-FOUR

EMMA

Sunday, May 19th, 2024

As Taryn and the girls deal with Diego and the pond, I pace in the master bedroom, staring out at the water thinking about the color of lies again. What colors are mine? Shades of gray, the kind told to protect rather than to harm? I've lied to protect my girls—all three of them. I've lied to protect myself. I've lied to protect my staff, my parents. I want to call my parents to tell them of my plans to divorce Nate, but I'm going to wait until the process is started. However, there is one other person I know who wasn't charmed by the behemoth of lies, deception, and manipulation, so I call her.

"Honey Bunch! I was just thinking about you," says Abby. "I just—"

"I need you. It's a full-on red phone emergency. Can you come over?"

She goes silent for a moment. "Will *he* be there?"

I chuckle. She's hated him from the get-go and refuses to come over if Nate's home. She even warned me not to marry him. I should have listened to her. Then again, I wouldn't have the girls. At least something good came out of the darkness of my marriage to Nate. "No, and I'm getting rid of him for real this time."

She lets out a long happy squeal and I have to hold the phone away from my ear. "Please, tell me you're not the girl who cried wolf. I can't go through that drama again—"

"I'm dead serious. The serial cheater that is Nate threatened to have me committed. And the girls overheard him say he wanted to marry them off to the highest bidder."

"What?"

"You heard me."

"Fuck, that's messed up," she finally says. "Still, I can't believe you finally did it."

"Did what? I haven't done anything yet, which is why I need your advice."

"You finally got your head out of your ass!" exclaims Abby in between snorts. "I'm bringing a bottle of champagne. I'll be there in fifteen minutes. Maybe less if I speed—"

Abby does have a lead foot. She'll probably be here in five minutes. I head into the bathroom to take a shower, walking by the mirror on the way. I grimace. Why didn't the girls tell me I looked like an extra in a horror film? And then I remind myself it doesn't matter. I can clean myself up, wash the grime off my face, but Nate will always be a dirty rotten bastard.

Like a hurricane, Abby enters the foyer, knocking into one of my orchids on the console. We grin at one another. "For a woman on the verge of a divorce, you're looking good," she says, gripping me in the tightest of hugs.

"I showered before you came over." I curtsy. "You're welcome and, as usual, you look amazing."

I scan her outfit—a flowing skirt Stevie Nicks would be jealous of matched with a lace-up top. I've always referred to her personal tastes as artist-chic-bohemian but her style has transformed into something more sophisticated. She still wears her big hoop earrings. Her red hair is occasionally unruly. She's rock star chic.

"Every time I see you, you get younger," I continue.

"What can I say? I still have the heart of a twenty-year-old."

"A very elegant twenty-year-old."

"Stop kissing my ass, Emma." She kisses my cheek and then puffs out a laugh. "No, keep on at it. I like it."

Taryn, Ava, and Grace saunter down the stairs. "Aunty A! You're here!"

Abby grins. "I am and I need some love."

After embracing the girls, Abby holds up a magnum. "And I really hope we're celebrating the end to a new beginning, Honey Bunch."

"We sure are, Sugar Pie," I say and we share a knowing grin.

We belt out the lyrics of the Four Tops "Can't Help Myself," just like we did together so many years ago when we were roommates, pointing fingers at one another and dancing. Our voices echo off the walls.

Ava puts her fingers in her ears. "Stop. Just stop. Neither of you can sing or dance."

"And neither can either of you," I say, looking over my shoulder. "What? You don't think I've heard you singing Britney and Taylor Swift in your rooms? Or seen you dancing?"

Abby cackles out a laugh. "Don't forget, girls, your mom and I were once young too."

I high-five her. "Come on. Let's head into the kitchen."

And to the kitchen we go. As Abby uncorks the bottle and commandeers glasses, we sit at the table in the atrium. The girls scroll through their phones and I look outside. It's a sunny day, a cloudless cerulean sky, and the pond shows signs of life. One of the koi jumps by the small pool at the foot of the waterfall. This is normal because he's new to the environment. I smile to myself: he or she is spotted. Diego smiles and waves and I shoot him the thumbs up.

My gaze locks on my butterfly garden—the only place where I actually get my hands dirty. When I was young, I used to garden with my mother and I find the whole process serene and calming—digging in the dirt, planting beauty. I've tried getting the girls interested in my passion, and they were budding enthusiasts when they were younger, but not so much anymore.

"Mom, you're zoning out," says Ava. "Trying to spot your obsession?"

"Just looking at the pond and the garden," I say with a melancholy smile. Butterflies are a symbol of hope, faith, freedom and transformation. From egg to larva, to caterpillar to chrysalis, they go through many life cycles, finally transforming into the beautiful butterflies. And, like a butterfly, I'm about to go through a rebirth. "You know me and my love of butterflies."

"Yeah, Mom," says Grace. "We've seen the living room and we've seen your tattoo."

Taryn looks up from her phone. "I'm thinking of getting one like yours."

Abby brings over the glasses, the magnum, and then turns to grab a bottle of orange juice from the fridge. "Don't get a butterfly tattoo, get a grape."

"A grape?" asks Taryn.

"Yeah, because when you're old and wrinkly it'll turn into a raisin."

We all burst into laughter and it feels good to laugh, the kind that makes your stomach ache. Once we settle down, Abby pours the adults champagne with a splash of orange juice and gives the twins plain old juice.

After updating Abby on almost everything, she sits with her mouth agape.

"He's the mental one. He's the one who should be committed. The psycho." She grimaces. "I can say that now, right?"

"You can call him anything you want, even in front of the girls," I respond, my heart pinching. "The girls hate him."

"We do," says Ava.

"Girls, it must have been so hard on you to keep your feelings bottled up. He needs to be stopped before he does any more damage to any of you."

"Oh, I think we all turned out OK," says Grace, smiling at me. "We have Mom. She's done a fairly decent job—don't you think?"

"Better than decent, you girls are amaze-balls." Abby meets my gaze, her shoulders slumping. "Since we're getting everything out in the open, there's something I need to tell you. I've kept it locked up for so long, right now I feel like I'm going to burst. But since you're really leaving the narcissistic fuck-tard of a lying cheating soulless bastard..." She pauses. "Too much?"

Ava and Grace giggle. Abby clasps both of her hands over her mouth.

"Don't worry, Aunty A," says Grace. "We've heard much worse from Dad and his friends."

"Our friends too," Ava adds. "Mom's the only one who uses the word sugar when she's stressed."

I pat Abby's hand. "And I won't even reprimand you for swearing in front of them." I place my elbows on the table, my hands cradling my chin. "Abby, you'll always be my best friend. No matter what."

She swigs from her glass of champagne, her words coming out in a whoosh. "He tried paying me off to stay away from you way back when."

I get that the manipulating son of a bitch could bribe me with a life that dreams were made of, but buy my friends? "How much?"

"Hundred and fifty thousand."

My face flames hot. "And you took it?"

Abby pours herself another glass of champagne. "No, I said fuck no. You don't put a price on friendship." Her hand flies to her forehead. "Crap. I swore again. Sorry."

"Right now I just want to know why didn't you tell me?"

"You were in love. You didn't want to hear it. Damn it, Em, I didn't want you to hate me." She takes in a breath and shakes her hands out. "God, I've been keeping that secret close to the vest for so long." She clasps onto my hands. "Please don't hate me."

"Never," I say. "I hate Nate. Besides, I should have been there for you too."

"Ah, my divorce wasn't that bad. You were there when I needed a shoulder to cry on; and I should have seen the signs in the first place."

A few years after Nate and I tied the knot, Abby married Stephen Grossberg, a trader on Wall Street. Out of respect for me as her maid of honor, she'd conceded to allow Nate to attend the nuptials, but he didn't go. I didn't like Stephen much, thought he was smarmy, but, knowing how I'd felt when she told me what she thought about my marrying Nate, I kept my opinions to myself. Abby's marriage lasted three years—until she caught him bonking his secretary in her own bed.

I gulp. "I should have seen the signs too. In my marriage. In yours. What good are we as friends if we can't be honest with one another?"

"The kind that protect each other's feelings without stepping on each other's hearts when we need support. Hey, we all make mistakes, but we can fix 'em." She shrugs, raises her glass, and we all toast. "Here's to new beginnings. L'chaim."

She doesn't know the extent of Nate's mistakes. But I'm hell-bent on fixing everything now.

I lift a brow. "For my new beginning, I need a really good divorce attorney."

Abby leans forward and lowers her voice into a growl. "I tried connecting you to the best one two years ago. They don't call her *burn them in hell Hedra* for nothing. Believe me, she's earned that reputation." She raises an index finger. "Hold that thought. I'm going to text her right now."

She swigs back her champagne with another l'chaim, sets the glass down, and then pulls her phone out of her purse. As the girls and I sip our drinks, exchanging glances, we watch her texting. A minute or so passes and Abby looks up. "I have good news. Hedra can see you tomorrow morning. And, before you ask, yes, I'm spending the night. We'll order in food and binge-watch romantic comedies like the good ol' days."

I huff. "As long as you don't say it all night long."

"Say what?"

"I told you so." I get up from the table. "And you know what? I'm not in the mood for a romantic comedy. I want to watch something with ferocious and powerful females—"

"Have you seen the series *The Queen's Gambit?*" asks Abby, linking her arm into mine. "It came out a couple of years ago."

"I missed that one. Is it good?"

"It's perfect," she says. "It's about a woman overcoming obstacles and preparing for her biggest challenge."

As we curl up on the couch and chairs with blankets in the media room, we drink more champagne and watch the first three episodes, but I'm antsy. I can't stop wiggling my foot. I want to put all of my pieces on *my* board, getting on with my life—a life without Nate in it.

THIRTY-FIVE

NATE

Sunday, May 19th, 2024

I'm sitting on the couch watching the news when I eye my wrist. I love this watch—it's still ticking and not ticking me off. At least Emma is on a path to her own self-destruction and she's making getting out of this marriage financially intact so damn easy. This week the CEO of our hospital is announcing the new medical director for the ward. And that person will be me—the decision based on my skills as a surgeon, my leadership skills, and merit. I didn't even have to bribe anybody. Emma's served her purpose and I don't need the facade of the perfect family life anymore.

For a moment, she had me when she pulled out her seduction tactics and I'd thought the Emma I'd fallen in love with all those years ago was back. But then she'd insisted on the DNA test. Does she take me for an idiot? No, Emma, you won't win this game you're trying to play because you are going to be institutionalized. I want you and your whiny voice out of my life.

Needing to relieve some stress, I pick up my phone.

> Want to have dinner tonight?

Three dots.

JANE:

> Yes! Where?

I chuckle. Funny, her assuming that we'd go out. As if I'd be seen with her in public. I always keep a low profile and order in, especially with divorce looming on the horizon. Save for Audrey and Irina, all my extracurricular activities come with expiration dates like milk. Three months—maybe four—and then I move on when they get too clingy. Nobody ever spends the night. If I count the blow job, this will be Jane's second spin with me. Lucky girl.

> My place. Like sushi?

JANE:

> What time?

> Now?

JANE:

> OK. I need a ½ hour.

> I'll be waiting.

I text her my address and then head into the bedroom and, after placing a stack of condoms in reach of the bed, I set up the camera. Hopefully, the time Jane needs will be spent preparing herself for me.

It's only a little after ten and it is time to send Jane home. I can't wait to get rid of her.

"Tonight was fun," I say as I pull on a pair of sweatpants

and a T-shirt. I hand Jane her clothes and her face twists with confusion.

Her eyes go wide. "Y-y-you don't want me to spend the night?"

I shake my head. If things continue with Jane, I'll have to tell her my rules. For now, I don't want to get into them.

"Sorry, I have some work to catch up on and I have an early start tomorrow morning—at four a.m. I need the sleep." I pinch her butt and wink. "Maybe next time."

She nods and then gulps, "OK."

She dresses and I walk her to the front door. She tries angling in for a kiss but I take a step back. "Don't tempt me. I'll see you tomorrow," I say, practically pushing her out of the loft and closing the door behind her.

I pour myself a Scotch and sink down on the couch, feet on the coffee table, pulling up a movie—the one I just made of Jane. I'm getting into the homemade film when Ben calls. I mute the sound and click the line open. "Still on for Tuesday night? Pearl & Prime? Seven?" he says before I can utter one word.

I turn the video off. I didn't have the right camera angle— worse than an amateur. Plus, she makes the oddest facial expressions, like she's about to die in a car crash.

"Yep."

"You finally gonna divorce Emma?"

"Harold's already drawing up the paperwork–serving her later this week." I exhale and then chuckle. "Remind me to thank Becks for posting that video."

"Becks will be thrilled. She never liked her." He snorts. "See ya Tuesday."

After we hang up, because Ben's mentioned her, my thoughts turn once again to Emma. I created this life for us, for me. And I can take it all away.

Emma will get exactly what she deserves: nothing.

THIRTY-SIX

EMMA

Monday, May 20th, 2024

The secretary leads the three of us into the conference room. I sit at the table waiting for the woman of the hour to arrive, Abby by my side, Taryn sitting across from us. Crystal glasses and chilled bottles of Voss water beckon to me from an elegant wooden trolley with brass handles. Although my palms are sticky with perspiration, Abby clasps my hand. "You've got this," she says with a cheery grin.

My response comes out as a gurgle.

A fiery brunette wearing cat-eye glasses bursts into the conference room. The moment she enters she walks with purpose. With the blood-red lipstick and thick eyebrows, her essence, right down to her stiff suit and sturdy shoes, reeks of a mess-with-me-and-I'll-cut-you vibe.

"Mrs. Landon, I presume," she asks and I nod, standing up to shake her hand.

"Please, call me Emma."

"I'm Hedra Siegel, divorce attorney extraordinaire." She bows and waves her arms out dramatically. "Abby, always a pleasure to see you." She focuses in on Taryn. "And you are one of the daughters?"

"Kind of." Taryn clears her throat. "But more of a family friend. Taryn Flynn."

"Got it. Before we get started, would you like a coffee or water?" Hedra grins and points to the trolley. "We also have champagne, wine, whiskey, Scotch?"

Abby leans over and whispers in my ear. "Told you she was hell on wheels."

"I'd love a water," I say, looking at my watch. It's too early to drink and, if anything, I need to keep a clear head.

"Sparkling or still?"

"Still," I say, and she turns and pours, handing me the glass.

"Taryn? Abby?"

"I'm fine," they chime together, phrases overlapping.

"OK, Emma. As you are aware, today's consultation is 5k. To retain our firm, the fee will be around 50k, give or take. Depending on how messy the situation gets, you're probably looking at 250k, maybe more. And with an estate the size of your husband's, I think we're looking at a real shit show." She sits down at the head of the table. "Any skeletons in your past, things he could use against you?"

"Oh my God, she's as clean as they come," blurts out Taryn.

"Not a speck," says Abby with a snort.

My eyes dart to both of them. "Remind me why I brought you here again?"

"We're here for moral support," says Taryn. "This is going to be tough."

"No, we're here to make you go through with this, because once you start the process you can't back down," says Abby.

"Abby is dead right," says Hedra. "Back to you, Emma. Is there anything he has on you?"

"Well, there is a video of me acting like a lunatic this past Saturday night," I say, cringing. "It's pretty bad."

"Show it to me." I take my phone out of my bag, pull up Instagram, and hand it over. Hedra chuckles as Abby leans forward to view the video, her mouth agape.

Abby blurts out a laugh. "You're really excellent at charades. *A Perfect Murder*?"

"Yep. And not funny. I think I also reenacted *Eyes Wide Shut*. I guess drama club in high school was beneficial." My fingers fly to my temples. "Will this hurt me in court?"

"My goal would be to settle out of court, but that would be a pipe dream given his worth. Is this the only thing he has to use against you?" she asks, and I shrug out an 'I don't know' with my palms raised.

Hedra lowers her glasses to the tip of her nose, meeting my gaze. "How far do you want Nate to fall?"

I growl so low the guttural and animalistic tone surprises even me. "The lowest pits of hell."

"When do you want to start?"

"Today. Right now."

"OK, then. I've studied the prenup you sent over last night," says Hedra. She taps the file. "I need to be certain. You need to be one hundred percent sure you're ready to go through with this." She shakes her head and meets my eyes. "You wouldn't believe how many wives change their mind at the last minute."

"She's in," says Abby. "Or I'll kill her."

"Abby, I can speak for myself," I snap. I meet Hedra's intense gaze. "I'm not going to change my mind." I point to Taryn. "And she's the proof I need. Nate had an affair with her mother. Her DNA results will prove she's his daughter."

"What?" exclaims Abby, locking her gaze onto Taryn's blue eyes.

"It's a long story," I say. "And the twins don't know, but they will when their test results come in. So, until then, keep your lips zipped."

"Emma's known for a while. My mom wrote her a letter

before she killed herself," says Taryn, her head down. "She finally shared the letter with me two years ago."

Abby slams a hand on the table. "Jesus, Em, how could you keep a secret like that?"

"Because she'd made a promise to a dead woman not to say anything until I found out. But she didn't know I already knew." Taryn looks up, meeting my gaze. "It was one of the reasons Gordon sent to me boarding school."

A long silence hangs in the air.

"Could work," says Hedra, clearing her throat. She thumbs through the papers. "Taryn, when were you born?"

"May twenty-sixth, 2004."

Hedra sucks in a breath. "Oh boy, it would have been the nail in his fiduciary coffin, but Taryn was born prior to your relationship with Nate."

"What about the harmful clause?" asks Abby.

"Nope. Wouldn't come into play here." She clucks her tongue. "I'm sorry to say but, after looking over this agreement, if you decide to file for divorce, you'll have to settle for the minimum amount of one million dollars for each year of marriage after the girls were born. Sadly, you'd lose all rights to the house."

"He'd fight to keep the girls," I say. "And I can't let that happen."

I groan and explain the situation with my parents, how they'd moved to be near us, how my father is in poor health—just had another stroke, how the medical bills are piling up, and how Nate also owns their house. Plus, there's also the staff to consider. Fourteen million may seem like a lot—because, let's face it, it is—but it won't destroy him. And he needs to be destroyed.

Hedra taps her pen on the table and then picks up the prenup, scans through it, her eyes flashing onto mine.

"I understand," she says. "But the cheating clause is still a silver lining. You'd get half—and keep the house. Maybe both houses." She grins like a Cheshire cat with a mouse in its paws. "You were smart to put that in."

"Nate put that in."

"I see. Interesting." Hedra leans forward, a gleam in her eye. "So, the real question is: can you prove he's cheated since your marriage?"

"Perhaps. But I'm not sure if what I've done is exactly legal."

Abby's head snaps in my direction, her mouth agape. "Emma, what have you done?"

I purse my lips and my eyes go wide. "I may have designed some lamps with hidden cameras in them. When the lamp is switched on, it may turn on the camera. And the camera might have a Wi-Fi connection." I pause and clear my throat. "The videos stream to my phone. There's a lamp in Nate's office, and a few in the loft." I swallow and meet Hedra's stunned gaze, getting back on track. "I have over a year's worth of his escapades stored in the cloud—some at the hospital, but mostly at the loft. Can we use the videos?"

"No, what you've done wouldn't hold up in court. It's called entrapment," says Hedra, and I see years of planning my preemptive strike fly out the window until she speaks again. "But they all get busted eventually. Sometimes they just need a little help," she says, wagging a finger. "We're going to bait him, catch him in the act legally. And I have the perfect private investigator who deals with these types of affairs."

I tap my chin in thought. "How much will he or she cost me?"

Not that it matters. I've been saving my pennies for this rainy day because I knew it would be a matter of time. Nate's going to bankroll this divorce with the astronomical allowance of 50k he deposits into my bank account every month. It's hush money, he says; to keep me from complaining. I've also made quite a few savvy investments, thanks to my financial advisor.

"Stella's fee is 4k a day, the girls she works with cost another 1k to 5k per set-up," Hedra continues. "Think of it as poetic justice. Isn't that what you're looking for?"

My lips curve into a half-smile. "Yes. Exactly."

"I love this idea," says Taryn.

Hedra clears her throat and taps the prenup. "Back to the topic at hand. Emma, we'll get everything you need for a clean break. Everything you need to secure your future. Of course, he'd be better off dead, make things easier on everybody, but that's a pipe dream." She blurts out a hard laugh. "Clearly, I'm joking."

Oh, I've thought about his death. That would be so much easier than a legal battle. My black widow fantasies churn around in my brain. So many ways that make me smile. I zone out, staring at the skyline; he could fall off a building. Splat.

"Emma? I lost you there for a moment," says Hedra.

"I'm sorry. Just thinking." I snap back to the present. "I mean, isn't this also entrapment?"

"Eh, it's kind of a gray area. We have to ensure no laws are broken while obtaining the evidence. But Stella knows her stuff and the laws regarding surveillance in New York." She claps her hands together. "Should I call her?" I nod. "I need to know if Nathaniel has any habits, places he might go?"

"Pearl & Prime on Sullivan. Every Tuesday."

"And does he have a type?"

"I'm thinking he likes young, pretty little things, as long as they have a heartbeat and a pulse," says Abby, and I glare at her. "What? I didn't say he was into necrophilia."

Taryn and Abby snort out laughs.

I sneer. "I honestly don't have the mental bandwidth for comments like that right now. I just want to catch the bastard."

And I want him to rot in hell.

Hedra grins. "Can you get out of town? The chances of baiting him are better if he feels like you're not around to catch him in the act."

"We can go to my place in Paris," says Taryn with a wink. "It's perfect."

"Paris is *always* a good idea," says Abby.

"Thanks for the cliché," I say.

"You're welcome. And if I'm not mistaken, there's a red-eye we can catch tonight," she says and I shoot her a look of confusion. "What? I'm going too. I can write it off as a business expense—go to the fabric showrooms and stores for Zala. She'll love the idea. Can the twins come?"

I'm so very thankful for the odd vacation schedules at Ivy Crest. The girls weren't happy they'd have to attend an all girls' private school—What! No boys?—and they were even madder at having to attend boarding school, but it does come with its advantages.

"The twins are already on summer break. Plus, I'd promised to take them on a trip," I say. "Paris it is. But we're not leaving tonight, we're leaving tomorrow. I have to take care of some things for work."

"Text Nate and let him know you're going," says Hedra, rubbing her hands together. "Let's set this plan into motion."

Oh, I'm ready to strike, I think. And he won't know what hit him.

THIRTY-SEVEN

NATE

Monday, May 20th, 2024

After reading Emma's text about taking the girls to Paris to get her head together, I grip my hair and then slam my fist on my desk. Just like Emma to mess up my plans. It's as if she knows she's about to be served divorce papers. And those smiley face emojis? She's using them to get under my skin. I'm thinking about calling Amex to put a hold on her card, but I don't want to sound any alarm bells. She can't know what I'm up to. Not yet. Plus, the twins will thank Daddy for footing the bill and I'll need them on my side to testify that their mother is a bona fide lunatic.

The moment I'm about to close out of my phone, another text chimes in. If it's Emma again, I'll claw my own eyes out. I look at the screen and relief washes over me: good ol' Ben.

> BGOLD:
> Did you receive your invite?

> I'll be there tomorrow.

BGOLD:

Not talking about dinner.

What the fuck are you up to?

BGOLD:

You'll see. And you'll be happy I'm your friend.
You're welcome.

Catherine knocks and peeks her head into my office. "Dr. Landon, something just arrived for you."

"Come on in," I say, and she does, stepping forward and placing a box on my desk.

After she leaves, I open the package to discover an iPad mini. The note taped to it reads: *Turn me on and we'll turn you on.*

Fucking Ben—always up to something—usually no good. No wonder I love the guy like a brother. I power the device on.

The start screen loads with a message:

You're one of the chosen ones. Click here to begin.

This is no ordinary iPad. Butterflies and dragonflies zip across the screen. A flash of a breast. Of sex. An orgy. This is my kind of app and it has my complete attention as the video fades out and a note fades in.

Welcome to the Sanctuary.

After an extensive background check and a referral from one of your dearest friends, your membership to join us in a world of unadulterated debauchery has been pre-approved. All of our members must have a minimum net worth of 100,000 million and you fit our very exclusive criteria. The euphoria you'll experience with the most elite hedonistic events in the world awaits— where you can be your most authentic self and live out your most wild and decadent fantasies. Whether you're into dominating or being dominated, role-playing, or just watching, we have something for every taste. Private affairs with a total of eight butterflies and/or dragonflies and/or a combination of both can be arranged at the location of your choice for the cost of 125k.

No strings. No attachments. Simple.

Safety, security, and anonymity are ensured, regardless of the location.

You have twenty-four hours to make your decision. Click <u>here</u> to sign the nondisclosure agreement to continue. A digital signature will suffice.

This could be one of Ben's pranks, but I'm more than fascinated. Why not? I click on the link and my personal information shows up: name, age, and address—details anybody could find about me. I scan through the NDA. The language is well written, protects all parties involved, but involves sex and acts, never disclosing other members, what we do, or locations. I can live with that. I'm a gambler and so I sign. Another message pops up.

Thank you, Nathaniel Booth Landon, we've received your information.

Feel free to explore our garden, consisting of our <u>butterflies</u> (a kaleidoscope of the most beautiful women in the world) and our <u>dragonflies</u> (a swarm of the hottest men on the planet).

All of our butterflies (15) and dragonflies (5):
• have a clean bill of health
• are cultivated by Madame Butterfly, our founder

• *are between the ages of 18 and 28*
• *have signed nondisclosure agreements*

Finally, what I'm looking for. I head straight to the butter-flies and my heart nearly stops with the group photo. Although the girls all are wearing masks, some with feathers, some with rhinestones, I can tell these women are supermodel gorgeous—some small-chested, some with breasts like cantaloupes, all of the asses sheer perfection, rounded and firm juicy peaches I want to bite right into.

It's like a buffet of sexual delights and it's all mine for the taking. Anonymous. No commitments. No stress. With people of my caliber enjoying a candy store of hedonistic pleasure. But I'm on edge, questioning why I'd even do this.

> Got the invite. I don't have to pay $$$ to get my rocks off.

BGOLD:

> But you do. Heard membership is limited and filling up fast. Better think quickly.

> Could be a scam.

BGOLD:

> It isn't. Got my invite from Jeff a couple of hours ago. Gave you a referral. You can thank me later.

> Fuck off. There's my thank you.

I laugh and shake my head. Ben is right. Sometimes I do pay to get my rocks off. I must be forking over at least six hundred thousand a year, probably more, depending how many women I have on my roster. But complications arise and life becomes frustrating and stressful instead of bringing me the release I need.

No strings. No attachments. Simple.

Yes, that sounds fucking incredible.

Oh, but how a man can dream. I look at the girls' individual pages. One of the women is heavenly—mile-long legs, long locks of auburn hair, and from what I can tell, emerald green eyes. She wears a large pair of gossamer wings like a Victoria's Secret model and I'm imagining ripping them off her.

I don't need Ben to convince me. I click on the payment link to read the terms and the wiring instructions. Then I click back on the butterflies—hotter and sexier than any of my sidepieces have ever been. I close out of the browser and call up my banker so he can wire the initiation fee of $25,000 to Mariposa Enterprises and then I text Ben.

> Signed up. Thinking of booking a private party for Thursday night. The whole crew. You in? My finger is on the trigger...

BGOLD:

> *I'll treat for the next one, you dirty bastard.*

THIRTY-EIGHT

EMMA

Tuesday, May 21st, 2024

On Tuesday, I ran a couple of last-minute errands in the morning and then came back home to work on the project for JenX, Luisa by my side. Once we've finished going through all the invoicing and purchases I'd made in Thailand on the client's behalf, I turn to her. "You are my rock."

"Gracias, Emma."

"I'm leaving for Paris later tonight with the girls. Why don't you Alba, Homa, and Kom take off for a few days. My treat. Use the card. Go anywhere you want."

Her eyes dart back and forth, glinting with fear. She blinks. "What about Mr. Landon?"

"What about him?" I shudder. "He'll be staying at the loft. And if he comes back here he'll be on his own. I couldn't bear to think about him bossing you around when I'm not here as a buffer. Nobody should have to face their monsters alone." I meet her eyes and lean over and whisper. "And he is a monster."

We go silent for a moment.

Luisa taps her chin. "We've been talking about heading

down to Atlantic City. Homa and Kom have never seen a show at a casino, and Alba wants to try that saltwater taffy. I don't know why, but she does. I told her it sticks to your teeth. But I do love walking down the boardwalk."

"So do it."

"When will you be back from your trip?"

"Sunday, so I'll see you next Monday."

Her lips part like she wants to say something more. She gets up and files the papers we'd been working on, her back to me.

"Was there something else on your mind?"

She waves a dismissive hand and turns to face me. "Just thinking. Atlantic City sounds like the perfect escape."

Believe me. I know. Sometimes we need to escape for some fun. And sometimes we truly need to escape our twisted lives. "You were going to say something else. I can tell by the expression on your face."

She lets out a breath. "Alba, Homa, Kom and I will go to Atlantic City. You are right. It's a good plan. Go pack. I'll take care of everything here."

After a long flight and clearing security, ten hours later, we arrive at Taryn's apartment in the sixteenth arrondissement, filled with swanky homes, foreign embassies, trendy restaurants and noteworthy museums like Fondation Louis Vuitton. Of Haussmannian design, Taryn's building is beautiful—cake white with wrought-iron balconies. As the driver unloads our suitcases from the back of the van, a beautiful woman of a certain age exits the building. Oozing class, she's dressed from head (sunglasses) to toe (ballet flats) and everything in between, wearing my favorite designer: Chanel. A silver vixen, her hair is slightly tousled, shoulder-length and the perfect shade of gray with elegant streaks of white.

"Bonjour, les filles," she says and air-kisses Taryn's cheeks.

She raises her sunglasses to the top of her head, turning. She eyes me up and down, giving me a sly once-over and an even slyer smile. "You must be Ava and Grace's mother. Taryn's told me about them and you. Enchantée."

"Enchantée."

She focuses her attention on Abby. "And you are?"

"Abby Hoffman, the mother's friend."

"Is that Zala you're wearing?" she asks, and Abby nods. "Aside from Chanel, she's one of my favorite designers."

"Abby is Zala's head designer, Madame Valois," says Taryn.

"Alors, I'd love a secret preview of the next collection, but unfortunately I don't have time," says Madame Valois, her French accent rising and falling. "My husband is in the film industry and we're traveling to Cannes for the festival. Malheureusement, I'm unable to use a box I'd reserved at the Palais Garnier Thursday night. They are performing Puccini's *Madame Butterfly*. May I offer you the tickets?"

Abby nudges me in the ribs and smiles. "Isn't that your favorite opera?"

"It is," I say. "That's a really generous offer, madame, and we'd love to go. I'd be happy to reimburse you."

"That won't be necessary." She waves a dismissive hand. "Taryn is like a granddaughter to me," she says, tittering out a laugh when my eyes go wide. "I'd also like to invite you to stay with us at our place in Cannes on Saturday after our first round of guests leave."

She raises a brow as Ava and Grace whisper excitedly to one another.

"That's so kind of you, madame, and another very tempting offer," I say, hesitantly. "But I'm afraid we'll have to pass on that one. I need to take care of some important things back in New York—"

"I don't have to get back, madame," says Taryn. "And Ava,

Grace, and I can change our return flights if the offer still stands —that is, if it's OK with Emma."

I shoot Taryn a look.

"What? I can keep an eye on the girls. They'll be fine."

Madame Valois lowers her sunglasses and winks. "I'll get you into the best screenings, bien sûr. Rumor has it Taylor Swift will be performing—not once, but twice."

Ava and Grace let out excited squeals. After Taylor Swift is mentioned, I know there's no way I'll be able to convince them to come home with me. And I do want them to have fun, staying away from Nate and the nightmare that will be waiting for me at home.

Abby nudges my side again. "I'm not sure this is a good idea."

"Oh, Taryn will be with them. She's like their big sister. It's fine." I smile and meet Madame Valois's steady gaze. "Well, I can't argue with two die-hard Swifties. Thank you."

"It's settled then," says Madame Valois and looks at her watch. "I must be on my way. I have a few last-minute errands to do before I leave this evening. Mathilde, my helper, will drop off the envelope later today."

Taryn kisses the woman's cheeks and rattles on and on in French. I can only make out merci beaucoup. I'm impressed with Taryn's perfect accent and fluency with the language. As Madame Valois says goodbye and sashays down the street, I suck in a breath, trusting that my girls will be safe with her. But I know they will be because I know exactly who she is.

THIRTY-NINE

EMMA

Then: May, 2022

I was working on a Parisian-chic concept for one of my clients—
a couple who had just won fifty million playing the lottery.
They'd wanted anything French! Only French! And they'd
insisted I fly to France to get the very best of the best design
ideas for the home they were constructing. Sadly, their tastes
leaned toward baroque, with a lot of gold, over-the-top
Versailles elements. But meeting my clients' dreams and
demands was what I worked for, my end goal.

I wasn't quite sure if my passport had expired or was valid
for the six months necessary for my return back to the US. If it
wasn't, I had two weeks to get a new one, using a rush service.
My passport was fine, but, while searching for it, I found
another document: Nate's faded and smudged birth certificate,
listing his mother's maiden name: Simon.

I don't know why, but curiosity got the best of me. So, I
headed to my computer and googled her. To my surprise, a
couple of results popped up, and one in particular caught my

eye, but it was in French, which I didn't understand. I opened up a new window and translated the words.

> Former showgirl Brigitte "Gigi" Simon marries film magnate Olivier Valois at an undisclosed location.

There was no mistaking it; Nate's mother—who was supposed to have died years before we met—was very much alive. Older, yes, but stunning all the same, with graying hair, the perfect shade of white, and steely blue eyes. I clicked through a few more results. Save for a few more photos of her with her husband Olivier at film events, dressed up in fancy gowns, nothing more about her or what she'd been doing all these years came to light. Of course, there were tons of articles about her wealthy French husband—a producer, director, screenwriter, and owner of a film studio, Lumière Corp, and tons more photos of him with practically every celebrity on the planet. I scrolled back and stared at her picture.

Nate was one big fat liar.

I printed the article out and confronted Nate the second he walked in the front door that evening. "Your mother lives in France!" I screamed, shoving the paper in front of his face. "You told me she was dead!"

He scoffed, tore the paper into tiny bits, letting them drop like confetti onto the floor, then he spat out, "She's dead to me."

Every muscle in my body felt like it was going to explode. "You're insane."

Before I knew it, his fist flew out, right into my face, and I was splayed out on the travertine floor. He stepped over me, grabbed the keys to one of his many cars, and said, "If you even think of contacting her, you won't live another day. If you want to divorce me—and I don't know why you haven't by now—this is the time to do it." He laughed, but I could barely focus through my pain. "And, like it says in the prenup, you'll walk away with nothing. The money and the house are mine—and so are the girls." He groaned. "I can't stand to be around you for one more second. I'm staying at the loft."

"I'm your wife!" I screamed.

"No," he said, "you're just a prop. I thought you knew that. Don't forget you signed up for this life."

The front door slammed behind him.

I passed out in pain, in shock. The following morning, Luisa found me bleeding—my lip split, my eye swollen to the size of an egg—and groaning on the cold travertine floor. When I fell, I twisted my wrist, probably bruised a rib, and I couldn't get up.

"No, no, no. He did this to you?" she asked, wrapping her arms around me.

I could only nod.

"You have to leave him. Before he gets rid of you," she said, shaking her head with concern.

"I can't," I cried. "The girls. You. Homa, Kom, Alba? My parents. Taryn. I'm responsible for all of you."

She clucked her tongue. "Well, you wouldn't do any of us good if you're dead. Or put into a mental institution." She swallowed. "I overheard him talking to Gordon and Ben. It was like I wasn't even there." Luisa took in a breath and continued, "That's the thing about us, the help. We slip into darkness, hearing everything, seeing everything. But our ears are always listening. We know everybody's secrets, including yours." She popped her lips. "But yours aren't so bad. You're a good person." She met my eyes and snickered. "Wishing somebody dead isn't the same thing as killing them."

I recoiled. "How do you know I've wished Nate dead?"

She shrugged. "You told me many times. When you had too much to drink."

"Getting loaded is the only way I can deal with the bastard," I said, my throat catching. "I have to report him."

"You can't call the cops. He knows important people and

he'd turn everything around on you." She took in a breath. "How do you think we got our papers to be legal? Think about it."

Think? I could barely breathe. The father of my children was truly a monster, just like Irina had written in her letter. This was the life I'd chosen?

I met Luisa's concerned gaze. "I've always had my suspicions, but every time I've tried broaching the topic you clam up. But I really need the answer now." I cleared my throat. "Tell me your story, how you ended up working for Nate."

Luisa nodded and shook her head again. "I will. But not here. Get up off the floor. We'll go to the kitchen. I'll whip up a batch of your favorite aguas fresca with the pineapple and ginger, maybe some turmeric for inflammation. Then, while you hold a pack of frozen peas on your face, I'll tell you everything." With her free hand, she made the sign of the cross. "I'm glad our baby girls, Ava and Grace, are at their school."

We sat at the table in the atrium, overlooking the pond and my butterfly garden, now showing signs of life. My beautiful butterflies. How I dreamed of flying free. Luisa brought over our chilled drinks and, as promised, a sack of frozen peas for my face. She nodded with a look of concern and a sigh, then began to speak.

"The year was 1997. I remember the date, the day. I remember everything. My family was very poor in Mexico and my mother died very young. We couldn't afford the medical bills. My sister, Camila, was eighteen and I was sixteen. We also have three younger siblings—two brothers, and another sister." She shrugged. "Catholic family. Lots of mouths to feed. So we worked at a beach bar in Puerto Vallarta to help my father out, and one day Becks Stark approached us."

"Becks?" I asked.

"Sí." Luisa's brows lifted. "I remember how I could feel her eyes scanning my body, giving me the chills, and feeling very unnerved when I took her drink order." Luisa leaned forward. "It surprised me. She spoke perfect Spanish. The two of us stood there and she asked us to turn around. She asked us a lot of questions about our lives. Then she said, 'What if I could promise you a better life in America?'

"'That is my dream,' Camila told her.

"Becks pointed to a big yacht docked in the harbor. 'That's where we are staying. We're leaving tomorrow morning, if the two of you would like to join us. Come by tonight and we'll discuss your dreams.'"

Luisa lowered her head and continued, her shoulders caving forward. I gripped her hand.

"Camila was very excited and so was my papa. We went to the yacht around dusk. I remember the birds flying, the cries of the seagulls. And the sunset, bursting in oranges, pinks and reds. On the level above us, a group of men sat around a table in deck chairs smoking cigars. I could hear them laughing and smell the smoke. When I saw Becks coming toward us, I wanted to turn around and run, but Papa clasped onto my wrist. 'Wait, Luisa,' he said. 'Let's hear what she has to say.'

"Somebody on the staff led Camila and me to the upper deck. Becks and my father disappeared. There were maybe a dozen young girls and boys splashing around in a swimming pool and two of the girls were hysterically crying. I told Camila, 'We have to get out of here. Something isn't right.'

"'Don't worry about it,' she said. 'Just look at this place!'"

I gulped, bracing myself.

"Fifteen minutes later, the yacht began to move out of the port. I ran to the side of the deck, thinking maybe I could jump, but I was afraid to. Then I saw my father standing on the dock. He had a big black duffel bag at his feet and in his hand was a bundle of dollar bills. He was smiling. It took me a minute to figure out what was happening and I couldn't believe it until Becks walked up behind me and said, 'Your father is an excellent negotiator. Consider yourself very lucky. He was planning on selling you to the cartel, until we came in with a better offer.'

"I turned to face her, woozy from whatever I'd been given to drink. 'H-h-he sold us?'

"She placed her hand on my shoulder, squeezing it hard. 'Don't worry. You and your sister will be in good hands. We've decided to keep you. Well, one of you.' Nathaniel Landon walked up behind me and Becks said, 'Luisa, meet your new owner, Mr. Landon. I'll leave the two of you alone to get acquainted. Camila, you are coming with me.'"

Luisa rubbed her eyes with the tips of her fingertips. "And that was that."

Her story was far worse than I ever could have imagined in my wildest nightmares. Tears slid down her cheeks. Tears were sliding down mine. I could feel my heart thumping inside my chest, slow and hard. I let her words, her story sink in.

"Why didn't you leave, try to escape?" I asked once I found my voice.

"Harold Katz keeps our papers locked up, unless we need them to travel or renew our driver's licenses. That—and they threatened to deport us or kill and replace us with somebody else if we said a word. We couldn't let that happen." She lowered her head. "And they would deliver on their promise. It's happened before. There was a girl who worked for the Starks. She's dead. Some guys picked her up and dropped her in an alley." She paused and shook her head slowly. "They called her Jane Doe on the news. Her name was Sofia."

"Do you speak with your sister?" I stuttered.

"Si, I do. She works for the Starks. You wouldn't have met her because you don't go to their house." Luisa blew out a long, hard breath. "For a while I hated Camila for the position she put us in. We've only started speaking again recently."

I felt like such an idiot. All of this happened right under my nose. Of course, I'd had my suspicions over the years, but hearing the words coming out of Luisa's mouth was another story altogether and my body trembled. Was I just as guilty as Nate? "And Homa, Kom? Alba?"

"I texted them while I was making our drinks," said Luisa. "You'll hear their stories from them."

I placed my head on the table, pushing the bag of frozen peas onto my throbbing face, but the pain in my heart couldn't be numbed. Light footsteps padded into the kitchen. Hands were placed on my back, rubbing gently.

"My story is pretty much the same," said Alba, swallowing hard. "Except Nathaniel purchased me from Becks and Mr. Flynn."

Silence settled over the room for a second or two. I could hear my heart beating, thumping in my brain.

"Ours is different," Homa finally said. "Kom and me grew up in villages north of Chiang Mai by the Burmese border. Like Luisa and Alba, all of our families sold us, but to work in the sex industry in Bangkok." She took in a sharp breath. "Kom and I are from the same village. When I was fourteen, my stepfather sold me for one hundred dollars to a police officer to support his opium addiction. Same for Kom, except her own father sold her. We ended up in a brothel in Bangkok. Becks found us there, just like she'd found Chariya, Ahn, and Daw many years before us. And now we are here."

My mind sifted through the past, to their arrival. During the construction of the main house, when I was three months along, we'd been living in Pound Ridge, and Homa and Kom had miraculously appeared at Nate's side. They were both so young then—only eighteen and twenty years old (at least that's what Nate told me)—and spoke broken English.

"This is Homa and this is Kom," he'd said, pushing each of them forward. "I've hired them to help Luisa clean, take care of you, and our child, once he or she is born." He crossed his fingers. "Charles. I like that name. Charles Peter Landon. It's got panache."

Anger flared in my neck.

"We don't know the sex of the baby. We'll discuss names when we find out." I sat upright in bed, swallowing back one drop of irritation at a time, not knowing I was carrying twin girls. "Shouldn't I decide who we hire to take care of me and our child?"

Homa and Kom exchanged worried glances.

"Where did you find them? A nanny site?" I asked.

"They came highly recommended from a friend of mine. They have childcare experience," he said flatly. "You're not feeling well, so I did you a favor. You don't have to go through any interviews." I was about to protest, but he cut me off. "The decision has been made. Unless you want to kick them out of the house after I've already promised them a nice home and jobs."

Infuriated he was putting me on the spot, I was about to argue when the morning sickness I couldn't get rid of or keep under control hit fast and furiously. My shoulders began to heave. I licked my lips repeatedly. Kom stepped forward with the garbage can I kept at the side of the bed. She pulled my hair back as I vomited, while Homa ran to the bathroom and returned with a cold washcloth, placing it on my neck.

"See," said Nate, turning on his heel. "They're already helping you. I'll leave you to get to know your servants."

"These girls are not servants," I'd wheezed. But he was already out the door, slamming it behind him.

Suffice it to say, Homa and Kom moved into the refurbished basement with Luisa that day. Alba showed up at the house a week later, bringing me homemade soups, urging me to eat and to stay healthy. I didn't question her arrival because I'd been so deliriously sick. Because Nate was a doctor, when I was put on bed rest at six months, thanks to undetermined vaginal bleeding, I was allowed to stay home. Nate basically ignored me after we found out I was having twin girls, and these four women took care of me. During this time, Luisa helped me oversee the construction of the main house, taking photos, going over the plans, wheeling me around in a wheelchair. Luisa was a house manager and a personal assistant—and my friend.

My head felt like it was going to explode, but I snapped to attention. "Why haven't you shared *any* of this with me? I would have listened. What's more, I would have done something about it."

"Like what? Emma, go look in the mirror. You can't do anything on your own," said Luisa pointedly. "He would have had you killed and made it look like an accident, or had you committed to a mental institution. We've all heard him talking about it."

Everybody nodded with emphatic agreement.

Luisa clasped my hand. "At least you know who and what you're dealing with now."

I wanted to scream. Instead, I clenched my teeth so tightly my jaw throbbed in pain. Fear no longer paralyzed me into submission, not with the wave of anger sweeping my entire system.

FORTY

NATE

Tuesday, May 21st, 2024

Ben is pacing out front of Pearl & Prime when I arrive. I hand him a gym bag and we enter the restaurant, our gazes locking onto a sexy young woman sitting alone at the bar. She lets an oyster slide down her throat and licks her lips. A sense of déjà vu washes over me. Ben pokes a chubby finger into my ribs, his beady eyes glimmering. "She looks a little bit like Emma. But with big tits. Might be a fantasy of mine."

"More like a nightmare," I say, nudging his side. "You really are a twisted fuck. Don't waste your time on that piece of trash. We have Thursday night to look forward to. My place. Nine o'clock."

"The loft?"

"No, the house. Emma's out of town with the girls. More space, not to mention more privacy."

"Got to love country life," Ben says. "You keeping the house in the divorce?"

"I paid for it. You bet I am. And I'm keeping the girls too." I laugh. "You've got to love boarding school and summer camps."

"Theme for the party?"

"You'll see." I shoot him a grin. "Did Becks take off to Cuba OK?"

"Yep. Back tomorrow." He glances at the gym bag. "And...? What did you get this time?"

"Ketamine."

"Perfect. She'll store the product in the warehouse until Friday." He slugs my shoulder. "Let's eat, buddy. I'm starving."

We knuckle-bump. A few waiting patrons grumble as we're ushered to our table before they're seated. And I'm thinking it's good to be us.

Wednesday, May 22nd, 2024

Exhausted, today I'd stayed behind, letting the girls and Abby explore Paris without me. I'd slept a little bit, but I'm now wide awake. I log into the Nest application on my phone, only to find Nate has turned the surveillance off, which means the bastard is home and probably up to no good. The last video is of him smirking into the camera. I check my texts.

STELLA:

Bad news. Nate didn't fall for the bait. What do you want me to do?

Shaking my head from side to side, I tap in my response.

Keep trailing him until Friday. He's at the house and he's turned all surveillance off, alarm too, so he's up to something. He'll leave for the hospital 6 a.m., usually home 7 p.m. Cameras? Legal?

Although it's 11 p.m. here, it's only 5 p.m. in New York and three dots blink almost immediately after I hit send.

STELLA:

With your permission. You're out of town. Need to check on house.

Got it 😊

We spend the next half hour chatting online, me giving her the layout of the property, entry codes, places to hide cameras. I'm signing off with Stella when somebody knocks on my door. "Emma-ma, I saw your light on? Are you awake?"

"I am. Come on in, love-bug."

Taryn gulps. "I'm so glad we're in Paris, far away from the shitstorm that's about to go down." She kisses me on the cheek and then links her fingers together. "Everything is crossed."

I pull her in for a hug and whisper, "Taryn, never forget, everything starts with a plan. Trust me, they're all going down."

"That's my hope," she whispers.

"The girls don't know who she is yet, do they?"

"Nope. And it's been a really tough secret to keep. Along with the fact I'm their half-sister." She groans. "I really hope your plan works. Because if something happens to you, I will die."

I squeeze her hand. "Nothing is going to happen to me."

Two years ago, I'd planted the seeds to get away from Nate. But it was only after I met Nate's mother—Madame Valois—that those seeds started to germinate and take root.

FORTY-TWO

EMMA

Then: May, 2022

I was to leave for Paris in a week and the bruise on my cheek and my right eye had yet to fade, turning that horrible greenish color, rimmed with a putrid purple hue. I was surprised that Nate could even look at me. Then again, I could barely look at him. Luisa, Homa, Kom, and Alba's stories weighed down on my heart. But I couldn't report him, not with all his threats hanging over our heads. Not with his powerful friends backing him up.

I met Abby for lunch in the city a couple of days later, not taking my sunglasses off. Abby picked up on my hesitation immediately. "Let me see your face."

"It's not pretty," I said with a grunt.

"You're always gorgeous," she replied as I lifted my glasses to the top of my head. She cringed. "I take that back. What the fuck happened?"

I mumbled, "I walked into a door. You know me. I'm a klutz."

"The door had a nice right hook." She clucked her tongue

and eyed me with worried concern. "Is this the first time it's happened?"

Hitting me in the face, yes. Grabbing my arms and squeezing tightly, and leaving small bruises or indentations in my flesh, no. I wore long-sleeved blouses to cover up the wounds from our hate making. Thankfully, it didn't happen often.

I sighed. "It's the first time. He didn't mean to do it."

"Jesus, Emma, don't make excuses for him. You're not a mindless robot. You've got to get away from him. Now."

A low groan worked its way out of my throat. "I'm working on it." And then I explained how he'd fight to keep the girls. Probably win. I did not share what I'd learned about my staff. At the time, it wasn't my story to tell.

Abby met my eye—the good one that wasn't all swollen and puffy. "First that debacle with Audrey Clark, now this? How much more can you take?"

"Not much more," I said. "I have to come up with a plan."

Abby pulled out her phone. "I'm texting you Hedra's details. Now."

"And she'll hear from me when I come back from Paris."

As luck would have it, Abby was going to be in Paris for fashion week, spearheading the show for Zala, which Taryn would be making her runway debut in. I'd commandeered two of the coveted tickets from Abby—one for me and the other for a guest.

Because, of course, I didn't keep my promise to Nate, regardless of his threat.

After dealing with my client's demands and working my tail off searching all the brocantes for antiques, I walked the red carpet, avoiding the cameras, and took my spot, watching the seat across the runway. Music boomed. My heart pounded to the beat. My nerves were in a tangle as I prayed for my special guest to arrive. My face also itched like crazy, thanks to the pints of foundation I'd slathered on to cover the bruises. I hoped my dark red lipstick and the flashing lights would prove enough of a distraction.

A half hour before the show started, Madame Valois took her place and my posture straightened. I sucked in a breath as she lifted up her chin. Her eyes met mine and then darted to the foyer. She stood up and surreptitiously ushered for me to do the same. Thankfully, the army of photographers were too distracted by the many celebrities in attendance to pay us any attention. Hesitantly sidestepping through the crowd, I made my way to the bar where Madame Valois waited.

"I was wondering if it was you who sent me the invitation," she said, her back to me. She called the bartender over, ordering two glasses of champagne. "Quite the risk, Emma, n'est-ce pas?"

She turned to face me as soon as the glasses were placed in front of us. Dressed impeccably in a turquoise dress I knew Abby had designed, she looked exactly like her photos—the steely blue eyes, the perfectly coiffed hair.

My jaw dropped. "Madame Valois, you know who I am?"

"Of course, I've been keeping tabs on you. And the girls." She tilted her head to the side. "Please call me Gigi. My driver is waiting outside. On y va."

Let's go.

"Where?"

"My car. We'll have more privacy there. As you must know, we really shouldn't be seen together. We'll go out the side entrance, where there are no photographers lurking." She held up a slender finger and pulled her phone out of her clutch. "My driver will pick us up. I'll go first."

I hesitated. She looked over her shoulder. "You can trust me."

I swallowed and followed her, her pace brisk. A minute or two later, a capped driver held the door of a stretch limousine open and ushered me over. I slid into the back seat.

"Champagne?" Gigi asked with a smile. "We didn't get to toast our meeting at the bar."

"No, thank you, I'm fine," I said, my body trembling. I placed my hands in my lap and turned toward her. "Nate told me you were dead."

"Do I look dead to you?" She shook her head, shaking it and laughing softly. "I did read my obituary and found it quite comical."

"Suffered from dementia?"

She scoffed. "I certainly hope I don't look demented."

Not one bit.

She pulled out an album, placing it on her lap, and flipped through the pages. I sat shocked, regarding clippings of every magazine I'd been featured in and photos of the girls. I noted that there were no pictures of Nate.

"Where did you get all these?"

"Since I couldn't be a part of your lives, I have been keeping tabs on you and the girls," she chortled, her French accent rising and falling in the sweetest of melodies. "I hired a private investigator. I hope you don't mind."

If I'd known she was alive, I would have done the same thing.

"I'm wondering why—"

"Why I've stayed away? Yes? I'd be asking the same question too. Believe me, it's been difficult," she said, her voice catching. "Not being in your lives was part of my settlement agreement when I divorced Peter—no contact with any Landons or any of their descendants." She shook her head with remorse. "I had to slip away quietly and never be heard from again."

"Is that why Nate..." How could I put this politely? "Has problems with you? Because he feels abandoned?"

"No, I wish it were that simple," she said, her eyes glazing over with sadness. "Nathaniel was always a horrible child—the kind that bit me when he was a baby, the kind that tore the wings off butterflies or threw rocks at cats." She cleared her throat. "The kind that killed his brother because he knew I adored Andrew more than him—"

I held up a hand into the stop motion. "Wait. I thought Andrew died in a car accident?"

"He did," said Gigi, patting my leg. "But who do you think was at the wheel? And who do you think covered everything up, paying off officials?"

I gulped. "Your husband, Peter—"

"And Gordon Flynn." She dabbed her eyes with a white linen handkerchief. "Andrew's death did hit me hard and I did lose my mind for a while. I couldn't move, couldn't leave the house. But after I found out they were buying and selling people, something in me snapped back to life." She leaned forward, meeting my eyes. "I threatened to go to the police with everything I knew. Peter threatened to have me committed or have me killed. I struck a deal with Peter. I would receive a healthy settlement. The divorce would be quiet. And I would disappear. Voilà." She shook her head, a strand of silky gray hair falling over her eyes. "In his own way, Peter did love me, but I'm not sure Nathaniel has any capacity for real love. He's an inhuman machine propelled by extreme narcissism—a sociopath." She lifted up an eyebrow. "Do you really think Peter died from a heart attack? Or do you think it may have been brought on by something Nathaniel—who was studying medicine at the time—played a hand in?"

I sat back in my seat, flabbergasted. My breath came hot and heavy. I was struggling to retain my composure when all I wanted to do was scream. Emotions—fear, shock, betrayal—were all hitting me at once. I was at a crossroads, facing Nate's true nature. And I didn't know where to turn. My body trembled, my voice shook. That night, I told her everything—about Luisa and my staff, his serial cheating, and how he'd hit me—not just because I needed to tell somebody, but because I could tell she understood what was at stake with every gasp.

Gigi's expression darkened as she listened. But I felt the darkness that had gripped me begin to lift. After all, she'd done it; she'd escaped. Hope fluttered in my chest. "I want to leave him. But I don't know what to do. Will you help me?"

Gigi grasped my hand, squeezing it tightly. "I was hoping you'd ask, but we need to be very careful..." She took in a shaky breath. "My husband has made many films with hit men in them, but sadly we don't know any actual ones."

A hit man. Yes, why hadn't I thought of that? I wondered where I could find one. They were hardly likely to advertise their services on Google. Maybe the dark web? But what did I know about that? Zero.

Gigi continued, "When you strike, and you have to strike hard, your plan has to be methodical, no stone left unturned, every detail accounted for. Because he can't know what you're up to." She shook her head, a dash of fear sparking in her eyes. "If he could take such drastic measures against his own brother and the father he adored, imagine what he'd do to his own mother? His wife? Or even his girls? It's the real reason I've stayed away." She paused. "Please, don't tell your girls about me until you're all safe and far away from my son."

Her words carried more than a weighty caution, crushing my brain as if it was pressed in a vice. He'd already threatened to kill me. Would he be so inhuman as to harm the girls to get back at me? And what about Taryn? The staff? My parents?

I had one more bomb to drop: "One of your granddaughters is modeling in the show."

Her head snapped in my direction and her eyes went wide. "Ava and Grace model? Aren't they too young? Only twelve years old?"

"They are. But I'm talking about your other granddaughter. Taryn Flynn. I believe she's Nate's biological daughter."

I cleared my throat and continued, telling her about Irina's letter, about Gordon, about how she'd killed herself to escape. And how I'd never let that happen to me.

"I should hope not," she said. "Because I'd like to get to know you and the girls better. That is my hope. 'Un bel dì vedremo.' One fine day we shall see." She smiled. "That's from one of my favorite operas, *Madame Butterfly*." She squeezed my hand. "I noticed your butterfly garden in *Vanity Fair*. I believe we have more in common than you think."

We both had to deal with a sociopath?

Her eyes met mine, steady and calculating. "For now, play the part of the loving wife. And, by all means, play it safe." She reached into her purse and handed me a phone. "I came prepared. This is how we can remain in contact. The bill goes to my husband's studio. Make sure Nathaniel doesn't find it. Keep the ringer on silent. I'm going to head back in now." She paused, kissed me on the cheek, and then opened the door, her perfume, Chanel No. 5, blowing in on the breeze and floating up to my nostrils. "Float like a butterfly. Sting like a hundred killer bees."

I watched her sashay into the building, deep in thought. After heading back inside to watch Taryn's debut, I took my seat, entranced. The lights flashed and the models practically floated on the stage—lovely as butterflies, their dresses silky and flowing.

I'd made a career out of drawing up beautiful plans. It was time to become the architect for my own life—for all of our lives. As a lone butterfly, I wouldn't stand a chance against Nate. But Gigi's words had set me thinking: what if I had a hive of killer bees for backup...

FORTY-THREE

NATE

Wednesday, May 22nd, 2024

Jane taps on my door and, without waiting for a reply, comes sauntering into my office. She smiles and I cringe. Suddenly, I hate the gap between her front teeth. A simpleton with great tits, she's nothing like the women I'll be playing with tomorrow night. And I really didn't enjoy her as much I'd thought I would. Time to cut her loose.

"I had fun the other night," she says, wiggling her brows. "When can we do it again?"

I look up from a patient's chart. "Do what again?"

"Have fun," she says with a wink.

She thinks she's being sexy; I'm thinking otherwise.

"I have no idea what you're talking about. I'm busy." She doesn't budge. I wave a dismissive hand toward the door. "Unless there's something you need regarding the care of a patient, you can leave."

Her mouth trembles. She clenches her hands together. "Why are you being so cruel?"

I point toward the door again. "Do I have to repeat myself?"

Her facial expression changes from utter shock to anger to understanding. "I'll tell everybody. I'll report you. I'll-I'll—"

"Do what?"

Jane is pushing her luck with the wrong person. Which is why I always have a contingency plan: I have the pictures and the videos. Like the one I took of her on Sunday night with her ass in the air. Who knows what I would do with them if somebody forced my hand? Post them online. Send them to employers, family and friends? Nobody can or will fucking blackmail me. Ever. I learned from the best, Gordon Flynn, and I know how to play it safe.

I lift my phone from the desk and flip to the photo of her, the one my face is not pictured in, but hers is. I shove the screen in front of her. "You'll do nothing. I also have the text from you asking me to give you a raise in return for special favors—"

Her eyes sparkle with tears. Her throat hitches. "That was a joke. We were sexting—and I can prove it!"

"Funny? Do you have any replies from me? At all? Even one?"

She pulls out her phone from her pocket and swipes the screen with her fingers, her eyes wide when she realizes she has nothing. Just her word against mine. I use the latest technology. Vanish mode. Everybody should consider it.

"I can't believe you'd do this to me. Not like this," she says, storming out of my office.

The moment the door slams behind her, I call Catherine. A couple of moments later, she pops her head into my office. "Dr. Landon? You needed something?"

"I did. It's about Jane. I don't think she's a good fit for our team."

Catherine nods, eyes wide. "Phew. I didn't like her much anyway—too chatty and a bit unprofessional, if you ask me. I see the way she's tried to cozy up to you. And she's a bit off-kilter, she just raced down the hall crying." She taps a pensive finger on her chin. "What about sending her over to geriatrics?"

"Perfect."

"I'll request a transfer right now."

"You're the best," I say.

"No, you are, Dr. Landon." She grins and looks over her shoulder before leaving. "I hear congratulations are in order, Mr. Medical Director."

I wink, look at my reflection in the computer screen, and smile.

FORTY-FOUR

EMMA

Thursday, May 23rd, 2024

For my own sanity, I've been trying to act normal. The effort to gather more information online had to be abandoned when my absorption in the task earned me stern glares from the girls, so in the end I gave up, clamped my phone shut, and joined them in perusing the art galleries of the Marais, and having a decadent lunch. Then it was back to Taryn's to get ready for *Madame Butterfly*.

Now, dressed to the nines in various shades of blue (Abby's idea)—heels, dresses, and makeup done to perfection—we climb into our limousine. This, I'm thinking, is what life is about. Art. Culture. And having the people I love beside me.

I really need this mental break.

We pull up to Paris's most renowned opera house, the Palais Garnier, and, arms linked, sashay up to the magnificent building. People shoot us approving glances and whispers of "who are they?" follow us. Excitement races in my chest and I can't help but share: "The Palais Garnier is probably the most famous opera house in the world and a true symbol of Paris, like Notre Dame, the Louvre, and Sacre Coeur—"

Ava and Grace shoot me the side-eye. "Here we go with architecture 101," says Ava.

"Girls, broaden your horizons." We stop before the main entrance. "Constructed in the 1800s by Charles Garnier, the style of the building is Napoleon III—and melds Baroque, Palladian, Byzantine, and Renaissance influences together." I pause and take in a deep breath. "Look up. So many artists—mosaicists, painters, and sculptors—lent their skillful hands to the ornamentation, using materials like bronze and tiles and stone—"

"It's truly amazing," says Abby. "I can't wait to see the inside. And, yes, that is a hint."

We enter the main foyer and head over to one of the ushers. I hand over the gilded envelope. "Ah, the Empress Box," she says, raising an impressed brow, her eyes wide. "Please follow me."

Abby nudges me in the ribs. "There's so much gold here. And you hate gold."

I shrug. "Not when people use it in the right way."

Taryn snorts. "What? You didn't like Gordon's golden throne?"

"God no," I say. "How much did he spend on that monstrosity of a toilet?"

"Four mill, I think," says Taryn.

"Money down the shitter," says Ava with a laugh, and I glare at her.

"Language!"

"Oh, sugar," says Grace, and the girls crack up.

As we walk through the main hall, the usher points to the statue of Pythia—the priestess of Apollo, god of the arts. We're all in a trance, taking in everything as we make our way to the auditorium. Gazing up at the bronze and crystal chandeliers, and a ceiling fresco painted by Marc Chagall, I'm in architecture and art overload.

The usher escorts us to our box, which is decorated with plush burgundy velvet furnishings and luxurious drapes. "Please make yourselves comfortable. A hostess will be arriving soon with your canapés and champagne."

"Merci beaucoup," says Taryn.

"I feel like royalty," says Abby, sinking into a chair.

I sit beside her, the girls behind us. Two glasses of champagne later, the opera starts. By the time the second act hits, when Cio-Cio sings her famed aria, "Un bel dì vedremo" (One Fine Day We Shall See), the song where she's waiting for her beloved to return, a lump has formed in my throat and tears stream down my cheeks.

In the third act, when Cio-Cio takes the dagger which her father had used to kill himself and commits suicide, choosing to die with honor rather than live in shame, I wipe the tears off my cheeks and straighten my posture. Over my shoulder, Taryn grabs my hand. She gulps and then whispers, "Cio-Cio is like my mother. I understand now why she did what she did."

So do I.

Nate has no shame. Nate has no honor. Nate has no morals. And he's not going to take my life away from me. I've never been more intent on destroying his.

FORTY-FIVE

NATE

Friday, May 24th, 2024

I arrive at Gordon's and enter his stately home to find all the usual suspects are already here, along with a few others, sipping from glasses of bourbon, Scotch, or champagne, served by one of Gordon's older servants. Forgot her name. And don't really care. She'll soon be replaced.

After smoking cigars on the terrace, Gordon leads us down to the grotto. The Jacuzzi tubs are lit up with lights that change color—blue, red, purple, and green. The sconces on the walls glow and flicker. I rub my hands in anticipation.

FORTY-SIX

EMMA

Friday, May 24th–Saturday, May 25th, 2024

STELLA:

> Got the bastard. (And his sick and twisted friends if you ever need dirt on them.) You'll have everything you need to negate the prenup you signed and more. Video is not for the faint of heart. Cleaning it up—although I'd rather not re-watch it.

STELLA:

> Quick Q: when can I clear out the equipment I hid? Thanks for all the details, by the way. Made my job so much easier.

> > He should be at work now. Left home around 6 a.m,, back around 7 p.m.

STELLA:

> Perfect. I'll be in and out again. Like a ghost.

> > Great. On the off-chance he's home, just say I hired you to look at the electrical outlets—that there was a spark before I left and he wouldn't want the house to burn down, would he?

STELLA:

Got it

I click out of our chat and put on Spotify. Moments later I'm howling out the lyrics to Nina Simone's "Feeling Good".

I'm belting out the chorus when Abby bursts into my room. She wipes the sleep out of her eyes as I'm jamming out in my pajamas. "I take it you're feeling better. But it's not even six in the morning. Do you want to wake up all of Paris? Please, stop jumping. You're a klutz. You're going to break something."

"I'm not going to break anything but Nate's balls." I clasp her hands and pull her into a spin. "She got him. Stella! Got! Him!"

She got his friends too. A couple of stones to throw for the price of one. Although I probably need more ammunition to bring them all down, it's a start. And I'm starting with Nate. For the first time in days, instead of feeling scared and flipped out, I'm hopeful.

Abby squeezes my shoulders, her eyes wide. "You have the proof you need?"

"I do. Well, not at the present moment, but I will."

A cough comes from the doorway—Taryn. "I'm up and I want to know what's going on."

The rest of the day and night is one big celebration.

On Saturday, the girls take off by train for Cannes and Abby and I head to the Louvre to find design inspiration. We walk through the museum's famous halls filled with sculptures and art and historical relics for hours, passing the hundreds of tourists trying to catch a glimpse of the *Mona Lisa*, and then find ourselves standing in front of Poussin's *Rape of the Sabine Women*, the painting depicting the moment Roman leader

Romulus raises his cloak and his warriors seize the women to force them into servitude as their wives.

"That's how Nate made me feel," I mumble. "That's what he did. He captured me."

Abby nudges me, shakes her head, and scoffs, "Are you forgetting that you're the one who tracked him down?"

I glare at her. "How could I forget when you're constantly reminding me of the fact?"

"Look, Emma, sometimes my words don't come out the right way. I say what's on my mind. The important thing is, you'll get through this."

"I know. I'm sorry for being so snappish," I say, scowling. "But, in addition to being married to a monster and terrified of going home, I can't take this museum anymore. I'm feeling rather cramped in here. There are too many people. Whose brilliant idea was it to come to the Louvre on a Saturday at the start of tourist season?"

A group of English tourists push into Abby without an apology.

"See?" I say as she recovers her balance and rubs her arm.

"You're right. Let's bolt."

Getting out of the museum takes grit, determination, and a lot of elbow-bumping. Finally, we're in the main square. People are standing in front of the glass pyramid-inspired triangular entrance, holding their fingers together, pretending they're holding the structure.

"Want a photo of you like that?" asks Abby.

"You're not funny."

Abby looks at her watch then points to a café across the street on Rue de Rivoli. It's très French, the terrace set under a limestone archway, the tables facing out for people-watching. "Let's grab an apéro. We have a few hours to kill before we head off to the airport. I'm kind of hungry now."

Hours to kill. I'm now thinking about killing Nate. This

thought is churning in my mind on repeat, like a twisted song I can't get out of my head. I want to scream the words out, but instead I take in a deep breath, then let it out with a grunt.

"Is something wrong?" Abby asks.

"No, I'm fine. Let's go."

We head over to the restaurant and ask for a table on the terrace, the only one left. Once seated, both of us face the sidewalk for the whole people-watching Parisian experience, and Abby pulls out a cigarette.

"You don't smoke." I wrinkle my nose. "You quit fifteen years ago."

"But we're in Paris. And rules were made to be broken." She grins. "Plus, I stole a couple from Taryn. They're really thin. It's like I'm not even smoking. Want one?"

Why not? When in Paris. I light up and, after my first inhale, start coughing and my eyes water. I snub out the cigarette in an ashtray. "Not for me," I say, and Abby sniggers.

Two men in their forties sit at the table next to us. They're well dressed in slacks and crisp button-down shirts and moderately good-looking. One has graying temples, the other is bald. They speak in another language; one I can't put a finger on. "Russian?" I whisper.

"No, maybe Serbian? Albanian?" She shrugs and shakes her head, lips pinched. "I have no idea. All I know is that they're not speaking French."

Our waiter arrives and we order two Aperol spritzes along with a charcuterie platter and cheeses. As he jots down our order, a young woman wearing a curve-fitting green tank dress walks up to our neighbors. She's holding a glass of champagne. As she sits down at their table, Abby and I eavesdrop on the conversation.

"Do you speak English?" she asks the men. They nod. The conversation continues. The girl laughs, flipping her long hair over her shoulder.

"I don't think she knows them," whispers Abby. "What's going on here? This is so bizarre. I feel like I'm watching a creepy scene in a movie."

The girl stands up and for some reason I have the urge to follow her. "Abby, I'll be right back." Abby shrugs and blows out a puff of smoke and then coughs. I trail the girl up a flight of steps to the ladies' room. When I enter the bathroom, she's staring blankly at her reflection in the mirror, brushing her hair like she's hypnotized. She's definitely on something. Pretty, with long auburn hair and green eyes, she's young—around Taryn's age. My motherly instincts kick in.

"Are you OK?" I ask and her unfocused gaze turns in my direction. "Do you need help?"

"No, I don't need help," she snaps. "I need for you to stop staring at me."

The girl turns on her heel. The bathroom door slams behind her. I shake my head with surprise. After washing my hands, I make my way back to our table to find the girl sitting with the men, her back to Abby and me. "I was just checking on my friends," says the girl. "They're upstairs. While I wait, I'm going to order another glass of champagne."

I whisper to Abby, my eyes wide. "There's nobody upstairs."

Her mouth forms a large O.

"I'd be happy to offer you one," says the bald man, eyeing his friend.

I sit silent, listening, watching. I want to do something when I can't do anything.

Abby snaps her fingers, right in front of my face. "Lost you there for a second. Do you think she's a working girl?"

"Yep. Or maybe trafficked." I take a sip of the spritz. "It's a systemic problem and it happens all over the world—even in our own backyards. Closer than you think." I raise a brow. "Much, much closer."

Abby's eyes go wide. She takes in a deep breath. "People like Gordon Flynn—the sex king of New York," she whispers. "God, this world is so messed up. I really don't understand anything or anybody anymore. How do they think they can get away with it?"

"Because they think they're untouchable."

For the next few hours, anxiety winds its way through me and, even with the aid of a Xanax and three glasses of champagne, I don't sleep on the flight back to New York.

ACT THREE: NOW
BREAKING FREE FROM THE WEB

The butterfly counts not months
but moments, and has enough time.

—Rabindranath Tagore

FACT: Tiny, individual scales form the iridescent colors and patterns on butterfly wings. When escaping sticky spiderwebs, the trapped scales break off, thus allowing butterflies to fly free.

FORTY-SEVEN
DETECTIVE ROSSI

Monday, May 27th, 2024, 9:12 a.m.

When I'd asked Emma to share what happened the week prior to Nate's death, I got way more than I'd bargained for. And I wasn't prepared for any of it. The four of us sit in silence, the only sounds our heavy breaths.

Now I know a couple of reasons as to why Emma wasn't forthcoming with me. Not that she should have told me anything. A bit cryptic, she'd tried telling me to look at Nathaniel's friends with a closer lens, but I'd been too focused on her and that damn phone call, my bull-headed stubbornness getting in the way, not to mention the twinges of jealousy for the life she leads and my initial aversion toward the woman.

The back of my neck is damp. So is my forehead. I've been clutching my hands, digging little crescents in my palms, listening to her brutal account of the past instead of tuning her out as she rambled on as I did yesterday.

What she's told us is blowing my mind. But although she's being more forthright now, it's almost like being spoon-fed information one morsel at a time, and I want the whole platter—

meat, potatoes, and all of the fixings. I shake my head. Maybe Emma is a victim? I look up. She's glaring at me. And I don't blame her. There was a point when she opened her mouth and then clamped her lips shut. She'd changed the subject, quickly moving on to how she suspects her late husband and his twisted friends of being involved in human trafficking.

Dirty people do dirty things.

"This is certainly a lot to process, Mrs. Landon."

Emma's eyebrows raise and she puffs out a breath. "I know it is, Detective."

"Why didn't you share any of this with me yesterday?"

She glares at me and crosses her arms over her chest. "I didn't have proof of any of it at the time. And without proof you wouldn't have believed a word I'd said. You'd already made up your mind about me. Wife planning on divorcing billionaire husband comes home to find him dead."

True. And maybe my instincts are off. But something still isn't sitting right and I'm wary. Just like when I'd questioned her, she's shifting the focus off of her and onto other people, not to mention the gravity of her accusations. "So, why are you bringing all of this up now?"

Dina slaps her hand on the table. "Detective, I think, deep down in your gut, you know why. Can we move on so we can get out of here? Unless, that is, you're charging my client with something."

"We are not," says CD with force. He shoots me a scorching look and mouths, "Back off."

I can't. I need answers. There's a lot to unpack here and I don't even know where to begin. But I have to start somewhere.

"I'll try to keep my questions brief," I say, and CD groans. "So, Taryn Flynn is Nate's biological daughter. And you already knew this, or had suspicions," I scratch my temple in thought, "because of Irina's letter, the one you hid in one of your gardening books."

And now I know why she'd gone rigid when I'd picked up that book.

"Unfortunately, Taryn was conceived prior to Emma's marriage to Nathaniel, so she needed to hire Stella for evidence to break the prenup," says Dina. "What you saw in the video."

A video I never, ever want to see again.

Tonight, I know I'll be having nightmares about Gordon Flynn's evil, puffy face. I take slow, purposeful breaths, willing the visions flashing in my brain to disappear, and get back on track. "You mentioned your spy lamps. Was the video we just saw procured legally?"

"Yes," says Dina. "Again, and to be clear, Emma gave Stella Kinkaid permission to place cameras at her home, since Mr. Landon had turned off their security system—"

"I get it," I say, turning my attention back to Emma. I lean forward. "You've told us you suspect Mr. Landon and his friends of being involved in human trafficking, that you overheard a conversation."

"I did. And I do." She rubs her eyes with the tips of her fingertips. "Unfortunately, I can't remember everything. That was the night of the party I snapped at, the one at Gordon Flynn's."

"But you do remember asking Nathaniel what he was investing in, and he said horses."

Emma lets out a caustic snort.

"Obviously a lie. He hates horses. Even when the girls were competing in equestrian events, he refused to buy them mounts of their own. But it wouldn't have mattered anyway. The bastard sent them to boarding school. At least they have riding stables there." She spits out her response, the venom in her tone reminding me of the call she made to Dispatch. She lowers her voice when my head tilts to the side. "After what I'd heard and what I'd discovered from Luisa and my staff two years ago, I've come to another conclusion altogether."

So have I. Nathaniel and his cronies are traffickers, bringing in people from Thailand, Mexico, Belize, and possibly Cuba, to buy and sell for their own amusement and personal gain. Now I just have to prove it, connecting the others in his little club to the crime. Connect the dots. This news weighs heavy on my heart and if I weren't sitting down I'd be knocked off my feet.

"Correct me if I'm wrong, but you were shit-faced. How can you possibly remember bits of this conversation?"

Emma looks at Dina. Dina nods. By the intense look in Emma's eyes, I know I'm in for a wild ride and it's one I'm not sure I want to be on.

"I told you I was trying to trap him. To get ammunition for my divorce, right?" she asks, and I wave a hand for her to carry on. "That new dress I'd bought? I'd ordered a wireless microphone from Amazon. Stuck it in my cleavage. Well, what little I have of it." She juts out her chin. "That was my gift to Nate, the one I was wearing under my dress. I wasn't talking about lingerie."

CD blurts out a surprised laugh and slaps his thighs. "You wired yourself? We should hire you."

I glare at my boss, although I have to give Emma credit when credit is due. "Do you have the recording? Considering the methods used to get it, it wouldn't hold up in court, but I'd like to hear it."

"I do," she says, pulling out her phone.

The moment she hits play every hair on my body stands on end. Although the voices are a bit muffled, the words are clear. Emma hasn't made up one word of the conversation she'd overheard.

CD mumbles, "We may need to call in the Feds."

One question nags and pulls at my brain. She could have survived on fourteen million. Her design business is doing well enough. People have survived on much, much less. "Why didn't you leave him?"

"I was terrified, and not only for my own life. I had others to think of." She pauses. "The girls. Taryn. My staff. My parents. I thought if I could trap him with cheating, we'd all have a way out. And I could take care of everybody."

This case just took on a new twist, one I definitely wasn't expecting. Part of me is excited, ready to go for it and bring everybody down. The other part is so shocked and dismayed my stomach is twisting into knots. And I still need to find out who killed Nathaniel. Emma? Somebody else? Although the devil on my shoulder is whispering in my ear, *He's better off dead, he deserved to die*, I'm not wired that way.

Is Emma capable of going to such lengths—killing her husband, or hiring somebody to do it—to protect her family? "You said that you wished him dead?"

She meets my eyes and leans forward. "With everything I've told you, wouldn't you fantasize about an escape? One without repercussions?"

I rub my forehead and look down at my notes. "I need to interview Luisa and your staff again."

Emma bangs her hands on the sides of her legs. "No. It's a sensitive subject. And I don't think they'll talk to you when they couldn't even speak to me about it for years—"

I nod. She's right. I'm one hundred percent certain they won't open up to me, given Luisa's reaction when I interviewed them yesterday. I clear my throat. If what Emma is saying is true, and I'm still wary, I'll need her on my side. But judging by her rigid posture, she doesn't trust one word I'm saying. That's my fault. I need to win her confidence. "OK, I'll let you speak with them first so they're not blindsided," I say in a soft, placating tone. "But I will be questioning them again."

"And I'll be there," says Dina with a fierce nod. "Unless you have a problem with that?"

"I don't," I say.

The connections are spreading out like the roots in a forest of trees, but the branches are pointing in so many directions I'm not sure where to direct my attention. I tap my pen on the table and Emma glares at my hand.

Dina stands up and indicates for Emma to do the same. "Are we finished here? I think my client has been through enough for one day. Maybe even a lifetime."

"I believe we are," says Chief Davis.

"Almost," I say, and CD's eyes send daggers in my direction. "One more question. Mr. Landon's mother is alive? And he threatened to kill you if you contacted her?"

"Yes," says Emma, preparing to stand up. She sinks back into her seat. "But, regardless of the risk, I didn't listen to him. In case you're wondering, I did update Gigi on my plans, Taryn too, once I'd figured out how it might be possible to leave my marriage. They both thought the spy lamps were a brilliant idea, but hiring the private investigator to catch him in the act was better." She tilts her head to the side again, eyeing me. "You seemed pretty judgmental about my decision to let the girls stay in France with Taryn." She lifts up her chin and folds her arms across her chest in defiance. "They are also with their paternal grandmother, but they don't know who she is. Happy? Now you know everything about my perfect husband."

Oh, I know there is no such thing as perfection, especially when it comes to that man.

If human trafficking wasn't enough to make my head spin, Emma's also told us that she thinks Nathaniel Landon may have killed his brother and his father.

I should have chosen my adolescent crushes better.

I'm getting a migraine, definitely on information overload. Maybe my brain is about to short-circuit. My breathing becomes shallow. I feel like I'm going to lose my balance and I have to place my hands on the table so I don't fall over.

Kowalski appears in the doorway. "Sorry to interrupt, but it's important. One of the screenings came back and it relates to Mrs. Landon—"

"Hand it over." I stand up and grab the paper from his hand, my eyes scanning the page. I slap my hand to my forehead and then massage my temples.

Dina clears her throat. "What's going on?"

"Apparently, the Xanax Mr. Landon prescribed Mrs. Landon wasn't Xanax. It was OxyContin, 20 milligrams. Which means—"

Emma's eyes go wide and she falls back into her chair, her cheeks flushed. "H-h-he tampered with my prescriptions?"

Oh, Emma, I think it's way worse than that. Nathaniel is pure evil incarnate. He thought he could get anyway with anything—maybe even murder. "I wasn't going to say that but, yes, I believe he did."

I stop talking and start to pace, shaking my head.

Emma's shoulders tremble. "What else were you going to say?"

"OxyContin and alcohol are a very, very dangerous combination. I was going to say he was either trying to drive you crazy"—I take in a deep breath—"or possibly kill you."

Her panic-filled eyes flash to mine but she doesn't say a word, just sits up straight staring blankly at the wall, breathing in and out. "I can't believe what I'm hearing," she mutters.

"Do you take it every day?" asks Dina with concern.

"No, only when I'm stressed," she whispers, her voice robotic. "I'd packed an emergency bottle in my suitcase. I took one this morning, and yesterday on the flight home. And last night." Dina places a gentle hand onto Emma's back. "I took one before that party at Gordon's! No wonder I snapped. No wonder I can barely remember anything! Oh my God! Oh my God! He's been poisoning me for two years! That was his plan!"

Emma slouches over, resting her head on the table, moving

it back and forth, mumbling something about not being able to sleep and heart palpitations. Everything she's saying is making sense and also explains the radical emotional shifts she'd had when I questioned her yesterday. I'm almost as shocked as she is, but I need to defuse this situation and calm her down if I'm to figure out who killed Nathaniel Landon.

"I just want to go home." Emma blinks and then swallows so hard I feel it. "To my home. I don't feel safe." She gulps. "At least my estate has a security system, video surveillance, and iron gates. I also need Luisa and the rest of my family. And—"

Dina's slick ponytail swings and slaps on her back when she turns to face me. "This isn't a goddamn request. It's happening today. Right now."

I'm wondering why Emma would even want to set foot in that house. But I'm not Emma and this is not my choice. Perhaps she can get her staff to open up to her some more. That's my hope. I need something to help me break this case.

"I believe we've collected enough evidence to link those people"—I indicate the photos spread out on the table with a wave of my hand—"to Mr. Landon's death. But we're not shutting down the investigation. I'll have the team finish collecting what they need inside the property, but they'll still need more time outside."

"I'll call 'em," says Kowalski. He's been so quiet I'd forgotten he was still in the room.

"Thanks, babe," I respond out of habit and Kowalski's eyes widen, flashing a quick glance of caution before he walks away.

Dina and Chief Davis are talking in the corner of the room. Thankfully, CD didn't hear me. But Emma Landon picks up on the slip. Her gaze follows Kowalski as he leaves.

"Hmmm," she mumbles.

I tap my index finger to my lips twice. "We all have our secrets."

"That we do. And no matter how careful you are, secrets

catch up with you," she mumbles. She exhales a sharp breath. "I'm talking about Nate and his friends, of course."

Her words give me pause. She's definitely keeping something from me. And, knowing what I know now, I honestly don't blame her for withholding information. We all have our dirty laundry, but hers will be hanging on the line for the whole world to see—the press will make sure of that.

"I realize what an ordeal you've been through, but I still have to investigate Mr. Landon's death. If I have any further questions about his"—I pull my fingers into air quotes—"*friends,* would you mind answering them?"

"Not a problem. But not today." She slowly gets up from her chair, her knees quivering. "And not here. We can do it at my house." Her eyebrows raise and her lips part. She looks like she wants to say something else, maybe tell me off. But she doesn't.

"One more thing. I'm stationing two officers at your home. To be safe."

Her eyes volley back and forth. "Safe?"

"As a precaution, in light of what you've told me."

"Good idea." She stands up, brushes her hands on her dress. "Can I go home now?"

I nod. "Thank you for your time."

Dina steps over and links her arm into Emma's. "Frank and Tony are waiting in the lobby. Ready to get out of here?"

"I am," says Emma, looking over her shoulder with a tight smile. "Thank you, Detective."

As I watch Emma and Dina leave, Kowalski races up to me and CD, out of breath. I ignore his bear-like grunts.

"Next steps?" asks CD.

"I'll start with Gordon Flynn. Then the Starks."

"That's going to be an issue," interjects Kowalski, and my gaze locks onto him. "Flynn's maid just called Dispatch," he pants. "She found him this morning. Dead."

I feel the blood draining from my face. Two billionaires in two days? This can't be a coincidence. Not when both of them are connected to Emma Landon—and Taryn Flynn.

All my senses are tingling. I'm thinking about webs, how sticky they are, how the threads capture the spider's prey. I'm also thinking about venom, how the neurotoxins directly affect the nervous system, particularly those of Black Widows—how they mate and then they kill. Spiders never get caught in their own webs—they have movable claws that release as they walk.

I've just let Emma Landon saunter right out of here.

I think I've been played.

FORTY-EIGHT

EMMA

Monday, May 27th, 2024: 10:36 a.m.

The bodyguards cover me with the black coat again, the hornets' nest of reporters buzzing around me with their stingers —a.k.a. microphones—shoved into my face. Frank thrusts me into the car, not so gently this time, and slams the door. As Dina pushes her way through the crowd, screaming NO COMMENT at the top of her lungs, I sink into my seat as low as I can, overcome with so many emotions my head spins.

Nate had filled my Xanax prescription two years ago, and I took the pills. I suppose all the stresses in life caught up to me— raising the girls (worrying about them), running my business (making sure everything went to plan), and dealing with Nate (pretending I adored him). Funny, when he wasn't around, which was most of the time, I rarely took the pills to alleviate my stress. But I did take one the night of that party and on the flight home from Paris. And I'd also taken one last night and this morning.

How long has he been tampering with my prescriptions? Since the beginning of our relationship? It doesn't take a rocket scientist to figure out that he'd probably replaced my birth control pills with placebos. The world according to Nate—and his timeline. Granted, I love the twins with every beat of my heart, but this news has rocked my mind. Hot tears stream down my cheeks to the corners of my mouth, scorching my lips with so much bitterness I can taste my anger. No more. I wipe the tears away with the sleeve of my dress and pull my phone out of my purse.

> I'm on my way home. Everybody meet me at the house.

LUISA:

> Thank the lord! We'll be there.

Dina snakes her way into the car and I do my best to block out the cries of the reporters as she settles into the seat beside me, slamming her door. "Jeez, those people are goddamn animals. No wonder celebrities wind up punching them." She breathes in through her nose, out through her mouth and then shakes out her hands. "Are you sure you don't want me to drop you off at the hospital?"

I tuck my phone into my purse. "With what I've just learned, I'm not all that confident with doctors anymore."

"I totally understand. But it might be wise to get some bloodwork done—"

"I'm fine." I meet her concerned gaze. "Really."

She clasps my hand. "You did excellent today."

I lower my head, shaking it from side to side. "I'm glad that everything is out in the open now."

"Oh, it is," says Dina. "It's a good thing you told me about Nate's activities yesterday, otherwise I'd have paled like Rossi did."

We sit in silence on the ride home, me checking my texts from the girls. There is nothing new. I look at the time. It's 4:30

in the afternoon in France and I'm wondering what they're up to. I send them a quick text, wait a moment, but don't get a response. Hopefully, they're having fun. I can't wait to hug my girls, to talk to them. They're safe. A sense of relief washes over me until the car rounds the corner.

A couple of reporters wait outside my estate, but most of them are in front of my nasty neighbor's house. I turn to Dina, my heart racing.

"Something must have happened to Gordon Flynn," says Dina.

That's what I'm praying. Because if Chariya or Ahn were harmed in any way I'll lose it.

"What a disgusting waste of a human being." Dina's eyebrows pinch together. She raises her hands and then claps them together. "Your husband and his friends all deserve to rot in hell—let's leave it at that." She pats my thigh. "I'm just glad you're not a suspect anymore. You should never have been a person of interest in the first place. That Rossi really had it in for you."

I know she did. Part of me thinks she still does.

Tony shifts the car into drive and we rumble down the driveway, Frank following on foot. Luisa, Homa, Kom, and Alba barrel up to me when I get out of the back seat. I barely have one foot on the ground before they wrap me in hugs, their words overlapping.

"We were so worried about you."

"We're glad you're home."

"We were so scared."

"So scared."

"What's going on next door? We heard sirens."

"Are you hungry? Thirsty?"

"What can we do?"

"Are you OK?"

"They're saying somebody murdered Mr. Landon."

"Are they going to come back to speak to us?"

I take a step back and smile, the first real one I'd had in days. "I'm fine. I'll answer all of your questions in a second." I turn to Dina. "See, I'm in good hands. You don't have to worry about me."

Dina grins. "I'll get out of your hair."

"Thank you for everything." I nod to Tony and Frank. "And thank you, guys. I was thinking of asking you to stay on, but—" I nod my head toward the Flynn estate.

A drop of rain splatters on my forehead. I look up to the sky, gray and cloudy now, a reprieve from the heat.

"If the circumstances change, call us. Because they could change like the wind." Frank steps toward me, handing over his card. "I wouldn't leave the house until things settle down."

"Believe me. I'm not going anywhere," I respond, tucking the card in my purse. "Thanks."

"You have my number." Dina gives me a brief hug and then hops into the car. "Ciao for now. Get some rest."

I watch the car drive off and close the gates, and turn to face the ladies, my smile turning into a quivering frown. I stare at the home I designed—a glass and cement prison of broken dreams and promises filled with lies and deception. And I don't want to live here anymore.

If I'm being honest with myself, designing homes gave me something to do, but I was never really fulfilled picking out expensive and useless things for people who wanted to one-up each other—like Nate. All the articles in the magazines inflated my ego for about 2.5 seconds. Don't get me wrong: I'm proud of my accomplishments, but did it do anything for the world, give me joy? I'm happiest when I'm in my butterfly garden, digging in the dirt, connecting with myself, connecting with nature. I'm happiest when I'm with my girls. I'm happy that Nate is dead.

Luisa places a hand on my shoulder. "You've been through a nightmare these past few days. You need to get some rest."

"Luisa, I'm not tired," I say forcefully. "I actually feel invigorated, like a giant weight has been lifted off my entire body. I..." I pause when Luisa gives me a look. "I know exactly what I want to do, what we all need to do." I clap my hands together. "Ladies, we're going to fumigate the house, clean every square inch of it. We're going to light the firepits and burn Nate's remnants away."

Save for Homa, everybody's eyes spark up. She grimaces. "But what about the kitchen? It's disgusting. And the pool house has been turned upside down and round and round. We would have cleaned everything up, but we weren't sure if we could touch—"

"I'll tackle the kitchen," I say, looking down at my dress. "I just have to change clothes first." My gaze shoots to the two officers patrolling the property. "And ask them if it's OK."

Luisa snorts. "You do realize that olive green is the color the inmates at the Bedford Hills Correctional Facility wear?"

My upper lip lifts. I didn't think about that when I chose my outfit. Rossi must have thought the same. I know that woman still thinks I had something to do with Nate's death. Although her words seemed sincere, the glare in her eyes told me everything, not to mention the way she ambushed me with the texts I'd sent to Nate and that damn Instagram video.

"You go change," Luisa continues. "And I'll help you clean the kitchen."

"Me too," says Kom.

"It's vomit," I say with a slight gag. "And it's probably congealed now."

Kom rolls her eyes. "I'm used to cleaning up vomit. The girls. The dogs. You."

I hang my head with shame, sobbing deeply. "I'm sorry."

"There is absolutely nothing to be sorry about." Luisa shrugs and holds her hand out to me. She pulses her grip. "I guess now is not the best time to tell you we all think he's better off dead."

She bursts into laughter and it is infectious.

The cops have given their clearance to clean the kitchen and the pool house; apparently, they've collected enough vomit. After we raid Nate's closet and change into his T-shirts and tight biking pants (my idea, because we'll be burning them in the firepit later), we snap on gloves and set to work, throwing bleach everywhere—the terrace, the hallway, and the kitchen—Kom, Luisa, and me working as a team while Homa and Alba tackle the pool house. Scrub. Polish. Scrub. My back aches to new levels, but it's a good pain, the kind that makes me feel whole—human.

Luisa stops throwing garbage in the trash, mid-step, and turns to face me. "We're missing something."

"What?" I say, gagging while trying to scoop something indefinable off the floor with a spatula. A spatula that I will be replacing—once I learn to cook.

"Music. Something appropriate."

"Music? Now?"

"Si," says Luisa. "Music is powerful. I recently read an article about the limbic system—it's the part of the brain that controls emotional and behavioral responses. So, when we listen to music it's a way to process our emotions or remember things —to feel joy or pain."

She's right. Abby and I had a way of connecting through music, each song bringing up memories from the past—some good, some bad. Aside from Chris Isaak and Bryan Ferry, Nate and I had completely different tastes. We didn't have a song. Come to think of it, we really didn't have anything in common. Good thing—because he was a narcissistic sociopath without a soul.

Luisa nods toward the sound system. "What do you want to hear? What are you in the mood for?"

Dancing on Nate's grave? I can't say that, though.

I tap my chin, thinking, finally deciding on the perfect song. "Alexa! On! Play Talking Heads—'Burning Down the House'."

After Alexa spouts out her introduction, the song blares from the speakers. I'm down on my knees, scrubbing and polishing, and belting out the chorus. But this moment of unbridled angry energy only lasts for a minute before I crumble against one of the cabinets. Luisa scoots down next to me. "You're not OK, but pretending you are for us."

I pinch my lips together. I know she's gone through far worse than I have. Bring out the tiny violins. Still, I can't help but have a pity party. I gulp. "Today, I found out that Nate might have been trying to kill me or drive me crazy. He tampered with one of my prescriptions—it's such a scary, mind-bending thought." I stroke the base of my throat. "What if he'd actually had me committed? What if his plans to get rid of me had worked?"

Luisa clucks her tongue and then squeezes my hand. "Thankfully, they didn't. You're here with us now"—she does the sign of the cross with her right hand—"and he is not." She points to the floor. "He's where he should be."

Hell. An even better vision than my twisted "black widow" fantasies. I can see him rotting in the lowest pits depicted in Hieronymus Bosch's famed painting, *The Garden of Earthly Delights*, now displayed at the Prado Museum in Madrid. Such a masterpiece of the ultimate nightmare. Nate, of course, had loved the debauchery pictured within the detailed brushstrokes. I love picturing him in the midst of the scene now, because, yes, that's exactly where he belongs.

"Do you really think somebody murdered him?" she asks. "I mean, it wouldn't surprise me."

"I guess his past caught up to him," I say numbly, staring at the pond.

Her phone vibrates. She pulls it from her pocket and flips the screen open, frowning. "Aye, aye, yai." She clucks her tongue and meets my gaze. "It's bad news. I'll tell you later."

"Tell me now. Seriously, what could be worse than finding out Nate was trying to kill me? Or pulling his dead body out of a pond? Or being interrogated by the police?"

Or finding out I'd married the devil.

She rubs her index and middle finger in between her eyes. "You've been through too much. We all have. Let's just get back to cleaning and burning down the house."

"Alexa. Off!" I hold out my hand, palm up. "Luisa, I can take it. Give me your phone."

Begrudgingly, she hands her cell over. My eyes scan over an email from JenX's personal assistant.

Luisa,

I'm sorry to say that we can no longer work with you, Emma Landon, or Atelier Em on the re-design of the Hamptons property. Jen loves the spotlight, but, considering the current situation with Mr. Landon, not this kind of luminosity. Please send us a final invoice for the work done to date, the materials and elements purchased in Thailand, and the designs we've paid for thus far. We'll be moving forward with another firm. Thank you for understanding.

Best,

Holly

Even in death, Nate is destroying my life. Sabotage from the grave. This time it's hitting my career, everything I'd worked for, the one thing that was truly mine—sort of. If Nate were alive he'd remind me that he paved the way.

"It's OK." Luisa grips my hand. "We'll get other clients."

My head drops and I squeeze my eyes shut. "No, we won't. But I don't care."

"You do care," she says as my breathing picks up. "Don't you dare waste one more tear on that monster. We'll scrub him away. We'll burn him out of our lives, and then we'll come up with a new plan. Bueno?"

She's right. In a way, even surrounded by turmoil, I feel myself growing calmer, maybe even stronger. I'll figure it out. I'm an architect and everything starts with a plan. My life could be beautiful.

"Bueno," I say forcefully. "And you don't have to help me clean—"

"But I do," she snorts. "I can't believe you used to work for your mother. She should have fired you because not only are you a terrible cleaner, you have horrible taste in music." She grins when I tilt my head with confusion. "What? I don't like your Talking Heads. Alexa! Play Luisa's mix."

FORTY-NINE
DETECTIVE ROSSI

Monday, May 27th, 2024: 11:05 a.m.

Kowalski and I arrive at the Flynn estate just as the coroner's van drives out of the massive iron gates. Reporters shove their cameras and microphones toward the car and I gun the engine, ignoring their loud pleas and the roar of questions. Circling in front of the Landon house like sharks, they'd obviously smelled fresh blood and swum right on over, jaws open and ready to suck in any morsel of gossip they can get. Fresh meat. Bone and blood.

A stark contrast to the clean lines of the Landon residence, the Victorian mansion is painted blood red, the towers and turrets chiseled into sharp points. An enormous fountain of Poseidon in a horse-driven chariot takes its place in the center courtyard, the circular drive surrounding it. Even the weather seems to be having a visceral reaction to the dread pounding in my heart. Dark clouds roll in, snuffing out the light of the sun, and the wind picks up, swirling dead leaves in the driveway. I blink back a couple of droplets of rain.

Before a storm slashes the sky open with a heavy downpour,

my gaze sweeps over the property and that damn video—his evil face, his cigar-stained teeth, the way he tapped his cane—keeps flashing in my mind. I shake my head, trying to clear the image. When I open my eyes, a peacock, his colorful plumes outstretched, struts by us. Another one roosts in a tree.

Kowalski hip-bumps me. "Look at *that* whirlybird." He whistles between his teeth. "Beautiful."

In the distance, the air fills with high-pitched shrills and squawks, reminiscent of a cat in heat. Meatball, my hefty furball, put me through the wringer, keeping me up all night until she was spayed. But the screams coming at me from every direction are not cat-made. Another peacock prances by, shooting me an evil eye, and I position myself behind Kowalski.

"I see the peacocks. Kind of hard to miss."

"Not those birds." He points. "That one."

Enormous, the Airbus H175—also painted blood red with a navy blue tail—is also impossible to miss on its landing pad the size of a football field.

"Should we check it out?" continues Kowalski, rubbing his hands together with childlike glee.

"Later," I say, wanting to get into the house and away from a potential attack. I've been nervous of birds since seeing Hitchcock's film. Don't get me started on ravens, gulls, and crows. "Let's head inside."

Sergeant Brenner waits for Kowalski and me on the front steps. He nods and we follow him into the foyer. "The pervert was old—pushing eighty-two," says Brenner. "With what he does for a living, I'm surprised his ticker didn't give out a long time ago."

"The maid, Chariya, found him?"

"Yeah. On his golden throne." He snorts out a laugh. "Twenty-four-karat gold-plated ceramic. And that's not the most messed-up part." He raises a brow. "He has a bunch of sex rooms in the basement—padded chambers with whips, handcuffs, you name it. The Jacuzzis are wicked nice, but it's creepy as fuck downstairs."

Instead of wasting my time yesterday at the Clark house, I should have been here, interviewing Gordon. And now it's too late. That mistake is on me.

My head spins as we make our way through the mansion. The hallway is lined with knights, not actual ones but the full armor they would wear in the Middle Ages, chain mail included. The richness of the decor—so much gold everywhere —is overwhelming, and not in a good way. Plush oriental runners patterned with shades of red and blue silence our foot-steps into soft muffles, but the floors beneath the carpets creak and groan with every step.

We pass by a living room with forged iron chandeliers that, along with the knights, must have been stolen from King Arthur. An Asian woman paces back and forth, wringing her hands. She looks to be in her early forties. Unlike Emma's staff in their designer clothes, she wears a uniform—a black top, edged with tan a collar, black pants, and sturdy shoes. Her inky black hair is twisted into a messy bun. A man, also Asian, also wearing a uniform, sits in a wing-backed chair, his head bowed and his expression somber.

I'm not about to ask where they're from, not after what happened with Luisa. Learned my lesson there. But my mind is working and stopping on one word: trafficking. Before I dance into that subject, I'll play it cool.

"Kowalski, you and Brenner scope out downstairs," I instruct. "I'll handle this."

"Got it, boss," he says with a smirk.

I roll my eyes and walk into the living room as they meander down the hall.

"I'm Detective Rossi," I introduce myself, extending a hand. She just stares at my outstretched arm and I pull it back, clearing my throat. "You must be Chariya."

"Yes," she replies, her voice strained. She points to the man. "And that's Ahn."

"I understand you found Mr. Flynn?"

"Yes, around nine this morning. I was getting worried because he's usually downstairs by eight thirty for breakfast." She points to a tray of uneaten fruit, eggs, and a coffee set on the table. She takes in a breath before continuing, her voice quivering, eyes wide. "So I went upstairs and knocked on the door. No answer. I knocked again harder. No answer. So I went in." Her gaze drifts and her shoulders contract. "That's when I found him, Mr. Gordon, on the toilet. Then I called 911."

"Did you notice anything out of place when you found him?" I inquire, watching her eyes.

"No, everything seemed normal," she says hesitantly, glancing at Ahn who still sits silently in the wing-backed chair, hunched over and clenching his fists. "Except, of course, for Mr. Flynn being dead. And the vomit. So much vomit. And—"

I have an overwhelming sense of déjà vu. I'm wagering a heart attack will be the cause of Gordon Flynn's death. Emma hated Gordon Flynn. Is it a case of two birds, one stone?

"Right." I nod, trying to make sense of the puzzle pieces set before me. "And nobody else was in the house?"

"I don't know." She sighs. "Lots of people here all of the time."

"Interesting," I murmur. "Does anybody else work for Mr. Flynn?"

She nods. "Big Guy, Lug, and the rest of his security detail. Plus, his pilots, Maverick and Goose."

Top Gun? The nicknames roll around in my brain. "Do these men have real names?"

"They don't talk to us." She shrugs. "Mr. Gordon just calls them Big Guy and Lug. And Maverick and Goose."

"Where are they now?" I ask.

Her eyes flicker to the side. "I don't know."

"This house is enormous," I say, a bit perplexed. "You clean it on your own?"

"I cook too." She scratches behind her right ear and then continues, "I have a schedule. Kitchen and Mr. Gordon's room every day. And I rotate the rest of the rooms. Ahn helps me when he's not driving."

Ahn clears his throat. "I'm his chauffeur. I only drive the limousine to pick up Mr. Gordon's guests," he says. "I drive the Rolls when Mr. Gordon wants to go somewhere or if Chariya needs for me to pick up something."

I note this down on my pad. "How long have you worked for Mr. Flynn?"

Chariya and Ahn exchange nervous glances.

"For a long time," Ahn finally says. "Since 1986. I was sixteen and Chariya was eighteen. So, almost forty years."

I'm astounded. 1986. I calculate the math in my head. That means Chariya is fifty-six and Ahn is fifty-four. Neither of them look their age. I'm wondering how long Flynn had been coloring outside the lines of the law and how everything connects to Nathaniel's death.

"Do you know Emma Landon well?" I ask, watching her closely for any changes in her demeanor.

"Yes, of course," says Chariya, nodding her head. "We love her. She's like family. I brought Taryn to her place all the time. Homa, Kom, and me, we raised her girls, Ava and Grace, with Taryn." She sighs, her lips forming the faintest of smiles. "Homa and Kom, although younger, are our best friends. They're also from Thailand—from the north, like us."

The conversation Emma recorded rings in my ears. Product from India and Thailand. And Cuba.

"About Taryn—how was her relationship with her father?"

"She doesn't have one," says Chariya, her eyes welling up. "She doesn't speak to him and doesn't come around ever since he sent her away when she was fifteen. I wish I could see her, but Mr. Gordon didn't allow it. I don't leave the house much."

I suck in a breath. A prisoner. I'll hold off on this line of questioning until later, mostly because I need to prepare myself for it. "And Mr. Flynn's fiancée, Veronyka?"

Her lips pinch together. "Mr. Gordon did not have a fiancée."

"Emma Landon told me she saw her at a party. Here."

"I remember that night. Emma was very drunk," says Ahn. "I saw her stumbling around outside in the parking lot. I raced up to her, grabbed her before she did something stupid, and then I drove her home."

Something stupid? "What was she doing?"

"Um, she was in front of Mr. Landon's car with keys in her hand. She kept saying, 'bastard.' I grabbed her wrist before—" His jaw drops. "I shouldn't have told you that. Emma was really drunk. I-uh—"

"I appreciate your honesty."

OK. Maybe Emma isn't a liar. Maybe the medications Nate had swapped out had turned her into a raging lunatic. I get it. She hated him and probably would have keyed his car. But I saw the video. Nathaniel and Gordon talked about this woman, Veronyka. Perhaps Chariya and Ahn don't know anything. Or maybe they're scared, protective of their master. Not that it matters; he's dead now.

As my mind races, Kowalski taps me on the shoulder. "We need you. It's important."

I turn to Chariya and Ahn. "Thank you for your time. Wait here, please."

Chariya sniffles and sits down on the couch. Ahn lowers his head.

Kowalski and I head downstairs, navigating through a twisted maze of sex rooms, each one more disturbing than the last. The walls are lit with iron sconces, spitting out a creepy yellowish-orange light that flickers on the walls. I can't stop picturing Flynn's demonic smile, watching. Brenner didn't lie; nothing is normal down here.

"Detective Rossi." Brenner interrupts my thoughts, his voice tense. I follow the direction of his flashlight to a metal door—could be a panic room or it could be something else altogether. The door clicks open. No alarm sounds. My eyes scan the large, sterile space: Linoleum tiles. A toilet. A hose. A small refrigerator. Three dirty mattresses. A pile of ropes. A wall with monitors linked to a computer system. And eight large safes.

This is *not* a panic room, but I do smell fear. My heart races and my lungs tighten.

Keep it together, Rossi.

"We've got to get those beasts open," says Brenner, pointing to the safes. "I think we'll need dynamite."

I hold up a finger. "Wait here, I have an idea," I say, racing back upstairs.

Chariya sits on the red velvet couch now. She looks up when I walk into the living room. "Detective? I didn't offer you a coffee. Would you like one? Or water?"

"Thank you. I'm fine." I'm panting, out of breath. "Would you, by chance, know the combinations to the safes downstairs?"

She shakes her head and disappointment takes over hope. I figured if she's worked here for so long it wouldn't hurt trying. But then she looks up, a glint in her eyes. "I do know where he keeps a paper record. He's old and forgetful sometimes. He likes to write everything down." She stands up and ushers me with a finger. "Come. I'll show you. Follow me."

Chariya leads me down the corridor and opens a large wooden door, the stench of stale cigar smoke hitting my nostrils immediately. Like the rest of the house, everything reeks of evil, rotten, and moldy under the surface. She walks over to a large black desk with a marble top and fumbles around with a lever underneath the base. A click. A thud. A drawer slams onto the ground. Figures, Flynn is old-school, going with a hidden compartment. Chariya hands over a paper with a bunch of codes and numbers written on it.

"Thank you. I'll meet you back in the living room," I say and race out of the room.

I'm not looking forward to going back downstairs, but I'm hell-bent on getting those safes open. Breathless, I make my way up to Kowalski and Brenner. I wave the paper victoriously above my head and hand it over to Kowalski. "The two of you get cracking."

Kowalski looks at the page. "There are a lot of numbers on here."

"And you're going to try them all."

Brenner grabs the page from Kowalski. "I can barely read this."

"Figure it out," I say. "This place is locked down. I'll be back in twenty minutes."

FIFTY

EMMA

Monday, May 27th, 2024: 1:47 p.m.

The storm has lifted, the sun whispers a little light through the clouds, and the kitchen and pool house finally sparkle—no remnants of Nate's demise. We've all changed back into our clothes and I've lit both of the firepits by the pool so we can burn what we'd been wearing of Nate's, currently crumpled up in a garbage bag by my side. But I still have so much to do to scrub my life clean of him.

Luisa steps onto the deck carrying a tray—a pitcher, glasses, and a crystal bucket of ice. "I mixed up a batch of pineapple, lime, and ginger aguas fresca, your favorite. Made a pitcher for the policemen too. They were very happy." She winks. "Are you hungry? Alba can whip something up."

These women. How much have they done for me? I have to do something for them to make amends for Nate.

"No, thank you. I'm fine." I throw one of Nate's T-shirts onto the flames. "We'll tackle the rest of his clothes later, but this—this is a start." I watch the fire slowly engulf the fabric, sizzling and crackling. Bye, Nate. Burn, baby, burn, in hell.

At that moment, the buzzer rings. And I'm thinking, *Now what?* I can't get a break.

Luisa steps over to the monitor. "It's that nasty detective lady," she says, turning with a scowl. "But she's with Chariya and Ahn. I see them squirming in the back seat of her car."

I prod Nate's burning clothes with a poker, trying to snuff out the flames. Plumes of orange and red fire rise, only making the odor worse and the smoke rise higher. The air smells of ash and chemicals. It doesn't matter. Burning clothes isn't a crime. "Buzz her in and I'll be right back."

I head down the flagstone path to the front of the house, watching Detective Rossi grind her Impala to a stop. Sprays of gravel shoot out everywhere and then she jumps out of the driver's seat. Chariya and Ahn sit quietly in the back. Rossi stomps her way toward me, eyes me up and down before speaking.

"Emma, is everything OK? Did you go to the hospital to get yourself checked out?"

Now we're on a first name basis? And she's concerned about me? I feel like she's instantly morphed from bad cop into a good cop. But I know better. I see the way she's looking at me with doubt.

"I didn't. We've been cleaning and the fumes got to me."

"Is something burning?" she asks, sniffing the air.

My life? She'll probably accuse me of destroying evidence. "We've been cleaning up all the garbage. And, yes, I cleared it with your men. I turned on the firepits to..."

"Maybe it could have waited." She shoots me a worried look and tsks. "If I were you, I'd get some rest."

Rest? No, I need to put the pieces of my Humpty Dumpty life back together. Purge everything.

"You saw the state of the kitchen, *Detective*. I couldn't leave it like that and, no matter what you think, I'm not above hard work. I used to work for my mother's cleaning service... And babysit. And waitress. And do a lot of dirty work." Like pretend I loved Nate. I point toward the distance. "I even garden—"

I don't know why I'm explaining this to her. Maybe because I'm not over how she treated me.

"Yeah, I noticed your Crocs and your butterfly garden, but that's not where I was going," she says with a sigh so long it could blow all the leaves off the trees. "Gordon Flynn is dead. I can't go into details, but Chariya found him this morning and the property is being processed."

Another monster—the unscrupulous leader of all the soulless derelicts—is dead. My lips curve into a tight smile and I can't hide the spark lighting up my eyes.

"By your expression, I'm not going to ask you if you're upset."

"With what I told you this morning, you know that I'm not." I raise my chin in defiance. "Do you need to know where I was? Is that why you're here?"

"No, I know where you were." Rossi looks over her shoulder. "I'm here because Chariya and Ahn need somewhere—"

This time, I cut her off. "Of course they can stay with us. They're like extended members of my—"

"Family. I know Chariya told me. Raised Taryn with your girls. Over here all the time." She shakes her head and ushers for Chariya and Ahn to get out of the car. "I'm going to have to come back and question everybody—them and your staff."

"Please, can we save the inquisition? I can't take any more. My staff can't take any more," I say with force. I look at the worried expressions on Chariya and Ahn's faces as they approach, carrying small duffel bags. "And I think they might need a break too."

"I've got to head back over to the Flynn estate anyway." She shudders then and hops into her car, rolling the window down. "Don't go anywhere. I'll be back later."

Can't wait.

The moment her Impala peels out of the driveway, I race up to Chariya and Ahn, pulling them in for tight hugs. "I can't believe Mr. Landon and Mr. Gordon are dead," Chariya whispers. She points toward the sky. "It's like we have an angel watching over us."

FIFTY-ONE
DETECTIVE ROSSI

Monday, May 27th, 2024: 2:33 p.m.

A woman sighs loudly as I pass the red leather padded room with whips and chains and sex toys on the walls. "There are too many prints here. Hundreds. Maybe thousands. All overlapping one another. None of them are clear."

I peek my head in before heading back to Kowalski and Brenner. "All we need are partials. Keep at it."

"I want to get the hell out of here," she says, turning to face me.

"Lori, believe me, so do I. But—"

"I know. I know. And I'm going to have nightmares for years." She grimaces and then gags. "Do I have to print everything?"

She hasn't seen the video I'd been tortured with this morning. Or the pictures on Nathaniel's phone.

"Yep," I say. "Sorry."

"Not as sorry as I am."

I rejoin Kowalski and Brenner. Four of the eight safe doors are open. And, much to my chagrin, Officer Roberts has joined them. "Rossi," he says with a nod and continues punching numbers into one of the keypads.

"What have we got?" I ask, ignoring him, and change into a new pair of gloves.

"Videos. Lots of and lots of videos," says Brenner.

"From his porn company?"

"Nope," says Kowalski, handing over one. "This one is marked Nathaniel. Another is marked Harold. Ben and Becks —" He clears his throat. "I don't want to make assumptions, but looks like blackmail to me."

I stare down at the CD cases, pieces of tape slapped onto the covers, black marker indicating the names. And I think Kowalski is spot-on with his thought.

"Find any marked Jeff or Claire or Harold?"

Brenner nods. "Yeah, how'd ya know?"

"Just a hunch," I say, not wanting to get into the details of my morning. "Bag and tag everything and get it all back to the station," I add, looking at the computer monitor, which is linked to the video camera currently recording the forensics team, the images flashing. "Anything on that?"

"Haven't had time," says Kowalski with a shrug. "Jeez."

"Well, let's make the time. One of you tech whizzes, see if we can rewind the footage to Friday night."

Kowalski shoots me a sly grin. "You got it, boss lady."

I glare at him and mouth, Stop calling me that.

As Kowalski and Brenner hunch over the computer, a click snaps me to attention and Roberts lets out a whoop, "This one has files and folders and papers in it. I think we hit the mother lode—"

He gets up and hands me a ledger and I run my fingers over the spine. Flipping through it, I find pages after pages of numbers and initials, presumably payments for something. People? Payoffs? Before I can ponder my theories, Roberts hands me another file.

"Last will and testament. I scanned through it quickly. Most of his estate and his businesses go to Taryn Elizabeth Flynn, his daughter. A small portion goes to Chariya and Ahn, his faithful staff."

"Taryn?" I blink. Emma and Chariya had mentioned that Taryn hadn't spoken to her father in years, not since she'd received her trust when she was eighteen. Emma had been under the impression that Gordon had cut her out of his will.

"Oh, for fuck's sake," yelps Kowalski, breaking me out of my thoughts. "We've got Friday night—it's pretty bad."

If it's another sex video of a messed-up orgy, I'll claw my eyes out. I gulp. "How bad?"

"Really bad. Take a look."

Brenner pulls up a video and the grotto comes into focus. He fast-forwards to a clip. I immediately recognize some of the people in the room—Nathaniel Landon, Gordon Flynn, Jeff Cox, Benjamin Stark, Claire Woodbridge, and Harold Katz.

Becks Stark leads a group of eighteen or so teenagers into the room. A rope tied at their wrists binds them together. Gordon Flynn taps his cane. One by one, the crowd pokes and prods them, fingers digging into their flesh. They open their mouths, inspecting them like animals. And, one by one, they are auctioned off.

"Stop," I wheeze, hunching over. "I've seen enough."

This is worse than really bad; it's a horror film. Yet, with everything Emma has shared, I want to run right into it. After catching my breath, I tap Kowalski's shoulder. "Let's go."

"Where now?" he asks with a grunt. "If you say the Landons', I'll—"

"The Stark house."

"Warrant?" Brenner asks, and I nod. "On it."

FIFTY-TWO

EMMA

Monday, May 27th, 2024: 4:57 p.m.

Freshly showered, before entering the media room, I listen to the beautiful mélange of Thai and Spanish. Chariya, Homa, Kom, and Ahn sit on the couch, watching *Real Housewives*. Alba and Luisa chat on the settee. Luisa looks up and smiles. "Come in. We've been waiting for you." She looks at the clock. "It's almost five."

Alba points to the coffee table, which is set up with a pile of crêpes, a variety of garnishes including sugar, lemon, chocolate, and freshly cut fruits.

"I wanted to surprise you when you got home from Paris. At least, I had one day with a French chef," says Alba, sighing. "Voilà!"

I can't remember the last time I ate. I inhale the sweet aromas and grab one of the little plates she's set to the side, choosing chocolate and strawberries. I roll up my crêpe and take a bite, my eyes popping open. "Oh my goodness," I say, holding my hand over my full mouth. "This is delicious! Spicy and sweet. What did you put in the chocolate?"

"Ah, a little chili powder." She tilts her head toward Luisa. "She made me do it. Such a bossy lady."

"And she was right!" I snarf down the delicacy and set my plate down, meandering over to my chair with the ottoman, sinking right into it.

Homa changes the channel and Maggie Pressly's voice chimes in, her image on our twenty-seven-foot wide television— another one of Nate's ridiculous extravagances. The definition is so clear it almost feels like Maggie is right in the room with us —larger than life, a blond behemoth with a piece of lint on her navy blue jacket I want to pick off. The room stills to a quiet hush. I settle deeper into the chair, picking my cuticles down to the quick.

BREAKING NEWS: SEX KING GORDON FLYNN FOUND DEAD

"Gordon Flynn, otherwise known as the sex king of New York, is dead. His maid found him earlier this morning and she immediately called 911. Mr. Flynn, a billionaire and owner of G-Spot Enterprises, was a close friend and next-door neighbor of Nathaniel Landon, whose death we reported yesterday."

A picture of Gordon and Nate golfing fades onto the screen. They're standing with clubs over their shoulders, dressed in khakis and polo shirts, laughing about something. I have to close my eyes. The two monsters.

"According to the initial coroner's report, a heart attack was the cause of Nathaniel Landon's death, the estimated time of death 10:37 a.m. on Saturday morning.

"Nathaniel Booth Landon was born in Pittsburgh, Pennsylvania in 1975, the son of Peter Banks Landon, founder of American Steel Corp., and former Rockette, Brigitte 'Gigi' Landon. An esteemed cardiothoracic surgeon at New York Presbyterian Hospital, known philanthropist, and single heir to his father's billion-dollar steel fortune, Nathaniel Landon is survived by his wife, Emma, and his twin daughters, Ava and Grace.

"Nicknamed the new prince of New York, Nathaniel Landon touched the lives of many people and he will certainly live on in our hearts. We at New York Live at Five send out our deepest condolences and prayers to the family in their time of need."

I laugh as the camera pans to the front gates of my home. And then I cringe.

"We're live on scene with Rick Meyers. Two billionaire neighbors die within days of one another. Is there a connection?"

"Here's what we know," says Rick. "Emma Landon was brought in for questioning earlier this morning and released a couple of hours later. She's currently at her home—the estate known as the glass house on the pond."

A video clip of me being pushed into the station by Frank with a coat over my head is followed by Dina holding up her hands and screaming, "No comment."

"Is Emma Landon a person of interest?" asks Maggie.

"My guess would be no. The forensics team packed up their gear and left earlier, but they're all here at the Flynn estate and there's lots of activity going on," says Rick. "We've been trying to get answers, but law enforcement aren't making it easy, refusing to answer questions. The coroner took Mr. Flynn's body to the morgue at approximately 10:15 a.m. According to the initial coroner's report, Gordon Flynn's death, like Nathaniel Landon's, was the result of a heart attack."

A clip shows the coroner's van leaving the Flynn estate and Detective Rossi driving in.

"Detective Gabriella Rossi has been called to the scene, so once again we can only assume the police are assuming foul play."

"Thank you, Rick. I'm Maggie Pressly and this is New York Live at Five, where we bring you, our faithful viewers, all of the breaking news first. We hope to have more answers on this evening's edition. Stay tuned."

A collective sigh fills the media room. I sit stunned, shaking my head, deep in thought until Chariya taps me on the shoulder. "Does Taryn know about Gordon yet? She's with your girls, yes?"

Sugar. I'd been so wrapped up with cleaning, I hadn't even thought to look at my phone. I hold up a finger, launch out of my seat to grab my phone from my purse. Five hundred missed calls and just as many texts. Most of them are from reporters. Damnit. I'll have to take my phone number off my company's website. Thankfully, my iPhone has two SIM ports, I have two phone numbers, and the one the girls use to get in touch with me is private.

I tap in Taryn's contact; she picks up on the second ring. The sound of loud club music booms in the background. "Thank God, Emma-ma," she says. "I was getting worried. I must have called fifty times and texted you as many. Hold on two secs. I'm heading inside." I hear feet clomp, a door open, and the music fades. "Sorry. I'm at a roof-deck party. It's much quieter in here."

She's partying in Cannes? "Where are the girls? I couldn't get in touch with them."

"Don't worry. They're at Gigi's, all snuggled up like bugs in a rug—a very expensive rug. It's almost midnight here. They're probably asleep." I hear her swallow. "How are you?"

"I'm fine," I say. "I'm home. Tell Ava and Grace. But that's not why I'm calling."

Chariya grips my hand. "Chariya found Gordon this morning—"

"And the repulsive old perv was doing what?"

"Nothing." I cringe. "Nothing at all. He's dead." My statement is followed by a long gasp. I let my words sink in before continuing. "Gordon's house is now a crime scene. Chariya is with me. So is Ahn."

"Emma-ma," says Taryn, her voice a steady whisper. "What do I do?"

And now I have my in. "Keep a low profile, get out of that club—or wherever you are. Get yourself and the girls on the next available flight and I'll have Frank and Tony pick the three of you up from the airport and bring you back home."

"Frank and Tony?"

"Bodyguards. Reporters are swarming everywhere. Taryn, it's too much to get into over the phone."

A long pause. My phone keeps dinging with alerts and I want to throw it across the room.

"What goes around goes around comes back around," she finally growls. "Frankly, I want to celebrate."

Although I agree, there's an edge to her voice, a sadness. She's not OK. My girls are not OK. Nothing is OK. The trajectory of our lives has taken a turn like a speeding train flipping off the rails, about to explode. "Get back to Gigi's and don't leave the premises until your flight takes off."

Chariya motions for my phone. "Taryn, Chariya wants to speak with you. Also, tell the girls to call or text Luisa if they need anything because, like my brain, my phone is about to blow up."

As Chariya takes the phone and heads into the hallway, she's not speaking English, but Thai. Raised by Chariya, I know Taryn speaks fluent Thai. And I also know they only speak the language when they don't want others to understand what they're saying.

FIFTY-THREE
DETECTIVE ROSSI

Monday, May 27th, 2024: 4:33 p.m.

Becks Stark paces frantically in front of their McMansion in Katonah, a four-story modern knockoff of the Landons', but smaller in scale and not as impressive. The moment we step out of the car, she races toward us. She looks the worse for wear, disheveled in an animal-print dress with her hair sticking out in clumps. She has a crazed look in her eyes, as if she's hopped up on something. Red lip-liner feathers around her mouth.

"You guys got here quick. I literally just hung up with 911. It's Ben, my husband—something is wrong with him," she says, her voice gravelly, her breath smelling of alcohol. "Follow me."

Kowalski and I share a look.

When she races through the front door, we follow and she ushers us into her kitchen. Lo and behold, Ben Stark is lying in a pool of vomit, his fat tongue lolling out the side of his mouth, his eyes unblinking. My hand flies to my nose and I pinch my nostrils. Kowalski gags.

"Something is definitely wrong with your husband," I say, eyeing him and then her. "He's dead."

"H-h-he was alive a minute ago!" She stands over him, blinking, and tries to nudge him with her toe. And then she screams. "What the hell happened?"

Good question. That's what I want to know. Because Emma Landon hated him too.

"Please, step away from the body," I say, noting the foil chocolate box by his side—red—and the round, dark candy melting in his hand. "Considering recent events, your home is now a crime scene."

Her entire body spasms. "What events?"

"Are you not aware that Gordon Flynn and Nathaniel Landon, friends of your husband's, are dead? It's all over the news."

"I, uh no, I didn't know that." She rubs her mouth and then her nose. "I've been somewhat occupied. I only returned home five minutes ago. And found him writhing around on the floor."

Love the way she's not crying over her husband's death, just grinding her teeth like a cokehead. I know the signs. This woman is a real piece of work and I can't wait to bring her down.

"And where were you?" asks Kowalski, his voice low and gruff.

"Delivering valuable pieces of art to another state," she says by means of explanation. "I'm an art dealer."

"Which state?" insists Kowalski.

"Does it matter?"

"It does," I say.

She crosses her arms across her chest and raises her chin with defiance. "I'm not telling you a damn thing. I know my rights. And, as for searching my house, I think you need a warrant for that—"

I can't hide my grin when Brenner radios in. "Good to go on the warrant. Judge Vitrano wasn't happy, by the way. We interrupted his golf game. I'll be there in a minute. Forensics in ten. Roberts is on scene now."

Perfect timing.

"Get the coroner over here too." I meet Becks's terrified eyes as Roberts swaggers into the kitchen. "As you were saying?"

"You have absolutely no right to do this! None whatsoever."

I follow her gaze to a door with a lock on it. Such a tell. Her lips clamp together and she turns her head, muttering swear-words under her breath. "I'm not saying a damn word without an attorney present."

As Brenner skids into the kitchen, breathless, Becks's posture crumbles.

I turn toward Roberts. "Watch her," I instruct. "Kowalski, Brenner, you're busting that door down. Unless"—I turn to Becks—"you want to give me the combination."

She doesn't respond, just clenches her jaw.

"I'll grab a crowbar," says Brenner, racing out of the kitchen.

He returns and levers the lock off with a loud crack, sending wood splinters flying through the air. We stomp down the stairs to find another basement set up like a sex dungeon. I take in a deep breath, preparing myself for the worst. The scent of fear—the same odors at Flynn's "panic" room—waft up to my nose. And the source makes my heart stutter.

A group of teen girls, Asian, Indian and Thai, and one boy, Cuban, according to the conversation Emma illegally taped and the video I'd seen in Flynn's grotto, huddle in a corner on a dirty mattress. Their eyes, although glassy and dazed, plead for help. They're half-naked in skimpy underwear. An older Hispanic woman, around fifty years of age, sits beside them, comforting them, stroking their hair. Her own hair is greasy and covered in sweat, her clothes damp. She tentatively raises her hands up in the air and the teens launch their bodies into her lap, wailing. "You are the police?" she asks, pointing to the ceiling. "They can no longer harm us?"

My throat catches. "Everything is going to be fine."

Everything but me.

I can feel my heart breaking one slow beat at a time, my blood pumping in my veins. Kowalski hunches over, placing his hands on his knees, and then he throws up. Brenner drops his flashlight and sinks to his knees. I swallow and turn to Kowalski and Brenner. "Arrest that monster. Now."

I squeeze my eyes shut as I listen to their footsteps clomping up the stairs. Kowalski's voice booms with menace as he reads Stark her Miranda rights. Tentatively, my eyes meet the woman's. "Let's get you all out of this room," I say, trying to keep my tone soft when I want to scream.

I lead the group upstairs. The teenagers cling to the woman like their lives depend on it. We settle in the living room and the woman says, "They need something to drink, eat."

I'm not trusting anything in this house. I nod and unclip my radio. My voice drops to a low hush. "Somebody bring food and water. Living room. Now."

I close my eyes, trying to regain my composure.

A few moments later, an officer brings bottles of water, apples, and bags of chips, placing them on the table. The kids dig right in, squealing with delight as they rip open their bags of Doritos. The crunches make my heart almost happy.

The woman's eyes open and close with a slow blink as if to say thank you. I take in a deep breath. I'm trying to keep my tears from falling, but it's so damn hard and one slides down my cheek. I wipe it away before continuing. Emma's story haunts my brain. "I'm assuming you're Luisa's sister? Camila?" I ask and she blinks with bewilderment. She obviously needs an explanation. "I heard about your story from Emma Landon."

Her lips dip into the saddest of frowns. "Yes, I'm Luisa's older sister." She takes a sip of water and then she points to the two Hispanic girls. "Mr. Landon, Luisa's boss, was storing the girls here until he was ready to pick them up. But that didn't happen."

Because he's dead.

"Mr. Stark locked you down there?" I ask, and her lips twist to the side. She's silent when she nods her head yes. "I was supposed to explain their new lives to them, give them a special drink to calm them down." She gulps. "They were very upset, crying. Very scared."

The boy taps her on the leg. She leans over and whispers something to him. She squeezes his hand and meets my eyes. "I told Juan—that's his name—the nice lady is here to help us."

Juan eyes me with suspicion.

Camila's soft voice snaps me to attention. "These aren't the only teenagers Mrs. Stark brought back on her latest trips."

The video in the grotto. At least thirteen other teenagers. I gulp so hard it hurts to swallow. "Do you know where they're being kept?"

Camila shakes her head and whispers something to Juan. As he speaks Spanish, I watch him pantomiming—plane, helicopter, truck, and then big scary room. "Las personas," he says and I understand.

"People?" I ask with a slight pause, trying to remember some of my remedial Spanish from high school. "Quién? Dónde?"

She asks Juan and then looks at me. "He doesn't know where they took the others."

In my gut, I know where some of the kids are.

Kowalski steps into the living room, holding up two bags— one a large plastic sack filled with white powder, presumably cocaine, the other a ground-up substance, brown in color. In his other hand, he holds a bottle filled with a thick viscous liquid— ketamine. "Searched her car. One of these has to be the murder weapon. I also found another iPad mini."

Becks Stark is Madame Butterfly? None of this is making sense.

My head spins. I've got to get back to the station, interrogate Becks, and track down the rest of the victims. As for Camila and these kids, I have to get them to a hospital and then arrange for them to be taken somewhere safe. My brain tingles and sparks with everything I've learned over the past twenty-four hours.

"Kowalski?"

"Yeah," he says, his expression pained.

"Loop in Scarsdale. It's out of our jurisdiction, but they'll work with us. Ask for Detective Madden. Before the news gets out, we need four more warrants and quick—"

He nods solemnly. "Cox, Katz, Woodbridge, and Weiner."

FIFTY-FOUR

EMMA

Monday, May 27th, 2024: 8:45 p.m.

I'm restless, pacing in my room, when the buzzer for the front gate rings. Luisa is staying in the house with me in one of the guest suites and she stumbles out of her room. She rubs the sleep out of her eyes. The buzzer rings again and again and again. We head downstairs and look at the monitor. A large police van sits in front of the gates, flashing red and blue lights.

"I think they're here for me," I say with a shudder.

"You haven't done anything wrong," Luisa replies with a sigh. "Let them in or they'll just keep ringing."

A spark of fear shimmies its way down my spine.

After pressing the button to open the gates, we watch the van rumble and bump down the driveway on the monitor and make our way downstairs. An officer unknown to me steps out of the van as I open the front door. I hold out my arms, my wrists overlapping one another. "Just get it over and done with. Luisa, call my attorney—Dina Fadel. I didn't do anything, by the way. Rossi has a stick up her ass."

Luisa nudges my ribs and scowls.

The officer takes a step back and chortles. He holds up his hands in mock surrender. "I'm not here to arrest you, Mrs. Landon. And I agree, Rossi definitely has a stick up her ass."

Oh, how I want to laugh, but refrain. I tilt my head toward the two patrol guys circling the property and I'm reminded that I'm still a prisoner in my own home. "Then why are you here?"

He points to the van and then meets Luisa's eyes. "Your sister thought you might take her in. The kids, too."

Luisa nods to the officer. "Thank you for bringing them here. Yes, they can stay with me."

After ushering the group to get out of the van with a wave, the officer's eyes meet mine. "OK, with you, Mrs. Landon?"

Momentarily stunned, my jaw unhinges as five skinny, malnourished teenagers crawl out of the back seat, followed by Camila. The kids look dazed and confused and I'd like to comfort them, tell them everything will be OK, but when I walk forward they grip each other's hands and shudder with fear, backing away with each step I take. My heart stutters. This just got so real.

"Mrs. Landon?" asks the cop.

"Of course they can stay here," I say with a little too much enthusiasm. "Luisa has her own home."

He salutes me and then heads to his van. Before he gets in, he says, "By the way, the two patrolmen won't be leaving the premises." He shoots me a sympathetic smile. "Rossi told me to remind you that neither will you—especially with the kids. She's trusting you and your staff."

"I understand," I say.

Rossi doesn't need to warn me. I know for a fact that she doesn't trust me.

Right when the officer pulls out of the driveway, a long, black limousine screeches in front of the house. A petite Asian man gets out of the driver's seat and races up to Luisa and Camila. His face has very feminine features—pretty with long black eyelashes and full lips. I've met Daw a couple of times, mostly when Nate had me go to Harold Katz's to sign papers.

"Harold was arrested," he says with a soft squeal and fans his face with a hand. "I tell the police I stay with Homa and Kom. OK?"

"Si, Daw," says Luisa. "Where else would you go?"

Luisa turns and then she points toward the kids. "Camila, Daw, and I have to get them settled in my house and then we'll all meet in the media room. Bueno?"

By the intense look in her eyes this isn't a question, but a demand. And I'm not about to argue with her. "Bueno."

I'm sitting in the media room, waiting for Luisa and the others, sadness coursing through my veins. The last text I received from the girls was sent a couple of hours ago and, after deleting hundreds and hundreds of messages, I'm only seeing it now.

> AVA:
>
> Flying private on MV's plane. Arriving at Westchester County tomorrow night around 9pm. Luv u.
>
> GRACE:
>
> Is it true what they're saying about Dad on the news? We're scared.

> Don't worry. I'll see you tomorrow.

My girls are on their way home and will get back safe and sound—the only positive thing I have to look forward to. And, as much as I'd like to avoid reality, maybe curl up in bed and never get out of it, I know I have to face it. Immediately, I call Frank, letting out a sigh of relief when he says that he and Tony are available.

> Frank and Tony will pick you up. Can't wait to see you. We'll talk about Dad tomorrow. Luv u.

I wait for a response, staring at my phone. Nothing. No dots. This time difference is killing me. While I wait for Luisa and the others, I turn on the news, my body rigid with stress. I circle my head and my neck cracks with a couple of pops as Maggie Pressly's image fills the screen.

BREAKING NEWS: THE BILLIONAIRES BOYS' CLUB MURDERS

"The Bedford Police Department has just confirmed that hedge-fund manager Benjamin J. Stark, a close friend of Nathaniel Booth Landon and Gordon Flynn, has died of a heart attack. Aside from the cause of death and being billionaires, what's the connection? You'll have your answer and more when we come back from commercial break."

I already know the answer. They were all disgusting excuses for human beings and deserved to die. As the segment fades back in, Luisa and the others saunter into the room, and we sit in silence, watching.

"I'm Maggie Pressly and we have startling news to share on this evening's edition of New York Five Live at Ten."

A clip of Becks fades in. A couple of cops drag her out the back of the cruiser and lead her into the police station. I hold my breath. Oh, this is getting good. I rub my hands together.

"A few hours ago, Rebecca Stark was arrested in connection with the Billionaire Boys' Club murders. Rick Meyers is on scene at the Stark house..."

The screen splits to show Rick, standing in front of a poorly designed home that's supposed to look modern and elegant, but comes off as a smaller, cheaper reproduction of my own.

"Good evening, Maggie, viewers. Earlier this evening we learned that, in addition to billionaires Nathaniel Booth Landon and Gordon Flynn, Rebecca Stark's husband Benjamin J. Stark is now dead.

"Rebecca Stark was arrested and taken into custody a few hours ago.

"We've tried getting in touch with Detective Gabriella Rossi to confirm the exact charges, but have been unable to connect with her, and the Bedford Police Department is not answering questions."

I'm rendered silent as my eyes dart to everybody in the room, listening to all the sighs of relief. And I let out one too, knowing Becks will not only be going down for murder but also for trafficking humans—the teens Camila brought to our home are proof of that.

"I can't believe our nightmare is over," says Luisa, making the sign of the cross with her right hand.

I sink into my chair, squeezing my eyes shut.

FIFTY-FIVE
DETECTIVE ROSSI

Monday, May 27th, 2024: 10:35 p.m.

When I return to the station, an army of black SUVs are parked in front of the building and my gaze locks onto the dozen or so men and women wearing dark navy blue jackets with yellow lettering on the upper arm and their backs: FBI. They are carrying out boxes and containers, loading them into the back of the trucks. My heart sinks. I know this is no longer my case, a fact that is confirmed when I walk into the precinct and CD ushers me into the briefing room with a forceful come-hither finger.

Two unassuming men in black suits with short black cropped hair sit at the conference table, standing up when I stomp in. My gaze shoots to CD, he shrugs. I shake my head, lifting up my chin, not saying a word. No, all I can do is grunt in anger.

"Detective Rossi, Special Agents Ambrose and Sullivan," he says, waving a finger at each of them so I know who is who, although, through my haze of anger, they both have melded into the same person, "are taking over from here."

"This isn't a federal case," I say with defiance.

"Agent Ambrose," says CD. "Can you please explain to Rossi what's going on?"

Ambrose leans back in his chair, placing his hands at the back of his thick neck. "This is a federal case now."

"I-I..."

I slump into a chair, disappointment pulling me down like a heavy weight. I can't look at these men. It's not my ego getting in the way. I don't need a big case like this to make a name for myself. It's the fight for justice, everything I staunchly believe in, and they are taking it away from me.

"You should think about joining the FBI. You did excellent work," Ambrose continues, and my eyes narrow into a glare. "Look, Rossi, we have more resources, more people than you. That substance you found in Stark's car? It'll be processed in a few hours at our lab at Quantico." He claps his hands together. "Your call for a tox screening for Flynn and Landon was spot-on —and we're pulling that one from the lab you sent it on to, getting it processed quicker. Hope to have a match in a couple of hours."

Match. Match. Match. And a veiled compliment. Honestly, I'm happy somebody will be held accountable, that justice will be served, but there are more victims.

"What about the other teens?"

One of them coughs out a laugh. Nothing about this situation is funny. I look up in shock, noting Sullivan has crazy-blue eyes, unlike Ambrose's dark hazel ones. At least I can tell them apart now.

"Stark has given us the names and addresses of all her contacts," says Ambrose.

Sullivan snorts. "She was hoping for a plea deal."

"And it won't help her one bit," says Ambrose, meeting my eyes. "From here on in, if you want to be involved, you'll be on the sidelines."

I figured that much out.

"Damn straight," I say, crossing my arms defiantly over my chest.

Anger zaps my body with electrical pulses.

The FBI has decided to detain Becks at Bedford PD. They're pushing for a bail hearing Wednesday afternoon at the federal courthouse in White Plains, after they process the grainy substance Kowalski found in the glovebox—presumed as the murder weapon. My head is pounding and it's late when I crawl into bed, dizzy from exhaustion, from stress, from pure terror. I spoon into Alex, hoping his breathing will settle my nerves, but he grunts and rolls away.

"You're mad at me," I say, stating the obvious.

"Who was right about Landon?" he growls sleepily.

"You were."

"And who was spinning their wheels and making rash decisions, reacting before thinking things through?"

"I was." What does he want? I've already admitted I was wrong. I sit up in bed. "Look, you've made your point. And if you're so mad at me, why are you here? Why don't you just break up with me?"

It wouldn't be a surprise. Maybe he just needs to get the last word in before he breaks my heart. I'm too bossy. I'm too bull-headed. I'm too much. I huff through my nose, waiting for his response. He stares up at the ceiling, a sliver of light from the streetlamps outside highlighting his square jaw.

"I may be mad at you. But I hope you've learned a huge lesson."

"I have," I say, confused. "That still doesn't explain why you're here."

"I love Meatball," he says, stifling a snicker. "She needed to be fed."

Meatball, hearing her name, jumps on the bed, settling in between my legs and purring her heart out like a little motorcycle revving its engine. I stroke her under the chin and her purrs roar to new decibels.

"You're here because you love my fat cat?"

Meatball chirps out a couple of meows, as if to say, Stop cat shaming.

Alex sits up, stares at me like I'm nuts. His chest heaves up and down. "Are you that thick in the head?"

I honestly don't know where this conversation is headed or why he's laughing. "I believe I am."

"Gabby, we've got a good thing going on." He grins and pushes my shoulder. "I'm not in love with Meatball. I'm in love with you, dummy."

I blink repeatedly. "Oh."

"Oh? That's all you have to say?"

I don't know how to respond. Those three little words, three little syllables, scare the crap out of me and I've never said them before to anybody but my family. "I—uh—I..."

"I know you love me too," he says, pushing Meatball off the bed. "Now, let's get some sleep. Tomorrow is another big, nightmarish day." He rolls over, turning on his side. "I'll spoon you if you want."

"That would be nice," I murmur.

Alex curls up next to me, his arm slung over my waist like a lead weight. Soon, his snoring becomes somewhat soothing, but I won't be sleeping because my mind is one hot mess. Something about Rebecca Stark's arrest is off. Way off. Too easy, it's almost as if she was handed to us on a platter and the server was Emma Landon.

FIFTY-SIX

EMMA

Tuesday, May 28th, 2024: 11:47 a.m.

Once again, we're all waiting for the news to come on and I bolt upright when my parents and Abby saunter into the media room. The three of them pull me in for hugs and kisses, followed by a barrage of questions and statements. "Are you OK? I can't believe Gordon Flynn is dead. I'm glad you're home. What are Chariya and Ahn doing here? Who are all these people? She looks like Luisa. What happened at the station?"

"Wait! I can't get one word in. You're all talking a mile a minute and speaking over one another." I take a step back, holding up my hands, palms out. "Now, don't take this the wrong way. I'm happy to see you, but what are you doing here? How did you get in?"

"You weren't picking up your phone and we were getting worried," says Abby. "So your mom called Luisa. Anyway, I wanted to check in on you, so I took a sick day, mostly because I've been watching the news, so I stopped by your parents and, well, we're all here now."

"But how did you get past the media circus?" Most of the reporters had moved on to the Flynn estate, but a couple of stragglers had stayed behind, pacing in front of the gates like big cats.

"Luisa buzzed us in through the back entry."

Luisa comes back into the room. "I was mixing up another batch of aguas fresca, and I forgot to tell you. I figured you wouldn't mind. Do you?"

"No, no, of course not."

"Alba's making more crêpes," says Luisa.

"Thank God," says Abby, flopping down onto one of the couches. "I'm starving."

My parents settle in, my mom next to me. Mom pats my leg. "I can't believe what we've been seeing on the news. How are you holding up?"

"Fine," I say. "Better with my family around."

"And the girls?"

"They're coming back tonight," I say.

"To a nightmare," says my dad, and I gulp.

Mom glances around the room. "Chariya, it's so nice to see you again, even under the present circumstances. I think the last time was at the girls' thirteenth birthday?"

"Yes, yes, I remember the day well. Taryn had just returned home. We had such a nice reunion, all of us." Chariya looks down, a melancholy smile on her face. "This time it's not so good, but I'm glad Emma is letting Ahn and me stay here."

"I can't believe what's going on," says my mom, fanning her face.

Understatement of the year.

"None of us can. Did you finish setting up the guest rooms in the pool house?" I ask, looking toward Kom.

"You mean room," says Homa, and my eyes go wide. "Emma, come on, after all these years you've never realized that Ahn and Chariya are a couple?"

Both Chariya and Ahn's faces turn bright red. "We've been in love since we were young," says Chariya, her head lowered. "We've been through the same things."

Ahn squeezes her hand. I can only imagine what they went through, and I'm not going to ask when my parents are here. Homa switches the channel and TMZ comes on. "Sorry," she says, fiddling with the remote. "I'll change it."

"No, don't," I say, leaning forward. A woman stabs the air. Spittle flies from her mouth. She has a crazed look in her eyes. And that woman is me. This is so much worse on my big screen, every detail, every pore, in high definition.

Abby squishes beside me, intertwining her fingers with mine. I sit in shock, not even realizing I'm gripping her. The camera sweeps through the studio, swapping from a thirty-something year-old guy wearing a gray T-shirt to a woman wearing her hair in braids.

"Here's the weirdest thing. Emma Landon is actually acting out *A Perfect Murder*. And she's at sex king Gordon Flynn's house. Did a game of charades transform into the real thing?"

The camera cuts to a chunky blond woman in yellow overalls. "She's clearly hammered," she says with a laugh. "And, while we're on the subject, so is Taryn Flynn—celebrating the news of her father's death in Cannes tonight."

An image of Taryn and another girl wearing the skimpiest of sequined dresses and drinking shots of tequila off a topless male model erupts onto the screen one pixel at a time.

The camera pans through the studio. "I'd be celebrating too," somebody says. "Taryn's going to inherit some major cha-ching."

The sound of a cash register. Laughter.

"Isn't that Anna Petrova with her? The model slash tech whiz?"

"Oh, *sure*, she went to Harvard," somebody laughs, mimicking Dan Aykroyd in *Trading Places*.

"She did. And I'm single," says a young guy. He holds his hand up like a phone and mouths, "Either one of you gorgeous babes. Call me."

My mom clucks her tongue. "Oh, Emma, this isn't good."

"Really, Mom?" I snap. "You think?"

Another image of the two girls partying fades onto the screen. Luisa and Chariya shoot me concerned glances. Everything we've planned could blow up in our faces like a Molotov cocktail. Taryn didn't listen to me when I'd told her to keep a low profile.

The sound of the report, all the people, turns into a garbled buzz of blah, blah, blah. My ears ring. My brain throbs. My body tingles. Somebody changes the channel as my heart races.

BREAKING NEWS: REBECCA STARK IS MADAME BUTTERFLY

"Hello. I'm Maggie Pressly and welcome to today's edition of New York Five Live at Noon. We have more news regarding Rebecca Stark's arrest—she's not only being charged with three murders, but with trafficking humans.

"An anonymous source has told us that all three murder victims were members of a private sex club, exclusive to billionaires and led by somebody calling themselves Madame Butterfly. With me via Zoom is one of the escorts hired to work a party this past Thursday night. A party the victims attended at the Landon estate."

The camera fades in, a blurry dot covering the woman's face. It's clear she's wearing a wig. Her voice, thanks to distortion, is a garbled mess.

"See, there are a lot of underground sex parties in New York. Selective memberships. Around six months ago, a woman named Veronyka approached me in a club. She said she was working for somebody to arrange private parties. Veronyka told me this new club was the most exclusive of them all. People with a minimum worth of 100 million. She came with cash. A lot of it..." She pauses. "She told me 10k could be mine, right then and there, and 20k a party if I could gather a crew of twenty people. The others would be paid 10k a party. I'd asked her who she was working for. She said she didn't know her name, but that she went by Madame Butterfly and that she was insanely rich. The first part of this job was a photo shoot. Honestly, it was a dream come true. So I took the money."

My heart is about to jump out of my ribcage.

"*Eyes Wide Shut* now has a new twist," says Maggie, facing the camera, her gaze intense. "This Veronyka? Has she contacted you recently?"

"Not since she hired me for the party at the Landons' last week. The phone number she gave me doesn't work anymore. But I know Rebecca Stark is the woman Veronyka was working for. She and her husband were always at the Kitty Kitty Bang Bang parties. I saw them talking with her. And when I saw the news last night, I wanted to come forward. Because they were there that night. At the Landon house."

My mother gasps.

"Am I going to be arrested?" the woman continues.

"No, we're not the law," says Maggie. "And we thank you for your candor."

The pixels of the girl fade out and Maggie's eyes blaze into the screen. "In addition to the murders of Nathaniel Landon, Gordon Flynn, and her husband, Benjamin Stark, Mrs. Stark is being charged with trafficking teenagers. Five victims were found at her home in Katonah yesterday evening. Scarsdale police have confirmed four other arrests in relation to these heinous crimes: attorney Harold Katz, tech billionaire Jeff Cox, governor hopeful Claire Woodbridge, and Judge Alfred Weiner.

"Apparently, Rebecca Stark made her millions buying and

grooming teenagers, selling them off to the highest bidder. And she went by the name of Madame Butterfly. The police and the FBI are asking other victims to step forward."

I slam my hands over my eyes when my mother screams, "What the hell is going on?"

"I think I'm going to have a stroke," whispers my dad, placing his hands on his chest.

And when the five teenagers saunter into the media room my mother faints.

Tuesday, May 28th, 2024: 4:15 p.m.

I storm into the station. "Who the hell leaked the news?"

CD crosses his arms over his chest. "I did."

"Why?"

"You know about rattling cages. And we want more victims to step forward. This is the case of the century."

"I don't think Rebecca Stark is Madame Butterfly. Did Tech find anything on Mariposa Enterprises? The iPad?"

He groans and then purses his lips but doesn't say anything for a moment. "Yep."

"Emma Landon?"

"No, not Landon. The account in Belize where the payments for the sex party were wired to was registered to one Rebecca Elana Stark. Now, can you stop with your twisted theories? God, Rossi, sometimes you're insufferable."

I clench my teeth. "I'm not."

He shakes his head. "You are."

I don't budge. "What about this Veronyka? Who is she? We need to track her down. Or question that party girl she hired."

"No, we don't, Rossi. Ambrose has already interviewed the escort," he growls. "Veronyka has disappeared into thin air. There's no trace of her. It's like she never existed. But the escort gave Ambrose a description. It's all he has to go on."

People don't just disappear. "What'd she look like?"

"Tall, blond, blue eyes—"

I gasp. Somebody else had a motive for wanting them all dead. "Taryn Flynn?"

"Nope, not Taryn. Ambrose asked that question too, brought a photo of her along with him," he said with a shrug. "Plus, Taryn was out of town—"

I nod like a know-it-all, my chin bobbing up and down. "With Emma Landon's twins."

He sighs and growls again. "Go home, Rossi. Let the Feds do their job. If you want to stay involved, come to the line-up planned for tomorrow morning."

"What time?"

"Eight."

"I'll be there."

I stomp out of the precinct, my mind reeling.

FIFTY-EIGHT

EMMA

Tuesday, May 28th, 2024: 9:30 p.m.

I'm in the kitchen, staring blankly at the pond, which is lit up at night, a cup of coffee in hand, when Ava and Grace race into the house, tackling me and wrapping me in tight hugs. I kiss their foreheads and breathe them in.

"Mom, thank God we landed at Westchester County," says Ava. "It's nuts out there. There are miles of reporters on the road. Helicopters in the sky."

Ava tilts her head to the side and an elegant woman rounds the corner. "By the way, with all she's done for us, we've invited Madame Valois to stay at the house."

Grace narrows her eyes into a death glare. "But you know exactly who she really is, don't you?"

Gigi steps forward and kisses my cheeks, the European way. "I told them on the flight home. After all, it's safe now—for them, for you, for me."

Ava takes a step backward and stomps her foot. "You've told us that keeping secrets is just as bad as lying. And you've been keeping some pretty big ones from us."

"Like the fact we have a half-sister," says Grace, glaring at me. "We got our DNA results back. I can't believe you knew Taryn was actually our sister and you didn't tell us."

Oh, if they only knew half of the things I haven't told them to protect them.

"For a very good reason."

"Yeah, Taryn told us why. You couldn't break a promise to a dead woman. But we've seen the news and it's flipping us out," says Grace breathlessly. "And we have some demands."

My eyes meet Gigi's. She shrugs.

Grace blows out a shaky breath. "A: We don't want to go back to boarding school. Ever. We can't face anybody we know with the things Dad—and I hate calling him that—has done. Is it all true?"

I grimace. "Yes, and some of the victims are staying with us."

Ava's head snaps from side to side. "Where?"

"With Luisa, Homa, Kom and Alba," I say. "And you'll meet them tomorrow. They're sleeping now."

"OK. On that, B: We can't believe Dad and his friends are so evil. And we want to change our last names," Ava continues, frowning. "Like, we don't even want to be associated with the Landon name."

Grace nods her head in agreement, jutting her chin out. The girls share one of their looks.

"To what?" I ask.

"Novak, duh," says Ava with a roll of her eyes. "And C: We want to move to Paris, go to the American School there, for a fresh start. That, and we'd like to get to know our grandmother better."

I go silent. Then I shrug. "Sounds like the perfect plan."

Grace sneers. "You're not even going to argue with us? Tell us all the reasons why we can't."

"I'm not," I say, bringing them in for hugs. "I agree. We just need to settle some things here first. OK?"

"Uh, OK," says Grace, her eyes darting back and forth. "Where are Harry and Potter? We were looking forward to cuddling them."

Sugar. With everything going on, I'd forgotten about the dogs. And I would let them upstairs because I don't care about my perfect house anymore. "With Ryan on his farm."

Ava tilts her head to the side. "Can they come home tomorrow?"

I nod and pull out my phone. "I'm texting him now."

Grace yawns out something that sounds like good. I glance at the clock in the kitchen. It's early in the morning in France—not even 4 a.m. They are going to be so jet-lagged. I kiss the top of their heads.

"Girls, why don't you show Gigi to her room and we'll discuss everything in the morning," I suggest, expecting an argument.

"Good idea," says Ava. "We can't wait to sleep in our own beds."

Grace links her arm around Gigi's. "Ready, Gigi?"

Gigi nods and blows me a kiss and the three of them head upstairs. Then it hits me. "Wait! Where's Taryn?"

Right on cue, she walks into the kitchen. "I'm here, Emma-ma."

My mouth drops open in shock. Because she isn't alone. Taryn and an unexpected guest enter. Taryn meets my stunned face and clasps my hand, her eyes wide. "Our minds are blown. We can't believe somebody is killing the monsters off and, in the process, busted their ring."

"I'm so relieved," says Anna, cringing. "I really didn't like being a blond."

We should not be talking about anything right now. And they know it.

"We are so freaking exhausted. Anna is going to bunk up with me in Grace's room. Ava and Grace are bunking up together. It's already planned." Taryn blows me a kiss as they round the corner. "See you in the morning, Emma-ma! Love you."

My spine stiffens and my legs go rigid. Save for my thumping heart, I can't move one muscle. Anna, a.k.a. Veronyka, could be the one crack in the foundation that brings everything I've so meticulously planned crumbling down to the ground.

FIFTY-NINE
DETECTIVE ROSSI

Wednesday, May 29th, 2024: 7:55 a.m.

I don't know how the FBI managed to pull off a last-minute line-up so early in the morning, but they did. We're sitting behind the one-way glass with the rest of the victims the FBI rescued last night sitting behind us. The five we'd gathered from the Stark house are at Emma Landon's estate. Apparently, Ambrose will question them later.

"Number six, step forward," instructs Ambrose.

One by one, thirteen trafficking victims point shaky fingers at Becks, confirming her involvement in their nightmare. Agent Sullivan leads the group of teenagers out, back to the hotel where they're being cared for until we—meaning the FBI—come up with a long-term solution. A tough dilemma. I'm hoping they won't be deported, returned to families who would probably sell them off again.

"We've got her for trafficking," I mutter under my breath.

Ambrose chuckles. "And that's not all we've got her for. We're also looking at three counts of murder. The results from the sack you guys found in the glovebox came back—

fingerprints on it, whole nine yards. She doesn't have a prayer."

I snap my head toward him, stunned. "That quick?"

He shoots me a smirk. "Told you we had resources."

My pulse quickens. "What was it? Crushed oleander?"

"Close. Pong pong."

I snarl, not sure if I'm hearing him correctly. "Ping pong?"

He laughs. "I know? Weird name, right? It's formally known as *cerbera odollam*. It's grown in southeast Asia, Thailand and India, and known as the suicide or assassins' seed—related to oleander but a lot more lethal. One seed can kill you in a flash and, apparently, it's a very painful death."

My mind mulls over his words, the facts. What was Stark's motive? The blackmail Gordon had used to control her and her husband? Did she want to take over Gordon's throne and become New York's queen of sex? Make millions to support her cocaine addiction? I realize Stark's DNA was found everywhere, but why would she kill her husband? And she'd said she was obsessed with Nate. Was this a case of "If I can't have him nobody will?" I'm back to wondering about Emma. She'd also traveled to Thailand and she hated all of them.

"Method of delivery?" I ask, rubbing my eyes.

"Ground up, and rolled into chocolate truffles, like nuts."

I tap my lips. "Nathaniel Landon didn't eat chocolate."

"Stark must have figured out another method. Regardless, her prints are everywhere—on the boxes, on the sack."

"Mmm-hmm," I agree. Becks did excuse herself from Nathaniel's twisted party with the escorts, heading into the kitchen. And she did refer to Madame Butterfly. I jump out of my seat, as a thought comes to mind. I'm pacing back and forth, thinking. Emma had said Nathaniel was a creature of habit—made his smoothie every morning around 6 a.m.

Ambrose taps his pen on the table. "What's going on inside that head of yours?"

"I don't think we processed the pantry at the Landon residence."

Aside from containers of tea, I know we didn't.

"Does it matter? Evidence doesn't lie. DNA doesn't lie—"

"But people do," I mumble and stand up. "And we have more trafficking victims at the Landon house. You coming?"

He gets up and brushes his hands on his pants.

"Only to see if they'll testify against Stark," he says, placing a sturdy hand on my shoulder. "We've arrested and detained the right person. She'll get what's coming to her. Life behind bars."

For trafficking, yes. For murder? The wheels of doubt run like hyperactive hamsters in my mind. And I want them to stop. My head can't take it anymore.

After pushing the press away with a roar of my engine, Ambrose and I pull up to the Landon estate and Emma buzzes us in with long groan. I hear her mutter, "Great. Rossi is here," before the line closes.

Ambrose chuckles. "Not your biggest fan, I take it."

"Nope."

She opens the front door and scowls when we make our approach. "Mrs. Landon, this is Special Agent Ambrose from the FBI. He's taken over the case."

She squints into the sun, her eyes adjusting to the light. She looks exhausted, her eyes tinged with red. "Yes, we've all been watching the news. Why are you here?"

Ambrose takes a step forward. Emma takes a step back. "Do you think your staff would be willing to testify against Rebecca Stark?"

"You'd have to ask them," she says, turning her back on us. "Everybody is in the media room. Follow me."

Ambrose shoots me a side-glance as we make our way

through the corridor. He whistles in between his teeth. "This place is—"

"A nauseating display of privilege."

"Not what I was going to say."

The moment we enter the media room all eyes are upon us. It's disconcerting being stared at with so much distrust. My weight shifts from side to side. "You certainly have a full house, Mrs. Landon."

"Where was everybody supposed to go? And you're the one who sent them here—which, if you need to know, I'm more than OK with." She nods her head. "You want to talk to my family? Talk."

Whoa, Emma is snappish. And not in a crazy way. She's pissed off. I scan the room—in addition to her staff and the other victims, the twins, and Taryn are home. But there are two people I don't recognize, an older woman—very elegant, oozing class from every pore. She nods her head in acknowledgment. Nathaniel's mother? The other woman is young, a pretty brunette, her hair almost black, with green eyes. I lock my gaze onto her.

"And you are?"

"I'm a friend of Taryn's," she says. "Just here to support her with everything that's been going on. We've modeled together. In Paris and New York—"

"Name?"

"Anna Petrova."

I recall seeing her and Taryn on TMZ. Maybe she's just an opportunist party girl? Taryn is coming into a big payday—over twenty billion dollars.

Ambrose steps in. "Save for you, Ms. Petrova, we need to speak to all of you—one by one." His gaze meets Emma's. "Is there somewhere we can interview everybody in private?"

Emma's lips curl into a nasty sneer. "The living room. Detective Rossi knows where it is, don't you?" She storms out of the media room, we follow, and she stops mid-step. "Dina Fadel is on her way over. I texted her the moment your car pulled up. She should be here in about twenty minutes. Not one question until then. Make yourselves comfortable."

Ambrose sniggers and takes a seat on the couch. I sit next to him, twiddling my thumbs, wondering why Anna is here. I go through all the facts in my head as Ambrose listens to a true crime podcast on his phone. I tap his shoulder and he pulls his earbuds out.

"I think you should question Anna."

"The only question I'd have for her would be wanna go on a date?" He tilts his head back and sighs. "That girl is smoking hot. And her brain is on fire too. Heard she's developing an AI program that's going to crush all of them."

"Wow," I growl. "You don't think she should be questioned?"

"I don't." He laughs. "She's a programmer. She'd have all the answers."

I glare at him. "What about the pantry?"

"Rossi, focus on the big picture. We have the evidence linking Stark to everything." He shakes his head. "Anna's not even a blip on our radar screen."

Ambrose goes back to his podcast while I sit seething, listening for Dina's arrival. Finally, Emma buzzes her in and greets her a couple of minutes later. I hear the exchange of air kisses. "Dina, glad you could make it."

"You are not going to believe this. Stark called me. She wanted me to represent her."

"I'm taking it you said no."

Dina spits out a laugh. "You're funny, Emma."

Two hours later, Ambrose has what he needs: all the victims will testify against Rebecca Stark, and tell their stories in written affidavits as well as in court if needed. I'd have cast some suspicion on Taryn, but like Emma and Chariya had said, she hadn't been in contact with Mr. Flynn in over two years, resenting him for shipping her off to boarding school after her mother died. She just took her trust at the age of eighteen and took off. Honestly, I don't blame her for cutting ties with that man. And it didn't help that Ambrose practically drooled when she'd sashayed into the living room. Emma's twins were devastated—crying over the trafficking news. As for Nate's mother, after telling me her story, simply put, she'd said, "Now that he's dead, that they're all dead, I don't have to live in fear anymore and I can be a part of my granddaughters' lives—out in the open and not hidden in the shadows."

We're in the car, heading over to the courthouse for Stark's bail hearing. "I know what you're thinking," says Ambrose. "I can practically see and hear the wheels turning around in your brain, but leave Emma Landon alone. She's been through enough. Again, we've arrested the right person."

But did we?

SIXTY

EMMA

Wednesday, May 29th, 2024: 5:00 p.m.

After Rossi and Ambrose leave, Taryn and Anna take off, saying something about a quick errand they need to run. I don't know where they're going, but I'm sure they'll be back. With what? Who knows? As Forrest Gump has said, "Life's like a box of chocolates. You never know what you're going to get."

The thought makes me laugh.

The girls squeal with delight when Ryan arrives with the dogs. They usher Juan, Lakshmi, Intira, Clara, and Benita outside. The teens have been warming up to us a bit more, now that they know they're safe and well-fed, thanks to Alba's amazing meals. I listen to the sounds of laughter, of them splashing in the pool. One thing this house doesn't have a shortage of is bathing suits, kept in the pool house for surprise guests.

The adults reconvene in the media room. I sit in my usual chair, my arms wrapped around my legs, my knees tucked under my chin, a permanent frown etched on my face. Homa clicks on the news. We wait in nervous anticipation, me wringing my hands.

Taryn and Anna saunter into the room. After Anna hands out bags of popcorn, she takes a seat on the couch, next to Gigi. Taryn flops down onto the ottoman in front of me. She rubs her hands together. "Now, we get to watch her."

My eyes drift from Taryn to Anna. With everything that's been going on today, I haven't had the chance to speak with them, to anybody really. But I will.

BREAKING NEWS: THE MOST HATED WOMAN IN AMERICA: MADAME BUTTERFLY REBECCA STARK IS BEING CHARGED WITH MURDER

"In a case that has rocked the nation, Rebecca Stark has been charged with the premeditated murders of Stark's husband Benjamin J. Stark, Nathaniel Booth Landon, and 'sex king of New York' Gordon Flynn. The FBI has confirmed that Stark poisoned these billionaires with *cerbera odollam*, or pong pong as it's called on the streets, also known as the suicide or assassin's seed, and grown in southeast Asia, where Stark had recently traveled.

"In addition to murder, Stark, fifty-nine, is facing twenty-six counts of human trafficking, with more charges expected to be filed once additional victims step forward."

Luisa whispers with a low growl, "And they will step forward."

"Going back four decades to the mid eighties, Stark allegedly collaborated with her husband, Benjamin Stark, Nathaniel Landon, and Gordon Flynn, the mastermind behind the horrific and very sophisticated ring, luring teenagers away with the promise of a better life."

Taryn leans back and grips one of my hands.

"In addition to seizing all of Stark's assets, including a bank account in Belize used to launder the money made from selling the victims, the FBI has arrested four other perpetrators in connection to these horrific trafficking crimes—including attorney Harold Katz, tech guru Jeff Cox, governor hopeful Claire Woodbridge, and Judge Alfred Weiner. Seven other government officials, four pilots, and six members of Mr. Flynn's security team have also been detained for questioning. More arrests are expected to follow."

We're all holding our breaths.

"Victims were intended to be sold to the extremely wealthy for a life of domestic and sexual servitude. Previous victims have come forward to tell how they were forced to work in one of Mr. Flynn's many shady businesses including massage parlors, porn cam sites, and sex films.

"As we wait for word on the bail arraignment, Rick Meyers is with us live at the Southern District of New York courthouse."

The screen splits to show Meyers on the courthouse steps. "Behind me, as our viewers can see, hundreds of people have gathered to voice their anger. A task force is trying to control the mob."

The camera pans to hundreds of protestors jabbing signs in the air. It's chaos.

She deserves the death penalty. The monster!

Stark should rot in prison for the rest of her life. In solitude.

She won't last in prison.

Rick Meyers comes back into view, his face filling the screen. "Detective Rossi has just exited the building." He races up to her. "Detective, Detective, you must be thrilled—"

She lowers her head, her eyes not meeting the camera. "I'm just happy justice will be served—"

Rick's hands shoot to his earpiece. He looks up, ignoring Rossi as she thuds down the steps. "We've received word that Judge Florence Adams has denied bail.

"Because of the gravity of the charges she is facing, and considering she's a flight risk, Rebecca Stark will be detained at the Bedford Hills Correctional Facility, a maximum-security prison in Westchester County. And in an unprecedented decision based on the amount of evidence, her court date has been set two months from today."

A collective sigh fills the room.

"That monster may be a madam but she's definitely not a butterfly," says Taryn. "They need to change her name to something more appropriate." She cackles. "I've got it. Pong pong killer."

"Everything starts with a plan," says Luisa, flipping her hair over her shoulder. "You taught us all that, Emma." She makes the sign of the cross. "But we weren't expecting this."

Anna laughs. "I, for one, am relieved."

"I think we all are," says Gigi.

My gaze drifts to every person in the room. There are ten of us, eleven including me.

I squeeze my eyes shut, thinking back to when everything started. Two years of meticulous plotting and planning... and oh, yes, how the plan has changed.

SIXTY-ONE

EMMA

THEN and NOW

After meeting Gigi, I'd texted her on the burner phone:

> Please keep an eye on Taryn.

I didn't realize how close they'd become; eventually, Gigi told her who she was, making her promise not to tell anybody else, especially the twins—at least not until my plan to get away from Nate was set in place. Taryn, of course, wanted in on the plan—and I needed a hive.

At first, Gigi, Taryn, and I were plotting to catch Nate cheating. That way, we could keep the lives of my staff and family intact. I was a mother protecting her daughters, Gigi a grandmother, and Taryn the girls' biological sister.

We shared a common goal. Get us away from the monster!

Taryn and Gigi thought my spy lamps were a brilliant idea —but getting them designed took about four months. Testing them took another two months. But after Chariya overheard Becks and Gordon discussing their trafficking operation, she told Luisa. And Luisa told me. Catching Nate cheating wasn't enough. It was then I decided we needed to do something on a much grander scale.

One by one, our hive multiplied and, well, the initial plan went through some major adjustments: get them all arrested for trafficking, ensuring that they would spend the rest of their twisted lives in prison.

Enter Anna.

Taryn introduced me to her childhood best friend. Anna's mother, Natasha, was brought over from Russia a year after Taryn was born. At the time, Anna was four. I'd heard Irina mention her friend and her beautiful daughter, but I'd never met them. Gordon moved Natasha to the West Coast to "act" in his films. Sick and tired of being used and abused, Natasha overdosed on heroine when Anna was eighteen.

Over the years, they'd kept in touch and let's just say both Taryn and Anna had very specific reasons for wanting to bring Nate and the rest of them down. The concept of The Sanctuary was born—a sex club so exclusive that if they didn't sign up, they'd feel like they were missing out.

A bit paranoid, we all agreed never to talk about the plan. What if Nate or the others had hidden cameras? We all communicated via burner phones, supplied by Gigi.

According to Chariya, we had around eight months to arrange our pieces on the board. She'd overheard Becks's travel plans—Thailand and India, sometime in May. We weren't sure of the exact date, but we'd be ready.

Anna recruited the escorts at Kitty Kitty Bang Bang parties, disguised in her Irina 2.0 persona. She set up the photo shoots, and the iPad invitation. We'd decided that anybody she enlisted would be doing it for the thrill, for the money. Gigi supplied the cash and the costumes, flown in on her private jet. Anna was never a webcam girl—her character was generated with an AI program. But Ben and Becks didn't know that when they met her at one of those parties. Through them, Anna met Gordon, using the name Veronyka.

Yes, she's a tech whiz with a beautiful face and, more importantly, a beautiful mind.

Without Chariya and Ahn, we wouldn't have discovered the bank in Belize used to launder the funds when buying and selling people. Gordon, apparently, wrote everything down on a slip of paper.

Our plan took on a life of its own.

For everything to work, Alba, Homa, Kom, Camila, and Daw also needed to be looped in. They were our eyes and ears. Camila confirmed the dates.

Alba had her cousin track down the bank in Belize. "Lots of dirty bankers," she'd said. And her cousin came into a nice, very anonymous, cash payday. So did the banker he'd paid off, thanks to Gigi's cash.

Anna linked the payment information for The Sanctuary to that bank in Belize, which also linked everybody to the account used to launder the trafficking funds.

Gordon had cut Taryn out of his will. Nate had cut the girls and me out of his. Luckily for us, their attorney Harold Katz always had Daw fetch his files. And Daw changed the wills.

Homa, Kom, and Camila bought more mini iPads—in cash.

Then we waited for everything to go down.

I was the wild card, the diversion. I didn't think I'd get so out of control at Gordon's party, but it worked out quite favorably for all of us. Because while I was doing charades, Anna (aka Veronyka) hacked into the computer in the grotto, linking it to a network.

The final part of the plan was for me to hire a divorce attorney and private investigator, and then get the twins out of town when the shit hit the proverbial fan. Gigi and Taryn would keep the twins out of harm's way when the FBI received a video and the iPad, sent anonymously.

On Monday, Anna, dressed up in her Irina disguise, sent out the iPad invitations via a messenger service. We weren't sure if Nate and his nasty friends would fall for The Sanctuary trap, but one by one they wired the funds and signed up. Regardless, we had Anna's link.

To be safe, we placed two spy lamps in Luisa's living room. She was to turn them on as a precaution, say if Nate found out about anything and tried to harm her, Homa, Kom, or Alba. I almost died laughing when I viewed the video of Rossi's questioning and Luisa pointed to the blue morpho prints. Amazon chic? Why, yes they are, because Luisa purchased them from Amazon. Behind one of the prints is a confession, written by me in case anything went awry. And in that confession I take full accountability for everything, and also the reason we used the name Madame Butterfly on the invitation. If anybody was going to go down for spying, extortion, or hiring escorts, it would be me. But after Detective Rossi left her home, Luisa burnt the letter. Nate's death changed everything and even the tip to the FBI was put on hold when I became a suspect for his murder.

SIXTY-TWO

EMMA

Wednesday, May 29th, 2024: 5:37 p.m.

Taryn brings me back to the present with a loud cackle. "You did say you wanted poetic justice. And you got it. We all did."

I look nervously around the room, my eyes darting to possible hidden corners.

"Don't be so paranoid, Emma," says Anna. She holds up a gadget. "I already swept the entire house. There are no hidden cameras or microphones. We can all talk freely now. We don't need to communicate through the burner phones."

Luisa smiles and pumps her fist into the air. "I can't believe it! The monsters are dead!"

I shake my head as if to clear it and wink at Luisa. "Nobody should ever have to face their monsters alone."

All eyes land on me, blazing with curiosity. They're expecting me to say something more. So after clearing my throat, I do. "Tomorrow we're announcing our foundation, Fly Free, to help victims of abuse and trafficking. But right now I think we should be celebrating." I grin. "Taryn, you know where the good stuff is in the cellar."

A cheer erupts in the room as I fumble with the remote, clicking on Ella Henderson's "Alibi" on the sound system. "Unlike the lyrics in this song, we don't have to run and hide anymore."

And, well, I don't need an alibi for anything I've done. It's over. All the weeds threatening to destroy our lives have been yanked out of our proverbial butterfly garden.

SIXTY-THREE

EMMA

Thursday, May 30th, 2024: 7:15 a.m.

After a sleepless night, I wake up to more than a few death threats. Basically, they express the same sentiments, worded differently.

You deserve to rot in hell just like your husband.

How could you have married a monster like that?

You're a waste of the air we breathe. You should die too.

I want to slice your neck wide open, you disgusting pig.

Watch your back.

The sun hangs low in the sky, casting eerie shadows across the graveyard as we stand before three freshly dug graves, Taryn and Luisa by my side, the others behind us. I told my parents and Abby to stay away from the madness, keeping the girls with them, and to turn on the news. Aside from the press seated on chairs, the police are keeping an angry mob under control.

Every news outlet is covering the story, and the media has descended in a frenzy with no end in sight. The sky is filled with the whirling of helicopter blades, tornadoes of dust and debris in the air.

I take in a steadying breath. The cacophony of voices and swearwords screaming into the wind is overwhelming. The tension in my jaw is evident as I clutch my purse tightly, my eyes locked on the dirt beneath my feet.

"Enough with the accusations, the death threats," I finally snap, turning toward the voracious crowd of journalists and protestors. My eyes flash with defiance as I raise my voice above the clamor. "We're giving you a statement, so listen carefully."

The press and the crowd quiet down, eager for any morsel of information from the woman at the center of the scandal.

"We are here today, not to mourn the death of these horrible men, but to celebrate our freedom." I take in a steadying breath, surveying the crowd's reaction. There's a moment of stunned silence. "I'm sure you have questions. And we'll take them one at a time."

And so it begins.

"Emma, do you feel any responsibility for what happened?" a reporter dares to ask.

"Responsibility? No and yes." I swallow, shaking my head. "I'm not responsible for the actions of my husband and his group of twisted, morally bankrupt friends. I'm only responsible for my daughters, my family, my friends, and myself. Which is why, together, we are all doing something about it."

"Are you scared for your life?" a concerned journalist asks.

"Terrified," I admit, my voice barely audible. "I've been receiving death threats every hour, the screen on my phone questioning my character. Questioning everything."

I grab Luisa's hand and she steps forward. Brave, powerful

Luisa. "I am one of the victims, but these two are among the first," she says, indicating Chariya and Ahn with swift nods. "And we're here to tell you that we are all survivors." She gulps, taking in a breath. "Emma, my friend, and also my employer, didn't know what was going on until recently. That's my fault. But I was scared to tell her." She grips my hand tighter. "But we, all of us"—she looks behind us, locking eyes with Camila— "are not scared anymore. They can't harm us now. And when I say 'us', that includes Emma too."

A reporter shouts, "How does it feel to be the richest woman in New York?"

It's hard to hold back the wicked grin that is threatening to spread across my cheeks. I swallow and lift up my chin. "I believe that honor goes to Taryn Flynn."

Taryn steps forward. "Our lives have been thrust under a microscope. But we want to leave the past behind us and focus on the future." She pauses. "Emma and I will be donating our homes and land to a foundation we're setting up to help victims of trafficking and domestic abuse. Luisa will be the voice, the chairwoman, of the foundation. We're also petitioning the government to help current victims. In addition to the funds Emma and I will be donating, we'd like for all items and monies seized to be divided equally among them."

"What's the foundation called?" someone asks.

"Fly Free."

With that, we turn on our heels and stride away, leaving the stunned media in our wake. We said our piece, stood our ground, and now it's time to pick up the shattered pieces of our lives and begin anew. To fly free.

I look over my shoulder before stepping into the limousine. A man with unkempt hair spits on Nate's coffin, his eyes bloodshot and full of rage. A woman follows suit, spitting on Gordon's casket as she screams out a few choice words.

Detective Rossi stands beneath a tree, shaking her head and muttering something under her breath. I think I see her mouth, *I know you're Madame Butterfly*, when my eyes meet hers.

I slam the door to the limousine closed.

ACT FOUR: TWO MONTHS LATER
FLYING FREE

The butterfly does not look back upon its caterpillar self,
either fondly or wistfully; it simply flies on.

—Guillermo del Toro

Fact: The scales of some butterfly wings contain pigmentations of ultraviolet colors to attract mates, unperceivable to human visual capabilities. Additionally, the light in these ultraviolet pigments are also used as a communication system, providing guidance for survival methods such as finding nectar or warnings against predators.

SIXTY-FOUR

EMMA

Wednesday, July 31st, 2024

Becks has been tried and convicted on over seventy counts of trafficking. And three charges of premeditated murder. Life in prison. No chance of parole. Thirty other degenerates are still waiting for court dates, including Katz, Cox, Woodbridge, and Weiner.

I've been overseeing the teardown of Gordon Flynn's estate, as well as making designs for the new construction. The girls and I have been staying with my parents—Harry and Potter included, the property now in my parents' names. Luisa, Alba, Homa, and Kom don't want to leave their home and they've got a full house with Chariya, Ahn, Camila, and Daw. My former home is a safe place for the victims Becks had corralled—thankfully the FBI agreed to release them to us, or rather to the foundation.

Last week, Taryn and I held an auction—selling off all of Nate and Gordon's cars, their watches, and anything of value. Funny, Kowalski, the big cop, won the bidding on the Indian motorcycle. I won't be cashing his check. You're welcome. All of the money will be donated to the foundation. And I'd been happy to see that Picasso go—at Sotheby's for twenty million—not to mention the robot of a coffee machine and that ridiculous TV.

Tonight, I have dinner plans with Abby. It's 7:30 p.m. and I can't wait to get back to her house and prepare us a home-cooked meal. Yes, for the last two months Alba has been teaching me how to cook. Although I'm a pro at making spaghetti, I've yet to master the pan flip when making crêpes. Cue J.Lo's "On the Floor," which Luisa played after my first disaster. I also haven't had a drink in two months. Amazing what freedom from a sociopath can do for the soul.

Abby's Tesla tears into the driveway and, once the rocks stop flying in every direction, I hop into the passenger seat.

"I can't believe you're moving to Paris in a month, Em-Dash. I'm going to miss you."

"You'll be in Paris all of the time, launching your label with Taryn and Anna." I shoot her a side-glance and narrow my eyes into a mock glare. "I thought money and friends didn't mix."

She laughs. "I like her, but Gigi isn't my best friend. She's an investor."

"I'm happy for you," I say, tapping the screen on her dashboard and pulling up Adele's "Rolling in the Deep." "And, on that, I'm in the mood for this."

"Why? It's a little dark. And we kind of have it all now," she says.

"Exactly."

As the car winds through horse country, we look at one another and belt out the chorus. When the song fades, we're careening off the exit ramp and Abby, like she always does, starts reeling off the names of the Bedford Hills Correctional Facility's most infamous inmates. "'Fatal Attraction' teacher Carolyn Warmus, 'Salt Mom' Lacey Spears, 'Long Island Lolita' Amy Fisher, 'To Die for Teacher' Pamela Smart, and

'Pong Pong Killer' Becks Stark." She tilts her head back in laughter, a rogue curl falling over her eyes. "Who would have seen that coming?"

"Mmm-hmmm," I agree and mumble, "I am Madame Butterfly."

"What'd you say?" Abby turns the music down. "I didn't hear you."

I sink into my seat and grin. "I said I'm happy I'm finally free."

She grips my hand tightly and nods. "Amen to that."

The music switches to Cyndi Lauper's "True Colors" and instead of humming along with Abby I lean back in my seat, looking out the window and find myself thinking about my true colors and the color of lies.

Leopards. Spots.

Liars. Cheaters.

Monsters. Fiends.

Nature. Nurture.

Nobody knows what my true colors are or what I did. What color are my lies? Gray. Life is about balance, helping rather than harm. A mother will do anything to protect her daughters, her family. Or maybe my lies are red, carved with blood and betrayal.

After I'd read Irina's letter years ago, I knew the name of the seed she'd used to kill herself, thanks to an article I'd found while searching the web: *22-year-old dies after eating seeds from "suicide tree."* It had come out a couple of years before Irina's untimely death and she must have seen it too, ordering the pong pong online.

Let's just say I'm a staunch believer in poetic justice. Sending Nate to prison wasn't enough for me. I didn't just wish him dead; I'd wanted him dead. And I'd figured out a way to bring them all down.

Instead of ordering the plants from a nursery in Hawaii, I'd smuggled the pong pong from Thailand, crushed up in a peanut bag in my carry-on. I wore nylon gloves—knowing my fingerprints wouldn't be left behind when I mixed Nate's premeasured chia seeds with pong pong. He is, or was, a creature of habit—although the wasps killing him would have made life easier on everybody.

I also had a couple of Becks's cocaine bags—saved with her fingerprints all over them. Perhaps she and Ben shouldn't have stayed at our loft after one of their twisted sex parties in the city. Am I crafty, or what? And, well, thanks to cleaning the frame of the Picasso, I could explain the gloves, worn under the elbow-length fancy ones at Gordon's party.

At Gordon's party, I knew pong-pong rolled truffles were the way to take out Gordon and Ben. And, although I was quite tipsy, I wasn't as loaded as everybody thought I was, because that night I was on a mission. None of the cars, including Nate's, were locked; they all had the keys in the ignition. Before Ahn found me stumbling around the driveway, I'd planted a bag of the crushed-up seed in the glove box of Becks's red Maserati, burying the package under the user manual.

Right after I'd completed my mission, the alcohol hit hard. Only then did I think about keying Nate's stupid car.

On the Tuesday morning before I left for Paris, I took the train into the city, Luisa dropping me off and picking me up later. I told her I needed to run a final errand for our client, JenX, at one of the fabric showrooms, but that's not what I was doing. On the train, I'd changed in one of the bathrooms, and then switched cars. I'd worn colored contact lenses, dirty clothes, which I'd bulked up, a baseball cap, and a gnarly wig—the whole nine yards. I looked like a bum and people steered clear of me. I paid for the truffles in cash and then rolled them in the crushed pong pong on a small plastic tray placed on my lap, the location a bathroom stall in Penn station, and then I dropped them off with a messenger service, spreading out the deliveries and paying in cash.

I wore my nylon gloves throughout, and, when needed, a mask. I changed into regular clothes, gave my disguise to a homeless man (who was thrilled), and then I took the train back to Bedford, wearing big sunglasses and a hat.

Nobody blinked an eye. Except for Rossi.

I knew that when Rossi questioned me, the guiltier I looked, the better. So many tropes in thrillers, and she fell for my pathetic act. Nobody sent me the text: *You don't know who your husband is or what he's done.* I made it up, looking for a diversion because Ben and Gordon wouldn't receive their special delivery until Monday. As for the gloves I'd worn over the nylon ones at Gordon's party and the tray, I'd disposed of them in Paris.

I've been thinking of sending Detective Rossi my framed butterflies, along with a note thanking her for all her hard work —signed by Madame Butterfly. But then I think better of this passive aggressive 'you were right about me' gesture. Soon, we'll be far away, making a new life for ourselves in the City of Light.

I blink when the song changes to Fleetwood Mac's "Little Lies" and Abby howls out the chorus. She grins, nodding her head up and down. "Isn't this the song you sang that night at karaoke, way back when?"

I grimace. "I don't remember."

"Yes, you do." She slugs my shoulder. "I can always tell when you're lying."

"Uh-huh," I reply, stifling back a laugh. She doesn't know how good I've gotten at it over the years—so good I got away with three murders, sending somebody who truly deserved to be in jail in the process. I smile when I think about Becks wearing olive green prison garb, not designer clothes. I hope her fellow inmates know how to spot a fake. I raise a brow. "So, Abs, tell me something sweet."

"I'm glad we're both starting over, living the lives we deserve." She cackles. "I'm proud of you, Emma, and that's no lie." Abby's eyes meet mine for a brief moment. She squeezes my hand. "I love you, Honey Bunch."

"Love you more, Sugar Pie—even though you're driving like an old lady."

Abby snickers and presses her foot down on the accelerator. I lean over and switch the song to Beyoncé and Shakira's "Beautiful Liar."

Float like a butterfly. Sting like a hundred killer bees. And fly away while you have the chance.

A LETTER FROM THE AUTHOR

Thank you for reading *The Lucky Widow*. I hope Emma's story resonated with you and opens up some very lively discussions or inspires you to think about Emma's journey on your own. Here are a couple of questions to get you started: What are your thoughts on poetic justice? Do some people truly deserve to die? What would you have done if you were in Emma's shoes?

If you'd like to keep up to date with all my Storm Publishing releases, you can sign up here:

www.stormpublishing.co/samantha-verant

And if you'd like to hear about all my upcoming releases and bonus content, including the occasional French recipe, please feel free to sign up for my author newsletter.

www.eepurl.com/UH8cP

If you enjoyed this book and could spare a few moments to leave a review, that would be hugely appreciated. Even a short review can make all the difference in encouraging a reader to discover my books for the first time. Thank you so much! Merci beaucoup!

Inspired by current events, the #MeToo movement, and the horrors of trafficking, the central themes threaded within *The Lucky Widow* simmered in my brain for years. I'd wondered what would happen if wealthy individuals like Jeffrey Epstein and Harvey Weinstein (among others) had pushed the limits of their illegal activities to even more atrocious levels. And what would happen if their victims decided to take down the monsters responsible for these crimes.

Thanks again for being part of this amazing journey. I love hearing from readers and I hope you'll get in touch!

All my best wishes,

Samantha Vérant

www.samanthaverant.com

The Lucky Widow Playlist:
www.youtube.com/playlist?list=PLxnchxt8uUw-WNApeiQ4iGH-YC2DT6kcLo

facebook.com/AuthorSamanthaVerant

instagram.com/samantha_verant

tiktok.com/@authorsamanthaverant

bookbub.com/profile/samantha-verant

ACKNOWLEDGMENTS

I am so very thankful to all the people who helped me drive this story into what it is today. First, a huge merci goes to my fabulous editor, Kate Smith, my partner in crime. Thank you for your editorial guidance, supremely detailed feedback, and pushing the book to become its very best version. Thank you for your enthusiasm! Additionally, I'd be remiss if I didn't shout out a hearty to thanks to trailblazer founder Oliver Storm (chief), editorial director Alexandra Holmes (word sleuth), copyeditor Anne O'Brien (detective), proofreader Liz Hatherell (forensics), editorial assistant Naomi Knox (technician), and cover designer James Macey (sketch artist). What a phenomenal team! I've found my hive! I can't wait to create some buzz with our fabulous marketing and publicity team, the dynamic duo of Elke Desanghere and Anna McKerow. I'm thrilled and proud to be a member of the Storm Publishing family.

On family, thank you to my husband, Jean-Luc. Thank you for listening to me brainstorming about my plans to kill off a husband and how I'd do it.

Thank you to my beta readers, thriller authors Lyn Liao Butler, Elle Marr, and Heather Chavez, as well as women's fiction authors Lori Nelson Spielman and Barbara Conrey. Merci for helping me with the structure of the story and asking the big questions! A huge thanks also goes out to the 2020 debuts. Thanks for all the advice and support you've given me throughout the years.

To Sergeant Fusco from the Bedford Police Department

and SSA Raymond Hall from the FBI, thank you for answering all my questions pertaining to arrests and murder with patience... and for not putting me on a watch list.

Finally, thank you to the readers I've connected with and those I've yet to connect with—thank you for joining me on this wild publishing journey. Happy reading! Cheers!

Made in the USA
Columbia, SC
26 October 2024